The Mistletoe

Bride

A Hal Westwood Restoration Mystery

CHRISTMASTIDE 1666

by Jemima Norton

TUDOR GATE
PRESS

LARGE PRINT EDITION

ISBN 978-0-9850753-3-0

LARGE PRINT EDITION

You will find the other books in this series at:
www.jemimanorton.com
www.halwestwood.com

For ordering information visit:
www.tudorgatepress.com

This book is dedicated:

To my Mother
who bought me so many books
when I was a child
that my addiction has lasted a lifetime

Prayer of Dame Julian of Norwich, English mystic
(1342-1416)

All shall be well, and all shall be well,

and all manner of things shall be well.

THE HOLLY AND THE IVY

The holly and the ivy,
Now they are both full gown,
Of all the trees that are in the wood,
The holly bears the crown,
Oh, the rising of the sun and the running of the deer,
The playing of the merry organ, sweet singing in the choir.

Though this traditional Christmas carol is considered to be more than a thousand years old, it is still sung regularly. In the early 20th century the music and lyrics were collected by Cecil Sharpe, a founder of the English folklore revival. There are many more verses.

Kingsholme †
Weston Revesby † † Haceby Hall
† Fordham Manor
† Bickmarsh Hall
† Harcourt Hall

✳ *Mawcester*

† Elmley Park

Sidworth Castle † † Westwood Hall
✳
Chawcester   *London*
✳

ENGLAND

Sidworth Castle

Sidworth Castle

Haceby Hall

Haceby Hall

Rushley Manor

RUSHLEY MANOR

Westwood Hall

Mistletoe Bride

CHRISTMASTIDE 1666

ir Henry "Hal" Westwood, 28

Justice of the Peace, guardian of the Sophie,
widower, gentleman of WESTOOD HALL

ophia Redcroft, 20

Hal's & Justin's ward, Cordelia's companion

dam Blackwell, 26

owner of BICKMARSH HALL

ordelia Blackwell, 19

Adam's wife, Hal's ward, Sophie's friend

imon Craven, 27

Cathy's husband; owner of HACEBY OLD HALL

athy Craven, 23

Simon's wife, Jack's sister, Madeline's daughter

arbara Craven, 52 *Simon's mother*

rabella "Bella" Craven, 18

Simon's sister, the missing bride

Nicholas Revesby, 22, *owner of WESTON REVESBY*

atherine "Kate" Westwood, 42 *Hal's aunt*

ir Richard Harrison, 45, *betrothed of Kate Westwood*

Jack Hollingshead, 25

owner of FORDHAM MANOR; kin to Cordelia Sandys

Madeleine Hollingshead, 48

kin to Cordelia Sandy, Jack's & Cathy's mother

Margaret Pauncey 47	*sister of Barbara, aunt of Simon*
Rosalind Pauncy 20,	*Simon's cousin, bridesmaid*
Beatrice Pauncey 17,	*Simon's cousin, bridesmaid*
Helen Pauncey 15,	*Simon's cousin, bridesmaid*
Mistress Pridow 54,	*cousin of the Cravens*
Louisa Pridow 28,	*her unmarried daughter*
Ezekiel Pridow, 38,	*her son, widower, the bridegroom*
Jacob Brendon, 52,	*friend of bridegroom Ezekiel*
Raife Jackson, 56,	*Steward of Haceby Hall*
William Tulley, 38,	*butler*
Cook, 36	
Rupert, 14,	*stableboy*
Jem Attwood, 40,	*farmer at Weston Revesby*
Nurse, 59,	*servant at Weston Revesby*
Coroner and his assistant	

OTHER WESTWOOD FAMILY:

Libby Westwood *deceased first wife of Hal Westwood*

Margery Kingscott, 62 *Hal's aunt, Kate's sister-in-law*

Harry Westwood, 6 *Hal's & Libby's son*

Francis Westwod *Hal's & Libby's infant son*

Ned Westwood, 21

Hal's brother, Cecily's husband, owner of THE OLD MANOR

Hetta Shearsby, 17 *Hal's sister*

Will Shearsby, 18 *Hetta's husband*

Thomas Kingscott, 49 *kin to Sir Henry Westwood*

Mary Kingscott, 45 *wife of Tom Kingscott*

Mary Armstrong, 28

Hal's elder sister; Guy's wife

Guy Armstrong, 29 *Mary's husband*

owner of ELMLEY PARK, brother-in-law to Hal

Bess Danvers, 21 *Hal's sister; Justin's wife*

Justin Danvers, 26 *lawyer, Hal's brother-in-law*

Stephen Westwood, 1 *Hal's French step-brother*

Glossary

OED- *Oxford English Dictionary*
BD *Brewer's Dictionary of Phrase & Fable*

acrostic — short poem or verse in which an initial, first middle or last, taken in order, spell a word or phrase *1587 OED*

Act of Settlement — led to Charles Stuart being proclaimed King of England, Wales Scotland and Ireland in May 1660.

ague — any fit of shaking or chilling, an acute fever *1595–1611 OED*

Bickmarsh Hall — home of Cordelia and Adam Blackwell

Edgehill — English Civil War battle *1642*

Elmley Park — home of Hal's sister Mary and her husband Guy Armstrong

entailed — to settle land or estate on persons in succession so it cannot be possessed by anyone as an absolute owner *ME OED*

enclosure	the fencing off or walling of previously open fields, held in common *OED 1587*
Fordham Manor	home of Jack Hollingshead and his mother Madeline
friends calling on you	was a phrase used (often in the heat of the moment) to indicate a duel would be fought at some time in the near future.
Haceby Old Hall	home of the Craven family
Harcourt Hall	home of the Harcourt family
hoyden	A rude or ill-bred girl *OED 1578*.
Ironsides	those who took arms against King Charles I in the English Civil War.
jade	term of reprobation applied to a woman *1577 OED*
kissing under the mistletoe	an English Christmas custom dating back to early *C17*. *Brewers Dictionary of Phrase and Fable.*
look nettled, nettled	to irritate, vex, pique *1562 OED*

Malignancy	disposed to rebel, disaffected malcontents—applied between 1641–60 by supporters of Parliament
Naseby	English Civil War battle 1645
Newbury	English Civil War battle 1644
Noll Cromwell	shortened name of Oliver Cromwell, Lord Protector of England, 1650–59.
out of long coats /in short coats	long coats childrens garments discarded when they go into short coats *1603 OED*
overset	to discompose a person. *OED 1533*
pother	a disturbance or tumult, a verbal commotion *1591 OED*
Puritans	took arms against King Charles I in the English Civil War.
relict	widow of a man *1450 OED*
Roundheads	took arms against King Charles I in the English Civil War.

scarlet woman	originally an abusive epithets applied the the church of Rome, later applied to women of dubious reputation *OED*.
sennight	contraction of seven nights; a week.
Sequestration	seizure of the possessions of a subject by the state, especially the act of a belligerent power in seizing debts owing from its own subjects to the opposing power. A Court or Committee to settle these matters. *OED. 1645*
taking	from that which takes the fancy *1483 OED*
The Old Manor	home of Hal's brother Ned and his wife Cecily Westwood.
toady	anything hateful and loathsome, *1584 OED*
Twelfth night	The feast of Epiphany, or the Magi or 6th of January
well-dowered	from a dowry or marriage portion. *ME OED*

For a glimpse of life
in the Shires of England
today...

you are cordially
invited to visit
Jemima Norton's blog at:

www.jemimanorton.com

Find out about a contest for our readers,
and other interesting delights

1666

Prologue

Nicholas reined in his horse. "This is hopeless," he said, with a catch in his voice. "Merlin is lame, we'll never make it to Lincoln."

Bella gave a little sigh, and swallowed the sob in her throat. "I fear you are right, Nicholas, what shall we do?"

"The devil of it is, Bella, I don't know. It all seemed much simpler when I planned it at home," he confessed.

She patted his damp back kindly. "You couldn't have foreseen the weather."

"That's the point. At this time of year, I should have considered it. Maybe your brother is right. Maybe I am too much of an untried fool to think of marriage," he replied glumly.

He looked so miserable, with raindrops spilling from the rim of his dark hat and his once-jaunty feather hanging limply to his shoulder, that her soft heart was wrung. "I think you are wonderful, Nick," she confided shyly.

A radiant smile lit his face. He was at once transformed from a sulky schoolboy into a bold adventurer. "I adore you, too, Bella!" he said, his voice echoing his feelings. "I'm sure I'll think of something presently, but in the meantime, I fear we must walk. I am not willing to damage poor Merlin."

"Indeed, no, poor fellow! He has carried us so gallantly, too. I don't mind walking one bit. Only, do you know where we are, Nick?" she asked, looking doubtfully about her.

"No," he admitted reluctantly, as he slid from the saddle and reached up to help her down, "but we should hit the Lincoln road almost any time now. Mind those brambles, now, Bella. I am sure if we keep to this path, we must soon find the road."

He absently patted the nose of his horse and led the beast forward through the undergrowth of the wood, in what he trusted was the right direction. He hadn't lightly persuaded Bella Craven to elope with him. He was only too well aware of the difficulties of his situation. Unless he could find the treasure hidden by his father, he would never keep his house and land. He had only until the last day of the year to pay off the mortgages which were due, or he'd lose everything.

He tightened his grip on Bella's hand and smiled into her enquiring eyes as she looked up at him. Her dark hair, misted with tiny droplets of rain, curled wildly about her lovely face. At least, if they got to Lincoln, that awful man Pridow wouldn't get his hands on her. Even if he did lose his fortune, he wouldn't let Bella be sacrificed to her brother's ambition. Pridow had made his late wife's life a misery with his mean ways.

"Don't worry," she said with her sunny smile. "Once we are married, we'll soon find your treasure, and even if we shouldn't immediately, I'm sure Simon will give me my dowry. Shall we be married as soon as we get to Lincoln? You do have the licence?"

"It is all arranged. We shall be married at St Mary's, by a friend of mine who used to be the curate at St Cuthbert's chapel."

"Do you think I look old enough?" she asked anxiously.

He thought she looked a mere child, and couldn't help smiling as he replied, "Yes, none will suspect anything is amiss, provided you don't giggle."

"Giggle!" she repeated indignantly.

"Yes, you do, you know…ah, look! There is the road!"
he cried as they pushed through the trees into a clearing.

"Is it the Lincoln road?" she asked anxiously.

"I don't think so…but it is a road…it must lead
somewhere," he replied.

"As long as it's not straight back home," she agreed.

Hal looked about him. The Hall at Bickmarsh Hall was
definitely old–fashioned—Spartan almost—yet metic-
ulously neat. The windows were high, built for defence,
with stout shutters pulled back to let in the sparse winter light. The walls were recently washed to a dazzling
whiteness, but devoid of any adornment—no tapestries
to create the illusion of warmth or wealth. The floor
was plain, flagged stones, which time had polished to a
gentle sheen.

He crossed to the fire glad of its warmth, noting the
logs piled high to one side, drying out, and took a seat
on a bench set there, to warm his numbed fingers. There
was but one chair, high-backed, dark and obviously old,
in that it had seen better days, but had been carefully
repaired to be of use for the new age. Likewise the pad-
ded cushions, which were placed gaily along the stone

window seat, were neatly patched and darned, told a tale of their own. Money appeared to be short for the young couple.

"Sir Henry, please take the chair!" Adam Blackwell, returning with a mug of steaming ale, was insistent. "I mended it myself to take my weight. It will serve you easily."

"Thank you, Mr Blackwell," replied Hal, taking the mug from him and cradling it in his hands as he sipped the heartening brew. "It grows cold as the sun goes down."

"Yes," Adam glanced anxiously skyward. "I expected Cordelia to be returned by now. She has but stepped out to talk to the vicar's sister. The light fades so quickly at this time of year."

Hal nodded, feeling weary and not inclined to put his host at his ease, slipped into silence. The fretting worries, which had driven him northwards at this inclement time of year, springing back into his mind.

Aunt Kate, and Aunt Margery too, to a certain extent, both had become part of the fabric of his life since his return from exile in France near seven years ago. Both in their very different ways had helped him adjust to the new life, so abruptly thrust upon him, and both were fond of him, as he was of them.

Now Aunt Margery was ill, very ill, if the truth were told, although she wouldn't hear of it. And Aunt Kate, although she was yet unaware of it, seemed to have a problem of her own. His errand at this time of year between Christmas and Twelfth Night was to collect Aunt Kate from where she was visiting in the neighbouring county and return her to Westwood Hall. On the face of it, it was to help nurse Aunt Margery back to health, but in truth it was to get her from what could become a difficult, if not dangerous, situation.

And all this had to be done without any offence to those concerned, or any admission of what was going forward, a hellishly trick situation, which Aunt Margery was convinced only Hal could accomplish. Was it any wonder then, that he had decided to break his journey at the home of his erstwhile ward, Cordelia Sandys, making the excuse that he needed to transfer various papers to her husband now she was married, but in fact to gather his wits and plan how his objective was to be achieved without Aunt Margery's frequently repeated instructions.

"I'm sure Cordelia won't be long," Adam repeated uncomfortably, remembering how, from his very first meeting at the inn in Chawcester, Hal Westwood had the power to make him feel like an ill-educated clod.

"And how is my former ward, your wife?" asked Hal, disturbed from his reverie.

"Cordelia is—is well, replied Adam with hesitation. "I am sure both she and Sophie will be back directly. I've sent a lad after them."

"Mistress Redcroft—or does she go by the name of Harcourt in these parts—she is still with you then?" remarked Hal, although he knew it was so.

"Sophie is still called Redcroft," replied Adam frowning. "Mr Danvers came to insist it was necessary. She never took the Harcourt name."

"And she obeyed him? How refreshingly unusual of her! It is not a name one would wish to be associated with, most certainly." Hal agreed coldly.

"Definitely not in this location," Adam agreed with a sudden grin. "The gossip was dreadful!"

"I can imagine it was," replied Hal, "but something Mistress Redcroft is well-used to, surely?"

"I don't know that anyone can become used to having lies spread about them," returned Adam, frowning. "Such ill-natured spite must always hurt, I'd think."

Hal glanced sharply to the other man, a little surprised by his words. "Do you find your local minister to your taste?" he asked, his manner thawing slightly.

Adam gave a wry smile. "He's one of the old sort," he admitted. "He tends his flock with fire and brimstone! He considers Cordelia to be the spawn of Satan, even though she is trying her best to fit her beliefs to that of our English Church."

"Cordelia has renounced her Catholic religion?" said Hal surprised.

"She was never a convinced Catholic," replied Adam, defensively. "She decided it would be politic to embrace the Church of England if we are to remain here. Recollect she was brought up by nuns in France. What chance had she but to be a Catholic? Besides, in her faith, our marriage is no marriage at all, and she is little better than a fallen woman. She has been receiving instruction from the local man and hopes to be Confirmed at sometime in the future."

"And in the meantime, must pay lip service to the Rectory, and its inhabitants?" said Hal nodding his understanding.

"Cordelia will always be devout," replied Adam. "Anything she does is the result of careful consideration and he added, as Hal cast him a quizzical look, "the vicar's sister is a great favourite with both her and Sophie. They seem to have a sincere affection for each other.

Sophie is so useful in helping Cordelia understand the English way of things."

"Yes, I can well see that one raised by French Catholic nuns, might find herself at a loss in Lincolnshire."

Adam pulled another face and came to sit opposite him. "It has not been easy," he admitted. "Cordelia and I represent all they fought against. The son of one Royalist and the daughter of another, brought up, as you say, by French Catholic nuns. Even Sophie, who is the only non-royalist, is spoken of with disfavour because of her disastrous marriage."

"So, none have called upon you, I suppose, or made you welcome?" Hal remarked, trying to keep the censure from his voice.

"Sir Charles Wicliffe came a few weeks after we'd settled in, to bring Sophie word of how things went at Harcourt, and Dury Southgate was a regular caller, until Lady Harcourt became so very ill."

Hal nodded. "Yes, it would be so," he agreed. "The local gentry would give you the benefit of the doubt and merely talk about you behind your backs, but your own people and the yeomanry, no. They'll make their feelings clear to your face."

Adam nodded grimly. "Not that I care for myself,

but Cordelia doesn't deserve all the ill-feeling, anymore than Sophie."

"Scandal dies away eventually. Usually when another greater scandal comes along," said Hal. "I well recollect how it was when my uncle was killed. Many pointed a finger at me, and there were those who claimed Will Longstaffe had been a convenient scapegoat. And then, more recently, there was the gossip at the death of my wife and before that over the furore at Chawcester."

Adam nodded, recollecting the ferment of scandal which had spread in the sleepy market town whilst the Justice lay recovering from the wounds inflicted by a murderer who had run amok. "Yes, I remember it, too, Sir Henry," he nodded. "Yes and how suddenly, when the churchwarden of St John's disappeared with the collection one Sunday and was found dead-drunk behind the abbey, it all disappeared overnight."

"No, it never completely disappears," said Hal. "People have long memories and are always glad to remember scandal, usually at the worst time."

Adam nodded again. "I am convinced Jack Hollingshead is at the root of all the ill-feeling," he confided. "Every time I give a direction to one of the people here, they straight away start on about what Master Jack would have done."

A faint rueful smile flickered across Hal's face as he recollected the first weeks of his return to England. "It is never easy to fill another's shoes," he agreed with reluctant sympathy. "But recollect, none had ever heard of Cordelia's existence. From what I have heard, her father, Sir Basil, wasn't the best landlord either. Most of his tenure was during the war, when he was at odds with the majority of the local population. Jack Hollingshead must have seemed like a dream come true to the tenants. He turned the property from a ramshackle..."

"Adam! Adam, are you there?" A slender young woman, her golden curls tumbled by the wind, rushed into the hall, her words, full of laughter, tripping from her lips. "You'll never guess what that...Oh, Hal!" She stopped in her tracks by the long, polished table, her hand going to her chest, as if to still her heart. "Sir Henry, what a shock you gave me. I never expected to see you here!"

Hal, who had risen to his feet and was as pale as she was red-faced, replied quietly: "Did you not? Yet I have a vast deal of business to transact with Mistress Blackwell, and some letters from my family for you, too."

"Sir Henry!" Cordelia, a shorter young woman with darker hair, entered the hall in Sophie's wake. "Sir Henry! This is a surprise!"

"You didn't see Jankin, then?" Adam observed, coming to relieve her of her damp cloak and basket. "I thought the rain might bring him back with you."

"Jankin? No," she replied, smiling up at her husband.

"I sent him to fetch you," he said with a resigned air. "He was to tell you Sir Henry was come."

"Jankin will have taken the opportunity to go back home," said Sophie, her eyes never leaving their visitor's face, as she tried to absorb what was so different about him. Then she realised that the major change was that he had abandoned his dark coat. Apart from the first few weeks of their acquaintance, she had only been in his company after his wife died and he had been in mourning. He now wore a coat of green cloth, handsomely laced with gold, in the latest fashion. But that wasn't the only thing she noticed. There was about him an air of sadness, a weariness, as if he found life difficult, and a loss of that expectancy, which had made him seem so very alive.

Hal, who had been standing looking into the bottom of his mug of ale, glanced up to smile slightly at Cordelia's expression of dismay. He was acutely aware of Sophie. He could see her beauty was undimmed, even when she removed her cloak to reveal a dull, grey gown, as befitted her status of a recently widowed bride. True, in typical Sophie style, it was a silk gown, edged in costly lace and fitted her slender figure perfectly, but it was mourning of sorts, and Hal was relieved to see that someone, probably Cordelia, had managed to persuade her of the sense of not offending local people.

"Yes, that is most likely," Cordelia was agreeing. "He said this morning he missed his mother. I really don't think we shall ever train that boy Adam, Sir Henry," she came to give Hal her thin hand, her smile troubled. "You are most welcome to our home. You must be weary after your journey. Can I bring you some further refreshment?"

"Thank you, but I breakfasted well at The George at Grantham," he replied. "And Master Blackwell has been most attentive to my needs."

She smiled fleetingly, seemingly at a loss. "We—we didn't apprehend a visit, sir, or we we would have..."

"Even though you married without my consent, Cordelia, I am still your guardian until such time as I pass over various papers and deeds to your husband," Hal replied with a distant air. "I beg pardon that I have been so remiss in my dealings, but when I returned home after the debacle of Sophie's wedding, I found my sons were ill. By the time they had recovered, my cousin, Tom Kingscott's wedding was almost upon us. In truth, I would not have been happy to leave them again, until I felt certain they were truly well, so at Tom's suggestion, we all—Aunt Margery, the boys and I—came up to support him. I was Tom's groomsman."

"Harry and little Francis have been ill?" Sophie cried in dismay, shaking the raindrops from her curls. "Dear heavens, what happened?"

"A common enough childhood illness, so my sister Mary informed me, but one which romped through her children and Bess's boys, and left little Harry with a nasty cough, which gave us all cause for concern."

"They are well now though, I trust, Sir Henry?" asked Cordelia as her husband brought both her and Sophie a mug of warmed ale.

"My two are—I thank you—but Mary's youngest also developed a weakness of the lungs which is giving her much anxiety."

"Oh, the poor little man," Sophie said. "'Tis no wonder Mary never replied to my letter." Then, not giving Hal time to comment, and glancing swiftly to her companions, whose faces mirrored their inward trepidation, she added bluntly: "So, Sir Henry, other than to lecture us upon our behaviour, and to settle outstanding affairs between yourself and Cordelia, has anything else brought you so far from home at this season of the year?"

"The necessity to settle Mistress Blackwell's outstanding affairs is sufficient," he replied coolly, not meeting her sparkling eyes. "It is my remaining duty, as her former guardian, to pass over certain documents to Mr Blackwell, although I am also on my way to collect and escort my Aunt Kate Westwood back home."

"We had heard that Aunt Kate was staying at Haceby Hall," said Sophie, a mischievous gleam in her eyes. "As Adam is Cordelia's guardian now they are married, it is only I who need your protection."

Hal's eyes rested coldly upon her lovely face. "Is the Harcourt name not proving protection enough?" he enquired tartly."

"You are well aware I have not taken the Harcourt name," she replied quickly. "It was your—and Justin's —advice that I did not do so."

"And you took that advice? I am amazed," he replied sarcastically. "It must be one of the few occasions you have done so."

"I am not a fool," she retorted. "I can see my best interests as well as the next man! Besides which, the Harcourts are so beset by trouble, I couldn't even think of bothering them."

"Sophie is part of our family now," said Cordelia firmly, then as Hal looked surprised, she added: "Poor Lady Harcourt is not like to see the spring, so they say. Dury Southgate is doing his best to keep everything together, and Mistress Kate is nursing her mother devotedly, but the events of last summer have left scars everywhere."

"Indeed, and not only on their family," agreed Hal sombrely. "What of the child, of Mistress Selby's son, Harry?"

"Dury Southgate is his guardian, at Lady Harcourt's insistence, and they have changed his name to Harcourt legally, but the child seems bewildered by everything, poor little fellow," said Sophie with compassion.

"So, she got what she wanted, Jane Selby," said Hal, shaking his head. "Her son did become Sir Henry Harcourt."

"We can but hope that Dury Southgate's influence will make him a better man than his uncles," Adam remarked with a sigh.

"Or, that he doesn't favour his mother," Hal agreed.

"Amen to that!" Sophie said with a shudder, then in an effort to shake off her melancholy, she asked again, "So, is it true, as Mr Danvers says, Sir Henry, have you forsaken your guardianship of me?"

Hal's eyes rested coldly on her face for a few seconds. "It has been agreed between us that Justin would take the majority of decisions with regard to the joint guardianship we hold," he replied. "As I explained earlier, my own children have required my attention recently. And as my record as a guardian was hardly enhanced by both my wards embarking on ill-advised marriages, which involved both their names and mine becoming the source of common gossip and scandal, I decided I'd better concentrate my efforts on my own affairs."

At these harsh words, Cordelia looked stricken and distressed, and Adam's face took on a pugnacious scowl.

"I will not have it said our marriage was ill-advised," he cried, his tone belligerent. "Not to your taste, Sir Henry, I"ll admit..."

"What of the promise you gave me, Mistress Blackwell?" Hal asked sharply, as Sophie also began to speak. "The promise I relayed to Madelaine Hollingshead, who told her son Jack–"

"I gave no promise to Jack, Sir Henry," Cordelia replied, her voice trembling over the words. "The promise I gave was to you, and for failing in that promise, I apologise sincerely. You have every right to reproach me, although you can hardly do so more than I do myself."

"What nonsense!" Sophie cried above Adam's hot words. "Hal knows he was exerting unfair pressure on you, Cordelia!"

"No, Sophie!" Cordelia intervened quickly, to prevent the quarrel Sophie seemed intent on provoking. "Sir Henry put no such pressure on me. Any blame rests fairly on my shoulders. I agreed to his suggestions merely to please him—to demonstrate how much I appreciated the difficulty of the circumstances, and to show how grateful I was for his rescue of me. It was only later I began to fully comprehend how much I should dislike the marriage. Then, to my eternal shame, rather than facing up to the facts and explaining my feelings, I ran away, leaving Sir Henry with an awful mess to clear up." She smiled up at Adam, who had come to clasp her hand, a ferocious frown marring his handsome face. "The most dreadful thing is, sir, that I have never been more blissfully happy in my life. Now, how can that be a just reward for such cowardice?"

Hal, who knew he was being unreasonable, and that her words were patently the truth, shrugged his elegant shoulders, ashamed of the petulance that had provoked the question. "I am the last person in the world, ma'am, to criticise moral cowardice." Then, as Sophie began to expostulate, he cried: "Enough, Sophie! In the face of such a comprehensive explanation, what can I say, but to beg pardon for my bad manners?" A faint quizzical smile curved his lips. "There never was a need for so great a sacrifice, Cordelia, but the situation we found ourselves in coloured our reactions, I do believe. You are a good girl and I would see you happy in your life."

"I am happy, Sir Henry, married to my dear Adam," she replied, "but for the method of our achieving it, and the way I abandoned you, I have no regrets."

"Then all that is left, is to wish you joy, my dear," he replied, in his polished manner.

"Your blessing would mean much to me, sir," she said quietly. "You cannot comprehend how much. I know you are not my father, indeed you are far too young to be such, but if you could count me as a member of your family, like one of your sisters or a cousin, my happiness would be complete. I did so hate the thought that my foolish actions had made you cast me aside."

Hal, who had come fully prepared to hand over the legal documents and do just that, in his simmering resentment, found in the face of her sweet humility he had no choice but to agree to her wishes. "Certainly you may have my blessing, for what it is worth, on your union," he replied, trying to force a more cordial tone into his words. "I cannot hold you to blame, Cordelia, for the machinations of others."

Adam held out his massive hand. "Thank you, Sir Henry, for making my dear wife's happiness complete, and I beg that you'll add to it and mine, sir, by agreeing to stand godfather to our firstborn!"

Hal blinked. "Good heavens!" he cried, submitting to a knuckle-cracking handclasp. "Is it truly so?"

Cordelia blushed a deep pink. "It is rather early to speak of it, but we believe so."

"You mean you are to have a child, Cordelia? Oh, how wonderful!" Sophie cried. "May I be a godmother?"

Adam grinned. "Do you have any idea of the task you'd be undertaking, Sophie?" he asked.

"Indeed," she replied, with mock dignity. "I shall make a very good godmother."

"Being so very aware of all the pitfalls which present themselves, I suppose," said Hal, and in the laughter which followed, the discomfort of the situation was eased. And in no time, Hal, who had sworn to keep his distance and maintain the demeanour of an aggrieved guardian, found himself, as they sat down to supper, slipping back into the old position of easy intimacy, which was the biggest danger of being an acquaintance of Sophie Redcroft.

❧

Chapter Two

"Aunt Margery is quite recovered then, Hal?" Sophie asked, as the broth was removed and a pair of pheasants, flanking a leg of pork, made its arrival.

He cast her doubtful look. "She is recovered somewhat from her ill health," he agreed. "Although she regularly declares she'll never recover from the shame of having her connections know of your marriage."

"How can I be held to blame, Hal, for my future sister-in-law murdering my bridegroom on our wedding night?" Sophie asked bluntly.

"I do not know, Sophie, but Aunt Margery most certainly holds you at fault," he replied, his face relaxing at her amazed expression. "Indeed, it was as well you remained here throughout the autumn, when the children were all ill, or you'd have taken the blame for that too. By the by, did you know Hetta is like to produce another child in the spring?"

"Hetta? No, oh, that is splendid," cried Sophie, as Cordelia echoed her pleasure, adding: "Indeed wonderful news, sir, such that will put Aunt Kate's mind at rest after the tragedy of last year."

"Indeed, I do believe she plans to…" He stopped as a thunderous knocking came upon the door.

"Good heavens!" said Cordelia nervously, her hand going to Adam as he got to his feet, casting his napkin aside.

"Who is it, Jankin?" he demanded of the imp of a boy, who had but recently returned, having been beaten by the cook into waiting at table.

"Stand aside, churl!" A voice they all knew well came to their ears, and as Adam took a step forward, Hal rose to his feet and Sophie put her hand on Cordelia's shoulder.

"'Tis Master Jack, sir!" called the boy, as Jack Hollingshead came into the hall, thrusting aside the short cloak he wore to protect him from the worst of the weather.

"Cousin Jack!" Cordelia cried faintly, as Adam advanced upon the visitor.

"Mr Hollingshead, well met," said Hal, sensing trouble. "Will you not take a seat with us? we are still dining;"

"Sir Henry, you are here! This is excellent news! For 'tis you I seek!" cried the young man. His glance, bright with dislike, flickered to Adam. "Mr Blackwell, your servant, sir." He made the most perfunctory of bows. "I beg pardon for this intrusion! Mistress Blackwell, Mistress...?"

"Mistress Redcroft!" Sophie snapped, as he hesitated over what to call her.

He shrugged his shoulders, and as the smell of the food hit his nostrils, he appeared to come to a decision. He surrendered his cloak and sword to the boy who still stood waiting, and crossed to the seat Adam was reluctantly indicating.

"Thankee, I'll take a cup of wine, if I may. The rain has turned cold, it's setting in for an unpleasant night, and I have been on the road since before breakfast."

"Indeed?" Cordelia faltered over the word, knowing good manners would oblige her to offer him shelter for the night. "You are not at your home then?"

"No," his smouldering look lingered on her pale face. "No, my mother and myself crossed into the county last week to attend the marriage of my sister Catherine's husband's sister. She was to have been married today."

"I trust it was a happier occasion than our last experience of a wedding, sir," said Hal politely, wondering where this was all leading.

"No, it was not," he replied absently, his attention diverted by Cordelia's suggestion that she help him to some of the roast pork. "The wedding never took place."

"Didn't take place?" repeated Adam, placing a platter of bread in front of his guest.

"No, let me explain. My sister Catherine's husband, Simon Craven's family, had arranged for Arabella to marry a local man, a Mr Pridow, a widower, with several small children..."

"Poor Arabella!" Sophie murmured mischievously.

Jack glanced to her, irritated that she should interrupt his story. "Your pardon?"

"A widower with several small children as a bridegroom?" She made her lovely face into a mischievous grimace of distaste. "A hideous fate, surely?"

"Indeed," agreed Hal, well aware of where her mockery was aimed. "Pray continue, sir."

"My sister Catherine has three of her own children, and the bridegroom is as I say the father of six, and his good friend and supporter had at least five! At all events there were brats everywhere it seemed to me—either that or babes in arms, so the bride and her cousins, who were to be her maids, you understand—three sisters— these girls arranged to play games with the children. Hide and Seek and such, at the feast for the tenants, which was held yesterday—on St Stephens Day."

"To help keep them occupied?" Sophie suggested, as he paused to take a further mouthful of food.

He nodded, swallowing. "It worked, too. Apart from the squeals of fear and delight, so that we could barely hear the fiddler to dance! Until, that is, the feast finished and the nursemaids came to take the children to bed."

"They got over-excited," said Sophie wisely. "They always do, you know. I expect it ended in tears."

"Much worse than that, ma'am," he said a trifle thickly, hastily finishing a mouthful of bread. "They'd gone!"

"Gone!" Hal repeated blankly. "The children?"

"No, no! Not them. The bride and one of her maids!"

"Disappeared?" asked Hal frowning.

"You searched?" Adam suggested, puzzled.

"High and low, every nook and cranny from attics to cellars! Far into the night!" Jack replied, nodding as Cordelia offered him a dish of pheasant.

"But no sign?" Hal asked, his attention caught by the tale.

"None at all," muttered Jack, through a mouthful of fowl. "And of course, all the old biddies—I beg pardon—the older female relations, all cried out in fear, because of the damned wreath which Bella had been wearing in her hair!"

"A wreath in her hair?" asked Sophie, bewildered by his manner of telling the tale.

"Aye! It was all some mummery or another, something about the wreath which Bella put in her hair that afternoon. She and the older girls had been out earlier picking holly and ivy to decorate the chambers, and it seems Bella had made a wreath of ivy and berries, and one of them had put it on Bella's head. Then her aunt and a friend had sworn on their lives that it was bad luck to bring mistletoe into the house. You know how females do make such a fuss!" He coughed as he caught Sophie's eye, and made haste to say, "This is excellent pheasant, Mistress Blackwell! The game at Bickmarsh is incomparable!"

"Pray, sir, eat your supper in peace," said Cordelia. "I am sure we can wait a little longer to hear all the details."

"Nothing more to say," he replied. "Females weeping and wringing their hands, brats screaming, servants in hysterics—I told my brother-in-law I'd ride to fetch Sir Henry at first light. He deals in mysteries, I told them. Your Aunt Westwood agreed I should fetch you. She said you were bound to break your journey at Bickmarsh Hall." His eyes travelled to Sophie as he spoke.

"I arrived a few hours ago," agreed Hal. "Aunt Kate knows I have business to transact with Mr Blackwell, and as you suggest, it makes a convenient resting place between my cousin's home and Haceby Hall." He frowned as he finished speaking, and then added politely, "I'm obliged to you, Mr Hollingshead, but I don't see how I can be of assistance to you."

The visitor put aside his empty plate and took up his mug of ale. "A female—two females—can't just disappear like that," he said flatly. "We were all there! All of us in the house! This curst weather has stopped any hunting. We searched the place…and there is nothing." His heavy brows creased into a scowl. "I tell you, it makes no sense!"

"What did the bridesmaids say?" Hal asked after a few moments reflection as he realised Jack was right.

"I tell you, we could get no sense from any of them! Hysteria set in, and it was spreading rapidly!" he sighed. "In the end, my mother, your Aunt Kate and I agreed.

It were best I rode to fetch you, Sir Henry."

"What do you, and indeed your mother, expect me to do?" Hal asked, for he did not expect to meet Madelaine Hollingshead with any pleasure.

"Come back with me now and discover what has occurred," he replied shortly. "You are expected within days anyway, to escort your aunt back to your home. Just arrive earlier."

Hal leaned back in his seat and looked the man over thoughtfully. It was plain he was set upon this course, and that he and his mother felt Hal should oblige them in this matter. Hal acknowledged he was under some sense of obligation, but his last meeting with Mistress Hollingshead was still in his memory. The contempt and scorn she poured upon his faltering apologies, the blunt remarks about his relationship with Sophie still had the power to make him squirm. Yet he knew he had to undertake the journey, not only to assist Aunt Kate, but to pay his debt to the mother and son.

"I've looked into some odd matters in my time since I was a Justice," he admitted, "but in my experience to do so often causes further trouble."

Jack Hollingshead frowned at this. "What further trouble could befall us?"

"Take the affair of Sophie's guardian, Edmund Benson," continued Hal. "He called in my brother-in-law because his journeyman had been killed in what looked like a tragic accident. In looking into the affair, not only Edmund Benson died, but four other, totally innocent men died also, and Sophie herself was put into great danger before we found the murderer. There is a school of thought that had we let it lie, those men might still be alive to this day."

"But I might have been dead," said Sophie, "for I might well have been tempted into marriage with the murderer."

"Indeed, your fortune was the cause of the evil," agreed Hal. "Is there money involved in this matter, Mr Hollingshead?"

Jack frowned. "Not to my knowledge. Bella will have a dowry, I imagine, but no, nor are there any murders. Just the disappearance of two foolish maids!"

"Depend upon it, it is a foolish prank by those two young ladies and by now they will have returned, and the wedding is now set for tomorrow," Sophie suggested.

"Returned from where?" Jack replied tartly. "I tell you we've searched and something isn't right!"

"Perhaps they are hiding in the gardens, or a hut," said Cordelia, as she glanced to the rain-lashed windows. "Perhaps if your kinswoman really dislikes the thought of the marriage, she has run away and hidden somewhere?"

Jack cast her an unloving look. "Aye, we thought of that, having recently experienced something of the sort, and I tell you everyone has searched! This was no half-hearted attempt. We searched every inch of that house, aye and the pleasure gardens, too, in the foulest of weather, whilst the tenants and farmers all searched their barns. There is not one inch of that place we've not searched, for it was hardly the weather for young women to be out of the house!" Jack Hollingshead scowled at them all as if insulted at any suggestion of neglect.

Hal shifted uncomfortably in his seat and Cordelia looked chastened. "I am not expected at Haceby Hall until later in the week," he began reluctantly. "I still have business matters to attend to with regard to both Mistress Blackwell and Mistress Redcroft."

"Was it not you who insisted the trail of clues must not be allowed to run cold when Justin Danvers was accused of murder? I recollect you saying haste was of the essence in murder," said Sophie.

"But there has been no murder," protested Hal. "Two young women are missing, that is all. Mistress Blackwell is of a like age and she has suggested the most likely cause."

Jack Hollingshead looked bewildered. "I know nothing of causes, though I observe most females to be changeable creatures with minds like weathervanes. I however..."

"You are still a bachelor, then, Mr Hollingshead," interrupted Sophie, as Cordelia looked distressed. "And like to stayed a confirmed one, if you are always so ready with pretty words!"

"And you still, for all your efforts, lack a husband!" he retorted, his hackles rising. "Not quite so many fellows clustering about you these days, are there? None quite so keen for the embrace of death marrying you promises, are they?"

"It will hardly advance your cause with me, Mr Hollingshead, if you insult my kin," observed Hal. "Instead of squabbling with Sophie, tell me what you fear."

Jack hesitated, his high colour fading. "I beg your pardon," he said reluctantly, recollecting his manners. "I meant no slight, Mistress Blackwell." Again he hesitated, trying to gather the words. "Mistress Redcroft,

I beg your pardon, that was ill-said." Then, turning to Hal he continued, "I fear death, sir, in a closed community. It is Christmastide; we are all kin of sorts, gathered for a wedding. You have experience of such matters—we all hide from the horror of finding a murderer in our midst. Your Aunt Kate Westwood understood at once, and said you'd not fail us."

Hal sat silent for a few moments and then capitulated. "If Aunt Kate has given me such a testimonial, the very least I can do is to attend the scene and hope to find the young ladies returned and the wedding going forward. Adam, Mistress Blackwell, Mistress Redcroft, I fear our business must be delayed, perhaps until after Twelfth Night, and I crave your indulgence in this matter."

"You are welcome back at any time, sir," said Adam swiftly. "I know I speak for us both when I say our home must always be open to you."

"I shall go with you to Haceby, Hal," Sophie interrupted Hal's expression of thanks, without compunction.

Hal turned to stare at her. "I beg your pardon?" he asked, at his most disencouraging.

"I shall go with you to Haceby," she replied, undaunted by his icy stare. "You'll need someone, not of the family, to help, and I will be able to talk to the children and young ladies so much better than you can. The little ones will be terrified of you, and the girls will fall in love, and be a nuisance trying to get your attention."

"I assure you the young women of my kin are well brought-up young ladies. They would never dream of making unseemly overtures to a gentleman!" said Jack stiffly.

"I'm sure they wouldn't bother with you," agreed Sophie unkindly, "but Hal's face will bring them like bees to a honey pot."

"Sophie!" Hal protested as Jack's hackles rose again. "I am going to investigate a disappearance, no such complications will occur. And you most definitely are not going with me. You haven't been invited," he added as a clincher.

"By the time Aunt Kate has told them how clever you are, and wonderful and handsome, you'll be a hero to them all," replied Sophie. "Your aloof demeanour will only confirm what they've already imagined and any investigations into the mystery will get bogged down in countless little details—true or manufactured—to get your attention. It's what I'd have done," she added, as Jack and Hal looked appalled.

"She is right, Sir Henry," said Cordelia, as Jack began to repeat that his kin were not pert, ill-mannered hoydens. "Young girls can be very silly, and you are unaware of the effect you create. Half the nuns of the convent of Saint-Sauvy spent the night on their knees after you left, you know."

Hal looked very taken aback as Adam chuckled, adding, "Aye, the maids of Chawcester still talk about you even now, and my step-mother sighs over the memories of the time you spent there."

Hal reddened. "I fail to see how an ageing widower can be of any interest to anyone, save that he may help in solving a problem," he said dismissively. "That, however, is neither here nor there. The invitation is not extended to Sophie, and so you will remain here."

"I am a married woman, it would seem," she replied, "I can go where I please until Justin sorts out the legal tangle of my life. And I was invited to the wedding, but I declined the invitation."

"You are not a married woman. You remain in the wardship of Justin and myself until such time as the legal tangle is resolved," replied Hal sharply. "And if you have already declined the invitation to the wedding, you cannot possibly arrive with me. I do not need assistance, and I do not care to spend the journey listening to you and Jack Hollingshead exchanging insults!"

"In fact, Sir Henry, your Aunt Westwood instructed me to fetch Mistress Redcroft too, should she be in your company," said Jack reluctantly. "She said Sophie was very good at stirring up a hornet's nest of trouble, so bringing facts that normally remain hidden to the surface."

"That settles it then," said Sophie gleefully. "I'll undertake not to squabble with you, Jack, however pompous you may be, and we'll be off at once! Come, Hal, don't delay, in an hour the day will be fading fast."

"Indeed it will," he agreed. "Another good reason for you to remain here. We shall get along a lot faster without you."

"I'll engage to keep pace with either of you," she replied getting to her feet. "Adam, Cordelia, we leave you to your pastoral peace, and will return anon to tell you all!"

❧

Chapter Three

Hal looked in dismay at the reception committee which had gathered to greet him. He gave a shiver and gratefully swallowed another spoonful of soup. "This broth is excellent, Mistress Craven," he said politely, glancing to the anxious faces before him. "Very welcome after such a journey. I don't know when I've seen so much rain!"

"We do get more than our fair share of it this side of the country," said Jack Hollingshead, from the other side of the fire. "The heavens opened as soon as we left Bickmarsh."

"Most surely several years' supply fell upon us this evening," said Hal with another shudder, glancing with some interest about him. Jack had mentioned Haceby was an old house, but his words had hardly prepared Hal for either the place, or these people who lives he had suddenly been precipitated into.

Simon Craven, his host, was of a similar age to Jack Hollingshead, and therefore, Hal himself. A quiet young man, under considerable strain, yet with an air of competence and what appeared to be an imperturbable temper. He was shorter than Jack and less highly coloured, but Hal felt an instant respect and liking for him. His wife, Cathy, was of course, Jack's sister, and she shared his ruddy colouring and direct manner, although it appeared to have mellowed under the influence of the Craven family.

"Sir Henry, I've just taken a tisane to Mistress Redcroft, who is sensibly taking a hot bath, assisted by your aunt, will you not try one of my brews?" Simon Craven's mother, Barbara, entered the chamber, already in a state of readiness for bed, but with an air of capability which was an echo of her son's.

"Mother, Sir Henry has a glass of my finest brandy-wine to follow Cathy's excellent broth," said Simon. "I know which I'd prefer."

"My thanks for your trouble, Mistress Craven," said Hal. "I'll put it here by the fire, if I may, and take it before retiring. In the meantime, whilst I finish the broth, perhaps you could recap on the day's events, Mr Craven?"

Simon Craven nodded and came to put another un-necessary log on the already blazing fire. "We've made no further progress since Jack left before daybreak this morning," he said, his voice much troubled. "We searched and searched, going back over the same ground, in case we missed something, until the rain began to fall in torrents and the light failed us. There was no sign of either of the girls."

Hal nodded, guessing as much from the anxious fac-es before him. Barbara Craven's face was white with fa-tigue, her eyes red-rimmed with weeping, whilst those of her sister, Mistress Pauncey, a middle-aged woman with a quantity of untidy hair tumbling down her back and a vague, ineffectual expression, showed how deep was their distress. As for her two remaining daughters, they sat ready for bed, too, yet unable to think of sleep-ing. They all looked as if they lived a nightmare.

"Can you tell me more of what occurred?" Hal asked. "I have no desire to distress you further, Mistress Cra-ven, Mistress Pauncey, and Jack did his best to explain, but when the rain came down so hard, we judged it best to just get here, out of the wet."

"Yes, the foul weather curtailed our searches, too," said Simon, walking the floor in a fret of anxiety. "I hope to God those girls have found shelter!"

"Rosalind will take cold if her feet get wetted," said the elder of the two girls, who sat with their arms about their mother, Mistress Pauncey. "Rosalind always takes cold if she gets wet, Mother."

"Bella is no fool, Beatrice," said Simon, with a tight smile. "She'll see her cousin is kept warm and dry. She'll know how to seek shelter from the rain."

"I take leave to doubt that, Mr Craven!" An older man, dressed in the dark colours favoured by those of a more Puritan persuasion, spoke harshly from his position on an upright bench at some distance from the fire. His long, thin face seeming to echo the general misery. "A sensible woman would not have ventured from her hearth and home at this time of the year! I cannot imagine what she can have been thinking of."

"Indeed, Ezekiel," cried a younger woman, sitting next to him, who by her distinct resemblance, showed her kinship with him. "One wonders what she can have been thinking to leave her home at all!"

"We don't know what has happened," said an older woman, who occupied the far side of the bench. "Bella may have set out when the weather was clement," she observed placidly. "She is a good girl and will not have taken her cousin Rosalind into danger unnecessarily, we know that, Barbara. She has always had a care for her weaker cousin."

"Indeed she has," said Madelaine Hollingshead, Jack's mother, with whom Hal was by now well-acquainted. Of an older generation, Mistress Hollingshead had the confidence and social position to speak her mind and know she would be heeded. A handsome woman, a great beauty in her day, she still retained much of the fiery temper which made her a force to be reckoned with. "Bella is a fine young woman, who always has a care for the feelings of others. She would never run off without a word and leave us all worrying needlessly. She is no headstrong hoyden—an accident must have occurred to detain them."

"Indeed, ma'am, so we concluded," agreed Simon unhappily. "I know Bella is young, but if aught had gone wrong, she'll give every care to her cousin."

"Tell me more about the circumstances in which the young ladies went missing," said Hal, laying aside his empty bowl, and taking up the glass of brandywine Simon had pressed upon him.

"It was yesterday, or St Stephen's Day, as it used to be called..." Simon began.

"Near thirty hours ago!" interrupted the older man —who Hal now guessed to be Mr Pridow, the deserted bridegroom—could contain his impatience no longer. "Yet we sit here talking like gossips! What accident can have delayed them for thirty hours? Why did they even leave the house?"

"We always have a feast on St Stephens Day," continued Simon, glaring at his would-be brother-in-law. "You know, for our tenants and their families and the estate workers?"

Hal nodded his understanding, thinking fleetingly of his own home and wondering how his family had enjoyed a like feast.

"There must have been about a hundred and thirty of us, all told," said Simon, his anxiety returning. "We had the feast, and the choir sang the usual carols and songs, and the fiddler from the village played for the dancing."

"It was quite like the old days," said Barbara Craven. "When your father was alive, Simon, back before the war…" she broke off, with a quick, guilty glance to her guests. "I'm sorry, Simon, I interrupted you."

"No matter, Mother," he replied calmly. "I agree, it was very like the feasts I dimly remember from my childhood."

"Pagan rites!," a grim-faced man, who sat slightly behind the bridegroom, muttered under his breath.

"An old-style Christmas," said Simon, whose hearing was sharp. "Perhaps not so agreeable to everyone, but my people and tenants enjoyed it. There was a host of children, who got very excited at one point, and Bella, who had been dancing, said she'd organise some games to keep them out of mischief."

"They should have been set to their prayers," said another man, with a sigh. "Christmas should not be a time of surfeit and drunkenness. It seems to me we have forgotten we are here to celebrate the joy of the birth of our dear Lord."

"We did that earlier in church, Sir Richard," said Simon sharply, and Hal's attention was caught by the name, knowing this to be the man his Aunt Kate was to marry. He glanced curiously at him, wondering how it was they had never met until now. Hal saw a man weary with ill health, exhausted by life, devoid of any spark of humour which Hal felt instinctively would be an essential in a bridegroom for Aunt Kate. Then as Simon continued, he returned his attention to the matter at hand.

"Recollect, sir, the Puritan ways are no longer law," he was saying politely. "Nowadays, if he should so choose, a man may drink a health on the day of Christ's birth, after he has paid due reverence in church! I do beg pardon, Sir Henry, for all these interruptions. As I was saying, Bella decided, with the help of her cousins and some friends, to organise the sort of games we used to play at Christmas."

"Friends?," the bridegroom cried impatiently. "I saw no friends! The only friend was Nick Revesby!"

"I beg your pardon, sir," said Hal firmly, "but I must ask you to let Mr Craven explain as swiftly and unhindered as possible. I left my cousin's home and have been travelling for some time before Jack Hollingshead asked me to come here. I am, I must confess, bone-weary, and my wits, of a consequence, are a little hazy. If you have a point to make, I'd ask you to wait until the end of the account."

Ezekiel Pridow's cheerless companions looked affronted, but remained ominously silent, as Simon continued, "I don't recollect all that followed." He grinned suddenly. "Perhaps my wits were a little hazy, too. I know there was a game of Blindman's Bluff at one point, for the shrieks of the girls drowned out the fiddler."

"That was when Nick was Blindman," said Barbara Craven, with a small smile. "He insisted on a kiss as a forfeit when he caught any of the girls!"

"It sounds like a wonderful occasion," said Hal, smiling at the silent Pauncey sisters. "Did you get caught?"

"No," said the younger, Helen, "but Bea did!"

"Licentious behaviour," the bridegroom muttered under his breath.

Simon Craven ignored the aside, and continued his account. "Well, the evening wore on and the tenants began to leave. They are, for the most part, farmers, and have beasts to tend the following day, not to mention the walk or ride home. They collected their children, by now considerably quieter, having raced about playing Hide and Seek. My mother gave out her gifts to them, a pair of new boots or shoes and some sweetmeats, and they departed on their way home."

"A drunken rabble!" said Ezekiel Pridow disagreeably.

"Some will have had sore heads, I agree, but they turned out to a man the following morning to help search for Bella and Rosalind," Simon snapped.

"Did you not discover they had gone until the following day?" Hal asked in dismay.

"Oh, no, it became clear they'd gone quickly enough," said Simon. "We were all tidying up, you know how it is after a party—you all say you'll leave it to the morrow, but there is always just one more thing to be done?

Cathy was putting the children to bed, and Louisa and Mistress Pridow helping to settle Mr Pridow's brood, when we suddenly noticed Bella wasn't there."

"She usually helps me with the children, and Rosalind and her sisters have been helping Louisa with Mr Pridow's poor, motherless, little ones," explained Cathy Craven. "I called to Beatrice to see if she knew where Bella was, and we soon agreed we'd not seen either Bella or Rosalind since the height of the games, when they'd all been playing Hide and Seek."

Hal nodded his understanding. "You searched, of course," he remarked, with some resignation.

"All night, until it became too dark," said Simon. "There was no moon and it became too dangerous to go much further than the immediate grounds, so we agreed to snatch a few hours sleep and be up again at first light. Raife Jackson, my man, summoned all the tenants, and we combed the estate, and all the fields and farms. We found nothing, nothing at all. So we all returned home to get fresh horses and a bite to eat, intending to go out to search again. It was then Jack said he'd ride to Bickmarsh Hall, to see if you'd arrived yet, Sir Henry, for your Aunt Westwood said she expected you any day."

"And you still found nothing at all?" Hal asked frowning.

"The rain fell in torrents," replied Simon in dissatisfied tones. "After a few more hours, the light was so bad again, we were forced to give up."

"And the house? You've searched the house?" asked Hal, although he knew the answer, glancing around in dismay, for although he knew the house to be old from Jack's laconic words, nothing had prepared him for how old it was, or how rambling. The hall they sat in was vast, the roof beams lost in the gloom, and although warm as they grouped about the huge fire, there seemed space aplenty beyond the dim shadows, where tall windows still showed lashing rain and wind-whipped trees blowing.

"We did that the night they went missing," said Cathy Craven. "I, mother, Mistress Hollingshead, Aunt Pauncey, Beatrice and Helen."

"From attics to cellars," said Mistress Craven tearfully.

"And nothing was found," concluded Hal thoughtfully. He glanced to the expectant faces. "It is my proposal that we all get some rest. It is still raining heavily, as black as pitch out there, and you are all exhausted. At first light, I'll search the house with you, Mr Craven. Yes, I know this has all been done many times, ladies, but I bring fresh eyes to the scene. I have no knowledge of your house and may therefore pick out something which strikes me as odd, which you would accept from custom. Then we'll search the grounds again, until we find them. Above all, do not despair, in my experience, people never disappear completely."

Chapter Four

Hal awoke next morning feeling groggy. For a few seconds, he was on horseback in the driving rain of the previous evening. The distance may not have been great, but the weather conditions and Jack Hollingshead's horse throwing a shoe some ten miles short of their destination, had made for a nightmare journey. He rolled from the bed with a groan, as he realised how stiff and sore he was, but twenty minutes later, just as light was dawning over a sodden landscape, he entered the hall to find his host—along with his host's wife and mother, and Jack Hollingshead—all sitting at a breakfast they did not eat.

They exchanged greetings and civilities as Hal drank a mug of ale and ate a piece of bread and listened to their fears, then he gently detached his host from his womenfolk, and got Simon to personally conduct him and Jack over the house.

"You will, I know, understand our concern, Sir Henry," said Simon, as he led them from the dining parlour into the huge hall, which gave the house its name. "It is now more than thirty-six hours since we saw either my sister or our cousin."

Hal nodded sympathetically. "This was where the young people were all playing, was it?"

"No, the dancing was in here. The children played all over the rest of the house. They were rather loud and excited, I'm afraid, but it was a feast after all, and so Bella—who had, as I told you, been dancing—decided to arrange a game for them all."

"And she went missing at once? Did none see her all the remainder of the evening?" Hal asked, glancing with dismay at the number of chambers, passages and odd staircases that seemed to lead in every direction.

"No, most of us were in the hall, as I said, dancing. The children were running and laughing in and out during Blindman's Bluff, then there were fewer, as they went off to play Hide and Seek. We just heard shrieks as they were found, and some came back to join us as we took a little supper. It got latish, and my guests began to depart. Cathy thought the little ones should go to bed, for they were tearful with overexcitement, so she sent her nursemaid to find Bella, but none seemed to have seen either her or Rosalind. Then my mother went to look, thinking the nursemaid was being too idle to look properly, whilst Cathy and the girl got our little ones settled and the other younger children were all sent to bed. This left only the younger Pauncey girls and Louisa Pridow. That was when we discovered Rosalind was missing, too."

"I see," said Hal. "And do you think they may be concealed somewhere in the house?"

"I do not know what to think," he replied wretchedly. "We have questioned the grooms and the servants. They swear no horses have left the stables," he continued as they followed him up a handsome staircase. "Yet surely they cannot have left on foot?"

"And you said you've searched the grounds and the gardens?" continued Hal disregarding his question.

"Yes, whilst Jack rode for your assistance, Ezekiel Pridow, the bridegroom, his groomsman, Jacob Brendon, Sir Richard Harrison, your Aunt Westwood's betrothed husband, and all the outside men, scoured every shed, barn, and shepherd's hut on the estate. I thought they may have taken shelter and been too cold or too afraid to call out. We also sent word to tenants and neighbours, asking them to do the same. They all sent word by last evening that nothing had been discovered and that no horses had gone missing." His voice trembled over the last words.

"'Tis surely strange that no beasts were missing," Jack, who was dogging their footsteps, observed.

"What was the character of your sister, Mr Craven?" Hal asked as they traversed a long corridor.

"Bella? Well…I don't know," he replied blankly. "I mean, my mother has always had the handling of her, especially since my father died. She's—well she's a biddable sort of girl, quiet, gentle. She always used to be laughing and singing about the place."

"Used to?" said Hal, a note of interrogation in his voice.

Simon Craven frowned. "That is my memory of her until now; this is her chamber."

Hal entered a smallish chamber, which contained a bed with dainty hangings, a chest, well-polished but of considerable age, and a cushioned stool set before a hearth, ready made up. It was lit by a window set in the far wall, and Hal, with visions of Sophie in his mind, crossed to it immediately. He opened it, letting in a blast of cold air and sleety rain. The aperture was small, and the drop considerable, with no convenient creeper or tree to assist a descent. In spite of the weather, he made a thorough inspection of the frame, but could see nothing to assist him in his investigation, but a few rubbed areas of wood, plainly the result of years of wear.

"Is your sister a well-grown young woman, Mr Craven?" Hal asked, glancing back to the man, who was surveying him doubtfully, as he struggled with the wind to close the casement.

"No, Bella favours my mother," he replied. "If anything she is shorter, and more lightly made, wouldn't you say so, Jack?"

"Aye," he agreed, nodding. "She's—she's like a bird," he added with a burst of inspiration, and then blushed at the fancifulness of it.

"Pretty?" Hal asked lightly, lifting items from the toilet table and carefully replacing them.

"Well, not a classic beauty like Mistress Redcroft," said Jack, as Simon Craven hesitated. "But she...she had a sparkle, if you know what I mean?" He blushed more hotly.

Hal smiled at him. "Indeed I do, Jack, thank you for your insight. Pretty then, rather than a great beauty?" Her brother nodded, and suddenly his eyes filled with tears. "She is a dear girl," he said, a catch in his voice.

"And the cousin—Rosalind, do you call her?"

"Yes," again, Simon Craven hesitated, "the complete opposite of Bella, really," he admitted ruefully. "A lump of a girl, bitter-tongued and ill-favoured. She is our cousin and has always been jealous of Bella, all her life. It was so typical of Bella that she never noticed it and was always so kind to Rosalind. Making her a bridesmaid was just another in a long line of sweet things Bella has done, yet Rosalind betrayed her trust each time with her nasty tongue."

"Are her sisters of a similar ilk?" asked Hal, frowning.

"No," said Simon. "No, they are pleasant enough girls, at least Beatrice is. I don't really know Helen, the younger."

"Part of the Hollingshead connection?" Hal asked of Jack.

"Yes, they are distant kin, I believe," he replied frowning. "Why do you ask?"

"The Shakespearean names," he replied. "I noticed it with Cordelia."

"Oh, yes, that's our common grandfather, I believe," agreed Jack. "He was something of a scholar. He was killed at Worcester, the same as Cordelia's father was."

Hal nodded, realising there was nothing here to tell him more. "May I see the chamber of the other young lady?" he asked.

"She is sharing a chamber with her sisters," said Simon doubtfully. "I'll just make sure it is unoccupied."

"Do you think she is dead?" Jack asked bluntly, as Simon Craven went from out of the room.

Hal frowned. "Strangely, no! Yet everything is here. It's as if she has just stepped out. Which usually does mean something untoward—and yet..."

"Yes?" Jack asked quickly.

"I don't know." Hal paused, glancing about the chamber. "I...it doesn't smell right, somehow."

Jack sniffed the air. "Smell?" he asked blankly.

Hal laughed. "No, no, I don't mean literally! I mean something's not in place...hello, what is that?" Simon Craven's voice was heard, calling imperatively and they hastened along the corridor in the direction of the sound, to find him staring at a few scattered mistletoe berries on the dark floorboards.

"What is amiss?" cried Jack.

"I've just remembered!" Simon replied, and Hal noticed the fear was back in his voice. "Bella had a wreath of ivy and berries in her hair that day! Did I not mention it last night? You must recollect, Jack, all the girls were helping Raife Jackson, the steward, decorate the hall and chambers with holly and ivy, and one of them, I don't know which, began putting ivy in her hair. I remember Bella's because there were sprigs of mistletoe in hers, and Mistress Pridow, the bridegroom's mother, cried out in horror at so pagan a berry in a Christian house."

"Yes, Jack told us about that, and it was spoken of when we arrived," said Hal bending to pick up three waxy berries. "Presumably these are not the same berries? Recollect how easily they become detached from the stems, once they begin to dry out."

"But they must be!" Simon cried. "Mistletoe is quite rare hereabouts and my mother is every bit as superstitious as Mistress Pridow. Raife Jackson and his men would not have cut any. Indeed, it only grows in Hollywell Wood on the edge of the estate."

Hal nodded his understanding, and frowned as he considered his host's words. Something wasn't being said, quite why he wasn't sure, but Simon Craven was concealing a secret from him. He glanced along the dim corridor and nearby chambers. All seemed perfectly normal, yet the feeling that he was missing something grew upon him. He considered what he had been told, quickly reviewing all the information which had been imparted in the last few hours. Yes, something was amiss, but what it was he could not think. He walked the length of the corridor and stood looking out over the rain-drenched landscape as he considered further.

Most people habitually told the truth. He'd noticed it frequently that when pressed for an answer to a question, nearly everyone he met gave as honest an answer as possible. The only exceptions were people who had committed a crime and sought to evade justice, and those who sought to protect a loved one. Those with criminal intent lied cleverly. Those who tried to protect loved ones were usually bad liars and held back vital evidence from a misguided sense of danger. Simon Craven was plainly not telling him everything and that suggested he was trying to protect his sister in some way.

Hal turned back to where his companions stood patiently waiting. He paused, hesitating, then recollecting how the time was passing, asked bluntly: "Mr Craven, do you have a hidden chapel, or something like, here at Haceby?"

Simon Craven looked very uncomfortable, for he was aware, not only of Hal's position as a Justice, but of the

Puritan tendencies of the Hollingshead family.

"There is a small chamber on the floor above, almost in the roof, that my ancestors, in the troubled times of Bloody Mary and Good Queen Bess, used to use," he admitted reluctantly. "It serves no purpose these days, but as a store for old furniture."

"So presumably you searched it yesterday?" Hal asked, with the lift of an eyebrow.

"No," said Simon, looking even more uncomfortable. "Pridow and Brendon were constantly at my side all day, and then when we went searching the grounds, it left my mind, what with the rain and everything. I meant to examine it later, but sheer weariness overtook me." Again he glanced uneasily to Jack Hollingshead. "We never speak of it, you see."

Hal smiled a little. "Lead on, Mr Craven, perhaps we have discovered our truants?"

For a few seconds, Simon Craven hovered on a refusal, then he made a recover and an apology for putting his companions to so much trouble. "I do beg your pardon, you will think me very foolish, but it has been drummed into me from a very early age not to speak of the priest hole." He glanced rapidly from one to the other, seeing nothing but faint surprise from Jack, and interest from Hal. "I meant to look myself later, but you see, as it is never spoken of, Bella could have no knowledge of it, anymore than Rosalind, for she has only recently been a regular visitor to this house, since my uncle died."

"In which case, it will be empty, and of no interest to either Jack or I other than as a curiosity of our past," said Hal in soothing tones.

In spite of these reassuring words, Simon still continued, as he led the way up a short flight of stairs and into a chilly long gallery, lined with tall windows, to explain why he had not mentioned the existence previously. From there, he opened a door into a suite of rooms, long unused, and crossed a handsome chamber.

To Hal's ears, it sounded stilted and unlikely. His host, it seemed, having opened the floodgates could not stop talking. He revealed a door cut into the panelling, which could hardly be called hidden, but which led to a narrow spiral staircase. This, as they climbed it, appeared to twist hard back upon itself and finally brought them out into the roof space. Simon continued to talk, excusing himself for his lack of thought, and propounding with some relief, of the likelihood of a happy outcome. Hal, however, had his doubts as they drew level with the leads, then they turned aside, to go down close by the huge chimney a few stairs and into what appeared to be a cupboard.

"Well, how amazing!" Simon, who'd put his shoulder to the door in the expectation of having to move a load of lumber, was surprised. "This was filled with clutter the last time I came in here! Mind, that would be some years back now. Good heavens, how was this done with none knowing of it? And look, this rusted broadsword seems to have fallen across the opening!" He wrenched the ancient weapon away, and twisted the hook on the back wall of the cobwebby cupboard which stood empty of cloaks.

Chapter Five

With a click and a small squeak of protest, the back wall of the cupboard gave way under the pressure of his hand, and all three crowded into the same doorway to get a view of the interior of the dim chamber.

Lit by a tiny window at floor level, which was covered almost entirely by ivy, and reached by a short flight of perilous steps down, they saw a space, decorated with paintings, but small enough only to house the figure of a young woman slumped across the floor, dressed in a bridal gown, with a wreath of holly and mistletoes berries in her hair.

"Dear God! Bella!" Simon Craven cried, crashing down the steep steps into the room.

Hal followed him immediately, his worst fears confirmed, whilst Jack hesitated at the top of the stairs, for the chamber was already overfull. "Is she ill, has she swooned?" he cried in dismay.

In reply Simon Craven gave a moan of despair, as he felt the coldness of the body he'd snatched into his arms. "Bella! Bella!" Simultaneously, as the head of the young woman fell back and they saw her face, he cried, "It's not Bella!"

"Then who, pray, is she?" Hal asked, desperately feeling for a pulse at her white neck.

" 'Tis Rosalind Pauncey—my cousin!" said Simon blankly. "Is she...?"

"Dead? Yes!" Hal replied tersely, as at his instruction, Simon laid the body back down on the floor, so Hal could look more thoroughly.

"Dead!" cried Jack, in dismay. "How?"

"That, I cannot say." Hal looked first at Rosalind's young face, noting there was no sign of pain or fear, then at her hands and nails with a puzzled frown. "She appears to have suffered no distress," he remarked thoughtfully. "I am very sorry, Mr Craven, you were indeed correct in your fears. There has been a fatality."

"But where is Bella?" Simon Craven cried in a distraught manner, glancing about him, as if expecting to see his sister hidden in a corner. "There is still no sign of Bella, and why is Rosalind dressed in Bella's wedding gown?"

"Come, let us lift her out of this place carefully, these are questions answered more easily in a less confined space," replied Hal. "Mr Hollingshead, please go down before us to make sure the way is clear. " 'Tis best none see this sight until well-prepared for it."

It took them some time to get the body out of the chamber and begin their perilous descent of the twisting stairs. Whilst Simon and Jack accomplished this, Hal took the opportunity to conduct a swift search of the priest hole. The chamber was fully lined from floor to ceiling with wooden panels,very old and beautifully decorated, with carvings and paintings of Biblical scenes now faded with age. It was obvious no expense had been spared in it construction. The only plain panel was the back wall, where clearly an altar had once stood, for a wooden cross hung centrally, flanked by a pair of carved angels still lightly gilded. Hal had crossed to examine these, when Jack Hollingshead called breathlessly, "Sir Henry, can you follow with the candle, please, the stairs are rather dim at this point!"

"Do not trouble with anything, Sir Henry, I'll attend to it all later," added Simon Craven.

With one last look, Hal, fearing another accident, closed the door and shed light on the scene below.

The first faint light appeared in the east heralding the dawn. Arabella Craven saw it, and blinked back her tears. "It's no good, Nick," she said hopelessly. "We just can't go on. See, here comes the dawn and we are both so wet and tired! I don't know what to do!

Nick looked to her, and then east in dismay. "We appeared to have wandered about in circles all night. We are still miles from Huntspill Parva! In fact, we are closer to home."

"Yes," she agreed with a sob. "Oh, Nick, why is everything so against us? If only we could have made it to your friend's house before dawn, but even then, he surely would not have married us without a fuss. Now it is light, and Rosalind will be telling them everything. I know she won't wait, she will be so eager to seem important and tell the news. Simon will be out looking for us, I know he will, he'll be so angry with us for causing such an uproar, and he'll fight you and kill you—or you will kill him! Oh, I am such a wicked girl to bring such trouble on us all!"

Nick, who had been wearily slumped in the saddle of his horse, sat up straight at this. "I'll not have you say that, Bella! You, wicked? That is nonsense! You are the sweetest, kindest of all people! I think we should still make a push to try to get to my minister friend Charles Pearson at Huntspill Parva, he surely will have got my letter by now, and it can't be more than five, six miles. How is your hack holding up?"

"It is the most hard-mouthed beast I have ever ridden," she replied with a shaky laugh. "That is what is making me so tired, fighting him. Oh, what shall we do? I am so wet and hungry and tired!" She gave a sneeze and wiped her nose despondently on a very damp handkerchief. "I thought if only we could be married, all our problems would be solved, but nothing has gone well from the very beginning. Do you think our love is ill-starred, Nick?"

"No, I do not," he replied stoutly. "It is a wonderful, precious thing, and I am angry that your brother's stubbornness has driven us to these straits!" He sighed as the dim light showed their way more clearly. "Oh, Bella, I'm sorry. I've ruined everything and most likely brought you to death's door, too, by my incompetence," he added, as she gave another sneeze. "I think we should go home to get warm and dry then have something to eat."

"Home?" Bella cried out in dismay. "Home, where they'll make me marry Ezekiel Pridow?"

"No, home to Weston Revesby!" Quickly, he caught her hands, holding them firmly. "Do you trust me, Bella?"

"With my life, Nick, you know that," she replied, blinking back her tears.

"Then I think we should go home and—and tell them all we are married," he said quickly. "I'll write again to Charles, and make arrangements for him to come and marry us privately as soon as possible."

"Oh, Nick!" she cried, shocked.

"Bella, I swear to you all will be well," he said earnestly, seeing her reaction. "You know you can trust me! I love and honour you! Under my roof, you'll be safe until we can be man and wife."

"And what if your friend Charles Pearson refuses to help us, as most likely he will, for Simon will have raised the countryside by now! A young, newly ordained, minister isn't going to disoblige a local family, even for a friend!"

Nick shrugged and their eyes met in despair. "I don't know what we'll do," he confessed, knowing in his heart that he had ruined her reputation in this mad escapade, but certain in his mind that if they could remain together, they were less likely to be parted forever. "The only other alternative is a flight to London, which neither of us want, but I do know if we are driven to such a length, we'll better accomplish it with warm, dry clothes and fresh horses. All of these can be had at Weston Revesby."

Bella returned his look, knowing as he did, that they were both ruined in the eyes of their families and friends. He was right, their only hope was to remain together—and even though she shied from the thought—become lovers or be parted forever. She knew there was no choice, she would follow her heart. "Weston Revesby it is then," she agreed, with a wobbly smile. "I shall be so glad to get warm and dry. I am damp to my very bones."

The body of Rosalind Pauncey was brought down from the priest's hole and laid out in a chamber before her family were summoned to mourn her with wholehearted grief and many tears. Hal, who had no desire to intrude upon this natural sorrow, took himself back to the dining parlour and was busy making notes in a small book when Sophie entered.

"You did not find Arabella, then?" she remarked, pulling out a bench and sitting opposite him at the table.

"No, but it is only just after cockcrow," he replied absently, finishing off his sentence.

"And there was a priest hole?" she asked curiously.

"Yes, rather unexpected in this part of the world…or is it?" He looked up in surprise at the thought, and met her eyes, unable to prevent a smile at the sight of her beauty, undimmed by the rigours of travel. "Perhaps, as I think again, it is the most likely place to find one, in an area known for its staunch support of Puritanism."

Sophie, much heartened by the smile, nodded. "Yes, that makes sense. And Simon Craven knew of it, did he?"

"He reluctantly admitted his knowledge, and with a sharp eye on Jack Hollingshead, led us to it, although I think he would have much rather not—only I took him by surprise by asking outright."

"What was it like? Was it dark and cobweb-filled?" Sophie asked with a shudder.

"No, it was not," he replied, suddenly struck. "It was rather beautiful. It was also clean. The floor was not only swept, but polished, only the window was a little dirty and creeper-covered on the outside. Well done,

Sophie, I'd have not even noticed that but for your insatiable curiosity!"

She smiled again, but less surely, "What do you next? Can I help in any way?"

"I must give her poor mother and sisters time to grieve before I look the body over, you might help me with that. It's a tricky thing to do, and there doesn't appear to be a scratch upon her."

Sophie frowned. "How very odd. Surely there must be some sort of injury?"

"One would imagine so," he agreed, "but it was not the time to find out. Simon Craven was distressed, and only further convinced he'd find his sister dead, too — and Jack anxious."

"Of course," she nodded her comprehension, "then I will try to speak with either, or both, of the sisters later, if I get the opportunity. Do you think I should try to talk to the children at all?"

"They appear to be very young," he replied with a sigh. "And as we don't know them, how can we ascertain their veracity? I know if I ask my son Harry a question he will answer it as truthfully as it is possible for him to do, but my sister Mary's eldest, he can scarcely be got to speak, let alone tell me anything."

"It might help, of course, if you could remember his name and didn't always squabble with his mother, whom he adores, on every occasion you meet," Sophie replied dispassionately.

"Of course I can remember his name," he snapped, then as she raised her brows in mockery, he made a face. "Oh, well, there are so many of them, and Libby always told me their names."

"There are, in fact, three, all boys, and the eldest, called Guy for his father, is about two years younger than Harry, and he speaks quite well, as long as he isn't terrified of his uncle."

He smiled wryly. "Plainly I am at fault and must cultivate my nephew's company when I return home. As for the children, you are a better judge than I. If you think they will have any information they'd be prepared to share, then see if they'll confide in you, but beware their parents. I can't see the bridegroom Pridow and his following being happy at any attempt to get information from their young."

"Especially from one so defamed as me," she agreed. "Yes, I'll take care."

He frowned at her. "Why did you insist on remaining it this area, if you are held in such low esteem?"

"Where else is there for me?" she replied quietly. "I have no home. I am weary of being a nuisance at everyone's beck and call. At least I know Adam and Cordelia feel genuine affection for me."

"There are others who feel the same, but you have rejected them all," he replied, his voice low. "I don't know what you want anymore, Sophie."

"Neither do I, and that is the problem," she said in a different tone. "Now if you'll excuse me, no doubt that poor girl's death has affected my spirits. I am going to assist Aunt Kate."

"Please do," he replied returning to his book, his manner dissatisfied. "Although I may need your assistance shortly in that quarter."

"I am yours to command, as ever, Sir Henry," she replied in formal tones, "Adieu."

Hal continued making notes in his book, but his heart was heavy, and he cursed the necessity of meeting with Sophie again. He'd thought yesterday that she had been glad to see him. He had convinced himself these past six months that his heart was immune to her charms, but it had leapt at the sight of her, and all his careful reasoning was in ruins. Hope had sprung up, and now it was dashed again, which was probably for the best. She plainly didn't want his company, for she'd appeared disinterested in assisting him with the body of Rosalind Pauncey. He'd have to get other help. He sighed and, having completed his task, went to find Jack Hollingshead. With the plainly reluctant Jack for company, they then repaired to the chamber where the body of Rosalind Pauncey was laid out.

Hal stood at the foot of curtained bed, his arms folded across his chest and his chin grasped thoughtfully as he contemplated the body before him. Jack Hollingshead, meanwhile, fidgeted about the chamber uneasily. He twitched the curtains; he looked out of the window; he paced the polished floor. "What are you at, Sir Henry?" he asked at last. "What do we here? What if one of the women should come back?"

"It is your task to see they don't. I need time to consider and inspect the body. Many clues may lie here. We must search carefully," he replied calmly.

"You cannot disturb her!" Jack cried in distaste.

"None can disturb her now, Jack; she is dead," said Hal gently. Then, as Jack shrugged, looking even more unhappy, Hal applied himself to the task at hand. What was it his friend the French physician Philippe Douay had told him? Fleetingly, he wished he were here with him to assist. Then he heard in his head again the near-perfect English of the man, "Observe, Hal; firstly, look to see what nature tells you. Look at the body. Maybe there is a sword thrust to the chest, or a bullet to the skull, yes? But then, look again. Observe which way the weapon entered the body. People do not die without cause. Even with poison, there must be some signs. Look carefully for these signs."

"Well," thought Hal with a sigh, "I defy even Philippe to find a clue on this corpse. Apart from the pallor, she might still be alive."

There was not a mark on her. No wound, no marks of strangulation, nothing to give him any idea of how she met her end. However, met her end she had, and he was sure somehow it wasn't a natural death, unless, perchance, she had died of fear. He took a moment to consider this, recollecting how many corpses he'd seen since his return from exile. Each face had, in some measure, reflected the manner of their death. There was the shock of his Uncle Henry, the pain-contorted mask of Sir Edward Jolyan, the amazement of his wife's stepmother, the fear of that woman his brother-in-law Justin Danvers had been involved with. Poor Edmund Benton with his tongue bitten through in his agony, the cooper swollen by the waters of the Avon, the baker drowned in a butt of ale, the preacher strangled at the pillory and his tongue cut out. These last four, if he had but realised, pointed so clearly to the contemptuous cruelty of the murderer.

That was what most murderers had in common, of course, a contempt for their fellow man. Somehow, their ideas became so contorted that they were convinced their personal convenience was of greater importance than that of the life which stood in their way.

Something must have occurred in this house to make one of it's inhabitants decide to take the step which would set him apart from his fellows. Who among those gathered under this roof for a wedding celebration would deliberately, or perhaps by an unlucky chance, kill a young woman at the beginning of her life?

Once again, he examined the corpse, stepping to look closely at her hands. There were no broken nails, to show she'd tried to free herself, not even any bruising where she might have banged on the door or window to try to attract attention to her plight. Surely she must have been afraid, yet her face showed no horror or fear. It was as if she had lain down and slept.

"Someone approaches!" hissed Jack Hollingshead.

"Go distract them," replied Hal curtly, glad of the opportunity to get him from the chamber.

Surprised at the sharpness of Hal's tone, Jack departed swiftly and Hal heard his voice raised in conversation and the footsteps dying away.

Hurriedly, Hal began his examination, moving swiftly over the whole body, aware he had but a few minutes before Jack returned. It wasn't something he liked to do, he felt it was an infringement on the person's privacy, but it was better that he did so and discovered any clues, rather than they be missed and a murderer escape justice. He noted how her cousin's gown was not a good fit, the laces at the back of the bodice were stretched beyond the full limit, and the linen of her shift showed through. No more were her ankles decently covered by anything but a petticoat of dusky pink which accorded ill with the ivory damask of the gown. It was plain the donning of the garment was a last minute, hasty decision, not something planned. Swiftly, he lifted the garments, noting how her garters had slipped, her stockings bagged and her shoes had come adrift. The sadness of the whole thing made him angry, how could someone abandon a young woman like this? As it was, he found little and was just smoothing back her hair as Jack returned. It was at this point he found the bruise on her temple, hidden by the contrived curls on her forehead.

"What is it?" Jack asked anxiously as Hal gave a grunt of surprise. "That was the woman come to wash her and lay her out, you know. She'll surely run to Mistress Craven with a tale of us being here!"

"A bruise to her head," replied Hal shortly. "Now we know it wasn't entirely an accident."

"Accident?" Jack repeated as if he'd never heard the word before. "How could it be an accident? How could she accidentally get locked in a priest hole?"

"A mischance, then," said Hal. "Recollect, the children were playing Hide and Seek. It could have been a mischance which took Rosalind to the priest hole. The door closed, trapping her, and perhaps she died of fear when she couldn't get any to hear her cries, but to my mind, the blow to her head suggests she may have been put there out of sight."

"Unless she fell," suggested Jack. "She might have got into a pother when none came in response to her cries, and tripped on her hem."

"Yes," agreed Hal, "but Simon Craven said the gown was his sister's, and it appears to be a little short for her, so I can see no reason why she should have fallen."

"How would she have known of such a place as this?" Jack continued. "I've been coming here for the last few years since Cathy married Simon, and I've never heard of it. In fact, why did you ask Simon if there was a priest hole?"

"I asked because I could think of no other explanation for the disappearance of two young women in the dead of winter. If no horses had been taken, and there was no sight of them anywhere else, they had to be hidden in the house," Hal said. "As for you not knowing of the existence of a priest hole, if I were connected by marriage to so staunch a Puritan as you, Jack, I'd not mention a priest hole either, in case you began to think you smelt incense."

Jack smiled faintly. "I would not have said I was so staunch a Puritan," he replied. "Are we not all King's men again these days?"

"Indeed we are," agreed Hal pleasantly, "but every so often, there is a Calvinistic gleam in your eye, especially when you look at Sophie Redcroft."

"That's not a Calvinistic gleam," he retorted, with a snort, "that's a fear of a witch!" Then, as Hal looked reprovingly he added quickly, "No, you are right, I shouldn't say so, not even in jest, but, by Heaven, Sophie terrifies me!"

Hal smiled faintly in agreement and bent over the body lifting Rosalind's shoulders a little. "Move this wreath thing, Jack," he instructed. "I need to look at the back of her head."

Jack reluctantly did as he was bid.

"Ah, there now, do you see?"asked Hal.

"No," replied Jack who was averting his gaze.

"I need a witness, Jack," Hal said gently. "See, here in her hair, blood and another bruise. Was that enough to kill her though, I wonder?" He sighed, laying the body back on its pillow, crossing her cold hands on her chest again. "I don't think there is anything else to be found here, but I'd appreciate an opportunity to examine the priest hole again, if it can be arranged."

"The Cravens are still rather anxious about Bella, you know," said Jack, as they closed the door on the dead girl and beckoned to the nurse.

"Yes," Hal nodded his understanding, and stood thinking as he looked from the window. "Somehow, I don't feel she is in any danger," he said at last. "The sense of urgency, the anxiety, has gone."

"You don't think there might be a further priest hole?" suggested Jack. "One even Simon doesn't know of?"

"How much of your house don't you know, Jack?"

Hal asked. "Could your sister Cathy have discovered a hidden chamber at your home? No, I think Simon knows his home very well, but didn't imagine that his sister did. The disappearance of Mistress Arabella is still a mystery. I think I probably need to talk to her cousins."

"The children?" Jack asked in dismay.

"I was thinking initially of the sisters of Mistress Pauncey."

"You'd need a chaperone to do so," said Jack in a discouraging tone.

"Jack, I am not trying to be difficult, but I did come here at your request," said Hal patiently. "I am aware that this could cause a scandal, but I was under the impression Simon Craven wanted his sister found. Children often know lots of things which they don't speak of. You and I are of a similar age; you'll remember the war. Silence, then, could be imperative, but now?" Hal shrugged his shoulders. "It was my intention to get Sophie to talk to Rosalind's sisters and then, if we still haven't found Mistress Bella, to ask the younger children if they knew anything. I do not intend any harm."

Jack looked embarrassed. "I beg pardon, Sir Henry, finding Rosalind Pauncey dead has unnerved us all. I would think if the children are to be questioned, Sophie would be the person to do it."

"I am glad we are in agreement," said Hal in some relief, "for with Sophie talking to the younger people, we'd be freed up to make an extensive search of the grounds and estate."

"It has already been done," said Jack. "We found nothing."

"It was done in terrible weather. It is easy to miss things when rain is pouring down one's neck," replied Hal. "I observe that the weather is improving and the wind getting up. I think if we get Simon Craven to take us over the ground, we might discover something."

"You'll not get anywhere without the bridegroom and his friends," said Jack.

"I imagine not, although we would do better without," agreed Hal. "Well, when the opportunity arrives, we must separate into two groups. I depend upon you to take control of the other group. Now, if you'll excuse me, I must seek out my Aunt Westwood, I have not yet exchanged a word with her. I'll meet with you in the stables in about half an hour."

❧

Chapter Six

Hal hastened to his Aunt Kate's chamber, knowing he must talk to her, but aware he did not have the time to deal with the errand immediately. He found her, as he guessed he might, in company with Sophie.

"Hal, I am so glad you have come to the aid of these people, and so sorry I wasn't able to greet you. But this morning brings more tragedy, that poor girl Rosalind! I cannot believe she lay dead when we were searching all over for her!"

"It was so very late, ma'am," he replied, kissing her affectionately. "That I was glad to hear you'd retired." He subjected her face to a careful scrutiny. "Are you well, Aunt Kate?"

"I am tired, Hal," she admitted. "I have found this visit something of a…but never mind that. I am so pleased to see Sophie and thankful she agreed to come here with you. She'll be a great help to us."

"I have been telling Aunt Kate of how you found the body, Hal," Sophie observed with a sigh, "and we were wondering if you seek the other?"

"No, I don't think we do," he replied thoughtfully. "I don't see any evidence of such violence as we have witnessed previously. The cousin, Rosalind, has a few small bruises on her head. The reason for her death is yet unclear, and may remain so until we can find Mistress Bella, who will probably know more." He paused, plainly thinking. "I don't quite know why, but I am becoming convinced this has all been an unlucky accident."

"Or a very clever murder," murmured Sophie. "Remember how we thought dear Uncle Edmund had died of his heart—how poor Robin Tripp fell into the fire?"

"Yes, I am mindful of how a murderer becomes more careless as time passes," he agreed, "but I don't see this as a deliberate murder, more an unlucky chance, an accident perhaps which panicked the perpetrator into concealing the body."

"What should we do, Hal?" Aunt Kate asked quickly.

"First and foremost, take great care, both of you," he replied with some emphasis. "By all means be sympathetic, and help the families as much as possible, but listen as you are with the womenfolk for anything which might sound amiss. You'll know it as soon as you hear it, but don't remark upon it. Listen, but don't be seen to listen, and if possible encourage them to talk. The key to this mystery is possibly back here in this house. Sophie, if you can try to do the same with the younger girls and the children, that will also help."

"Yes, I will try, but do you know, Hal, that the coroner's man has come?"

"Has he?" Hal looked thoughtful for a few seconds. "This must delay our search of the estate. It should just give me time to write a few lines to Ambrose. If you'll excuse me, we'll talk again later."

Rather to Aunt Kate's surprise, Sophie merely nodded, and Hal, mindful of the time, hurried away in search of writing materials. He counted it unlucky then, to enter a dim parlour and find it inhabited by Madeline Hollingshead, Jack's mother. He stopped short in the doorway, and hastily bowed. "Mistress Hollingshead, your pardon, I didn't expect to find you here. How very delightful, I only wish the circumstances were less unpleasant."

"Sir Henry," she replied, with an abrupt nod, and a satirical glance. "You find me hidden away from the coroner's fellow and his grisly business."

"Yes, I had heard he was come," he paused, and added hastily, "Madam, I am aware I owe you an apology for the debacle at the Harcourt wedding six month ago."

"You apologised at the time, Sir Henry," she replied curtly. "I imagine you cannot be held to blame for the thoughtlessness of your wards."

"I rather fear I can, but I am obliged to you for your kindness in saying so, ma'am," he replied.

"The past is past," she said, in a manner to end the discussion. "Little good can come of replaying it, I find."

"How very wise you are, ma'am," he said with a wry smile. "'Tis not a common fault in general."

She laughed abruptly. "I'd forgotten your charm, Sir Henry," she observed. "Come, sit down do, and tell me what is afoot. How do your enquires progress?"

"Badly, ma'am," he replied, obeying her command. "I fear foul play with regard to Mistress Pauncey."

"And Bella Craven?" she asked quickly.

"Her fate is not yet clear, but at least we do not have the evidence of another body," he replied candidly. "Mistress Hollingshead, you are in a unique position here. One of knowing all the people in this house. Neither are you bereaved nor anxious. May I trespass upon your good nature, and ask you questions I hesitate to put to your fellow guests?"

"I thought Jack was assisting you," she replied, unwilling to be drawn.

"Yes, he is, most ably, but he does not, I think, have your particular insight. I admire your son. He is quick-witted and steady. I imagine he runs his affairs with precision, but the nuances of emotion would, I feel, be a closed book to him."

She smiled faintly. "True enough," she agreed in more amiable tones. "Jack will make a fine husband for a sensible, steady wife. Alas, they seem thin upon the ground these days."

"Jack is yet a young man," replied Hal pleasantly. "Time enough to be wed when the right person comes along."

Madeline Hollingshead frowned. "Jack is in fact but a little younger than yourself, Sir Henry. He needs to be settled in my opinion, but as you suggest, Jack is his own man. What can I tell you?"

"A little about your fellow guests would greatly assist me," he replied promptly. "They are, I believe, all your kin?"

"In varying degrees," she nodded her assent. "My daughter Cathy, married Simon Craven some four years ago, and has produced three children in rapid succession. Simon's mother, Barbara, is a cousin of mine on my mother's side."

"You know them well?" Hal asked politely.

"Tolerably so, since Cathy and Simon married. Before that, I had not seen Barbara since her marriage and her husband's death. My husband had no great liking for Lewis Craven. There was talk of Royalist leanings in the family. John was not eager for the match for Cathy, but after his death…Cathy always favoured Simon, and the Cravens are a wealthy family."

Hal nodded. "And the Cravens' kin, the Paunceys?" he asked.

"Margaret Pauncey is Barbara's younger sister and, therefore, my cousin too. I believe we also share a common ancestor on her husband's side," Madeline Hollingshead replied. "I've met them, perhaps half a dozen times, since Cathy wed Simon. They are pleasant enough people."

"Is there a connection with Mr Pridow?" Hal continued.

"Possibly," replied Mistress Hollingshead, wrinkling her nose slightly. "But one cannot be responsible for all one's kin! Some of my second cousins seem to have been driven to desperate straits. The war, you know, left many widows and orphans unprovided for."

"Indeed, ma'am, my own family was just such a case," Hal replied. "But for the skill of my uncle in rescuing what he could, and taking in my brother and sisters as if they were his own, I doubt I should be sitting here today."

She nodded, thinking how skilful he was at making himself agreeable, and wishing he could teach her son some of his ways to improve his manners. "Yes, I recollect your Aunt Margery telling us how pleased she was with your progress."

"I fear that must have been some time ago, ma'am," he said ruefully. "Of late, I have become something of a disappointment to her."

"Never that," said his companion, "but her concern for your future is at the forefront of her mind, rather like mine for Jack."

"Yes," he smiled a little. "Between them, she and Aunt Kate have assumed the maternal role in my—and my siblings' lives. We count ourselves very fortunate indeed, I can assure you, ma'am, for between them I think we chanced upon perfection."

"Hmm," she replied. "Honey-tongued indeed! They certainly both hold you in high esteem."

"I am honoured they should say so," he answered.

She nodded her head. "Yes, I sense your impatience, you would have my impertinent enquiries over."

"Indeed, ma'am, I am happy to answer any of your questions and deem them nothing but neighbourly interest, were it not for the fact a young woman lies dead."

"How right you are, Sir Henry, to remind me why you are here. Pray continue."

"At the risk of rousing your ire again, ma'am…Jacob Brendon?"

"No kin of mine!" she declared roundly, and then relented, "but kin of kin, if you understand."

"Indeed, ma'am," he replied promptly. "The ties which bind our nation and bring me hence in a time of trouble."

She smiled. "Acknowledging kinship with Sir Henry Westwood's family could never be akin to acknowledging kinship with a man like Jacob Brendon."

"You dislike him?" Hal asked with a frown.

"What is there to admire?" she returned candidly. "Times of war bring strange bedfellows, Sir Henry, often ones which cannot be easily shed when peace comes. Permanent alliances have been forged, and all at once these people, or their descendants, have a claim on one, especially at a wedding."

Hal nodded his understanding. "So, it was to celebrate the wedding that all are assembled, not the season?"

"Jacob Bredon and Sir Richard Harrison would probably sooner walk over hot coals than celebrate a pagan feast. Their idea of Christmas, they made very clear, was three sermons and a fast," she retorted. "It was that pair which stirred up Mary Pridow to react against the mistletoe in Bella's hair. Until that point, they had merely been disapproving and gloomy, like the Puritans they are. The berries on the mistletoe seemed to excite all their superstitions and prejudices."

Hal frowned. "I know it is disliked in churches to this day, but apart from being poisonous, I cannot see any harm in it. Tell me, is it true that Mr Brendon holds the mortgages on young Revesby's land?"

"It is said he picked up a lot of land during the war —a farm here, a field there. Then, when Christopher Revesby, young Nick's grandfather, came to take charge of the boy, he had to mortgage more to pay off his fines to Parliament. But of course, bereft of the land to support it; they soon fell into further debt. Enough is now owed to make it possible for Brendon to foreclose, and he intends to do so, I gather, on Twelfth Night. I must say, Sir Henry, you seem to have picked up all the relevant details very quickly."

He smiled briefly. "I encouraged Jack to tell me everything he could remember as we waited for his horse to have its loose shoe refitted. One becomes rather like a squirrel, ma'am, picking up nuts of information here and there, and storing them up for future reference." He looked up and smiled at her again. "One final question, ma'am, which you don't have to answer, for it is merely curiosity on my part: was I wrong to think you and your son were Puritans?"

Madelaine Hollingshead looked affronted, and then smiled reluctantly. "Do we not all hold different views on certain subjects, Sir Henry?" she asked. "I practise my religion in a manner which suits me. You—or indeed Jacob Brendon—practise it each in yet another fashion. Until the late, unlamented King chose to take issue with such matters, we were all allowed the freedom of our own conscience. The war forced us to make a choice on which side we stood. The resultant conflict drove us further against each other. So many wounded; even more dead! Children fatherless, mothers widowed! I don't think I ever considered myself a Puritan, but I was against, and will always be against, any King who could bring such grief to his people."

Hal nodded and bowed over her out flung hand with respect. "Ma'am, on this matter we are at one. I have never heard the case against the late King stated with more clarity. My father, as you will know, was one of his and his son's trusted associates. In my youth, I was often in our present King's company, but young as I was, my heart always grieved for the wanton destruction of our country. There is nothing more senseless than Englishmen fighting Englishmen, and such behaviour can never be condoned."

"Nor allowed to happen again!" she agreed.

"Amen to that, ma'am!" he replied. "Let me tell you I am convinced by my, admittedly limited, association with our present King that he is of a like mind. Although he is a decade my elder, I saw, as he did, enough to convince me of the waste of lives and happiness to ever go to war again."

"Amen to that thought," she replied. "Although there seem to be discontents everywhere these days—what with the plague which so afflicted us—and then London almost destroyed by fire. It makes you wonder if the Lord isn't trying to tell us something. The Dutch seem to be forever at our elbow. We've had fire, pestilence, and the sword…a period of peace would not go amiss."

Hal nodded, "But our navy grows stronger. When I was last with my father before his death, I went with him to see an acquaintance, and at his house we met such an odd man, who was fanatical about the navy… but I digress. Thank you, Mistress Hollingshead, for such able assistance. Now I must find some writing implements and send a letter to my brother-in-law in London."

"Allow me to show you to Simon's book room, Sir Henry, you'll find all you need there," she replied, ushering him to the chamber, and leaving him in peace to write his letter to Ambrose.

❧

Chapter Seven

"I do apologise, Mr Craven, for keeping you waiting," said Hal, as he finally joined the group of men in the stable yard. "I heard the coroner's man had come, so I took the opportunity to send word to my brother-in-law in London."

"No matter, Sir Henry, I had just this minute arrived, as you say I was delayed by the coroner's man. It would seem the coroner himself is too ill to attend upon us, but his man tells me he will call his court for the day after tomorrow, and says you must attend as one of those who found the body."

Hal nodded in acknowledgement, and raised his hand adding, "If you'll excuse me one moment, Mr Craven, here is someone I have yet to meet, an omission I must repair immediately." He walked across the yard to a man garbed in a thick cloak, with his hat pulled down to shield his face, who seemed to be intent on ignoring the proceedings.

"Sir Richard, well met, I am Hal Westwood, nephew to the lovely lady who has consented to become your wife. I do not know how it is that we have never met, but I am most anxious to shake the hand of one of the most fortunate men in the world."

The man, who looked as if he'd rather have turned and run than take the hand extended to him in so friendly expression, bowed his head formally. "Sir Henry," he said with all the enthusiasm of an overcast day. "I am delighted to finally make your acquaintance."

"And I, yours," replied Hal, taken aback by his lacklustre behaviour. "Do you join us in our search for the missing bride?"

"Alas, such is my ill health that I cannot think to get wetted again," he replied. "I did my best to assist the cause yesterday, but it is generally agreed I'll only delay matters today."

"Then I'll bid you adieu, and hopefully continue this conversation at some later, more convenient time," said Hal, feeling rather dismayed. "Mr Craven, I am now totally at your service."

Simon Craven nodded and made haste to explain, "We've been listening to my steward's report from the outlying farms. Raife, tell Sir Henry what you've just told us."

The elderly man, whose face was battered by wind and rain to the colour and texture of a walnut, nodded his head in deference, and in spite of the sighs from others of the group, launched into an explanation. "I've just been saying, Sir Henry, as how me and the lads have been up all night long, scouring the barns and fields with lanterns, just in case something were missed yesterday, and we haven't found hide nor hair of the lass."

"And I've just told Raife to stand his men down for some food and rest and to get dry," continued Simon. "They also know that our hunt through the house discovered the body of my cousin."

The old steward shook his head sadly, and cast his master a doubtful look. "That do be a great shame, sir. Mistress Rosalind were not a strong lass, 'tis true, but seems wicked she should be dead." He hesitated and then added reluctantly: "You mind the old tales, Master Simon, of a tunnel which do come out in Hollywell wood."

Simon smiled a tight smile as Ezekiel Pridow sighed again. "Yes, Raife, I know them well. Did I not drive you mad one summer, in my search for the tunnel, as I dug holes all over the wood? I dug up so many foxes with my friends that we all took naturally to fox hunting that autumn." His smile faded and he shrugged his shoulders. "I pray God we don't fall down one in our search today, but at least the rain is easing off a little." He glanced uneasily to Hal, his face difficult to read. "Do you think Bella might have succeeded where I failed?"

"Given the continued absence of your sister, I am prepared to consider any possibility," Hal replied politely. "Although if your sister is anything like mine, she'd need to be accompanied or at the very least, met in the tunnel. I find the fear of spiders and bats, or getting a gown dirty, is usually paramount in their minds." He smiled a little as the bridegroom muttered under his breath and added,"Far be it from me to sow discord amongst us, but was Mistress Bella eager for this marriage?"

"Indeed she was!" Ezekiel Pridow could be silent no longer, as Simon Craven hesitated over an answer. "Only the day before yesterday I presented her with the prettiest mare as a bridal gift, and she is exceptionally fond of my children. She says she prays God she will make them a good mother. There can be no suggestion of flight, and I resent the implication of such! An accident has occurred, or she has been abducted!"

"Abducted?" Hal glanced to the man in surprise, and then to Simon Craven. "Have I misunderstood the situation? Is Mistress Bella an heiress?"

"No," said Simon Craven quickly. "Bella has but her dowry, which is handsome enough, but she is not an heiress."

"Not an heiress, but the family is wealthy enough to tempt Nick Revesby into yet more outrageous behaviour!" Jacob Brendon cried. "He has nothing to lose, and he still thinks he'll find the treasure that his grandfather was ever seeking!"

"Aye, if his treasure ever existed, if Christopher Revesby ever had a penny that wasn't gambled away," replied Simon Craven dismissively as he glanced to Hal again. "Nick Revesby is a nice enough lad, Sir Henry, but he adores Bella, he'd never harm a hair on her head."

"And Mistress Bella, how did she feel about him? Saving your presence, Mr Pridow, but you'll agree all avenues must be investigated?" Hal said politely, as the bridegroom bristled.

"Once I told her there was no question of a marriage between them, that Nick Revesby had no money to support a wife, and was never likely to find a groat of his grandfather's money, she agreed a match was out of the question," said Simon firmly. "Bella was always a dear, biddable girl, Sir Henry."

"Then perhaps sometime, in the course of our search, we might find our way to Hollywell Wood," said Hal thoughtfully.

"Not to look for tunnels!" interrupted Ezekiel Pridow, with a snort of derision.

"No, we search for footprints and hoofmarks, the suggestion, perhaps, of a meeting, even more mistletoe berries or ivy leaves," returned Hal. "If your sister is alive, Mr Craven, then she didn't leave the house alone. It is winter; she is not a fool; she knows she'll need food and shelter. Few people, however much they may want to escape a situation, will set out in winter without some sort of destination. Mr Pridow, I mean no insult, I assure you, I merely say something must have happened to make Mistress Bella run away. If she is not dead, then her continued absence can only give us hope. Perhaps we might also visit young Mr Revesby in due course?"

Meanwhile, back in the house, Sophie was making an attempt to follow Hal's orders by talking to the women of the family.

"This must be quite dreadful for you all," she observed politely, to Louisa Pridow, the sister of the bridegroom, as they found themselves alone in the hall together.

The older woman turned a sour gaze upon her companion. "Dreadful?" She repeated the word as if it had no meaning for her. "To my mind, it is more inconvenient. Dreadful is the wrath of the Lord."

"Inconvenient?" Sophie stared, her mouth dropped open, her mind upon the corpse found in the priest hole.

"Yes, Bella's behaviour has always been inconsiderate," the woman replied, looking down her long nose at Sophie. "She has kept my brother Ezekiel waiting all summer on a decision, and then suddenly insisted the wedding be held at this inconvenient time, rather than at Michaelmas as suggested. I knew he'd live to rue the day he thought of that flighty Miss!"

"Rather more than inconvenient for poor Mistress Rosalind," retorted Sophie sharply.

"I'm not surprised she made a bad end. An unpleasant girl with unpleasant ways," replied Louisa. "There wasn't one piece of tittle-tattle that young lady didn't nose out from the servants and repeat to whomsoever she met!"

"Oh, a gossip, was she?" Sophie disliked the woman before her more and more, but forced herself to keep talking. "What a pity! Gossips can do such damage to other people's reputations."

"Indeed, and usually without any foundation," returned Louisa. "The lies that girl spread were notorious, but people are always ready to give credence to gossip, as if it were the Holy Writ!"

"Indeed," said Sophie, wondering who the other woman had in her mind. "I don't care for gossip myself. I mean, I enjoy a good talk with people, but I hate the malice of gossip."

"Malice!" Louisa cried sharply. "That young miss was so full of malice, spite and envy...but there, perhaps I shouldn't speak ill of the dead!"

"No, indeed no," said Sophie. "It is always best not to, I agree." She hesitated and then asked gently: "Was she nasty about you, then?"

"Well," sniffed Louisa, "no more than others, saying that I am an old maid, and will never get a husband because of my sour tongue."

"Oh, I am sure that is not true!" Sophie said swiftly. "Why, you cannot be much older than my own age, I am sure."

"Not a vast deal," she agreed smugly. "Although, of course, I don't have a damaged reputation."

"Indeed!" Sophie bit back a sharp reply. "I'm sure you are just a little more dainty in your requirements of a husband."

"I have a decent dowry," she replied, with an air of self-satisfaction. "I am in no hurry to make myself a man's slave at bed and board!"

"Indeed," agreed Sophie, running out of pleasant things to say.

"Rosalind Pauncey was jealous of Bella Craven," confided Louisa, as Sophie fell silent. "She'd set her cap at Ezekiel almost as soon as his wife died in child-bed last year."

"Oh, the poor woman," said Sophie, thinking of the children. "Did her baby die with her?"

"No, the baby was born strong and healthy enough, but Susan was ever a weak, puling sort of creature, laying abed and moping with the headache and the fuss she made over childbearing! As if it wasn't her duty and she'd not done it half a dozen times before!"

"Good heavens, I knew your brother had children, but so many! Did they all survive?"

"Oh, yes, there are seven of them, one for each year

they had been married, but all Susan could say was that six were enough!"

"Were they all girls?" Sophie asked curiously.

"No, they are mostly boys, just the one failure of a girl, and Ezekiel was very generous about it, I thought," said Louisa, with an air of complacency.

"And Simon Craven thinks this a good match for his sister?" Sophie was unable to hide her amazement.

The other woman drew herself up haughtily. "My brother has a handsome estate, a very good reputation and is not ill-looking!" she snapped.

"I have heard it said the Cravens are very wealthy," observed Sophie blandly.

"They certainly like to think they are of importance in the country," her companion agreed, with a sniff.

"What do you think has happened to Bella?" Sophie asked, tired of trying to get a pleasant answer from the other woman.

Louisa glanced about her to see if they could be over-heard. "She has run off with that rackety Nick Revesby from Weston Revesby," she hissed. "I told Ezekiel back in the summer they were too close, always riding out to-gether, and Nick allowed the run of this place with his tales of finding his fortune. Both Ezekiel and I blame

Simon Craven. He has always been too soft with Bella. She should have been made to marry last spring when Ezekiel asked for her. She'd be too busy nursing her first child by now to put us all to this trouble!"

Sophie, thinking back to her own disastrous wedding last summer, repressed a shudder. Simon Craven had allowed his sister more indulgence than she had been shown. "So you don't think Bella is dead then?"

"No! This is all so typical of Bella," she cried angrily. "She's made Ezekiel look a fool and defied both her mother and brother, yet it will all be about poor Bella being so frightened! Frightened to face real life if you ask me!"

"Which of us isn't ?" Sophie asked blankly. "If you were offered the choice of a widower with half a dozen children, would you take that offer over a younger man?"

"I'd take it any day over an offer which involved Nick Revesby!" Louisa replied sharply. "A rackety family, the Revesbys—Weston Revesby has gone to rack and ruin. Nick's grandfather Christopher was a notorious rake in his day! His women were a legion and he gambled every acre of the estate away. Lucky, the Hall was entailed, but it is now laden with debt."

"I understand, so he and Bella couldn't be wed," Sophie nodded her comprehension of an age-old problem. "I see, yes, marriage with your brother would be the prudent step."

"Naturally," agreed Louisa smugly. "We don't owe a penny to anyone." She glanced to Sophie thoughtfully. "I am told you are an heiress," she remarked.

"Yes," agreed Sophie, following the direction of her thoughts, "but my dowry is tied up in a legal dispute with my husband's family. I have little chance of being married with my unfortunate reputation."

"From what I've heard, you were lucky to escape with your life!" Louisa retorted. "Jack Hollingshead said Sir Henry got you off a charge of murder, if not worse! Is it true you and Sir Henry are lovers?"

Sophie took a deep breath to control her urge to shake her companion. "No," she replied swiftly, "we are not lovers! Sir Henry is still my guardian and, of course, he is a widower himself, with a vast estate in Gloucestershire. Perhaps he is somebody worthy of your consideration for a husband?"

"I had heard he is very wealthy," Louisa replied thoughtfully, "but he has only the two sons, doesn't he? I'm not sure I want to wed any man only to be a brood mare for him."

"Oh, well, he's not the man for you, then," said Sophie realising Louisa was so convinced of her superiority, as to be impervious to insult. "I've heard him say he wants at least another half-dozen children. His wife lost several infants, you know."

"Yes, I heard talk that he murdered her, too, or was that you?" Louisa asked maliciously.

Sophie blinked, sudden tears filling her eyes. "I would certainly count myself responsible in some measure for her death," she agreed, conceding defeat in the face of such malice. "Although such a thing had never been my intention. Will you excuse me? I must attend on Mistress Westwood. She requires my assistance."

Sophie hurried away, much discomposed by the encounter and needing the solace of Aunt Kate's company. In this, she was unlucky, however, for Hal's aunt was with the bereaved mother, so, mindful of her task, she sought out the sisters of Rosalind Pauncey, tapping on their chamber door with some trepidation.

"Your pardon," she said, putting her head round the door. "May I come in for a moment?"

"If you wish," replied a red-eyed girl, who sat in a window seat, whilst her sister occupied herself sewing erratic stitches on a fine linen shirt.

"I am most terribly sorry about your sister," said Sophie coming further into the chamber. "You must be so shocked."

"Yes," said the younger, Helen. "We are—we can't believe it."

"No," agreed Sophie, approaching the window and glancing sidelong to Beatrice, who still sat silently sewing. "It seems almost impossible, doesn't it?"

"It is so, however," said Beatrice in a shaking voice. "We'd best get used to it."

"Your poor mother must be so distressed," continued Sophie, taken aback by the elder sister's manner.

"She is laid upon her bed," replied Beatrice. "I believe Aunt Barbara and Mistress Westwood are with her."

"Mistress Westwood is so kind in such situations, she is surely the best of persons to be with the poor lady," agreed Sophie.

"I want to be with Mother!" said Helen fretfully. "She loves me best. She'd want me with her!"

"I've already explained it to you, Helen," said Beatrice firmly. "Mother is greatly distressed, it will hardly help her if you go and have hysterics with her."

"It will be better than sitting here with you!" Helen snapped spitefully, tears spilling from her eyes again.

"Look at you sewing on that old shirt, as if you've not a care in the world! You're glad Rosalind is dead. You've always hated her!"

Beatrice's hand faltered and tears slipped from under her red-rimmed lids. "How can you be so cruel, Helen?" she asked, her hands trembling as she used the sleeve of the shirt to wipe away her tears. "Really, I thought you promised Mother you'd try to be a brave girl."

"I'm tired of trying," she replied flatly. "Why is it better not to weep? Why must we be stoic?"

Beatrice sighed and blinked away fresh tears. "It does none of us any good to cry until we are sick, Helen. It won't bring Rosalind back, will it?"

"No," cried the younger girl passionately. "Nothing will bring her back, and you are glad because now you'll be able to wed Hugh St John, instead of waiting until Rosalind found a husband she could tolerate!"

"Oh, go to Mother, then!" Beatrice cried, stung by her words. "Go, add to her misery by your tears, and leave me in peace!"

Sophie stood awkwardly, as the younger girl fled from the chamber with a squeal of triumph. "Would you like me to leave you also?"

Beatrice wiped away fresh tears, and shrugged her

shoulders helplessly. Sophie, aware there were many questions which needed answers, took up Helen's seat in the window. "She is very young, you know," she remarked. "I expect she'll be sorry by and by."

Beatrice attempted a watery smile. "I doubt that. Both Rosalind and Helen are—were—known for their self-centred ways. I was only trying to give Mother a little time to rest and gather her composure."

"Of course," agreed Sophie. "I expect your Mother relies upon you heavily."

Beatrice nodded. "Ever since Father died," she agreed. "He was an invalid for many years. He could be difficult, too," she added as an afterthought.

"Sick people often are," observed Sophie. "I helped to nurse my guardian's sister when she was very ill. She was most difficult, but then she was in great pain, poor lady."

"One of Sir Henry's sisters?" Beatrice asked with a flicker of interest.

"Oh, no, Sir Henry has not always been my guardian. I was speaking of my kinsman, Edmund Benton. I have only been in Sir Henry's care for about eighteen months."

"Does he not frighten you to death?" Beatrice asked,

as she laid her sewing aside. "He came to speak to Mother, and to ask us all if we knew anything about Rosalind going off as she did. I felt so guilty as he looked at me, I felt I might almost have killed her myself from neglect!"

Sophie smiled gently. "Yes, he does have the power to make you feel as if you are at fault, but I tell you, he is a good and gentle man. He'd never do any harm, but he does care—really care—about justice."

"Does he?" Beatrice asked sadly. "I don't see how it matters. Rosalind is dead!"

"It matters how she died," replied Sophie. "If she fell and hit her head in helping Bella to elope, as it seems most people think, that is one thing, although poor Bella will carry the guilt to the end of her days."

"She will anyway, if she's run off to be married to Nick Revesby," said Beatrice flatly.

"Is this Nick Revesby so very bad?" Sophie asked, wrinkling her nose in puzzlement. "I mean, from what I have heard, he is much of your and Bella's age. Wouldn't you have chosen him rather than Ezekiel Pridow? I don't mean to be rude but…"

A small smile, quickly hidden, flickered across Beatrice's face. "I believe him to be a good man," she replied primly.

"Aye, and a very dull dog, given to lengthy sermons on almost any occasion, I'll be bound," said Sophie, and was rewarded with a ghost of a smile again.

"You should have heard him on Christmas day," she said quickly. "Huffing and puffing as we decorated the hall with holly and ivy. He called it pagan trappings! And he refused a kiss when we held the kissing ring over Bella. If it had been Nick, there would have been no hanging back! Mind, I think Bella was quite relieved when Mr Pridow refused, she says his embrace has all the warmth of a dead herring!"

"How very unpleasant!" Sophie laughed and Beatrice joined her, stopping after a moment in a horrified manner.

"No, no, don't feel ashamed that you've laughed," said Sophie, catching at her hands which had flown to cover her face. "Your sister liked to laugh, I don't doubt, and wouldn't want you not to because she is dead."

Beatrice was silent for a few seconds. "Rosalind usually laughed at another's misfortune," she said, with some hesitation. "She wasn't a very loveable person." She bit her lip in dismay. "Not that I am any better for saying such a thing, when she is so lately dead!"

"When loved ones die, they don't become saints,"

said Sophie wisely. "Soon, you'll forget Rosalind's worst traits, but until that time, you'll still be irked by her unkindness."

"She was very ill as a child, and made much of by my parents because of it," said Beatrice. "I think perhaps I was always a little jealous of all the attention she used to get."

"I can understand that," said Sophie. "To my great misfortune, I never had any sisters. I've no kin at all really, now that my Uncle Edmund is dead. He took me in for my mother's sake, out of the kindness of his heart, whilst my father, who was a preacher, was imprisoned for fermenting unrest. My present guardian, Sir Henry, had me foisted on him at Uncle Edmund's death. So my only knowledge of how families work is from the observation of Sir Henry's brother and sisters."

"Do you not like them?" Beatrice asked curiously.

"I didn't at first," she replied candidly. "They held me to blame for something and were very cold, although Mistress Westwood was always kind. Later, when I knew them better, I came to like and then love them all. What ailed your sister when she was a child?"

"She had a terrible fever about the time I was born," replied Beatrice. "They feared for her life. Indeed, I grew up with her always sickly, for the physicians said her heart was affected and that it was unlikely she would live. My parents, mindful of this, greatly indulged her, so that she grew up always expecting to have her will. It remained so until my father died. Then our half-brother, who is older by ten years, inherited our home and moved in with his new wife. Life became much more difficult for us. Isabella resents having so many dependants living with her. She and mother are not happy in each other's company."

"Oh dear!" Sophie felt instant sympathy for the family, "It is so difficult when a loved one dies and the situation changes abruptly too, isn't it?"

"Yes!," suddenly the tears were falling from Beatrice's eyes. "Yes, I do miss Father so!"

Sophie came to sit beside her and patted her shoulder gently. For a few seconds, her companion sat rigid, then she abandoned herself to grief and sobbed in Sophie's arms for some minutes.

"Oh dear, oh dear," she said as soon as she could speak. "Here I am making the very fuss I scolded Helen about!"

"It doesn't matter," soothed Sophie. "It is better for you to be rid of your grief."

"But it is for Father, not for Rosalind!" She wept all the harder. "I feel so dreadful that I can't mourn Rosalind. I am relieved that…that…"

"Never mind," Sophie hugged her again. "Our reasons are never clear, you know. I suspect you were too busy helping your poor mother, when your father died, to grieve properly, and the shock of Rosalind's death is making you do so now."

"No, no, it is much worse than that," she confessed, in a horrified whisper. "Helen was right, I am glad in a way, for now Hugh and I can be married! Oh, I am such a wicked, wicked girl!"

"You are no different to the rest of us," replied Sophie, holding her close. "There is nothing wicked in seeing the advantages that inevitably result from disasters. Everyone does, but Helen, being so young, speaks openly of them. Have you loved your Hugh for a long time?"

"Oh no," she replied. "We only met him properly when Father died. He is Isabella's brother, you see, and he came on a visit. Then he started to come regularly, and Isabella was furious when she discovered he came to see me, not her. She is angry that he makes no secret of his affection for me, for she doesn't consider me a great enough match for her brother. Hugh says we should be married soon, and asked Mother, but Mother said I was a not old enough, although I know it is because she fears to annoy Isabella. And she said I must wait until after Rosalind was married, as she couldn't afford two sets of bride clothes so quickly."

Sophie nodded. "That is a great expense," she agreed. "Mine cost me a king's ransom and now I am condemned not to wear them, as my husband was killed."

"Yes, I heard all about it from Mistress Westwood. Was it not the most terrible thing?"

"Yes!" Sophie said and could not stop a shudder. "I try not to dwell upon it. It was six months ago now, and the horror is fading a little. I honestly do not know what I would have done if my dearest friend Cordelia, and Sir Henry had not been with me. Sir Henry organised everything and found the murderer."

"Does he think Rosalind was murdered? Will he find out who did it?" Beatrice sat up and wiped her eyes, her own worries disappearing in the greater trouble.

"If it is humanly possible to find the truth, Sir Henry will do it," said Sophie confidently. "If there was a murder, or if it was just an unlucky chance that Rosalind died, then Hal will find out, that we all may be easy again."

"I don't think we will ever be easy again," sighed Beatrice.

"The important thing now is not to give way to despair. There is much to be done and if I may speak bluntly, it is better that we try to do it as cheerfully as possible, just as you have been doing. From my own experience, to dwell on the past, to constantly try to find out where mistakes were made, serves no purpose other than to make one miserable. We all must grieve, yes, but we must try as you have been doing, to be sensible about."

Beatrice smiled faintly, looking gratified, "I just try not to be a trouble to my mother," she said, "but thank you for telling me I am doing the right thing. It is so difficult to decide what to do for the best, isn't it?"

"Indeed it is, and I must go and assist Sir Henry further," said Sophie. "If he comes back, wet through to the skin, and finds I have spent my time in idle chatter, he will not be pleased with me. No doubt we'll meet up again anon."

Sophie hurried away, leaving Beatrice to her own reflections, pleased enough with the progress she had made, intent on a period of solitude to gather together all she had learnt before passing the details onto Hal.

"Oh, I do beg your pardon," She entered the small parlour where she and Hal had spoken earlier, and found her sanctuary already inhabited by an older man. He was sitting at the table with an open Bible before him, a quill held between his fingers, a blank sheet of paper before him, and an expression of torment on his face. He turned his gaze upon Sophie without a glimmer of recognition.

"Sir Richard Harrison?" Sophie said uncomfortably, encountering his lacklustre eyes. "I am Sophie Redcroft. You might recollect I arrived with Sir Henry Westwood late last night? I am sorry if I have disturbed you, I was seeking somewhere I could write a few notes."

"Mistress Redcroft," he replied, with all the enthusiasm he might have employed on encountering a stray dog. "Yes, Katherine said you would be accompanying Sir Henry. She was pleased at the thought," he added, in a puzzled manner, half to himself.

A smile lit Sophie's eyes. "When is Aunt Kate ever anything but pleased?" she asked simply.

"Aunt Kate?" he repeated, a query in his tone. "Was I not told you were the ward of Sir Henry Westwood?"

"Yes, I am," she admitted, "but Aunt Kate is such a dear person, and I have lived with the family for quite a long time on terms of informality—indeed, it was Aunt Kate herself who insisted…"

"Yes," he interrupted her, "Kate is like that. One meets her, knows her, loves her, all in the space of what appears to be a few minutes."

Sophie warmed to the man, rewarding him with one of her dazzling smiles. "The orphan's mother!" she said, then as he looked taken aback, she made haste to explain: "Hal—Sir Henry says that she attracts orphans—those desperate for a mother's love—like a lodestone!"

Once again a blank, anguished look flickered across his face. "A lodestone of goodness in a wicked, wicked world!"

Sophie smiled at the thought, but her heart was troubled by him. Hal wanted her to talk to as many of these people as possible, but this man appeared to repel conversation, indeed he exuded misery, yet she felt she owed it to Hal to persevere.

"A wicked world indeed," she agreed with a sigh. "How weary it must make her, dealing with it as she does. Even now she is sitting with poor Mistress Pauncey, trying her best to ease her suffering in any way she can."

"There can be no ease for a parent robbed of the life of a child," he replied heavily.

"Or of a child robbed of the love of its mother," she agreed. "Yet such is the fate of so many."

"Indeed," he nodded quietly.

"I am minded that your own wife died but recently, Sir Richard. I am sorry for your grief," said Sophie formally, thinking only this could account for the man's manner.

He nodded again, appearing overwhelmed by the thought of it. "Kate taught me to hope again," he said in almost a whisper.

"I believe she told me you have children, too, back in Virginia," said Sophie, determined to obtain some information for all her trouble.

"I have several children," he replied. "Three sons who are older, on the verge of manhood, and then four younger daughters."

"Good heavens, so many for Aunt Kate to be mother to!" Sophie cried in surprise, for she had never mentioned it. "How do they fare, so far away, without either a mother or father?"

"My wife's family—my late wife's family—her sister and her husband, have them in their care," he said quickly. "My brother-in-law is one of the elders of our settlement." He hesitated, and then added, "Life in the settlement is hard; conditions are difficult. Death is a constant companion. We have suffered many occurrences of fevers. Both children and parents have died. It is the way of things in the New World. Survivors get absorbed into other families."

Sophie nodded her understanding but she frowned over the words. "It is your intention to return to the New World?" she asked.

"I must," he replied simply. "I have a duty to those there. It is most unfortunate that continuing ill health has delayed my return."

"Does Aunt Kate plan to accompany you?" Sophie asked rather appalled at the thought of it, and by the hopelessness of his tone, as he spoke of his home.

"Yes, it is her intention to do so. She has such strength of character, that she says she cannot wait to take my children to her heart, but I could never allow that. She is by far too precious to risk in such a wild, hostile land. Yet, by my desire to keep her safe am I not showing my lack of faith in the Lord?" He sighed heavily to himself. "Am I not fixing my love on a flawed creature and forgetting my salvation? Is she perhaps the temptation of the Evil One? I must go back to see what must be done, and pray for assistance in the task before me. If it can be contrived, my hope was to bring the younger children back here, to the safety of a home with Katherine, but again is that not the Evil One at my elbow, filling my thoughts with my own wicked desires? True my sons are of an age to make their own decision—but no…" He hesitated, then suddenly aware of Sophie watching him anxiously, he added, " You find me seeking guidance from the Lord."

"God grant you that," said Sophie uncomfortably.

"Amen," he replied.

"I understand you are a minister," she continued as he said nothing more, trying not to be overwhelmed by his manner, but determined if possible to discover what lay behind this man's seeming despair.

"I took holy orders many years ago, and then found my inclinations were for a less formal church. Since that time I have been what is commonly called a Puritan," he agreed reluctantly.

"My father was a preacher," said Sophie. "Like you, he favoured the new religion. He believed one could only be saved by devoting oneself totally to the Lord and his works. We spent much of my early years on the road, but when my mother died of a fever, her uncle took me in, and gave me a home. He had no opinion of my father, he said his thinking was muddled and his preaching uninspired. I mostly remember being cold and hungry, and people throwing stones and setting dogs upon us. I felt much safer with Uncle Edmund."

"Children seldom understand the Lord's work," he replied coldly. "They are like wild beasts, only consulting their own pleasures. They must be taught to bend their will to that of the Lord. What pity your kinsman intervened, in time you might possibly have come to love the Lord and be his handmaiden forever."

"Or I might, like my mother, be dead in a ditch," said Sophie bluntly.

"If you had embraced the Lord, you would understand there is no greater felicity than being gathered into His fold," he replied sharply.

"You preach a doctrine I cannot follow." said Sophie, losing patience with his narrowness of outlook. "It seems all you would rejoice in is death, yet here you are, alive."

"I do not question my God," he cried angrily, "I obey him. If I am not gathered unto Him, then he has some purpose for me here on earth! Perhaps to bring unrepentant sinners before me to a recognition of their hopeless iniquity, perhaps to send women about their household duty!"

"Perhaps," she agreed, remembering belatedly, how Hal had warned her to mind her tongue. "Thank you for your insight, Sir Richard, I'll leave you to your meditation and seek out young Mistress Craven that I might be given a task to follow."

"Better that than you waste your time in idle chatter," he returned, picking up his Bible again.

Sophie curtsied and left the chamber hastily smothering her chagrin, knowing that she had invited his censure by her questions. She returned to the vast hall and settled in a window seat by the fire to make some notes in its light, pondering anew on what had made Hal's aunt choose to ally herself with such a man. Aunt Margery she could easily understand consenting to marry a man whose views were so similar to her own and who shared a staunch belief in the Lord, although she doubted their political views would be quite so in tune. But Aunt Kate, although every bit as devout as Hal's senior aunt, had a lightness of touch and a sense of humour which would surely be lost on Sir Richard Harrison.

❧

Chapter Eight

For what seemed several hours longer than the actual time, Hal, Simon Craven and Jack Hollingshead, accompanied by the deserted bridegroom and his glum friend, scoured the ground that had been gone over the previous day. The mood was one of settled gloom, and Hal could feel the despair of Mr Craven who rode alongside him, and wondered if this was not, after all, an impossible task.

"Well, this is Hollywell Wood," said Simon Craven bleakly, as they came to a halt in a clearing. "As we've not discovered anything fresh, perhaps you'll find something here, Sir Henry."

"My desire to see this place springs from your mention of mistletoe, Mr Craven. It struck me that plainly, as you all spoke of it, it may be one of the few clues," replied Hal, glancing up into the bare trees. "If you will all be so good as to spread out, we are looking for hoof prints, where horses have stood. Luckily the ground here is yet still quite firm, unlike the quagmire we have encountered elsewhere this morning."

"As we are all damp and muddy, surely it can no longer signify," said Jack Hollingshead as he jumped down and began looking about the clearing.

"You are a master of understatement, Mr Hollingshead," said Jacob Brendon, irritably. "I am more than damp and muddy, I am soaked to the skin and chilled to the bone!"

"You are at liberty to return to Haceby at any time, Mr Brendon," said Simon Craven, as he, too, got from the saddle, and began examining the ground.

"The significance, Jack, is that if the soil is free-draining, and not churned up under foot, we might find some hoof prints—ah! There is the mistletoe! Behind you, Jack!"

Jack Hollingshead turned about, glancing first up into the trees and then looking down. "Yes, so it is mistletoe, and here beneath, Sir Henry, are the hoof prints as you say!"

Hal rode over to inspect them, as the remainder of the group exchanged startled glances. He jumped down from the saddle in company with Jack. "Yes, here indeed are mistletoe berries and ivy leaves. What a convenient berry the mistletoe is. It falls from its branches so very easily and remains as an indication that someone met here."

"It is a berry associated with evil!" cried Ezekiel Pridow. "One which indicates pagan rites and devil worship!"

"Devil worship!"exclaimed Simon Craven incredulously. "I have never heard such a thing. Not that I know much about devils anyway!"

"We are constantly surrounded by evil, Mr Craven," said Jacob Brendon looking down his long nose. "We must always be on our guard, lest the devil tempt us with cunning."

"Well, somebody met here," said Hal, finishing a thorough examination of the ground with Jack. "See, here are footprints mixed in with the hoof marks…a man's boots I'd say, and smaller, daintier feet over here."

"Bella's?" Simon Craven suggested, a catch in his voice, as he too dismounted, and came to their side.

"Possibly," said Hal gently, "but, see there is no disturbance, no deeper hoof marks, no scuffing of the soil. Rest assured, Mr Craven, there was no abduction of your sister."

"You mean she went willingly?" Ezekiel Pridow demanded, anger in his voice.

"If anybody went anywhere, Mr Pridow, there was no violence," replied Hal sharply. "So we can be easy on that score. Mistress Bella was not taken by an unknown attacker."

"No, we all know it to be Nick Revesby!" snapped Jacob Brendon.

"Do we?" Hal replied shortly. "Well, that is more than I can say. All I will say is that Mistress Bella took no harm here. That being the case, the likelihood of finding her safe is increased."

"We should ride at once to Weston Revesby," Ezekiel Pridow cried. "We'll find her there, being held by Nick Revesby!"

"I can't think Nick would be that foolhardy," protested Simon Craven.

"The Revesbys were ever rakes and libertines—like father, like son, like grandfather!" Jacob Brendon snapped.

Hal glanced to the unhappy Simon Craven, saying in an undertone, "We are in your hands, Mr Craven. A trip to Mr Revesby's home might prove fruitful. Given that we seek your sister and the whole countryside knows it, it seems odd that Mr Revesby hasn't come forward to offer assistance."

A gleam of comprehension entered Simon Craven eyes. "I have been so worried that I never even thought of that, Sir Henry! Good heavens, of course! In the natural way of things, Nick would be the first person to be at my side to find Bella!"

"Then he most probably knows where she is," Hal concluded quietly. "May I suggest any meeting might progress more smoothly if we managed to keep the bridegroom and his gloomy friend from accompanying us?"

"By heaven, you are right, Sir Henry. If we are to stop this descending into fisticuffs, Pridow and Revesby must be prevented from meeting."

Hal turned to Jack Hollingshead. "As we surmised earlier, Jack, we need you to remove the bridegroom and his friend to another place," he said in an undertone. "If you'll be so good as to lead them back to Haceby, and once there, seek out Mistress Redcroft for me and tell her I shall need her assistance at Weston Revesby. We might need someone to persuade Mistress Bella to return home, I believe."

"There is no need to bring Mistress Redcroft out in this weather. Bella will return forthwith, Sir Henry," said Simon Craven stiffly. "I cannot tell you how grieved I am by her behaviour."

"Let us not judge the matter prematurely," said Hal pleasantly. "I always find it better to wait and see how matters progress when dealing with young ladies. Too much censure and judgement merely engenders an even more rebellious spirit."

Simon allowed a ghost of a smile to chase away his haggard frown. "I've heard you've had plenty of rebellious spirit to deal with Sir Henry."

Hal smiled but turned his attention to assisting Jack Hollingshead in persuading the other men to return home to inform the women of the good news that Bella was probably unharmed. For some minutes the matter was disputed hotly, with Ezekiel Pridow losing his temper and speaking harshly, then a sharp increase in the biting wind accompanied by rain so cold as to seem to freeze on impact, changed their minds, and the desire for warmth and shelter overcame the sense of chagrin.

Jack's group set off in the direction of the road back, whilst Hal and Simon examined the hoof marks and footprints again, trying if possible to assess the direction they might have taken. They had just remounted when they heard shouts echoing through the woodland and the thunder of hooves. Quickly they rode forward, to meet Jack and his party.

"We sighted them on the road!" Jack cried, as soon as he saw them. "They were on foot, leading a lame horse. Mr Pridow shouted out in anger, and they disappeared into the thicket on the edge of Revesby Wood." He glanced to Hal, his face mirroring his disquiet. "I judged it best to come to report to you, rather than give chase and risk an encounter, or danger befalling Bella." He edged his horse closer still, then hissed, "Brendon has pistols. Given the chance I believe he might use them."

"Whither were they bound?" asked Hal.

"They were already on Revesby land," explained Jack, adding over his shoulder, as the disgruntled bridegroom came along side. "Which was another reason, Mr Pridow, for not giving chase, but coming here to Mr Craven and Sir Henry!"

"That's all very well!" he snapped as Simon Craven gave thanks that his sister was alive, "but there was no occasion to jostle Brendon's elbow as he pulled his pistol—nor to wrench my horse's head about! It's not your betrothed who has been abducted!"

"Nor yours!" Jack snapped back, aware his actions were a little high-handed. "I've never seen a bride so keen to put space between herself and her intended bridegroom! She crossed the meadow like a deer, scattering cattle as she went, and disappeared into the wood before we could blink!"

Hal hid a smile. It was plain Jack's forthright manner wasn't reserved only for Westwood family. "If Mr Brendon had pulled a pistol, she had every reason to panic," he said in soothing tones. "So, that makes our task more easy, Mr Craven. We go to Weston Revesby, and perhaps, Jack, you continue as we decided, accompanying Mr Pridow and Mr Brendon back to Haceby to reassure the ladies, who must be in a sorry state of fear by now, that Mistress Bella has been found and is well. Indeed, Mr Pridow, I must insist. Plainly you are much disturbed by all that has occurred," Hal added firmly, as the bridegroom began to protest violently and Jacob Brendon to threaten to beat the life from Nick Revesby. "After all, was not our initial idea to keep this affair from becoming a scandal and a nine-day-wonder?"

Both men fell silent, and Brendon nodded sullenly, whilst Pridow glared at them before snapping, "Very well, but my patience is not inexhaustible! I know that young women can take fright over the thought of a wedding, but I tell you this, Craven, if your sister isn't back at Haceby by sunset, with a reasonable explanation for her bad behaviour, there will be no wedding!"

Simon Craven sighed as the group turned away and exchanged a grimace with Jack, the last to leave.

"Never fear, Mr Craven," said Hal. "Your mother will soothe his wounded sensibilities, and provided Jack Hollingshead doesn't favour him with any more opinions on the way home, all will be well."

"I doubt it," he replied, as they turned their mounts in the other direction, riding swiftly through the wood and out onto the highway. "It would be quickest across country," he continued as he waited for Hal to catch up, "but if I am going to quarrel with Nick, I'd prefer to ride up to his front door to do it."

"If your sister has taken such a drastic step as she has," remarked Hal placidly, "I'd try not to quarrel with the man she will in all probability eventually marry." Then, as Simon Craven looked at him in affronted incredulity, he smiled faintly and added, "When my uncle died, I found myself, by default, almost the sole guardian of my younger brother and sisters. My father was often abroad on the King's affairs, and quite frankly, he has always been rather disinterested in all of us, unless it were to find totally unsuitable—but advantageous for him—marriages."

"Oh!" Simon Craven was taken aback by his companion's candour.

"Myself and my elder sisters were given little choice in our marriages," continued Hal, as they proceeded along the roadway. "Mary, the elder, was married to a brute of a man near three times her age, who used her ill, but who had enough influence in the dark days of 1659 to allow my father to return to England. I, myself, married an heiress, which I was pleased to do, make no mistake, for in doing so, I became my uncle's heir. I was also more fortunate in that my Uncle Henry arranged my marriage to a good, sweet young woman. My sister Jane, however, endured several years of torment and misery at the hands of a vicious young fellow, before consumption relieved us of his presence. My next sister, Bess, threatened with an equally unpleasant suitor, eloped with my wife's brother, Justin, a lawyer, whilst Mary, the eldest, at the death of her husband, waited no longer, but married her choice incontinently, before my father had time to arrange another bad match."

"Good heavens," said Simon, blankly. "Your aunt said you were well practised in smoothing the path of troubled lovers, but I thought she was talking about your wards!"

"No," said Hal ruefully. "That was an entirely different matter. My sister's husband and I fell in with a merchant in the nearby market town of Chawcester, when he called upon my brother to look into the matter of his journeyman dying in odd circumstances. Unfortunately, we impressed Master Benton so well, he made us the joint guardians of Mistress Redcroft before he was killed himself. The following year I found Mistress Sandys—Mistress Blackwell as she is now—in France, when I was searching for my father's last child, who had been born there shortly after my father's demise."

"Good heavens," repeated Simon, "and I thought we'd had an unsettled time of it in this part of the country!"

"It can't have been easily hereabouts," agreed Hal pleasantly.

"No," Simon Craven assented ruefully, and then added in a burst of candour, "We are, as you noticed, Sir Henry, descended from ardent Catholics, who ran all the risks that meant at various times in the past. My grandfather was not of their persuasion. A phlegmatic man, he reasoned that the good Lord probably had a vast deal more sense than us mere mortals, and that belief, not form, was the key to a life of peace and prosperity. He shrank from the excesses of both sides of the argument, always trying to steer a middle course. The middle course of the Church of England suited him best, and indeed led to a little trouble for us with our neighbours in recent times, although now, naturally, things have improved."

"Yes, one must always have a sharp eye for trouble," agreed Hal.

"Indeed," he replied grimly, "marriage to Ezekiel Pridow would have been so much safer for Bella than an elopement with Nick Revesby. "

"Purely in financial terms?" asked Hal.

"No, not completely," said Simon Craven sharply. "Financially, it is not a wonderful match. Ezekiel has several sons to provide for. Any child of Bella's would have to make his own way in this world. But Pridow does have good connections, and enough wealth, which is more than can be said for Nick Revesby. His estates are about to be wound up, and he comes from a long line of scoundrels and womanisers."

"Yes, they'd have to be possessed of considerable charm," agreed Hal. "But surely this Pridow fellow is a dull dog, and his friend Brendon is little better. Good men, I am sure, but with little cheer! Nor, to be candid, can I think what my aunt Kate is about, to think of wedding Sir Richard, if these are his friends."

"I find Sir Richard a good man, but my knowledge of him is limited, although reports make him wealthy, with holdings in the New World." Simon replied, frowning over the thought. "I hadn't truly considered either character in great detail. My mother had the arranging of Bella's match, although until recently I believe she had her eye upon Jack Hollingshead."

Hal laughed. "Poor Mistress Bella, she has all my sympathy! I like Jack Hollingshead, but he has no time for the softer side of life. Marriage to him would be secure—indeed, I too, had hoped to settle my ward, Mistress Sandys as she was then, to a match, but at the last moment she felt they wouldn't suit. I must confess I was irritated about it, but when all is said and done, I'd have no hand in forcing any female—let alone one I had a fondness for, as you must do your sister—into such a big step as marriage."

Simon Craven was silent, as the rain began to fall again, and looked taken aback. "Well, no," he agreed finally. "I am fond of Bella. She is a dear girl, but why let it go so far? Good heavens, she was supposed to have been married yesterday!"

"I expect, being so young, she thought it would never

happen," said Hal wisely. "I expect, like you, she shrank from the fuss, from the questions, and the anger of everyone, trusting that something would intervene to stop it happening. Both Mistress Bella and Nick Revesby are very young, are they not?"

"Yes," he replied, "Bella was eighteen last week, and Nick only attained his majority just before his grandfather died. It is a pity in some ways he couldn't find this treasure he talks of. My mother helped Nick's grandfather with rearing him when he was younger, you know. He was in and out of our household since he could sit the back of his pony."

"He was, in fact the natural match for your sister," observed Hal, with a sidelong glance.

"Well, I suppose so. Only Aunt Pauncey and Mistress Hollingshead kept saying Bella could do better than a penniless scamp."

"Certainly Jack Hollingshead is a wealthy man," agreed Hal, "but do you truly think Ezekiel Pridow the right man for your sister?"

"I must confess I'd not met him above three times when he arrived for the wedding," replied Simon awkwardly. "I don't know how it came about, but before I knew it everything was settled."

"You are a very busy man," said Hal kindly. "These things are usually left to the women of the family, but after a bad experience or two, I've found it best to try to get to know any man who is to be part of my family. We so very nearly made a terrible mistake with my ward, Mistress Redcroft's marriage."

"That surely was a shocking thing," agreed Simon. "Poor lady, to awake to find her bridegroom dead."

"Yet worse still, I do believe, had he lived," said Hal, as the house, a sprawling, half-timbered mixture of part house, part ruinous castle, appeared out of the misty rain. "We found out, my brother-in-law and I, in our investigation, that the young man in question was nothing like the man he'd presented himself, but was instead a drunkard, a womaniser and a gambler, who wanted Sophie's fortune to pay off his debts."

"Yes, your aunt, Mistress Westwood, was telling us something of the matter," he replied absently, his eyes on the house. "Dear God, I would that this interview were over!"

"Try to remain calm, Mr Craven, and if possible, utter no hasty words you'll come to regret," suggested Hal. "Both will be defensive and upset. If we can come out of this meeting with no drawn swords or irrevocable family split, we will have done well."

❧

Meanwhile, Jack Hollingshead had pulled his horse to a halt before the front of Haceby Hall and abandoned it, hurrying into the house, his footsteps dogged by Ezekiel Pridow, whilst Jacob Brendon, rode off to the stable yard with the horses, and instructions for fresh horses to be saddled.

"Mr Hollingshead!" the man cried, "Whither are you bound?"

"Sir Henry said I was to find Sophie Redcroft and send her to Weston Revesby, and that is exactly what I shall do," he replied through gritted teeth, as he hurried across the hall in the direction of the staircase, scattering raindrops in his wake. Then, as Sophie, who had been watching from an upper window, appeared at the head of the stairs, his face cleared.

"Mistress Redcroft! Thank Heavens! Sir Henry Westwood extends his compliments and begs you will ride across to Weston Revesby at once. I've sent a message to have a horse saddled for you. Sir Henry desires your assistance with Mistress Bella."

"Mistress Bella is found? Oh, thank heavens! Everyone will be so relieved!" said Sophie, her glance going from Jack Hollingshead, to Ezekiel Pridow, who stood behind him, his face like thunder. "Sir Henry is at Weston Revesby then?"

"And Mr Craven with him," agreed Jack. "Sir Henry bade me ride to fetch you, and to tell Mistress Bella's mother all is well."

"All is not well!" Ezekiel Pridow exploded. "I have been treated infamously! Sent back here as if I am a child! How can all be well when Bella has been missing two days from her home, and is still in the hands of that scoundrel, Nick Revesby?"

"Sir Henry assures me all will be well," snapped Jack, over his shoulder. "I have great faith in him. Mistress Redcroft, I was given to understand time is of the essence!"

Sophie nodded her understanding. "Thank you, Mr Hollingshead. I'll fetch my cloak," she said, and hurried off back down the corridor.

"I'll await you in the stables and accompany you, naturally," continued Jack, then turning to his companion, he added curtly, "There, sir, I trust you are satisfied. Sir Henry was ahead of you. Mistress Redcroft goes to be with Mistress Bella in her distress."

"Mistress Redcroft is little better than Bella Craven!" the man replied angrily. "I would have thought an older woman, like her mother, or mine, would have been more suitable, one who could bring Arabella to an understanding of her crime!"

"Possibly, but an older woman would have required a coach, and at least an hour of preparation. Mistress Redcroft will be ready in—here she is, indeed."

"Mr Hollingshead, Mistress Craven desires your attendance, as does your mother, to assure them Mistress Bella is well. Pray do not concern yourself, sir, I will take the escort of a groom, if you will permit it. Sir Henry did say you were to set Mistress Craven's mind at rest."

"I'll accompany you," cried Ezekiel Pridow, as Jack reluctantly agreed this had indeed been Sir Henry's words.

"Thank you for the thought, sir, but I rather fear the ladies are in some confusion. Your mother and sister require your attendance, too," said Sophie, passing him with a smile. "Believe me, I shall do very well with one of the lads from the stable who knows the way."

❖

Chapter Nine

The approach to the house at Weston Revesby was through an ancient gatehouse, across a narrow bridge, up a very steep incline to the fortified entrance of the house proper and finally into the inner courtyard. Simon Craven brought his horse to a halt before a rather battered, but magnificent oak door, which was abruptly flung open by Nick Revesby, who cried, "Welcome, brother, to our home! Bella, my love, we have our first callers!"

"Nick," said Simon, sliding from his horse, as an old manservant hobbled across the courtyard to take the reins. "You have Bella here? She is safe?"

"My wife and I have just this moment arrived home, Brother!" he replied brightly, his light, damp hair tumbling about his face. "Come in, gentlemen! Sir, I fear you have the advantage of me, but you are welcome!" He bowed politely to Hal as he ushered them over the threshold out of the drizzle.

"This is Sir Henry Westwood," said Simon, taken aback and flustered by his manner. "He came to help us find Bella."

"Congratulations, sir, you have been successful!" Nick cried, with brittle gaiety. "Please allow me to introduce my wife—Bella, my sweet!"

A young woman came down the dark staircase that led directly from the vast hall in which they were standing. Garbed in an ill-fitting gown of at least twenty years before, she was exactly as Jack had described: small, dainty, with a mass of wildly curling dark hair that seemed quite wet. She hesitated, her red-rimmed eyes flying from Hal—as he removed his hat in a flurry of raindrops, and bowed—to her brother. A deep red colour stained her face.

"You find us all awry," continued Nick bravely. "We have but these last ten minutes got out of this rain, and we are wet through!"

"Simon," faltered Bella, "please don't be cross!"

"Cross!" he exploded angrily, "Bella, have you any idea of the absolute uproar you have caused? Half the country has been searching for you for the last two days, and you ask me not to be cross!"

"A little less heat, Mr Craven, if you recollect," said

Hal, gently pulling at his sleeve. "Little will be achieved if we allow hot words to run away with the situation."

"Hot words be damned!" Simon roared, his pent up fears giving way to fury as Bella collapsed on the bottom step of the staircase, weeping. "It will be more than hot words for you, young lady!"

"Mr Craven, I must beg you to moderate your tone when addressing my wife!" Nick said sharply, stooping to put his arm about his beloved in comfort.

"Bella, stop this nonsense!" Simon moved to confront the pair, his anger only fuelled by their words.

"Mr Craven, a word, I beg," said Hal, getting a firm hold on his sword arm. "Now, you asked me to assist you and I shall, by insisting I ask the questions! Mr Revesby, your actions have caused considerable distress to Mr Craven, his family and his guests. No doubt you'd like to apologise, and perhaps explain in part, how Mistress Pauncey came to die?"

There was an abrupt silence, words dying on Nick's suddenly ashen lips, whilst Bella, her tears stilled in horror cried, "Die?"

"Rosalind Pauncey is dead?" asked Nick blankly. "How?"

"She was found in the priest hole the day after your

disappearance, Mistress Revesby. She was dressed in what I believe was to have been your wedding gown, wearing the wreath of ivy and mistletoe you had worn previously," Hal replied in cool, measured tones.

Tears streamed down Bella's cheeks and she shook her head. "I don't know," she whispered. "I can't think— she—Rosalind, came with me to the priest hole, during the game of Hide and Seek, as we planned, and she insisted in coming down the staircase and talked of going along the passage to Hollywell Wood with me, because I foolishly said I was afraid the lantern might go out and leave me in the dark with the rats..."

"Passage, what passage?" cried Simon in exasperation. "Don't tell me you found the secret passage! It is a thing of the past, I know because I helped to pull the roof down! There is no secret passage!"

"Yes, there is an underground passage which leads to your house from Hollywell Wood," said Nick, his young face still showing the shock of the news. "My grandfather knew of it, and Bella and I found the entrance many years ago. Well, we found the Hollywell Wood entrance when we were children, and explored it often, but as you say it had caved in nearer to your house. So last year, when your mother started all the furore about Bella marrying Jack Hollingshead, I dug it out and shored it up again, knowing that if necessary we could still meet in secret—and because I also thought it might be a place where my treasure was buried," he added honestly.

"You mean you've been planning this since last summer?" Simon cried, only further infuriated by the casual way they had found something he thought so well hidden.

"No," replied Nick, "first off I thought to find the treasure. If I found that, I could ask you for Bella and there wouldn't be a problem. Then, when I didn't find anything but mud and stones and rotten wood, and you and your mother started to discourage my visits, I thought I'd put it to another use."

"By heaven, you scoundrel!" Simon cried furiously. "You've been sneaking into my house to meet my sister! If she weren't married to you, I'd kill you for this!"

"But I am not!" she cried, then as Nick turned to her in dismay, she added: "It's no good, Nick, I'm sorry, but I should never have agreed to say we were already married. Not now we know Rosalind is dead, and it being all my fault!"

"Your fault!" he cried in anguish. "How can it possibly be your fault? Oh, Bella, by rights we should be married. If that curate hadn't fallen from his horse and broken his leg, we would have been married!"

Simon Craven's face cleared of its anger. "You are not married?" he cried. "I thank the Lord for that! Come, Bella, we are going home!"

Bella looked from his forbidding face to Nick's one of despair, and promptly burst into tears again.

"Mr Craven!" Hal grasped his cuff as he started forward, and Nick rose to his feet, his hand going to where his sword should be. "Mr Craven, the situation is dire, but we need no further deaths on our hands. Step back, I beg of you!"

"I ought to spit you on my sword, you worthless dog!" snarled Simon Craven, disregarding Hal's words, as Nick, white-faced, stood his ground. "Don't ever set foot on my land again, or I will—I swear it! Bella, get your cloak, we are leaving!"

"Bella, remain where you are!" Nick's voice trembled, but his chin was up, and he met Simon's eyes. "I'll forget your insults, Mr Craven," he continued formally, "for we are to be family. Your sister, through no fault of her own, has spent the last two days in my company, honour demands I make her my wife, even if my undying devotion had not demanded it first!"

"Honour?" Simon Craven spat the word from him contemptuously. "Devotion? What devotion ruins a young woman's reputation? My friends will be calling on you, sir! Bella, come, you may have my cloak. If I get you back home before sunset, we might yet achieve this damned wedding!"

Bella gave a wail of utter despair, and turned her face from them all, weeping into the treads of the staircase, whilst Nick stepped forward to stop Simon Craven approaching her, his hands upraised in fists. "I'll see you in hell first, Simon!" he spat through gritted teeth.

"I've no objection!" snapped Simon, his hand on his sword, as Hal caught his arm again.

"Well!" Sophie exclaimed, stepping over the threshold. "Whatever is going on here? Oh, you must be Nick, and this is Bella, no doubt? My dear!" She pushed past Hal and Simon Craven, thrust Nick gently aside, and stooped, lifting the hysterical young woman into her arms and compelled her to walk with her up the stairs. "Hal, prevent Mr Craven from making a fool of himself, lest he do something very rash like getting into a fight— send him home. His mother is in a fret of anxiety!"

"Bella, if you don't leave with me now, I'll never see

you again!" Simon Craven cried. "Come home with me at once, or I have no sister!"

"Don't, don't, Mr Craven," said Hal, retaining his hold on Simon's sword arm. "Never back yourself into a corner! Of course you are angry, but pause, take thought. This is not worth all this grief!"

"Not perhaps to you," he snapped, "but I prize my family honour, Sir Henry!"

Hal's face changed. "Then I advise you, Mr Craven, as Justice of the Peace, to leave this house at once, before I demand you surrender your sword!" he snapped.

For a few seconds they stood face to face, then Simon Craven, his face like stone, bowed and turned, going back out into the rain. Hal turned to Nick, who was still breathing rather heavily, not entirely sure of his next action, so amazed was he at the turn of events.

"That was Mistress Redcroft," Hal said, as if in explanation.

"Yes," Nick's breath came on a sigh of relief. Their eyes met, and a grin swept over Nick's face.

Hal was suddenly aware, with a lessening of tension, that he had accomplished his task. Both young women were found, one, alas, was no more, and he knew that would need investigating, but Mistress Bella was, it seemed, unharmed, and the impetus to go on suddenly receded.

"Well," said Nick, shrugging his shoulders, as if suddenly released from a great weight. "What to do now?" He glanced to his guest uncertainly. "We were about to break our fast," he suggested tentatively.

Hal discovered he was suddenly ravenous. "What a capital idea," he agreed. "I snatched a few mouthfuls of food at dawn, and although that wasn't that long ago, it seems an age, and it will help to pass the time until the ladies reappear."

Nick nodded, his brow furrowed. "I do hope Bella will not weep herself to distraction. Do you think I should go to her and tell her Simon is gone?"

"Best to leave her alone and let Sophie deal with the matter," Hal replied quickly. "Mistress Bella needs some rest, primarily. She can examine her feelings later, when she is less overwrought."

"You are probably right," agreed Nick, leading the way to the dining chamber, "but I feel rather guilty, sitting down to eat whilst Bella is still so unhappy."

"It will not help Mistress Bella if we starve ourselves," said Hal calmly. "The sort of experience we have all just gone through usually drains one. Good food will stop us from becoming irritable with each other."

Without more ado, they attacked the substantial breakfast laid out before them. Hal waited until Nick had consumed a good meal and his own needs had been satisfied, before saying politely, "Thank you Mr Revesby, suddenly my view of the world is much improved. Now, I don't want to spoil your breakfast, but it is imperative that I ask you some rather important questions."

Nick sat up, suddenly alert. "Of course, Sir Henry, I am obliged to you for giving me a breathing space. I do understand that I shall have a lot of explaining to do."

"Perhaps I should make it clear that your elopement with Mistress Bella has little to do with me," said Hal. "My concern is purely with the death of Mistress Pauncey."

"Which would seem is a direct result of our flight," Nick replied, frowning. "Yet in all honesty, I can't think what have can occurred to kill her!"

"What was her demeanour when she arrived with Mistress Bella? Was she assisting you, or trying to prevent her cousin from taking a step she saw as disastrous?"

"Oh no, she'd been helping us all along—well, hindering really—but that is unkind. However, she didn't arrive with Bella. Didn't you hear Bella say she left her at the foot of the secret stair?"

Hal nodded thoughtfully. So there was no conspiracy between the young couple. They were as patently open as they appeared. "Yes, I believe I do recollect that. So, you did not see Mistress Pauncey once you had left the house?"

"No, I was the first Seeker in the game of Hide and Seek by design, to get the game going. Then I caught Bella, and she became the Seeker, whilst I went out through the priest hole and down the stairs to make sure my horse was ready and to wait for Bella to join me. Which she did, but rather later than we'd planned."

"And how was Mistress Bella when she arrived?" asked Hal, his eyes never leaving the young face before him.

"All of a pother!" Nick replied, frankly. "She was as white as a sheet, and trembling all over. Thanks to Rosalind, she'd come through the tunnel in the dark, and Bella is terrified of the dark."

"You say thanks to Mistress Pauncey, how so?" Hal asked, his eyes veiled, wondering if Bella Craven's agitation had another cause.

"Well, because she followed Bella to the priest hole.

It had been agreed she'd stay and organise the game of Hide and Seek, to cover our disappearance, but when it came to it, Bella said Rosalind claimed to be tired, and so Beatrice became Seeker, whilst Bella slipped away— only Rosalind followed her."

Hal nodded, thinking privately that Bella's distracted appearance could also mask a horror of what had gone before. So easily he could imagine an anxious young woman desperate to get away from a situation long out of her control, finding herself either by accident or design, with a corpse on her hands and seeking only to escape further.

"And did she soon recover, Mistress Bella? Or was she still agitated?"

"Oh yes, once we got going, she soon calmed down. Bella hates to be doing something which would hurt or distress another, so she was still a little unsettled by the thought of an elopement, but we had come to the conclusion we had no choice."

"Yes, it was not the best step to take in the circumstances," said Hal, thoughtfully, "but I can see how you came to take such a regrettable decision."

Nick looked taken aback. "It was the only choice we had," he said with a dignity which Hal found quaint, but somehow very believable. "We agreed we did not wish to so disappoint Bella's family, but none seemed to be heeding her, so we did what we had to do."

"Unfortunately Simon Craven doesn't share your views of things, but as I say, that is none of my affair. I purely wish to discover why Mistress Pauncey was left for dead in the priest hole."

"Do you think she died from climbing back up those stairs?" he asked anxiously. "I know Bella was worried about her, but then she always is. She says Rosalind shouldn't do too much, but it seemed to me, Rosalind could always do what she wanted. It was more the unpleasant things in life she couldn't attempt."

Hal hid a smile. "Yes, you are undoubtedly very perceptive, Mr Revesby, but there are some things in life which are probably better unsaid."

Nick grinned. "Yes, my grandfather used to say I'd never make a diplomat, or a plotter!" he sighed. "He wasn't wrong either, I seem to have made a terrible mess of this affair."

"Yes, that is something of an understatement, Mr Revesby, but let us discuss this further, perhaps there is a way forward," replied Hal.

⚜

Chapter Ten

"Dear me," said Sophie as she half-carried the weeping Bella along a wide, dim corridor. "What an amazing house! Where should we go?"

Bella indicated a heavy oak door with an uncertain wave of her hand, still unable, in her distress, to speak. Sophie opened the door wide and light flooded over them. "Oh!" she cried in surprise, "what a charming chamber! This must surely be part of the old castle, but it is so light and airy."

"It is the Tower chamber," whispered Bella, wiping her tears away with a damp handkerchief. "It was Nick's mother's chamber. I like it—it is like a chamber of a princess in a fairytale."

Sophie smiled, cheered that she had got the young woman to speak. "Yes, it has exactly that air! One can so easily imagine a dragon or a knight in shiny armour at that window."

Bella nodded and then began to sob afresh.

"Now, now," soothed Sophie. "Tell me, where will I find a cup of water? Aunt Kate, Sir Henry's aunt—you must know her, of course—gave me some drops to soothe you. I need only a—ah, yes, thank you," she said, as Bella, now weeping copiously, indicated a water ewer and a goblet set upon a tapestry-covered table. "How very handsome everything is! Mr Revesby doesn't appear to be impecunious."

"His servants are very good," she replied in a broken whisper. "There are only a handful of them left and they are old, but they have always been part of the family…"

"Drink!" Sophie instructed, as Bella's voice ended in a wail. She held out the goblet to her. "Please drink it down. It is not unpleasant and will help you to feel a little better."

Bella did as she was bid, obediently downing the mixture, and then seeking a dry corner of her handkerchief in an attempt to mop her streaming tears. Sophie handed her a clean, dry one, and observed sympathetically, "You are worn down by worry, my dear. Ideally you should sleep on that beautiful bed, but instead come to sit on this window seat with me, and tell me what has occurred. I walked in to hear your brother and

Mr Revesby shouting at each other. Why are men so silly? As if that helped anybody. I do devoutly trust Sir Henry has stopped the brawl which appeared in the making. I am Sophie Redcroft, by the by, Sir Henry's ward."

"I've heard of you," Bella stammered, eyeing her over the top of the goblet, her eyes wide.

"And nothing to my good, I'll be bound," replied Sophie with a comical grimace. "Not if Mistress Hollingshead or her son Jack were your informants!"

A faint, furtive smile flickered over Bella's lips, then her eyes filled with tears again. "I expect they'll be saying that I'll be an outcast, just like you!" she wept.

Sophie looked out of the window as the girl dropped her head into her hands, sighing a little and biting at her lip, as she wondered if the censure of her conduct would ever end. "At least I am not dead as my bridegroom and most of his family are," she replied starkly. "I may not always be welcomed by everybody, but I am alive and I am not part of that evil family. That would have been a living death."

Bella looked up, as the words echoed in her mind. "A living death! That is what I felt I faced," she cried piteously. "Tied as I would be to that dreadful man! And none would listen to me when I said I could not like him! Not Mamma, not Simon, not even Rosalind, she just wanted to be married to anyone. She said it didn't matter who the husband was—and now she's dead, and they all think it's my fault!"

"Yes," Sophie said, thinking rapidly, "Sir Henry has told you about your cousin, has he?" Then as the girl nodded weeping all the more, Sophie leaned forward to touch her hand, adding kindly, "Knowing Sir Henry's methods, I'd think it was done to shock and to test your reaction. Obviously if you had known of her death or been aware of any foul play, you would not have reacted as you did—neither you, nor Mr Revesby. Your very shock and dismay showed your innocence of the offence. It was plainly news to you both."

"Oh, I see," Bella said, her tears stilled for a few seconds as she considered the matter. "It was so horrid to hear Rosalind was dead like that, I felt as if my heart stopped. You see, I was irked with her as we left. She had overheard Nick and I talking a few days ago and insisted on knowing all our plans. She said if I didn't tell her everything, she'd probably get confused and say something before Simon or Mamma which would betray us. So I told her everything and she said she would help us. Which meant she had a hold over me to make me do as she bid." Her tears welled up again. "Rosalind could be such a cat at times! She was determined to come with me, saying that I'd need a chaperone, but I said she couldn't because of the weather, and how she'd make herself ill, so she just came with me to the priest hole, and then she insisted on following me down the staircase to the tunnel. Only, once we got there, we quarreled and I insisted she go back. I knew Nick would be angry if she arrived with me and we'd waste time whilst he took her back to safety, but I was anxious, for I felt sure she would go at once to betray us to Simon, and we'd not have had time to get away to Lincoln. Then it seemed like a miracle when none followed us. I never thought that we could get so lost in the rain and mist!"

"That must have been dreadful," said Sophie, observing that in making an explanation, Bella's tears were lessening.

"A nightmare," she agreed, with a shudder. "We went round and round in circles and I began to be afraid Simon would come up with us. I was so relieved when we finally found the road and were able to hire fresh horses at an inn. I thought perhaps our troubles were over, but they were only just beginning."

"But you did finally get to Lincoln?" Sophie asked curiously.

"Yes," said Bella wearily, "in the middle of the night! The landlady of the inn was most suspicious of us at first. She wouldn't give me a chamber, then when I wept from sheer weariness, she relented, and gave me the worst room in the inn, at the highest price! Nick had to sleep in the stables with the horses!"

Sophie nodded sympathetically. "And you'd missed your time to be married?"

"Yes," she sighed heavily. "Nick went to the church at dawn, only to find the vicar abed with a broken leg and head. He had always been doubtful about performing the marriage, and Nick thought perhaps it was just his way of getting out of it, but the servant took Nick to see his master, telling him he had fallen so heavily on the wet cobbles as to make the physician fear for his mind. He was to have no visitors until he had come to his senses, and even then it would be weeks before he could be back at his duties." She gave a shuddering sigh. "We didn't know what to do for the best. There seemed no choice but to return home, and try to find a local man to marry us."

"Not an easy task," observed Sophie.

"We knew in our hearts what would happen," she replied, her voice flat. "We knew coming back, even if we had been married, would be difficult. We were only driven to take such outrageous steps by despair. None had listened to me before. We knew they'd still try to push me into marrying Mr Pridow! That's why Nick said we should pretend to be already married!"

Sophie hugged her as she began to weep again. "I know, I know," she soothed. "They say really foolish things like, 'Oh, you'll be happy enough once you have a child of your own', and 'It is merely a matter of enduring a little discomfort and pain.'"

"Yes!" Bella cried. "I told Mamma the thought of Mr Pridow being my husband gave me the terrors, and she reminded me of how much I liked children, and said I'd soon come to love all of his and especially my own!"

Sophie nodded and squeezed her hand in sympathy. "When in truth you've given your heart to Mr Revesby, and want only his arms about you, and his children to tend?"

She nodded and wept into her shoulder. "We should have been married by now," she confided through her tears. "If only we had been married, I'd have had nothing more to fear. That's why Nick said we should pretend we were, but I couldn't tell a lie and I can't live with him a fallen woman either!" Sophie patted her back in comfort as her tears fell again. "Yet neither can I go back home! Oh, what shall I do? What shall become of me!"

"You must put your trust in Sir Henry," replied Sophie kindly. "He'll find a way of sorting out this tangle, and in the meantime, a sleep will do you good."

"But Sir Henry thinks I am responsible for Rosalind's death!" Bella protested. "I know he thinks it is all my fault, yet I tell you, Rosalind would not let me go alone as planned. She insisted on going down the stair with me, saying she had to, as I'd be afraid to go into the dark, but I knew Nick would be waiting for me, and it wasn't dark, for I had a lantern, but she would not listen and now she's dead."

"Hush, hush!" Sophie soothed her as she began to get hysterical again. "Come, no more tears now, no more thinking. You must rest. Once you've slept everything will seem a lot better."

"Oh, I am so tired," she agreed. "I can't recall the last time I slept properly. I still feel I am on that endless journey to Lincoln and back!"

"Come, get into bed, then," said Sophie, going to

pull back the heavy counterpane. "Get under the covers to keep warm and sleep to give Sir Henry time to decide what must be done for the best."

"If I sleep in Nick's house, am I not compromised?" she asked as she took off her boots. "If I sleep in one of his beds, won't everyone think the worst of me?"

"My dear, Mr Revesby is a gentleman, that much must be plain to all. He may, like you, have been driven to despair, but you need have no fear to take your rest. I am here as a chaperone, that is why Sir Henry sent for me. Rest easy, close your eyes and sleep," she continued, as she assisted the young woman into the bed and covered her tenderly. "I promise you I'll remain here with you. You shall not be left alone."

Sophie sat back down on the window seat and watched over her charge until finally her tears were stilled by sleep. Once she was sure Bella slept, Sophie sat back and looked about her with interest, taking in the good old-fashioned furniture and how well tended everything was. This was not the home of a rackety young blade, with no thought in his head but the ruination of Bella Craven. She frowned in concentration and only had time to begin considering what could be afoot, when a tap came upon the door and an elderly woman enter the chamber.

"Ah, she sleeps, does she, Mistress Bella," she remarked with simple satisfaction and a toothless smile. "She'll be a lot better for it!" She glanced brightly at Sophie. "Now, Mistress Redcroft, I've sat young Master Nick and Sir Henry down to some breakfast, won't you go and join them?"

"Thank you kindly, but I promised I'd stay at Mistress Craven's side," replied Sophie, although the thought of food made her realise how hungry she was.

"Bless you, my dear, I'll sit by her and keep her safe," replied the older woman with a chuckle. "I've known Mistress Bella since she were a little one come visiting with her brother on her first pony! Though how this matter will end, I dursan't say, what with Master Simon rampaging off like that and Master Nick in such a fury! Thank heaven for Sir Henry Westwood, I say, or there would have been blood! He sent Master Simon off and no mistake. Now he and Master Nick be sitting down to breakfast and a discussing what's to be done. Sir Henry, he said as to ask you to join them—a female point of view, he said, would be an asset at this juncture." She repeated the words with some relish and a grin. "He do talk like a book, don't he? But an agreeable gentleman, so they say."

"Yes, they do," agreed Sophie. "Well, I will join them if I am sent for. Pray, tell Mistress Bella I didn't desert her, but I must admit the thought of food is attractive. Sir Henry's message came as we were sitting down to break our fast at Haceby."

"Away with you then, my pretty," said the old woman, limping across the chamber to drag the hangings over the weak daylight. "Never you fear, I'll not desert Mistress Bella, but send her down to join you when she awakes."

"Thank you, mistress," said Sophie, hastening to the door. "Where will I find Sir Henry and Mr Revesby?

"In the parlour, just off the hall, at the foot of the staircase," she replied taking a seat, and settling herself comfortably. "Hurry along now, both gentlemen looked as if they'd not seen food in a sen'night."

⚜

Chapter Eleven

"Mr Craven!" Ezekiel Pridow stepped out of the archway as he rode into the stable yard of Haceby Old Hall, and stood in the sullen drizzle. "You have returned alone—yet surely we saw your sister in company with Nick Revesby!"

"You are correct," Simon replied stiffly, jumping down from the saddle, and giving his horse a pat, as the boy came running to take her away. "Give her some oats, and see she is well rested," he added, then turning back to the man who stood insistently close. "Stand aside, sir, I am wet through, and will not linger to parry words with you in the rain."

"But your sister, sir!" Ezekiel Pridow reluctantly let him pass, and followed him into the back of the house. "Surely, you have not returned without your sister!"

"I have returned home at Sir Henry Westwood's instruction, " he replied sourly.

"Sir Henry Westwood? Do you tell me he has remained with your sister?"

"He and Mistress Redcroft—I passed her and one of the stable lads on the road," Simon snapped irritably. Then as his ashen-faced mother hurried to meet him, he went to her, his arms outstretched. "She is found, mother, alive and well!"

"Oh, thank God!" she collapsed into his arms, weeping with relief. "Jack said she was found—but I didn't dare believe it, and I was so afraid you'd get into a fight with young Nick!"

"We are both well enough. Sir Henry saw to that," he replied grimly.

"But you didn't bring her back!" cried the bridegroom. "How can all be well, if you didn't bring her home? She is still at the mercy of that fellow, Revesby!"

"How can she be at the mercy of Nick Revesby if Sir Henry is there and Mistress Redcroft is with her?" demanded Simon, his patience at an end. "Now, if you'll excuse me, sir, I am for a hot bath and some food before I go down with the ague!"

❧

Sophie was still smiling at the woman's words as she left the chamber and made her way down three stairs cut from the trunk of a huge oak tree, and then down the handsome staircase into the hall below. She took the opportunity to look about her as she went, and arrived, favourably impressed, in a small parlour where Hal and a handsome young man, whose face bore witness to his weariness and anxiety, were still seated at a table well-provided with food. Sophie hesitated in the doorway, observing the notorious young man as he was talking to Hal. She saw that he was handsome, with a smooth, bronzed skin and slender physique under light blonde hair. His hazel eyes were well-spaced, and crinkled at once into an attractive smile as he saw her.

"Ah, Sophie," Hal, seeing Nick's smile, got up at once. "Come, meet Mr Revesby, whom you passed on the stairs earlier."

"Mistress Redcroft," Nick got hastily to his feet. "Tell me please, how is Bella?"

"She sleeps," Sophie replied, as Hal handed her to an ancient chair. "Sir Henry's aunt gave me some drops for her. I persuaded Mistress Craven to take them, and then as she talked to me, she grew sleepy, and finally she lay down on the bed and slept."

"Oh, thank heavens," Nick cried. "I swear she has barely closed her eyes these last forty-eight hours! I am vastly obliged to you, Mistress Redcroft. Firstly, in coming so promptly at Sir Henry's request, to our aid, and then in tending Bella so very well. I have been in such anxiety over her. I know how I have injured her good name by my foolish, precipitate actions. I don't know how I'll ever repay you and Sir Henry for your intervention."

"A good breakfast would go a long way, Mr Revesby," replied Sophie frankly, glancing about her, further fascinated by the house, and looking with admiration at the ceiling, which was heavily timbered in oak to form squares. The centre of each was painted in the coats of arms of various branches of the family. "I was about to break my fast when Sir Henry's message arrived, so I am famished."

"Rather like poor Mr Revesby here—and no doubt young Mistress Craven—we have barely eaten in the last two days," Hal observed. "I find now that I am in possession of a full stomach, things have begun to look a little more rosy."

"Do they, sir?" Nick asked anxiously, as he assisted Sophie to some bread and beef. "I must confess, for all that I've eaten, I still find myself faced with a daunting prospect—if not a duel—with Simon Craven."

"There will be no duel," Hal said firmly, smiling a little as Sophie attacked her breakfast with alacrity. "I give you my word on that, Mr Revesby, although it will hardly enhance our attempts at a reconciliation if I am forced to arrest Mr Craven, I must confess."

"Especially as it was he, via Jack Hollingshead, who sent for our aid," agreed Sophie, shaking her head firmly at the suggestion of wine.

"Yes, of course, Simon Craven, poor fellow, was mad with worry for his sister, having been with Jack and I when we found his cousin's body in the priest hole," remarked Hal. "Which accounts for his outburst earlier. As he sees it, Mr Revesby, through your folly his sister is ruined and a young woman of his kin is dead. He has spent the last few days riding in search of Bella in the pouring rain. Then as he might to have hoped to rest, he had to deal with half a dozen anxious women, all weeping and clamouring for him to do something."

"Not only females, Hal," said Sophie as Nick Revesby look dismayed. "Mr Pridow and his friends were enough to give old women a bad name."

This brought a sudden grin to Nick's pale cheek,

as Hal laughed abruptly. "I must confess," Hal said thoughtfully. "I am still bewildered by Craven's choice of bridegroom for Mistress Bella. I know Craven said he'd only met Ezekiel Pridow a few times before he arrived at Haceby for the wedding, and that his impression of him was not favourable, but I'd have thought he would have shown more interest in his sister's future husband." He sighed thoughtfully and then added, "I expect it was a case of everyone being over-optimistic, and probably the Craven family's anxiety that just what has happened, might occur."

"A masterly summing up, Sir Henry," said Sophie dryly. "What shall you do to resolve the problem?"

Hal glanced at her suspiciously innocent face, his lips twisting into a faint smile, as he realised how much he had missed her sharp wit these last six months. As usual, Sophie cut through all the talk and furore surrounding a subject to reach the heart of the matter.

"First, we must affect a reconciliation between ourselves and Mr Craven, and then between Mr Revesby and Mr Craven. Then we must get Mistress Bella back home without delay, that her reputation is not tainted, and we must do all this by sundown."

"A mere four, five hours to accomplish so much?"

Sophie said with a grimace, as she glanced toward the December day.

"I beg your pardon, Sir Henry," said Nick sharply, "but I will have no hand in giving Bella back to her family to be married to a man she hates."

"I give you my word, Mr Revesby, none shall force Mistress Craven against her will into a marriage she has no stomach for. Indeed, I rather think the bridegroom may be having second thoughts."

"No," said Sophie quickly. "He was huffing and puffing over all the trouble, and generally making a fuss, but he wants this alliance badly. He is such an odious, oily creature, that he'll convince Mr Craven he's such a good, kind, forbearing fellow that he is prepared to overlook the faults and folly of his young, wayward bride, and they'll still force her to marry him. You know only too well, Sir Henry, of the pressures put upon young women to marry as their family dictates."

"That is because most times her family have her best interests at heart," replied Hal swiftly.

"No," returned Sophie sharply. "Mostly the family are more concerned with getting a good bargain in return for her dowry, than her happiness!"

The grin returned to Nick Revesby's mouth. "I see

you favour plain speech, Mistress Redcroft! 'Tis no wonder you are considered a firebrand, to be avoided!"

Sophie fixed him with a look. "I have but recently escaped the fate Mistress Bella faces," she replied sharply. "I did it at the cost of my good name, and probably a considerable loss to my fortune, by the time the lawyers are done. Yet, I tell you to your face, I am prepared to sacrifice both—and will probably spend my life unmarried—rather than be tied to a man I can neither love nor respect."

"The difference being between you and Mistress Bella, Sophie, is that you are yet a wealthy woman, and, save for me and Justin, you have none who seek to control your actions," observed Hal. "In the plain terms you claim to favour, you have the money to become an eccentric spinster if that is your whim. Mistress Craven does not have that freedom."

"Neither Bella nor I care about money!" Nick cried at once. "We'll be happy to be poor, as long as we can be together!"

"Mmmm," said Hal dispassionately. "Justin, my sister's husband made similar claims when they married clandestinely and ran off to London together. Six months later, I found them living in a hovel, both slowly losing their health from lack of food, and Justin working himself into an early grave, in an effort to see his bride had but the basics to support life."

Nick blanched at this graphic picture. "I have hopes of retaining something of my estate," he said, his face suddenly pale. "And I am still, even at this late date, looking for my treasure."

"Somebody mentioned your treasure earlier," said Sophie, feeling sorry for him. "What is it, and how came it to be lost?"

"I would that I could answer either of those questions, Mistress Redcroft," he replied frankly. "I know there is a treasure. My father spoke of it frequently when I was a small child, and I know it was lost, because I imagine I was too young to understand when he died, and my grandfather was still in exile in France."

"But did he not know of it?" Hal asked, diverted by his words.

"No, my grandfather, if anything, was inclined to dismiss it all as one of my father's tales. My father was a scholar, you understand, and my grandfather very much a soldier, a man of action."

"So, you don't know what it is, or where it is?" Hal asked, glancing sidelong to him. "Forgive me, but surely it is just a tale, told by a loving father to a small child?"

Nick smiled bitterly. "Ah, once again the voice of reason, Sir Henry! Indeed, events would seem to bear you out. A fairy story told by a dying man to amuse a grief-stricken child! I'm sure my neighbours dismiss me and it as such!" He sighed heavily. "And they are probably right—but in my heart, I know it is there! My father spoke of it endlessly—it formed the whole basis of our brief life together after my mother's death."

Hal nodded thoughtfully, and would have sought to turn the focus of the discussion back to a more practical matter, but a step was heard in the hall and in a moment Bella Craven was with them.

"Mistress Craven, are you well enough to have arisen?" asked Hal, as Nick leapt to his feet in delight.

"Yes, yes, thank you, Sir Henry," she gave Hal a timid, fleeting smile, which immediately won his heart. "I must beg pardon for my earlier behaviour. I am afraid I was in sore distress."

"Come, sit by me," said Sophie, as she hesitated. "Are you not hungry?"

"Do you know, I am—and thirsty, too," she replied. "No, Nick, not wine, I have nothing in my stomach. I'll be talking nonsense in no time. Just some bread and milk, please."

"We have been discussing matters, Mistress Craven," said Hal, as these commodities were supplied for her. "Lingering over our own breakfast, to try to find a way out of the problems which face you and Nick."

"There is no way," she replied swiftly. "My brother has told me I am no longer welcome in his house. I must throw myself on Nick's mercy, and pray that as a gentleman, he'll not refuse to marry me."

"You know there is nothing I want more, Bella," said Nick quickly. "The protection of my name you must and shall have, but Sir Henry has been telling me that I will condemn you to a life of penury, if we persist."

She turned to him, her eyes sparkling, "I care nothing for that. Do you, Nick?"

"No, I don't," he replied simply, "and so I told Sir Henry."

"And I pointed out that my sister and her husband married clandestinely and eloped to London and both near died of exhaustion and starvation before we found them," Hal returned. "True, the same fate most probably won't befall you, but life is difficult if you are forced to become a pensioner of your family. In the struggle to live, love gets worn away like a rubbed fabric, and with it, goes all the joy of life."

"You paint a grim picture, Sir Henry," said Nick, frowning. "Surely, if we can hold onto some land, we can farm. Perhaps Mr Craven will allow Bella her dowry, so she can keep a maid?"

"And if he doesn't?," asked Hal.

"I am not afraid of hard work," said Bella stoutly. "If Nick can farm, I can cook and clean."

"And raise chickens and make cheese?" asked Hal, smiling a little at their innocence.

"If need be," she returned, a little less surely.

Hal decided it was time for a dose of reality. "In all this you are forgetting your Cousin Rosalind," he said gently. "There are questions which must be answered. The Coroner will come. You will be called, both of you, to give an account of what occurred. You will be under oath. If it is possible—if you will permit me—I should like to ask you a few questions, about the last time you and your cousin, Mistress Pauncey were together?"

"No, Nick, do not fuss, I am quite able to reply," said Bella, as Nick expostulated. "I am sure Sir Henry will bear with me if I am a little tearful." She resolutely gripped her bottom lip between her teeth to stop it trembling. "I just never expected such a thing to happen. I must confess I was worried about her, but she insisted on coming down the stair with me, talking all the time, and I was late because I had been remonstrating with her. Then she decided she had better come with us, to protect my good name. I had been quite sharp with her, telling her she would only slow us down, and in the end I lost patience with her and told her not to be so foolish, which she took ill," Bella's eyes filled with tears. "She could be so very unkind sometimes, but I never expected to come back to find her dead."

"Did she fall on the stair, perhaps?" Hal asked, his eyes never leaving her sweet face.

"I do not know. Did she?" Bella asked unhappily. "It was in my mind, that it might have happened so."

"But you did not push her, perhaps, when she spoke to you so unkindly and tried to detain you further?" Hal suggested sharply.

Bella's face showed her shock, and tears filled her eyes, but she controlled them. "As God is my witness, I did not," she replied, trembling. "I swear to you, sir, I left her by the cellar at the foot of the stairs and told her to return to the games, and please not to say a word to anyone."

"Sir Henry, I beg you will desist," said Nick sharply. "I will not allow Bella to be interrogated, when she is so shocked!"

"Hold hard, Mr Revesby," said Sophie. "Bella is not a simpleton. She knows she must help find out what happened to her cousin, and she has nothing to fear."

"But that often we must deal with less than the cleverest of mortals," said Hal, "who arrive with preconceived ideas, and prefer to put the blame on the easy suspect."

"Never mind all the dire warnings, Hal," said Sophie, as Bella's eyes filled with tears again. "Bella knows she has some explaining to do, but wouldn't it all go so much easier if we found Mr Revesby's treasure?"

"Oh, yes!" Bella's face changed from despair to anxiety. "That was to have been our task on our return, Nick. Most of our problems would be solved if only we could find your treasure."

"Something I feel certain Mr Revesby has sought endlessly these past months," said Hal, determined to keep to the practical.

"Years, sir—and please call me Nick, if you will," he replied. "Most people do. Yes, I've searched from attics to cellars for my father's treasure, but I've had little luck. I was hoping Bella might think of something new—or indeed yourselves."

"What are the cellars like?" Sophie asked quickly, well aware Hal was about to crush the young couple with more cold, hard facts. "Surely that is the most likely place?"

"Most of the house is so old, we have few cellars, and I've searched them," he replied.

"I thought of the attics, Nick. They go on forever, and are full to overflowing with discarded items. Any amount of treasure could be hid up there!" said Bella.

"Which was your father's favourite chamber, Nick?" Hal asked, intrigued in spite of himself, as the other three fell into a dispute.

"My father's favourite chamber?" Nick repeated the words blankly, and then remembering his manners, continued, "well, he was forever in his library. Even when he was ill, he would be in there, reading or writing. Indeed, at the end it became his bed-chamber too—he died there." His voice faltered and he frowned. "I imagine that's why grandfather and I never went in there. It was too full of ghosts for us."

Hal nodded, his own emotions stirred, and seeing that until they had attempted something, neither of the lovers would listen to reason, he added, "Well, that's where we should start the search."

"Do you mean it, sir?" asked Nick, as Sophie flashed Hal a smile of understanding. "I mean, I'm obliged to you for your interest, but it is merely a dusty chamber full of piles of old books! I've been looking for a secret panel or something."

"I'm sure you have," said Hal sympathetically, "but in my experience things are best hid in plain view."

"Well," Nick cast him a doubtful look, still not sure if his guest was all that he seemed, "as far as I can recollect, there isn't even a large chest in there."

"What? Not even one with a sign which says, *Treasure This Way?*" asked Hal, with a slight laugh.

Nick grinned. "No, not even that," he agreed, relaxing a little. "It just piles of books and papers, and my mother's lute."

"All the things you'd prefer to forget, no doubt," said Hal kindly, his liking for the young man increasing in the face of his good manners and amiable temper, "but I do think it might bear investigation. Sophie—Mistress Redcroft—will tell you I have just such a chamber, filled with books and papers, and I keep most of my precious possessions there."

"Only most of your precious possessions, Sir Henry?" Sophie asked impudently.

"Yes," he replied evenly. "My sons are forbidden it, being too young to understand the value of that which is within."

"Well, we are losing sight of our objective," said Sophie quickly, "which is the finding of Nick's treasure! Come, shall we not at least view this library? If Sir Henry says we should look there, then I am minded to follow his instructions!"

"That must rate as a rare occasion," Hal murmured, as he reluctantly followed Nick back across the hall and along a dim corridor into a chamber, which looked out on an overgrown garden.

⚜

Chapter Twelve

Hal looked around with interest, seeing a chamber lined from floor to ceiling with books of all shapes and sizes. Most were neatly placed on shelves with others stacked in piles alongside, and all were covered in a fine film of dust. His eyes finally came to rest on the faces of his companions, whose expressions aptly mirrored their feelings.

"Oh," said Sophie in a daunted voice, "what a beautiful library, so many books!"

"Indeed," agreed Hal, managing to hide the amusement which threatened to bubble up. "A wonderful library, Nick, you are to be congratulated on so valuable a source of information. I wish mine where half so large."

"Yes," said Nick unenthusiastically. "It was my father's pride and joy, so they tell me."

"Well, Sir Henry, where do we begin our search?" Sophie asked, as she glanced about her with interest. "Do you truly think what we seek will be here, rather than in other parts of the house?"

"I imagine, from what Nick has said, other parts of the house have been tried many times in the past," Hal replied fixing his eyes upon his host, who nodded. "By his own admission neither he nor his grandfather came here very often, meaning most likely it is still as it was when Nick's father died."

Nick nodded. "Yes, somehow we never had the heart to look much in here, although we searched everywhere else, when my grandfather returned from exile, and again each time we found ourselves pressed for money, in the intervening years. He was convinced my mother must have known where it was hidden as well as my father, but all that my nurse could tell us is that my father used to say he'd left my grandfather instructions, and that the treasure was hidden where no God-fearing Roundhead would ever find it!"

"So, take us through it once again, Nick," said Sophie, making room for Bella to sit beside her on a day bed. "Your father was badly wounded at—Naseby, was it?"

"Yes, his leg was broken when he was shot off his horse. He was left for dead, because he had hit his head and was stunned, but Jem Attwood, the father of one of our tenants found him, and brought him home. He set the leg first as best he could, and stole a cart to get him back, but by the time they got here, my father was in a high fever. He recovered, but it was slow work and his health was impaired. He always walked with a stick and was frequently in great pain thereafter. He spent much of his life on that daybed, Mistress Redcroft."

"Poor man," said Sophie, with her ready sympathy, "but he had your mother to tend him?"

"Until the birth of my brother," he sighed, "then even that solace was denied him."

"She died?" Hal asked, knowing the answer.

"And the baby with her," Nick agreed. "My father, broken-hearted, followed within the year. That was when my grandfather was forced to return from exile, and all the trouble started with Parliament levelling fines upon us. We were known to be wealthy, you see. Granted, a goodly sum had already been sent to swell the King's coffers—all the silver and such—but until grandfather returned, all the beasts and land remained. Once grandfather was back, it was a succession of sacrifices, with one farm after another sold off to pay endless fines, and the best beasts run off or stolen in the next round of fighting. And all the while we knew my father had hidden away a treasure somewhere so cleverly, none of us fools could find it."

"Do you remember nothing of your father, Nick?" asked Hal, becoming interested, in spite of his burning desire to get Bella back to the Cravens.

"Not really," he replied, with a small sigh. "I was hardly out of long coats when he died. I can dimly remember how he used to take me up before him on his horse and ride out each day. My nurse hated him to do so, and grumbled all the time in case we should take a fall, but my memory is that he sang to me as we rode along." He laughed abruptly, his eyes suddenly filled with tears at the painful recollection. "Christmas carols mostly. He died at that time of year, of course."

"Poor Nick!" Bella squeezed his arm in sympathy as he perched on a chair beside them.

"So, tell me more of your father—if it isn't too painful, Nick. He was an active man, in spite of his injuries?"

"So my grandfather said. I don't remember him as active," he replied. "Apart from riding out each day, most of my memories are of him lying on this bed reading, his face lined with pain, as my mother brought him a draught to ease it."

"And this was his favourite chamber?"

"Oh, yes, he was a great scholar, you see. He and my grandfather quarrelled often when he was a young man. My father wanted to go off to university, but my grandfather didn't hold with too much learning. He was of the opinion that too many books addled a man's native wit."

Hal smiled. "Yet there are books here aplenty," he observed.

"Yes, that was the compromise they reached. My father was allowed all the books he wished to study in the evenings, but he had to learn to run the estate and to marry in exchange."

"I see," Hal nodded thinking of all such compromises forced upon people in their day-to-day living. Then, as everyone fell silent, rather sobered by the tale, he smiled, "Well, I think if you wish to find your birthright, Nick, you must start here."

"Here, but what is here—in this chamber?" asked Nick.

"By your own admission, you and your grandfather seldom set foot in this chamber," said Hal. "A man who has no time for book learning, wouldn't even consider the hiding places that could be in a chamber lined with books."

"Goodness me!" Sophie cried. "You mean you think the treasure is here?"

"You say your father had difficulty in walking, Nick," said Hal, "and that he took great pains not to have an accomplice, for you must remember those were very difficult times. Somebody with a hint of knowledge might have inadvertently given the hiding place away."

"Oh, this is splendid!" said Sophie, getting excited at the prospect. "So all we need to do is to look for a book with treasure in the title—or no, perhaps—who was your father's favourite author, Nick?"

"I think both those ideas are a little simplistic, Sophie," said Hal with a smile. "Remember, this is a scholar we speak of. How are your Latin and Greek, Nick?"

"Bad," he replied bluntly, scanning the shelves with some doubt, as Sophie and Bella approached a shelf each and began lifting off huge tomes. "But surely the treasure my father spoke of would be much bigger? Surely it couldn't be contained in a book?"

"What makes you think so, Nick?" Hal asked, chuckling, as Sophie, full of zeal, returned to the bookcase and took out another volume, staggering as she began to sneeze repeatedly.

"I don't know." He turned to help her lay the book

upon a table, his young face creased into a frown. "I really couldn't say, but you know, I always had the feeling it would be so valuable that all our problems would be solved."

Hal grimaced and resisted the impulse to tell him that problems were seldom solved, merely shelved, or that if they were solved by some miracle, a fresh set appeared immediately. "Well, I am sure there is something of value to be found here," said Hal cheerfully. "Even if it were only the knowledge that the chamber has been thoroughly cleaned!" Then, as all three turned to look at him in horror, he smiled again and said gently, "It's a good story, Nick, but we must face facts, and Bella must be got back to her family. You've forgotten that there is still Rosalind's death to look into."

"But I told you how Rosalind was alive when we parted at the entrance to the tunnel," said Bella quickly. "She'd insisted on coming down the staircase with me. She was chattering on about her plan to don my wedding gown and pretend to be me on the morrow, and what fun it would be to wear a veil and then surprise Mr Pridow at the last moment, but I told her not to be so silly, and how everyone would be so cross if she did such a thing, and she said they were going to be so cross with me it didn't matter. Then we got to the tunnel entrance and I only had one lantern, for she wasn't supposed to be with me, so I made her turn back with it, and went on by myself in the dark." She shuddered at the memory.

"Yes," said Nick, "as I told you, Bella suddenly arrived out of the blackness of the tunnel, to where I was waiting with my horse. She was trembling all over, and I'm afraid I cursed Rosalind for being an interfering jade." He looked troubled at this confession. "Of course, we had no idea she'd be dead by the time we returned."

"Yes, we were certain there would be some logical explanation, but you don't take my point," said Hal. "The Coroner will return tomorrow, and you will both be required to give your evidence under oath. It is essential for Mistress Bella's reputation that she be returned to her home before that time."

"No, it is you who are missing the point, Hal," said Sophie, as the Nick turned away to hide his feelings, and Bella hovered on the verge of tears at the thought of going back home. "If Bella goes back to Haceby, she'll have no say in her future. No, don't tell me about her brother's threats, I heard them for myself. Bombast mostly, and irritation that he found himself in a difficult situation because he hadn't made sure the man his sister was to marry was the right one for her!"

"I bow to your superior view of the matter," Hal replied coldly. "However, I rather think my view is the one most of Mistress Bella's family will endorse. If she can be returned home by sunset, there will be little scandal, and I have Mr Craven's word Mistress Bella won't be forced to marry this man against her will."

"Yes, well, I know my thoughts on the likelihood of such an occurrence," Sophie retorted, "but I'll not take further issue with you. Instead I'll repeat your own words: Bella must be home by sunset. We have five hours to set to and find this treasure. A lot more will be accomplished if you stop disputing the matter, and start helping to look."

"Do you imagine we will find the treasure within five hours?" Hal demanded sharply.

"Who knows," she replied, "but we most certainly won't if we don't even look!"

As Nick and Bella exchanged horrified looks, Sophie turned her back on Hal and continued with her task. There was an abrupt silence whilst the others expected an explosion of wrath, then Hal shrugged and slipped off his elegant coat. "If it is a task we must attack, then it is best we do so at once—but we must return before dusk, Mistress Bella, I think you see that. Meanwhile, may I suggest we take a bookcase each, so that we don't fall over each other?"

For the next hour, they all worked feverishly, with many stops for bouts of sneezing. After ten minutes, Sophie had got Nick to send for cloths to dust the books as they went, for Hal's words made sense, as did his insistence that each book was returned to its rightful place, or they'd end up in a terrible muddle.

"Well, it would seem we are making progress" said Hal, as they paused for the ale a servant brought to soothe their dry throats.

"Are we?" Nick asked, sneezing repeatedly. "By heaven, my grandfather was right, books are nothing but dust gatherers!"

"Nay, Nick, never say so," said Hal returning the last of a series to its shelf. "The knowledge held here is worth a king's ransom!" As he said it, he turned back to them, his eyes suddenly filled with enlightenment. "Perhaps that is it, Nick—" he said slowly, "perhaps this is your father's treasure! Recollect he was a scholar. To a man of learning, this represents all earthly delights."

"You mean they are valuable, Hal?" Sophie asked,

looking at the book of maps she was dusting, unaware of the smudge of dust on her nose and a cobweb caught in her curls.

"Not perhaps in the manner Nick is imagining," said Hal slowly. "Each man's treasure must, of course, be different. Mine, I believe, is my home, my family and friends. Perhaps, Nick, this represented your father's most cherished possessions. The thing he'd most want to leave to his baby son—the knowledge of how to deal with life."

"You mean there is no gold," Nick cried in dismay, "no money to pay off all the debts!"

"Did you think it would be gold, Nick?" asked Bella, understanding Hal's words and squeezing Nick's arm in sympathy. "I was thinking more of fabulous jewels: diamonds and rubies and ropes of pearls!"

Sophie sighed. "Oh dear, I think you are right, Hal, but what a pity to see that bright vision of greed fade and be faced with the truth of the mundane. Yes, Nick, this is most certainly treasure!" She waved Homer's *Odyssey* at him as she dusted it, and as the cover opened a loose sheet of paper, fluttered to the floor. "Oh, I am so sorry, now I grow clumsy!" Swiftly she bent, picking it up, a frown forming between her eyes. "No, it is not a page from the book, thank heaven, it's a poem, handwritten. Nick, do you remember your father's handwriting?" she asked suddenly.

Nick had sunk to a stool in dismay as his cherished dream of finding his fortune and marrying Bella evaporated. He was left to face the fact he had lead the woman he loved astray to such a degree that he had ruined her reputation or condemned her to a life of poverty as his wife. "Handwriting?" he replied dully. "Yes, yes, it's in the account books."

"What is it Sophie?" Hal asked, observing his host's demeanour with sympathy, as he understood how he felt.

"A poem, I think, but the hand is crabbed and the ink faded—*My fist is in Heaven...*"

"My first is in Heaven," Hal corrected her, leaning over her shoulder. "Bring it over to the light, Sophie, do."

Sophie obediently followed him to the window, observing that although the rain was slowing, the day was past its zenith. *"My first is in Heaven and yet in Hell"*... goodness me, this sounds tortured!"

"My second is in Song but not in Bell," Hal continued. *"My third is in Fall but not in Trip"*...good heavens, Nick this is a cipher!"

"A cipher?" asked Bella, coming to look. "Do you mean a puzzle?"

"Perhaps," agreed Hal. "Nick, come and look, then send for some candles. We may have found a treasure map."

Nick leapt to his feet, calling for a servant to bring candles, hope suddenly back in his dark eyes. "A treasure map!," he cried, then as his eyes fell upon the manuscript Sophie held, he sighed. "It's only one of my father's poems. He wrote them all the time. Nurse says my mother used to weep over them."

"So it is in his handwriting?" Hal asked.

"Oh, yes, it's his writing," agreed Nick glumly. "There is a casket in my chamber full of love poems to my mother. They are very nice, of course," he added belatedly. "Only I thought..." His voice cracked, and he turned from them in distress. "Oh, Bella, Bella—what have I done to you!"

"Nothing I didn't agree to, Nick!" she hurried to his side, her arm coming about him in comfort, smiling up at him through her own tears of disappointment. "Please, don't be so upset. I don't care if you are rich or poor, I love you!"

"If I have nothing but debt, I cannot ask you to marry me," he whispered desolately.

"You already have, Nick, and I consented," she replied, with a wry smile. "But for the cruelty of fate, and Merlin losing a shoe, we should have been married by now. I have no care for money, you know that. We can live, retired from the world, on my dowry."

"Live where?," he cried. "You know that rascally Jacob Brendon has taken up the mortgages on this house and is threatening to foreclose at Twelfth Night! In nine days time I will not have a home to offer you!"

"This is odd, Hal," said Sophie who was still reading the poem. "What do you make of it?"

"I think it is an acrostic, Sophie," he replied, "each clue signifies a letter. Let me read it out to you:

'My first is in Heaven, yet also in Hell
My second in Song, but not in Bell
My third is in Fall, but not in Trip
My fourth is in Yule as the year doth slip.
My fifth is in Down, but never in Out,
My sixth is in Every, as you look about.
My seventh is in Swell, as the white berries do,
My eighth is in Love, which I leave unto you.'"

"A letter from each clue? Oh, I thought the first clue

meant Lucifer, as he was in both Heaven and Hell," she said pointing to the relevant line and taking the sheet. "And the second one is the church tower, see, *in Song but not on Bell* Nick?" she turned to see the young couple embracing. "Oh, I beg pardon, but is there a carving of Lucifer in the bell tower, do you know?"

"Lucifer? Do you mean the devil?" Bella asked, her eyes wide with horror, as the maid brought in the candles. Hal took the paper from Sophie and went over to sit at the table where there was an inkwell and pen.

"Yes, because the third talks of a fall and not a trip, and Lucifer was certainly a fallen angel. Although, I can't think of why Yule and the year slipping is relevant—unless it is a timescale? Yes, perhaps that's it! You must discover the treasure before the end of the year, because the sixth is down but never out—although why you'd need to look about? Oh, yes, of course! You'd need to look about in the bell tower—look down but not out. Oh, this is clever! Hal, what are you doing? We have nearly solved this!"

"I have a slightly different view of it, Sophie," Hal said, putting down the quill he'd been using. "Nick, think back, as hard as you can. Where did your father take you when you used to ride out together? Do you remember?"

Nick looked at his guest blankly. "We rode out over our land. My father had got into the habit of riding the boundaries. I think it might have been part of the promise he gave my grandfather. I think he swore he would ride the estate once a week to be sure nothing was amiss."

Hal nodded his understanding. "And he sung to you as he rode, is that correct?"

"Yes," said Nick with a slight smile. "Carols mostly, or so I remember—he died at this time of year. Sir, should we not give heed to Mistress Redcroft?"

"In a moment or two, if you please, but first answer me this—was there any particular place he went to repeatedly?"

"Oh, yes. Wherever else we went, we always ended up in Hollywell Wood," he replied, adding with a smile for Bella. "I still ride there most days."

"And that is where the white berry grows," said Hal nodding. "Indeed, where you met up to elope together?"

"But, Hal, what is all this talk of woods?" Sophie cried impatiently. "It is as plain as day the clues lead to a picture of Satan in the bell tower!"

"And the song, Nick?" Hal asked, ignoring the interruption. "The carol he sang most often?"

"*The Holly and The Ivy*," he replied blankly, glancing from one to the other, as Sophie barely restrained her impatience.

"*Now they are both full grown, of all the trees that are in the wood, the holly bears the crown*," said Hal reciting the first verse of the carol. "Is there a holly tree, Nick?"

"Well, of course there would be, Hal!" Sophie cried in exasperation. "It's a holly wood!"

"No, Sophie, it is a holy well wood," said Hal. "Recollect, the treasure is hidden where no God-fearing Puritan would go."

"A holy well!" Nick said in an awed voice. "Oh, sir, may I look?"

He took the piece of paper Hal held out and began to scan the lines; his brow furrowed. He came to the end and hesitated, looking uncomfortable. "Begging your pardon, Sir Henry, but it seems to me, with respect, Sophie—Mistress Redcroft—is on the right track."

"Indeed," Hal agreed, "and that is why it is such a good puzzle, because it makes sense on several levels. Tell me, what was the last thing your father said to you?"

"Well," Nick glanced about, looking embarrassed. "My nurse insists he said I was to mind my books—but

I recollect he held me in his arms and told me that he loved me," he replied, tears filling his eyes again, before he hastily blinked them away.

"As a father myself, I can imagine he said both," replied Hal gently. "May we speak to your nurse?"

"Yes, I will call her," he said, quickly going from the chamber.

"Hal, what is this? "Sophie cried impatiently. "We do not have time to waste with all this nonsense about books! We have all the clues we need here!"

"You have the first, most obvious clues that someone without a scholarly mind might seize upon," he replied calmly. "Recollect, Nick's father was first and foremost a scholar. His mind would work in a certain way, whereas young, impetuous youth would work another, and thus he safeguarded the treasure from anybody who hadn't the full set of instructions."

"Oh," said Sophie, taken aback "so you don't think he was talking about Lucifer?"

"Sophie, how often have you seen the devil depicted in a church?" he asked.

"The gargoyles are devilish," she replied defensively

"Indeed they are," he agreed, "and the fall of Lucifer makes an excellent story in stained glass or a wall painting, but the local church here will be devoid of both. This is Puritan country, and the chapel here has no bell tower."

"Nurse is coming, but mostly to scold us," Nick announced, coming back into the chamber. "She says you must go home, Bella!"

Bella blushed hotly. "I don't have a home anymore," she replied. "Remember, Simon said if I didn't go back with him, I was no longer welcome as his sister!"

"Your brother spoke in heat, Mistress Craven," said Hal, in soothing tones. "I am sure he'll be glad to welcome you back."

"But I am not happy—" Nick stopped talking as the elderly woman Sophie had met earlier, limped into the room.

"Sir Henry, Mistress Redcroft, Mistress Bella," she said with a stiff curtsey. "Sir Henry, young master says you be wanting to ask me a question."

"Indeed I do, Nurse," he replied politely. "Nick tells me you were present when his father died, and that your recollection of his last words to his baby son are probably more accurate than his."

Her stern face softened. "Indeed it would be, Sir Henry, Nicholas was yet in short coats, and such a mischievous child. He never gave heed to a word anyone said to him, and the poor dear Master in such agony as he was, with Master Nick wriggling and leaving mud all over the counterpane."

"Was there a last message for Master Nick?" Hal asked.

"Indeed, Sir Henry. He told him to mind me, love his books and obey his grandfather in all things," she replied promptly, in the manner of one who had learned something by rote.

"Love his books," repeated Hal. "Just that?"

"Well, 'twas a powerful long time ago now, sir, but there do be something a niggling at me. Something about them there foreigners or some such, but I don't pay no heed to foreigners."

"Foreigners?" Nick asked blankly. "You've never mentioned that before! Do you mean Frenchies or Spaniards?"

"No, no, no! Not them pesky Frenchies! Nor yet them devils of Spaniards! I know—it were them dead foreigners, the old ones, them as wrote the Bible before ever we were allowed it in our own tongue!"

"Italians?" Sophie asked, even more puzzled.

"The Greeks!" Hal cried his brow clearing. "Can you

remember his exact words, Nurse? It might be vital!"

She shook her grey locks regretfully. "No, I can't that, sir. None of it made any sense to me."

"Indeed, it was all Greek," he murmured, then added swiftly—"perhaps not to fear Greeks bearing gifts?"

The nurse looked at him in astonishment. "By heaven, they said you were a clever man, Sir Henry, but I do believe they were the very words!" she cried. "It made no sense to me, you see, when would you ever see a Greek man in England anyway?"

"Indeed, Nurse," he agreed with a smile, "and doubtless your master's head was turned with the pain."

"Oh, indeed, sir," she cried, her old face troubled. "In a rare old torment he were, what with the pain and the worry about the boy, and things so unsettled as they were! I were glad to see Master Christopher, but his coming only added to the trouble. Not that it were his fault, sir, but people hereabouts were powerful agin' the King, and Master Christopher, he'd not have a word said about him. 'Heaven's Anointed,' he'd say, not just a jumped-up squire with no book learning! Why, his own son, Master Nick's father, had more learning than Noll Cromwell!"

"It is plain Nick's father was a man of great learning," Hal agreed.

"Aye, and that difficult about his books. I see you've been dusting them. That will be years of dust, for he'd never let a maid in here to do any work. 'They'll leave it all in a muddle, they will and I'll never be able to find anything!,' he used to say. Even after he died he'd left instructions that we were to only lightly dust the outside of the books."

"Yes, thank you Nurse," said Nick. "Well, we've done a good bit, and we'll continue tomorrow. You can go now."

"Go, can I? And what about Mistress Bella?" the old woman demanded. "I saw Mr Craven leave. He were most put about!"

"Mistress Bella will be returning to Haceby with us, Nurse," Hal replied in soothing tones.

"Well, mind you don't leave it until the fog comes down, or you'll get lost again," she retorted as she went.

Hal glanced out of the window. "She is right, the light will begin to fade soon, although it has finally stopped raining, thank heavens. However, come, let me quickly show you what I mean."

He sat back down at the desk with the sheet of paper he'd been writing on. "See, you read out the clue, Sophie, and I'll write down both how you see it and my answer."

"Oh, what a good idea," she replied. *"My first is in Heaven and yet in Hell."*

"Yes, well, we'll put down Lucifer in your column, Sophie, for as you rightly say he was in both places—and in my column, I'll put down an H and an E" said Hal.

"Oh, I see," said Bella. "There is an H in Heaven and in Hell, and an E too."

Hal darted her a smiling nod. "Next line, Sophie."

"My Second is in Song, but not in Bell," Sophie read obediently.

"And you assume that means a bell tower, Sophie?" Hal asked, writing it down.

"Well, yes, or a choir, I suppose, if there isn't a bell tower," she agreed, as he wrote down an O. "Why an O?" She queried. "Why not an S, N, or a G?"

"Because if it is a word in the English language, it must have a vowel," Hal replied. "So it's an O."

"Oh," said Nick blankly, "I'd have never thought of that!"

"My third is in Fall, but not in Trip," continued Sophie. "Now, that's what convinced me it was about Lucifer, you see—the Fall!"

"Yes, indeed, Sophie," said Hal. "On the first level it

would, but using my method it becomes an F or an A, or an L." Carefully he spaced his letters out.

"I see," said Nick peering over his shoulder, "and the fourth?"

"*My fourth is in Yule as the year doth slip*," said Sophie. "I thought that referred to the expiry of Nick's mortgages."

"But this was written many years ago by Nick's father, Sophie. Nothing was secured against the estate in those days," Hal explained. "It was only as Parliament imposed more and more fines, that Nick's grandfather was driven to take such desperate measures."

"*My fifth is in Down but never in Out*," Nick read it over Sophie's shoulder as she was rendered speechless for a few seconds. "What does that mean?"

"Well, I took the Y from Yule in the fourth clue," said Hal, who had written out the whole word. "For by this time I could see a pattern emerging, and as the fifth is Down, I took the W."

"Oh, yes!" breathed Bella in excitement.

"*My sixth is in Every*," said Sophie, regaining the power of speech. "It's the E, Hal, it's the E! The seventh is the L in swell and the eighth is the L in Love!"

"Holywell!" cried Nick.

"So, Nick, now you know why it was so important for you to mind your books, not to fear Greeks bearing gifts, and to know that the holly is the tree in the greenwood which bears the crown," Hal smiled at the amazed Nick.

"Hollywell Wood!" cried Sophie. "We must go there at once!"

"It will be getting dark soon, not to mention the mist coming down," said Hal putting aside his pen.

"All the better, for none will see us," she replied. "Where do you think we should dig?"

"I don't think we do dig," Hal replied. "We need to find the well."

"Oh, we know where that is, don't we Nick?" Bella cried, her eyes shining. "It's close to where the passage comes out."

⚜

Chapter Thirteen

Hal glanced about him with resignation in the gathering gloom. "Well, I hope you know the way, Nick, for all I can see is a mass of damp vegetation."

They had spent some fifteen minutes, arguing as to the suitability of going out this late on a December afternoon to seek treasure, but Hal knew in his heart he had no chance of convincing any of the others to take the sensible course. He also feared if Nick was left alone, he would attempt to find it anyway and probably come to grief.

"Yes, it's supposed to put off the curious," replied Nick slipping from the saddle, and leading his horse forward. "No, stay on horseback, just duck your head, Sir Henry, as we go under the trees."

"How on earth did you find this place?" Sophie asked as she followed Bella by ducking under a low bough, which reached almost to the ground, as it was being held back by Nick.

"We came here as children," explained Bella as they made their way through a longish passage of undergrowth, and emerged into a small clearing.

"I rather think my father let this part of the wood go wild," said Nick, tying his horse up to a tree. "I've never allowed anyone to come here, and there is a tale abroad in the villages that the wood is haunted by monks."

"Monks?" Sophie shivered and glanced about her, as Nick came to help her down from the saddle, and Hal tethered the other beasts.

"Yes," said Nick cheerfully. "Legend has it that the monks were expelled from my home, which was once part of an abbey, and driven into this wood, where they were set upon by soldiers, and beaten to death. I have never seen anything myself. Grandfather used to say the sightings probably had their roots in a collective guilty conscience, as the abbey was certainly looted by the locals."

"Most likely," agreed Hal, "I do hope you can find this place easily, Nick, before it gets too dark."

"It's not far," he replied, collecting some lanterns, and a coil of stout rope, from his horse. "It is close to the entrance to the tunnel, so if it should come on to rain we can take shelter."

For a few moments nothing more was said, as he led the way amongst the trees, only stopping when he came to what appeared to be another bank of thick, dripping foliage. "See, here concealed is the entrance to the tunnel." He pulled aside some bushes, to reveal a low opening.

"It certainly is most effectively screened," agreed Hal, following Nick in, and assisting Sophie and Bella, as Nick bent to kindle a light in the lantern, which was hidden there. A soft glow illuminated the area, revealing a cave no more than seven feet in height, but going back a very long way into the blackness.

"Is it a cave all the way to the house?" asked Hal, taking up the lantern and advancing a few steps.

"No," replied Nick, "if you follow the path to the back of the cave, eventually the way is blocked by a vast rock. The entrance to the passage to the house is concealed behind that, but once again it is very well hidden."

"Are there bats?" asked Sophie anxiously.

"Only a few," said Nick in soothing tones, "and asleep, now it is colder."

"So where is the well?" Hal asked, grinning at Sophie's look of terror.

"Oh, that's back outside," said Nick. "I brought you

here to see the way back to the house, so that if time should get away from us, you could go with Bella, whilst I continue to look for my treasure. Indeed, if they wished the ladies could remain here, whilst we go and look, Sir Henry."

"Stay here with bats and ghosts for company," Sophie cried indignantly, "and miss all the excitement—never!"

"I think we should proceed, Nick," said Hal, "before the last of the day is upon us."

"If only the clouds would part a little," said Bella, as she pulled her hood over her head. "There would be light a plenty, for the moon is very nearly full tonight."

"A perfect time for ghosts and bats," remarked Hal, as he helped Sophie back out of the cave.

"The wind is freshening," said Nick, "the clouds could yet be blown away. This way, Mistress Redcroft, do take care of your gown on those brambles."

Conversation was stilled for a few moment as they went in single file behind Nick, following the lantern through more undergrowth, concentrating on where they put their feet, and keeping the soaked boughs from giving each other an unpleasant shower.

Finally, Nick came to a halt beside a mass of tumbled stones, and a low, broken down wall. "Well, this is it," he announced, putting the lantern on the wall, and illuminating the scene, "this is the holy well."

"It is very ancient!" Hal said, in surprise.

"Is it?" asked Nick. "Yes, I suppose it must be. Certainly all the carved bits are very worn." He frowned. "I believe my grandfather told me that my father, who liked antiquities, thought it was part of a building just after the Norman conquest," he said, sounding as if he was repeating something he'd heard many times and never thought about before.

"Older, even than that, Nick," said Hal, lifting the lantern to examine a partially broken circular cross which was placed above the well. "This must go back to the dawn of time, almost, when Christianity was but a fledgling religion in this land, perhaps to when people worshipped the very water of life itself."

"Well, it's certainly been here a good while," agreed Nick. "I wonder how deep the well is?"

"I wouldn't think so very deep," said Hal. "Surely this was once a spring, coming from the rock? Drop a pebble in and listen."

Nick picked up a stone, and dropped it over the edge, whilst Sophie took the lantern, to see it fall into the darkness.

"Not too deep," agreed Nick, as the splash came back. He took off his feathered hat and coat handing them to Bella. "Now, what to secure the end of the rope to? "

"The cross, I should think, with apologies to Our Lord," Hal said, glancing about. "Here, Nick, give me the end, I'll thread it through the only surviving piece of the circle of the cross left intact, and add my weight to it. You'll be safe enough, that way."

"So long as the stone isn't rotted and gives way," said Sophie anxiously.

"No, the other pieces have been deliberately broken, this is hard stone, probably granite. There is no obvious wear," said Hal inspecting it carefully.

Nick nodded and tied the other end of the rope securely about his slender waist, unable to repress a shudder. "Dear God, what do I do if it's nothing but another package of books?" he asked suddenly.

"Your father was a scholar, Nick, he would never have put books down a well. He'd have known the damp would ruin them," said Hal logically as he, too, removed his feathered hat.

Nick glanced up, his teeth flashing in the lamplight as his grin returned. "Thank you, Sir Henry, what would I do without your common sense? Bella, my love, give me a kiss. I'll return with a fortune or merely a name for fearlessness."

"Oh, get on with it do!" Sophie cried impatiently, leaning over the edge with the lantern. "The dratted mist is coming down again, and the damp ruins my hair. It will be a miracle if we don't all die of inflammation of the lungs after this!"

"Getting too old for adventures, Sophie?" Hal asked, with a lift of his eyebrow, as Bella complied with her lover's request.

Sophie's head came up and she fixed him with a stare. "No," she said defensively, then as he merely smiled at her mockingly, she repeated, "No, but—oh, thank heavens, he is on his way!"

Slowly, Nick, lantern in hand, let himself down the side of the well, whilst Hal braced himself to support his weight. Equally slowly the rope played out over the wall which began to show signs of the strain.

"Anything yet, Nick? " cried Bella, leaning over the wall with Sophie.

"No, nothing at all, apart from a dank smell and some very pretty ferns," he replied, once the echo had died away. "Hold on tight if you will, Sir Henry, I don't like the look of the water beneath me, it—oh—oh—hold,

Sir Henry! There's a niche cut in the wall of the well just here! It's just a little way beyond my reach—give me a little more rope if you please, sir. Oh—oh! "

"What is it?" Sophie called, leaning further forward, trying to see what Nick had spotted.

"Have a care, Sophie," cried Hal, "or you'll be joining young Nick in the murky depths!"

"Hey! That hurt," cried Nick, as some rubble loosened by Bella and Sophie's anxious movements fell on him.

"But what is it you see, Nick?" Bella called, craning her neck, as she leant over the edge of the well alongside Sophie.

"It looks like an iron-banded chest," he called back. "A small, iron-banded chest, and it looks heavy! Sir Henry, what should I do for the best? Should I attach it to the rope, and try to hang on somewhere, whilst you pull it up, or can you manage to pull both it and me, back up?"

"No, don't take the rope off, Nick," Hal replied quickly. "I'll try to pull you both first. I'd sooner not risk you falling into the water."

"It is further down than you'd think," agreed Nick. "I don't know that the rope would be long enough to reach me, if I did fall! I am lifting the chest now, Sir Henry. It is heavy. What do you think?"

Hal grunted in reply, and not wasting breath with words, began to pull the rope slowly back across the width of the low stone wall.

Sophie cast a look to Nick, dangling precariously over the evil-looking water, clutching a rusted chest. She handed the lantern to Bella and swiftly crossed the damp, slippery grass to help Hal with the effort of pulling. He managed a faint smile, the muscles in his neck showing as he pulled again, "Take the rope behind me and lean back," he said through gritted teeth, "use your weight to hold it."

She nodded and took the rope as indicated, almost slipping on the damp grass, as she understood how onerous the task was. "Bella," she called, panting a little. "Put the lantern down on the wall, and come and give a hand! Whatever is in that chest is very heavy!"

"Books are heavy," said Bella doubtfully, as she did as she was bid.

"Not this heavy!" Hal muttered through clenched teeth, as he strained at the rope.

With the added weight of Bella, the load began to move again, and soon Nick's wet hand could be seen, the knuckles white as he clung on, followed by the appearance of the rusty chest, which he struggled to slide onto the unstable wall, anchoring it well back from the edge. Once the chest was safely in place, Nick came up quickly, and scrambled over the loose stone, to lie panting on the wet earth.

Hal slumped against the tree, and then, with Sophie's help, tied off the rope to the tree, and attached the other end to the chest. Only then, did he approach where Nick was now sitting up, smiling at Bella.

"Well done, Nick," he said, still breathing heavily, but frowning as he looked over the edge, trying to make out in the gathering gloom, the niche where the chest had remained hidden for so long. "I wonder how your father, a sick man, managed to get that down there ?"

"He must have had help," replied Nick, frowning at the thought. "Probably Jem Attwood's father, Joshua, my father's steward. He was killed a few months after my father died, I believe. He was out in a storm looking for scattered sheep, and was struck by lightening or something. He wasn't found until the next day, poor man."

Hal nodded and grimaced, glancing at the chest. "Hmm, no key to the lock, of course. But if we lift it to the ground, one of those stones should shatter a lock as rusted as that one."

"Yes," agreed Nick, with a smile. "You know, I am half afraid to do so! It has been so long, and so well waited for, that if it contains nothing, I'll not know what to do."

"Best to find out quickly, then," said Hal reaching for a suitable stone. "Here, Nick, never be afraid to embrace tomorrow."

Nick got to his feet, still breathing deeply and lifted the chest off the side of the well, bringing it back to where he had sat, kneeling before it.

"Oh, Nick, do open it! " Bella cried, as he still hesitated. "You know it won't make any difference to me, I love you whether you are wealthy or poor!"

"It makes a difference to your brother," he replied, lifting the stone, "so it makes a difference to me, too." He brought the stone down with all his might onto the lock, which shattered with a crack.

Nick pulled up the stiff hasp, and grunted with the effort of throwing back the lid with rusted hinges.

⚜

Chapter Fourteen

"Gold!" Bella cried.

"Gold indeed, Nick!" Hal added, in honest delight. "My congratulations, you are indeed the wealthy young man you deserve to be. Doubly wealthy, as you have the love of a good woman."

"Gold, Bella now we can be married!" Nick cried jubilantly.

"We were going to be married anyway," she replied, as he ran his fingers through the gold coins, which packed the chest.

"But no jewels, or ropes of pearls?" Sophie asked, with a mock sigh of disappointment.

"You are a romantic, Sophie," laughed Hal, a little light headed with relief that the risk they'd taken had paid off. "What are the papers in the lid, Nick?"

"I don't know, legal documents by the look of them, or some such thing—but these are sovereigns, I do believe!" as he handed one to Hal.

"Elizabeth the first—*A Domino Factum Et Istud Est Mirabilis In Oculis Nostris.* This is the Lord's doing and it is mirabilis—marvellous in our eyes." Hal translated, adding with a laugh, "Well, Nick, it would seem even the Lord is with you, for it is marvellous in all our eyes."

Nick glanced up to him, his eyes suddenly wet with tears of relief. "Sir Henry, I can't thank you enough!" he cried. "Left to me, I'd have been off all over the country, looking for this clue and that, whilst all the while it has lain here at my feet. It was to this very spot my father brought me everyday. Here to this well!"

Hal smiled. "Poor fellow, how it must have chafed him that you were so very young that you couldn't be told the secret."

"If only I had heeded his words," said Nick sadly. "If only I had minded my books and read Homer, I'd have found the paper earlier, and grandfather need not have died worrying that all his land was about to fall into the hands of rascally Roundheads."

"I think, Nick, perhaps your father was the wisest of men," said Hal gently. "Perhaps he knew in his heart, that had your grandfather found the money, it would have gone the way of all the other."

"On wild dreams of reinstating the King, and gambling you mean?" asked Nick bluntly as he frowned over the thought and then bit his lip to stop it trembling. "I don't truly remember my father, and I loved my grandfather, without thought for his folly." He paused, taking stock, and added, "I shall always love him for his kindness, his warmth of heart and his enthusiasm, but I have the suspicion you are right, Sir Henry. My father was the better man."

"If you can see that, Nick, I am a happy man," Hal replied. "For I had qualms that your finding this treasure might convince you that your wealth was endless."

"No, sir, I know this will only be enough to pay back our debts, and set us straight with the world—that and marrying my Bella is all I ask."

"This is curious," said Sophie, who had been turning over the documents, as Bella examined the gold coins. "These are the title deeds to Larkspring Farm, Holiwell Farm, Stanton Hollow Farm and others. How come they to be here, Hal?"

"Let me see," he commanded, getting up and coming to take them from her. He stood frowning a little, "You are right, Sophie, this is indeed curious! Nick, are these not some of the farms Jacob Brendon holds?"

"Yes, Sir Henry," said Nick, exchanging one last kiss with Bella before coming to look at the documents. "Swallowford Farm, Baileys Piece, Jankin's Knoll and Home Farm—all the deeds are here!"

"Then I am sure none hold these farms but you, Nick," said Hal, frowning. "Tell me, was there a time lapse between your father's death and your grandfather's return?"

"I believe so, sir," he replied, "some months, I think, although I don't actually remember."

Hal nodded. "Then perhaps that is what happened. Your father, determined that your grandfather should not gamble away all the land—for most probably sacrifices had already been made—decided to hide the deeds to what was the most valuable land, so that there would always be a solid heart to your inheritance." Hal frowned again, "Did you not just tell me your father's steward died in an accident shortly after your father's death?"

"Yes, sir, I am not sure when, I only know his son, who now farms Home Farm as a tenant, took over from him until my grandfather returned." He glanced up to meet Hal's eyes, a puzzled look on his face. "How is it then, that Jacob Brendon has held these farms for most of my life?" he asked. "I seem to remember when I rode out with my father it would take us many hours to ride the land. Nurse would be cross, for often I had fallen asleep held clasped by my father. Yet by the time I rode out with my grandfather on my first pony, it would only take us the morning, and a lot of that time was spent drinking a mug of ale with the tenants. I thought it was more that a child's flawed memory, but now I wonder."

"Yes, these are questions that cannot be simply answered, Nick, without further investigation," said Hal, shaking his head. "Land was, of course, sequestered—taken in lieu of fines by those damned men of Parliament—but if that were the case, then it should have been returned to you, Nick, once the King returned." He frowned and shook his head again. "If your father, who was not a well man, had help in hiding the chest down the well, then isn't it odd that the one man, who was so vital in keeping the estate going after his death and probably who knew where it was, died shortly after?"

Nick looked up from the papers he had been turning over, as if by doing so he might discover their secret, and frowned as he considered Hal's words. "It does seem odd, Sir Henry, I agree, but accidents do happen. I would that I could remember more about it, but Jem Attwood, Joshua's son will probably remember much more than I; he is some years my senior."

Hal nodded, "Yes, probably consulting him would clarify the situation. As it stands, it doesn't make sense, for any person your father trusted enough to help him would have your interests at heart and would have told you of the chest. Why, it is well known you were looking for your treasure, or so Simon Craven said."

"Yes, even before Grandfather died there was talk of treasure hidden away," Nick agreed. "I really can't help thinking that if Jem Attwood knew anything, he would have told me long ago. He is a good fellow."

Hal nodded again, plainly considering things. "Simon Craven said Brendon used to be an attorney years back."

"I believe he started out as such," said Nick. "Certainly I've heard men call Clerk Brendon after him, if they'd felt they'd been worsted in a deal at the market."

"Hmm, we need to talk to somebody of an older generation, I think. It's a great pity your man died, but there must be someone who will remember the old days, surely?"

"Oh, yes, I am sure there will be," he said, glad to be able to answer a question fully. "Jem Attwood will know of someone. He has been a tenant of ours all his life. He used to run Home Farm for us. A big fellow, he is, softly spoken, and kindly to me as a boy, but a bit of a tartar with erring tenants, as I remember. Grandfather said it broke his heart to pay lip service to Brendon."

Hal nodded grimly. "As you say there will be somebody who will remember," he said firmly. "Memories are long in the country. Either way, as I see it, these properties are yours, Nick, for you hold the original deeds."

"I am glad, sir," he replied uncertainly, "but what if my grandfather had new deeds made out? He wasn't above doing things that were not—well, he'd lived a rather odd life abroad after the King was killed. He used to say that one could only play fair with men who knew how to play fair."

Hal smiled in sympathy. "My father lived in exile too, Nick, and for many years, I was with him, living the life of the next best thing to a vagabond. I hated the way we lived, and was so relieved when I returned home to live with my uncle, who was a man one could admire for his probity. I am sure your grandfather, like my father was often driven to desperate straits, but if new deeds were made out, I am not certain as to their legality," said Hal.

"But the obligation would still be there, sir," said Nick unhappily, "Especially if my grandfather lost them gaming."

"I agree with you, Nick, provided it was all done legally and in an above board manner. However, let us reserve judgement on this matter until we find out more."

"And it the meantime, should we not go back to the cave out of the damp?" asked Sophie. "Then we can rejoice that whatever else happens, Nick won't lose his home and he and Bella can now be married."

"This is all very well, and I am very glad you have found your treasure, Nick, but we can't pretend it solves every problem," said Hal as they stood just inside the cave to shelter from the rain which had suddenly come back with a vengeance.

"Doesn't it?" Nick asked, glancing with delight to the chest at his feet. "It means I can keep my home, which means so much! I really can't thank you enough, Sir Henry. I would never in a thousand years have worked out what that paper meant."

"And I would have sent you on a fool's errand," sighed Sophie, looking at her muddied boots with disgust.

"I am speaking of the wider problem of your marriage," said Hal gently. "If you will cast your mind back four or five hours, your brother, Mistress Bella, is enraged with you both, and was talking of sending his friends to call on Nick. Now, whilst as Justice of the Peace, I am obliged to stop any such duel, I don't feel my relationship with Mr Craven will be enhanced by my having to tell him so in front of his guests. Neither will it assist us in our endeavour, which is to secure your marriage. Anymore should we, in the midst of all this triumph, forget Mistress Pauncey."

"Oh, no!" Bella's face crumpled, as she realised in her joy she had done just that. "Oh, my poor aunt, she must be in such distress—and Mamma and my poor cousins too!"

"Yes," said Hal, "the time has come for you to return home, Mistress Bella, and we have at hand the means to do so." Hal waved his hand to the interior of the cave, which stretched away into the darkness.

"No, Bella, don't go!" cried Nick as they all peered into the blackness. "I know I'll never see you again if you go back! Simon will have you married to that pig, Pridow in the twinkling of an eye!"

"Be assured, Nick he will do no such thing" said Hal

quickly. "I give you both my word I will ensure Mistress Bella is neither forced nor coerced into a marriage she doesn't want. Come, you must see, that if we are to seek a happy outcome, she must return home. Then tomorrow, Nick, you must come across to Haceby, you must seek out Mr Craven, whom both Sophie and I will have spoken to, and you must apologise. I will remain with you, to ensure there is no repeat of this morning's foolishness. Then you will inform Mr Craven you have found your treasure, indicate you have come with the funds to pay off Mr Brendon, and ask him, as a favour, if he will witness the transaction. Then, and only then, do you ask formally for his sister's hand in marriage."

"Oh, that is an excellent idea, Hal, especially in asking him to witness the handing over of the money," Sophie cried, her eyes sparkling. "How clever you are!"

"But what if Bella is already married to the old fool!" cried Nick anxiously.

"She won't be, for I shall stay with her," said Sophie. "You will have to be strong, Bella, and insist I remain with you. Have hysterics again, if Mr Craven tries to make me go!"

"Oh, what will Mamma say?" Bella whispered tearily.

"She'll be so relieved to have you safe and well, she'll

forget to be cross until later. This must be a lightening strike, Hal, it must be accomplished before all the re-criminations start!"

"Indeed, Sophie," he agreed. "Mistress Bella, the time has come for you to take us back through the passage, and retire to your chamber, with Sophie as your companion. You are too heartbroken and distressed to be in company. You will see only your mother until you've had a good night's sleep."

"Unless Aunt Kate comes, Hal," suggested Sophie.

"Yes, I might be able to send a message with my aunt," he nodded slowly. "Now, are we all agreed upon this plan? "

"What if it goes wrong?" cried Nick reluctantly. "What if Simon Craven won't even listen to my proposal of marriage?"

"That is possible," Hal agreed. "He was very angry and no doubt the other guests will have added their mites to his anger. We can but try, and if it should fail, then we think again."

"Don't worry," said Sophie cheerfully. "If it goes awry, I'll come up with a new plan!"

"I pray God we are not driven to one of your mad-cap plans, Sophie!" Hal exclaimed devoutly.

Nick was still uneasy, as he accompanied them to the back of the cave, his hand firmly clasping Bella's. When they arrived at the big rock, Hal halted, and suggested firmly that he took his leave.

"Best make your goodbyes here, Nick," he said kindly. "It is only until tomorrow, and you have my word Mistress Bella won't be forced into marriage over night. Sophie will remain with her until you return tomorrow, I promise. Come, Sophie, we'll walk on to give Nick and Mistress Bella a little privacy."

"How kind you are, Hal," said Sophie in an undertone, as they walked around the rock.

He laughed lightly, "Oh, I have an interest in star -crossed lovers. Put up your hood again and keep stooped over from now on."

"Why?" she asked indignantly, then gave a shriek, as she saw the hibernating bats hanging.

"That's why," he replied, as she swiftly did as he suggested. "Please also remember that it is likely this passage will go past chambers where people are, so silence will be imperative."

"Do you think there will be rats?" she asked, trying to sound nonchalant.

"It's possible," he agreed, with a sight smile, "but they

are usually much more worried by us, and will run in the opposite direction, unless cornered." He turned as Bella came to join them, with tears in her eyes. Hal turned back to wave the lantern at Nick, who stood white-faced in a pool of light, looking as if his last hope were gone. "Tomorrow morning, Nick!" he called. "Don't oversleep after all the excitement and fail us!"

This brought the grin back to his face. "I'll be there," he promised.

"Please look after my horse for me," called Sophie. "I am very fond of her."

He nodded, and reluctantly turned away as Bella cried, "I love you, Nick, I promise I'll never wed another."

He spun about again. "I love you too, sweetheart! Do have a care on the way back and I'll be with you again in the morning. Goodnight!"

⚜

Chapter Fifteen

"Now," said Hal, as they approached the tunnel proper, "you'd best lead the way, Mistress Bella, with Sophie following, and I'll come at the rear."

"Are there rats?" hissed Sophie, in an undertone to Bella.

"Yes, horrid things," she replied, "but they usually run away from the light."

"Is it far?" Hal asked lifting his lantern, as they entered the tunnel. "Good heavens, it is a well made structure!"

"Yes, it seems my great-great-great-great grandfather had it built in the time of the young King Edward. He spent a lot of time and money on it. My father, who, apparently shared a passion for antiquities with Nick's father, seems to have found all the accounts. He listed the names of all the men who worked upon it in a book Nick and I discovered in Simon's book room. It stretches about a mile and a half from the house, which is why, we believe, it was never discovered by Cromwell's men. Mother says they spent ages searching around the house but never found anything."

Hal nodded. "We can only be thankful such days are over and that with the King's return, most of us are allowed to worship as we choose."

"Do you think such times could ever return, Hal?" Sophie asked.

"I think whilst what we lost remains fresh in our memories—all the family members killed, sons, brothers, even in some parts, wives and daughters—whilst we remember the damage done to the fabric of our society, then I think we shall never fight again. But if the terrible lesson be forgotten, if we become complacent and dismiss it, if we should ever belittle the sacrifices made by our forefathers for our present freedom, then I think we would again stand in real danger. Unfortunately, it seems every three or four generations, we do forget, and have to suffer anew." He smiled briefly at them. "You two young ladies must remember to tell your children, and your children's children, of all the pain and suffering endured by your fathers, or it will be so soon forgot."

"Will you tell Harry and Francis, Hal?" asked Sophie.

"I already do, "he replied. "Unfortunately, they love my tales of wandering footloose through France and the Low Countries. Harry seems to think it was all an exciting adventure. I swear if he was questioned, he'd see little difference between my father and I, and Sir Galahad and his squire." This was said with comic wryness and had the effect of making them chuckle, and so keeping their spirits buoyed with recollections of the more farcical incidents of his travels abroad, Hal got them through the increasingly narrow tunnel, to where he was forced to walk in a crouched manner.

"I do hope you are not too cramped, Sir Henry," said Bella anxiously. "It is not as bad, I do agree, as hiding in the barrel as the inn-keeper's wife looked for your father, and it isn't much further now. We are deep underground in this part, which is the bit Nick had to dig out again. We are close to the house now and they went deeper, we think, to deter any digging from above."

"Lead on swiftly, Mistress Bella! Aunt Kate will have a rub for my aching back, I am sure. Your words relieve an anxiety that I shall be permanently deformed," he replied.

"Only about another hundred yards, and then we

must keep a silence," said Bella. "For although in places there are still caverns, in others there are but wooden walls where the cellars are, and the stair itself is built near the stone of the chimney. So as we rise through the house, the other side of the stair backs onto various chambers, some of which may be inhabited and, of course, voices carry so well up a staircase shaft."

"Thus giving credence to the tales of ghosts in the night?" Sophie suggested.

"Probably," agreed Bella. "Here, Sir Henry, just ahead we enter the undercroft of the oldest part of the cellars, and you shall be able to stretch your full height again."

"Thank heaven!" he said, as they finally entered a low vaulted chamber, where he could at least stand upright, even through his hat brushed the arches. "And on the credit side, we saw very few rats, Sophie."

"Remind me never to go adventuring with you again, Sir Henry, my nerves are not up to it," she retorted.

Hal laughed, "Dear me, you are getting too old, Sophie, if you begin to talk like that! Harry would be ashamed of you, and that would never do."

Sophie smiled briefly but glanced anxiously about her, as if looking for the stairs.

Bella led the way across the shadowy undercroft and

ducked behind a ancient wine rack. "Now we must be silent, for this is, I do believe, the back of the cellars." She grimaced, whispering, "Often as I come through here , I hear the steward, Tully, singing. I've told Simon the man is a drunkard, but he pays me no heed." She swung her lantern to illuminate stone stairs, stretching steeply away before them. "Remember," she continued, "to be as quiet as humanly possible and do take care, it is a steep, long climb. I usually pause at every turn of the staircase to listen."

They nodded silently and in single file began the ascent.

After the first stone staircase, the way grew narrower, so that Hal was forced to take care that he did not brush against the woodwork of the panelling in some places. At each turn, Bella paused for them to catch up, for she, knowing the way, was fleeter of foot.

On the fourth turn, just as Bella was well ahead, a mouse ran across the stair in front of Sophie, who gave a squeak of dismay, and in a second, Hal's hand flew to cover her mouth. She turned her head to him indignantly, and as he nodded toward the panelling at her shoulder, they heard voices.

"I tell you, that damned wench overheard

everything!"cried a male voice edged with hysteria.

Sophie, clasped in Hal's arms with his hand over her mouth, scarcely heeded the words, as she rested her head against his broad shoulder. How many months had it been since she'd felt his touch, smelt that scent particular to him, felt the latent strength of his arms, the security of his embrace. Love so long denied, swelled swiftly in her heart.

"She was a long-nosed, tiresome jade," another voice cried angrily.

Sophie started as she recognised the voice and Hal held her tighter, his lips whispering, "Hush!"

Her world seemed to whirl at his nearness and she moved her head closer so that his lips were but a fraction from her cheek. With satisfaction she heard his intake of breath and felt its warmth on her cheek.

"I did nothing!" the first voice quavered, "all this is none of my affair!"

Sophie moved her lips against his open palm, and kissed Hal's hand, as she melted deeper into his embrace. She felt a tremor go through him, as his lips responded.

"I vow it was none of my doing that the wench fell as she did and hit her head—I wasn't the one shaking her!" the first voice continued, fretfully.

Hal, fighting his own emotions, realised he wasn't concentrating. Abruptly he moved away from the enticing softness of Sophie's cheek, but in compensation, he clasped her even closer to him, as if he would never be parted from her again

Sophie, content with the reaction she'd provoked, lay back against him and stifled a chuckle knowing her power undimmed. His lips could say what he chose, but his arms ached for her, too. They stood locked in a timeless embrace, as the men continued to quarrel, both shouting at once so that only occasionally could phrases be made out.

"Well, 'tis none of mine!" shouted the second voice, in a fury. "If you had but done what she wanted and taken her to wife, rather than Bella Craven, we'd not be in this fix!"

"I tell you, that damned Justice has a long reach!" cried the second man, on the verge of hysteria again.

"Aye, it's so typical of Jack Hollingshead to go charging off without a word, pompous fool that he is!" cried the other.

The opening of a door on the other side of the panelling brought the conversation to an abrupt halt. The third voice was a mere whisper which they couldn't catch, and the other men also dropped their voices, so that soon they could hear nothing. Hal shrugged, and reluctantly released Sophie.

"Hurry on up and don't speak until we reach the priest hole," he whispered into her ear.

Sophie smiled to herself and catching up the hem of her gown, skipped on to the next turn of the stair, where Bella waited anxiously. Hal nodded as he joined them and indicated for them to continue. Only when they reached the security of the priest hole, did he speak.

"That was a revelation," he said at once.

"Yes, wasn't it?" Sophie agreed demurely, glancing about her with interest.

He reddened and cast her a frowning glance. "We heard voices, and stopped to listen," he explained to Bella. "It would seem our suspicions are confirmed. Your cousin was killed, but not with malice aforethought. More because she was a nuisance."

"Does that make it any better, Hal?" Sophie asked.

"No, it does not," he replied shortly. "I shall write out my findings and leave them for the local people to deal with."

"We'll probably be called as witnesses," said Sophie.

Hal glanced to Bella, recognising the horror in her eyes. "Yes, perhaps we can find another way, but we must both write out independently what we heard, and give the papers into Simon Craven's hands then he can decide the best way to deal with the matter."

"I don't know that I had my full mind on their words," smiled Sophie mischievously. "I was a little distracted by the rat—and the circumstances."

"Give it a little thought," he replied blandly, "and it will return to you. In the mean time, we have a task before us. We must get Mistress Bella back to her bedchamber unobserved. I shall go ahead and make sure the way is clear. Sophie, you stay with Bella, so that I can signal to come or stay." He smiled cheerfully as Bella began to look dismayed. "Keep your heart up, we are very nearly there. Once you are safe in your chamber, you need not reappear again until Nick has arrived in the house."

She nodded and helped him with the lock which released the door in the back of the cupboard.

"Stay there," he commanded, "but don't chatter, for I shall call to you, if all is clear."

It was the work of minutes to get Bella back down the narrow stairs and along the dim corridors as day light faded, and thence into to the safety of her chamber.

Hal lingered at the door, his hand on Sophie's arm. "Don't allow any in except Mistress Craven," he said, unable to stop his heart leaping, as she turned her hand over to grasp his. He met her eyes squarely. "Keep safe, both of you, and we shall talk anon."

"Good night, Hal," she whispered, "may you have pleasant dreams."

Chapter Sixteen

"You mean Bella is back here, in her own home? Simon Craven's face relaxed its stern lines of worry, into blank relief.

"Is that not what you wanted?" Hal asked, with an air of innocence. "I thought you wanted your sister returned to her home, without an outcry or any shame."

"Well, yes," he replied, still rather dumbfounded. "But how was it achieved? I saw none ride in and I have been watching the gate all afternoon."

"Not easily," replied Hal. "I shall have to send a groom over to collect the horses in the morning. I am sure you will recollect, Mr Craven, how frank I was with you on our ride to Weston Revesby? How I wish you had paid more heed to my words. You cannot fail but remember how quickly the situation became inflamed and how you so far forgot common sense in justifiable anger, and called out your neighbour?"

"Yes," Simon looked shamefaced, "not the cleverest of moves in front of a magistrate," he admitted, through clenched teeth.

"You forced my hand, unfortunately," Hal sighed with inward relief. Like most Englishmen, Simon Craven obeyed the law with the same simplicity that he embraced his faith, and honoured his King. They all went hand in hand. "The result was that I, too, was forced into high-handed methods," he continued. "Having dispatched you, I—with the aid of Mistress Redcroft—was able to soothe your sister, and young Nick Revesby finally calmed down. We spent some hours in a wide-ranging and at times frank discussion, which culminated in Mistress Bella's decision to return to her mother. I reminded her of the tragedy which had occurred in her absence, and how afflicted her family were. Mistress Bella, being the sweet, biddable young woman she is, could not deny she had to return home. Once we showed her how we could overcome the shame of a public return to her family, she consented to return immediately, especially, when I informed her that I would not allow her, once again in my lawful capacity, to be coerced into a marriage she found abhorrent."

Simon blinked and looked nettled. "It has never been

my intention to coerce my sister into matrimony," he said sharply. "If she had but said one word…"

"You'd have ignored it, "Hal interrupted as he smiled limpidly at his affronted companion. "The object of my openness yesterday, Mr Craven, was to illustrate that none of us are immune to the pitfalls of family life. Human nature doesn't change. Young ladies will be forever changing their minds about marriage. Or in this case, remaining true to the love they'd chosen early on."

"You are speaking of Nick Revesby," Simon said, with a sigh, "but after the way he has behaved…"

"Do you know how he has behaved, Mr Craven?" Hal had no compunction in interrupting him. "Have you ever talked to him man-to-man—or have just assumed because of his grandfather's reputation that he is a rackety young man? If anything, having been in his company for a few hours, I'd say he was rather like you. After all, did not your mother have a hand in his education? Although he has had few of the advantages of family life that you've had."

Once again a look, compounded of shame and irritation, flickered across Simon Craven's face. "Yes, I've rather avoided any closeness to young Nick, because my mother said not to encourage him in a match that would only cause heartache."

"So, because the poor young fellow has had the misfortune to inherit an estate encumbered by debt, his loneliness has been compounded by being deemed not a suitable match for your sister? Mr Craven, Nick Revesby has no living family." Hal saw an expression flicker across his companion's face, and laughed abruptly. "Yes, I have often wondered, in my more irritated moments, if that might not be a blessed relief, but trust me, it is not! I huddled many a night over a foreign fire in exile, longing to see home and familiar faces of my childhood."

"Yes, your aunt, Mistress Westwood, told us you spent many years in exile with your father." He hesitated, and then said, "I must thank you, Sir Henry, for your patience and your delicacy in returning Bella to us without any knowing. But what to do next I do not know. Everyone has come for the wedding, you see…"

"Which could never have gone ahead anyway, once Mistress Pauncey was found dead," Hal interrupted .

Simon Craven's worried frown cleared miraculously. "What have I been thinking of, of course it couldn't, could it? How foolish of me not to think of that!"

"I think between us we should be able to manufacture some tale to account for your sister being missing," Hal continued. "Something like her falling in Holly-well Wood or spraining her ankle, not knowing that Mistress Rosalind had already fallen and hit her head. I'll talk to Sophie—Mistress Redwood about it. She is a great manufacturer of half-truths which sound cred-ible. I have left her standing guard over your sister, by the way, with instructions she is to admit none but your mother to Mistress Bella's chamber. I am sorry if that offends you, but I had to give her that promise to get her to consent to return home—that and the further promise, that you'd not force her into a marriage for at least six months—but again, mourning for your cousin, Mistress Pauncey, would make a marriage before that time unlikely."

"Yes, so it will, thank heavens!" Simon exclaimed, looking happier. "If only I'd thought of it earlier, I could have said so to Ezekiel Pridow. He was here not half an hour ago, telling me that he was fully prepared to overlook, what he termed as 'youthful folly' provided we went ahead with a private marriage within the next few days."

Hal frowned. "What very odd and unsuitable be-haviour! You have looked into his financial affairs, have

you, Mr Craven? To push for a marriage in these circumstances, to my mind shows very poor taste, or an
ulterior motive."

"Well, he phrased it as if he were doing us a great
service," Simon replied, frowning over the recollection
of the meeting. " 'To assist us in covering up the shame
of my sister's unmaidenly behaviour' is how he put it.
He said he was prepared to overlook the failings in her
upbringing."

"Yes, he does have an unerring turn of phrase," remarked Hal drily. "He is so very determined for this
alliance to proceed yet, if you'll forgive the observation,
he doesn't strike me as a warm man. I have not seen him
genuinely grieved or worried by your sister's disappearance. He was more affronted by the inconvenience."

"Yes, he is exceedingly pompous," agreed Simon,
whose feelings were plainly still chaffed by his encounter with his guest.

"Now, from my point of view, I have completed the
task set me on my arrival," continued Hal, as Simon appeared to become lost in thought. "Both young ladies
have been found, and returned to their families. Mistress Pauncey however, was not unharmed, and though
it grieves me to be the bearer of greater trouble, it ap-

pears she did not die as the result of an accident."

Simon's attention was arrested immediately. "You mean you think she was killed?" he asked in dismay.

"I greatly fear so," Hal replied. "I took the opportunity to examine the body in some detail—possibly more carefully than the coroner's man with the aching head did. And Jack Hollingshead and I agreed, that although there was little appearance of violence, she did have two bruises. One to the temple, which is generally assumed she got when she tripped and fell—and another well concealed in her hair and by the wreath she wore—at the back of her head. Now, it might well be possible that she slipped and hit either the back or front of her head, and I suppose, if one wanted to stretch disbelief, she could have fallen, hit her head and then staggered about, concussed and fallen again, but none of this can easily explain how she came to be locked in the priest hole."

Simon looked grave. "No, so the fact that the priest hole was locked means we are all under suspicion?"

"Yes," said Hal simply. "Any who knew of the existence of the priest-hole must naturally be suspect, so we have to assess who actually had such knowledge."

"Once I would have said only me but now I don't

know. Clearly Nick Revesby and Bella knew, Rosalind herself, and possibly her sisters, perhaps even my mother, and Aunt Margaret Pauncey?"

"What you are saying is that only the more Puritan members of your household can be in the clear—but is that so? I suppose if we are thinking of a group of clever scoundrels, the mere knowledge that you possess a priest hole, would make you more inclined to hush up the affair, which is what they want. I understand the coroner's man is supposed to be making some enquiries, but I gathered from his patent lack of enthusiasm, they would be perfunctory to say the least."

"Yes, naturally we'd want to hush up the affair," agreed Simon. "Even if Bella's reputation were not compromised, there are always those ready to suggest that though the family is no longer Catholic, there is no smoke without a fire."

"Indeed, so we are seeking a man with few scruples, it would seem. someone with something to hide; someone who will turn whatever presents itself to advantage; An adventurer, in fact."

"That brings us back to Nick Revesby," said Simon.

"But for the fact that Nick Revesby was in company with your sister, on an abortive attempt to be married," said Hal sharply, thinking how his hosts mind seemed to run on predictable tracks. "And quite frankly he is rather too innocent for such elaborate machinations. Indeed, upon reflection, I doubt there is much planning in this affair, more just increasingly fraught reactions to a situation spiralling out of control."

Then, as Simon Craven looked puzzled, Hal took out his notebook, saying, "Could you outline once again the events of the day your sister went missing? I have been writing down the main elements of what occurred but I seem to have heard so many accounts: from Jack Hollingshead's rather terse recollections, to your excellent report, to the chaotic ramblings of the bridegroom, so that in truth it is difficult to discern vital details from obscure facts."

Simon frowned over his own memories. "It was, as you know St Stephen's Day, the day we traditionally hold a feast for our tenants. We were all up at dawn and there are small children in the house, so there is little time for quiet reflection, it would seem. We broke our fast and began to make ready for the arrival of our guests. They came after the service, and we all sat down to the feast, which was as lively and noisy as these occasions usually are. Once the meal was over the tables were cleared away and dancing commenced. After a while, Bella began to arrange some games to entertain the many children, some of whom were growing fretful. Blind man's Bluff was a favourite, and then later, Hide and Seek."

"One moment, can we go back to earlier, before the feast? Is this not when the holly and the ivy were being put up around the house?"

"Yes, I'd been doubtful about it, because of our guests, but Bella and the other girls wanted to put up the greenery. That was earlier on, after breakfast, and before church." Simon explained.

"And your sister was there for that?"

"Oh, yes, she was directing Raife as to where things should go. She and Beatrice were making long garlands and winding them about the staircase, tying them up with red ribbon, and telling Raife where to put the holly boughs. I seem to remember her making wreaths to go about the candlesticks and Aunt Pauncey getting into a fret about burning the house down. They were all in such high spirits."

"Then you all went off to church—everyone?" asked Hal, who was making notes.

"Yes, and then after the service, everyone came back

to mulled wine, and then the feast itself. By the time that was over, dusk was coming down. You know how short days are this time of the year."

"What was the fuss about the mistletoe? "Hal asked. "Who started that?"

"We usually have a kissing ring," said Simon reluctantly, "at least, we have these past few years. A ring of ivy and mistletoe, which lovers can kiss under? Do you have a similar thing?"

Hal smiled as he glanced up. "Yes, usually we do, mistletoe grows very well in our woods."

"Well, it is not so common here. It seems to prefer the old woodland, with ancient trees, and there has been much clearance in these parts since the enclosure laws. Anyway, the girls had brought a basket of mistletoe, and they made their ring as they always do, with much laughter and teasing, but mistletoe is such messy stuff, the berries fall off and the sprigs, and there were lots of small pieces left over, so Bella added them to the candle wreaths. It was when Rosalind put one upon Bella's head, saying she should wear it for her wedding, that my aunt and Mistress Pridow, Ezekiel's mother, got into a fret of anxiety, saying it was ill-luck to bring it into the house, and that it was an evil, pagan berry."

Hal nodded as he made a note of his words, asking "What became of the wreath, do you know?

"Bella put it aside on the table to please my aunt, who was talking of a ceremonial burning. I never saw it again until we found Cousin Rosalind's body," he replied with a sigh.

Hal nodded as he reviewed his notes. "According to Mistress Bella, she stole away during the game of Hide and Seek and went straight to the priest hole, only to find her cousin following her. Anxious that she should get away to join Nick Revesby, she and Mistress Pauncey fell into a dispute, which culminated in her going with your sister down the stair to the passage which leads to Hollywell Wood."

"I can't believe Bella knew all about the passage, and said not one word to me," said Simon, shaking his head. "Or that Nick dug it out again. My father impressed on me how vital it was to our safety that the priest hole and the secret stair were kept secret and never discussed, so I thought I had been successful in keeping the whole thing hidden. I feel such a fool that Bella and Nick were back and forth through it for years!" He added in slightly aggrieved tones. "Now it becomes plain Rosalind knew all about it, so why did she go too? And if she went with Bella, how came she to be back in the priest hole? "

"It would seem she accompanied your sister, because Bella thought Rosalind might betray her if she didn't allow her to go. Mistress Bella confesses she had a dislike of traversing the passage, but she was so anxious for Mistress Pauncey not to take cold, that she sent her back up the staircase, with the lantern, and went on in the dark, alone, confident Nick Revesby would be waiting for her at the entrance. She says there was no need for Rosalind to go as far as she did, but she was telling Bella of a plan she'd hatched to take Bella's place at the wedding the following day. It seems she was going to put on Bella's wedding dress, and proposed to hide her face behind a veil." Hal sighed, "It explains why she was dressed as she was, but not who killed her."

"So she didn't go all the way along the passage with Bella?" asked Simon, bemused.

"No, Bella is firm that she made her turn back. The plan was that Rosalind was to re-join the game, and to tell any that asked that your sister had taken to her bed with the headache."

"And then Rosalind hoped to turn up to the wedding next morning as Bella?" Simon cried blankly, reviewing the tale. "Even though she is at least three inches taller than Bella, and a good deal heavier?"

"I don't think your sister had any faith in the disguise either," Hal agreed with a small smile, "but her plan was to be in Lincoln marrying young Nick."

"What went wrong?" Simon asked curiously. "Why didn't they marry? Did Nick ever have such a plan, or was Bella just taken in?"

"Oh no, Nick is totally besotted with your sister. He has no thought of anything but marriage, it was all a chapter of errors," replied Hal, ruefully. "The fog came down initially, and they got hopelessly lost. Then, one of the horses went lame and when they finally arrived in Lincoln, they were too late for the marriage, and then the minister Nick had arranged everything with, wasn't there. It seemed he'd fallen from his horse, hit his head and broken his leg, and was in a high fever, so they couldn't be married. They decided they had no choice but to turn back and go to one of Nick's friends on the way home. Then Nick's horse lost a shoe, and it became too late. They were so wet through, Nick decided they must go to his home to get dried. After which, it would seem, they had thoughts of eloping to London, only at that juncture, we arrived."

"As you say, a chapter of misfortunes," remarked Simon dryly. "Yet after all that, she is still intent on marrying him!"

"She insists none of the misfortunes were Nick's fault," admitted Hal, with a smile. "She plainly worships him, and she has such a sweet nature. And you know, although young and untried, Nick is himself, a fine young man. He adores your sister, and with the help and guidance of an older, more sensible, mentor, would soon become an asset to the community."

"Do you truly think so? "Simon asked, his voice echoing his doubts, then as Hal nodded, he sighed and added, "Well, if there is no choice, I suppose something could be contrived for them. If Bella is set upon this regrettable course, I expect I could do something for them. She has quite a handsome dowry, you know."

"I didn't know, but I suspected as much when you said Mr Pridow was still willing, indeed anxious, and pressing for the marriage."

"Yes," Simon glanced to him, rather embarrassed. "I've plainly been stupid in my dealings with the man. You see so much more than I do, Sir Henry."

"It is merely a by-product of being a Justice, Mr Craven," he said pleasantly. "One is forever seeking hidden reasons for the other person acting out of character."

Simon subjected the words to consideration, and then suddenly smiled, "Yes, I think it is called wisdom."

Hal laughed abruptly. "I would that it were! I think, as it doesn't pervade all my actions, it is more sudden flashes of insight."

Simon Craven was still embarrassed. "Sir Henry, I don't know how to thank you for all your trouble. You have given my thoughts a whole new direction."

"I am pleased that I was able to assist your understanding," replied Hal. "Do I have your leave to continue looking into your cousin's death, or do you wish to let it lie?"

Simon Craven sat thinking for some moments. "I'd like to say let it lie," he confessed, "but if Rosalind was killed—and it does seem likely from what you say— then it would be very wrong to let her killer go scotfree, wouldn't it? "

"Ah, now you place me in a dilemma," said Hal. "As a Justice of the Peace, I am obliged to agree, but as an ordinary citizen I have observed that often, when we begin to delve into these matters, many things, often best kept hidden, rise to the surface, and become general knowledge. People get hurt, mentally and physically. Yet, who can say what might happen if wrong doing were allowed to go unchecked? The Lord charges us to root out evil, and not suffer the murderer to live amongst us. So, on balance, I say we should proceed."

"Yes," Simon nodded his head, "I think you should too, sir, I am happy to assist you, but do you think I might be allowed to see my sister briefly, to set my mind at rest?"

"I think in spite of her fears of your anger, she'll sleep the better for it," Hal agreed. "Just tell Sophie—Mistress Redcroft—that you come at my suggestion, and she'll allow you in to see her charge."

Simon smiled, plainly relieved as he got to his feet. "I understand you and Mistress Redcroft are to be married, Sir Henry. May I wish you joy? You and your bride would seem ideally suited to each other."

"You are in error, Mr Craven," Hal replied, all the warmth suddenly gone from his face, leaving it stark. "Mistress Redcroft and I are on easy terms. She has been my ward these past eighteen months, but we have no plans to marry. Mistress Redcroft has declined to be my wife."

"Truly?" Simon Craven stared in astonishment, "yet, even a dullard such as I, can see, now my wife has pointed it out, that Mistress Redcroft adores you, and that you entertain warm feelings for her. "

"I cannot deny it is so, but it would seem some things are just not meant to be. We have on several occasions, very nearly come to an agreement, but something usually occurs to prevent a match being made. Until quite recently I was in mourning for my late wife, and now Sophie must observe a similar period of mourning after her unfortunate marriage, and of course, she is of rather a volatile nature." He shrugged his shoulders, and smiled a smile which didn't reach his eyes. "Some things are not meant to be," he repeated.

They parted company, Simon to visit his sister, Hal to read through his notes before joining the rest of the company at supper. He entered the hall as Sir Richard was meandering through a prayer in thanks for the food provided, and took his place opposite Mistress Hollingshead, who opened one eye to survey him and the other followed, with an uplifted eyebrow. Hal smiled slightly and nodded, heartily joining in the "Amen!"

"Amen, indeed, Sir Henry, you are returned," she said at once. "Am I to congratulate you on a successful mission?"

Hal smiled, glancing to Simon who had come to take

his place at the head of the table. "Friends," said Simon, his voice a little uncertain as he began to get lost on his emotions, "before we break our bread, let me give us all cause for rejoicing. My sister is found, safe and although not entirely well, as she has sustained an injured ankle, and contracted a nasty head cold, from the inclement weather, which prevents her joining us in celebration, she is..."

"Safe," interrupted Mistress Hollingshead taking her seat so that the servants could begin to bring in the food. "Praise be the Lord! Our thanks, Sir Henry, that we do not face a double tragedy. The one has overset us enough."

"I did very little, ma'am," replied Hal, swiftly. "I merely...."

"You mean Arabella is back here at Haceby?" Ezekiel Pridow interrupted Hal rudely, his eyes fixed on Simon, as the men also took their places.

Simon nodded, as the servants quickly laid the table with food. "Friends, let there be no ceremony tonight, we are, I suspect, for the most part, weary to the bone. Let us eat and give praise for God's mercy, never forgetting our dear cousin Rosalind." he added with a nod to his young cousins, Beatrice and Helen, who sat quietly with his wife at the foot of the table.

"Amen," said Sir Richard, who sat between Mistress Hollingshead and Aunt Kate.

"Then the wedding can go forward as planned," said Ezekiel Pridow, amidst all the exclamations, and expressions of relief.

"Well," said Simon uneasily, " I am…"

"Surely you forget, Mr Pridow, this is a house of mourning," interrupted Hal, as Simon began to get lost in a muddle of words. "A wedding cannot go forward with so many grieved as there are in this house."

Ezekiel Pridow frowned. "Not, perhaps with the same unnecessary celebrations, but the contract can still be sealed."

"A wedding without unnecessary celebration is hardly a wedding," said Hal swiftly. "A wedding does not rank with the buying of a beast at market; it is much more than a contract. I am sure you agree with me, Sir Richard? Is it not a matter for God's holy ordinance and not to be entered into unadvisedly, lightly, or wantonly?"

Sir Richard choked on his spoonful of broth, and the next few minutes were spent in Jack slapping his back, and Aunt Kate holding a cup of water to his lips, thus giving Simon time to organise his thoughts.

"No, Mr Pridow, the wedding cannot go forward as planned," he said firmly, once the furore was over and everybody had settled down again. "My family has suffered a tragedy in the death of one of its members. We still await the Coroner's deliberations on the matter, and if our natural grief did not hold us back, then surely good taste would."

"I would have thought after the behaviour of your sister you'd be glad to see her married, and off your hands!" Ezekiel Pridow snapped angrily.

"The marriage of a member of one's family can never be a matter of the disposal of a nuisance, surely?" said Hal, with a smile for Mistress Hollingshead. "Otherwise, would it not take place, as I suggested earlier in the market, rather than in a church? Are you recovered enough now, Sir Richard, to give us your thoughts?"

"I am, sir, no longer a minister of the Church of England, but of a new reformed church. In our settlement, there is no need for elaborate rituals, no time for decadent feasting, and displays of finery. Marriage is the communion of two souls before God." he replied, quietly contemptuous.

"How very laudable, sir. Is it legal in a court of law?" replied Hal sharply.

"Indeed it is," he replied at once.

"I only ask because when we had such a system recently in our country, during the unlamented Commonwealth, there was also a legal requirement. I gather those wishing to be married were required to go before a magistrate, and solemnly swear an oath that no previous contract was held. With the return of the King, everything reverted to the old accustomed ways, we have our usual form of marriage, and it is all part of the service again. But there, these are such nuances as can be discussed another time. As our host suggests, this is a time for quiet rejoicing that a loved one is safely returned to us." Hal raised his voice a little and changing the subject, called down the length of the table. "Mistress Beatrice, how does your mother this evening?"

Beatrice got hastily to her feet, looking a little frightened at being addressed by so august a personage. "She is yet in deep distress, and suffers greatly with the pains in her head, Sir Henry" she replied quietly, " but I thank you for your enquiry."

Ezekiel Pridow glared at them all, breaking in on Hal's pleasant reply. "What is going on here?," he demanded. "Am I to be palmed off without an explanation? Where is Mistress Craven, perhaps she will give me an answer to my questions?" He turned to address Cathy Craven, who was sitting at the foot of the table, talking quietly to Helen.

"She sits with her bereaved sister, Ezekiel," replied his mother, as Cathy Craven looked amazed at being so addressed. "Louisa told you so earlier. She sits with her grief-stricken sister. Be at peace now, I beg you. This is no time to start a tumult. Eat your supper."

"I disagree, Mother," said Louisa Pridow, glancing about the table. "Ezekiel is right something is afoot here, and we are being pushed out of it. All this nonsense about Bella Craven falling and twisting her ankle that explains nothing! The question is why had she left the house? And if she fell and twisted her ankle, why wasn't she found at once when everyone was out looking for her?"

Simon glanced to his guest. "There is nothing afoot here, Mistress Louisa, my sister, has behaved in a foolhardy way, and in doing so twisted her ankle. She admits it freely. To save her pain and discomfort, she is keeping to her bed until it will bear her weight. It has been agreed that she has a slight fever, and that a good night's sleep, would be of value. Tomorrow, if she is improved, she will feel more equal to any explanations which should be required of her."

"She doesn't need to stand to be married," said Ezekiel Pridow. "I thought we'd decided all this earlier. Explanations as to her conduct can come later. I came here to be married to your sister, and I've tolerated a lot of frivolous nonsense for this wedding to go forward, Craven, and now suddenly, it is no longer a priority. I will not tolerate such treatment!"

Simon looked amazed at his words. "Your pardon, Mr Pridow," he said his voice suddenly icy, "but I really must decline to discuss this matter further at this time. As I said earlier, we are all weary, and would, I think, benefit from a period of reflection and rest."

Jacob Brendon, who had been glumly munching his way through his food, caught the cuff of his friend Pridow's coat, and whispered something in his ear. Pridow became further incensed then thrust him and his words aside, pushing back his stool, with a scrape, "I beg to be excused!" he snapped. "I find I have no stomach for food! Madam, your servant." He bowed then stormed from the chamber without another word.

"Pridow is suddenly taken ill," said Brendon in prosaic tones, as Mistress Pridow looked deeply distressed and embarrassed, "he begs to be excused." He managed a grin, which was such a rarity as to contort his face, as he, too, got to his feet. "If you'll excuse me, I'll keep him company. There are few things unhappier than a disappointed bridegroom."

Simon exchanged a doubtful look with Hal, wondering if he should follow and soothe the man, but Hal shook his head, confident that Sophie would have no trouble in stopping anything Pridow had in mind. So the meal progressed, with most being a little embarrassed at first, then everyone relaxed as the warm food and wine began have their effect.

⚜

Chapter Seventeen

A thunderous knocking on the door awoke Sophie from the light doze the substantial supper and the warm fire had engendered. She got hastily to her feet as Bella stirred, but confident the drops Aunt Kate had given the sleeping girl would keep her quiet, she went to the door, as the handle was rattled furiously.

"Who is it?" she asked softly.

"Mistress Redcroft, open this door immediately!" Pridow cried angrily. "I demand I have some speech with my bride at once!"

"Mistress Bella sleeps, Mr Pridow," replied Sophie, in soothing tones. "She has a fever and is in some pain with her twisted ankle, so Mistress Westwood gave her something to aid her rest. Please lower your voice or her efforts will be in vain."

"I do not hold with the easing of pain!" he cried furiously. "Pain is the physick the Lord sends to try our

Faith! Pain should be welcomed as a test of our fortitude, not put aside with craft and the wiles of the devil!"

"Sir, I am not here to bandy words with you," replied Sophie sweetly. "I am merely here to relieve others, that they might take rest and enjoy their supper in peace and tranquillity. Pray address your words to another, and perhaps moderate the noise you are making, if you do not wish to disturb the many children and infants?"

"Do not think to order my conduct, woman!" he cried furiously. "Do not think I have not seen through your wicked lures! I know a Spawn of the Devil when I see one! Do you know of the torments of Hell which await you?"

"No," murmured Sophie under her breath, "but I suspect you are about to tell me." She glanced to the bed where Bella twisted in her sleep, murmuring uneasily. "Oh, do go away, you silly man, before you disturb her," she added in a whisper.

"Mistress Redcroft! Are you still there? Mistress Redcroft, I demand you answer me!" Pridow cried, rattling the handle again.

Sophie went back to the door. "Mr Pridow, are you aware of the object of ridicule you are making of yourself?," she asked softly through the crack. "Can there be anything more derisory than a rejected suitor, banging on a locked door? You are too late, Mr Pridow, your threats, your unpleasant blandishments are fruitless, and Bella has given her heart to another, far more worthy man."

"Provided she hasn't given her body to that worthless fornicator, I care nothing for foolish fantasies!" he snarled. "Hearts, what nonsense is this? She is to be my wife. This is a matter of contract! Was she with that cur Revesby all that time? Or had he found her in the woods and kept her prisoner at his home?"

"These are questions I cannot answer, Mr Pridow," Sophie replied. "I suggest you seek enlightenment of Mr Craven in this matter, if you need reassurance."

The sound of another voice came to her ears, and she gave a shudder as she recognised the soft sibilants she had heard earlier, while paused on the stairway. Then as there was no more whispering and the sound of retreating footsteps, she went back to keep watch over the sleeping Bella.

Hal, having finished his supper left the hall after Aunt Kate, who had departed earlier in company with Sir Richard, still anxious about his health. He wondered how Sophie had dealt with Ezekiel Pridow, and thought of enquiring, but knew even as he hesitated outside the door to the chamber his aunt was occupying, his duty to her came first. He knocked and entered when bidden.

"Aunt Kate," he murmured, surveying her doubtfully, dreading the coming interview which he had delayed as long as possible.

"Hal, at last we get a moment to catch up," she cried, coming to embrace him. "How busy you have been, and you are still damp from your ride back! You must go and change into fresh linen at once, or you'll take cold and then where should we be?"

"I shall do very well, ma'am," he replied. "Pray don't fret for me, I am only a little damp, but first I must talk to you."

"I have seen Sophie, and was on my way to assist her with young Mistress Bella, but it seems she is sleeping soundly, so I thought to delay my going a few minutes. Tell me, Hal, how is Margery? Her letters are rather fewer than I would like."

"She has been rather ill, as you know, ma'am…"

"And?" Kate's head came up immediately as he hesitated, picking his words and her keen glance settled on his face.

Hal hated to lie, but Aunt Margery, of all people, had insisted he prevaricate, saying it was essential they got Kate away from her betrothed and back to the safety of Westwood. "Her physician isn't pleased with her recovery," he admitted baldly. "He says that unless there is some progress, he cannot predict a happy outcome."

Kate's face registered her horror. "A happy outcome—you cannot mean—?"

"He says her lungs are affected," said Hal, trying to keep as near to the truth as possible. "She has developed a dreadful cough, which can't be soothed. It just won't go away. In truth, ma'am, her spirits are very low." He smiled in a troubled way. "She misses your company very much, although I am forbidden to tell you so, and I think when these low spirits are upon her, she fears she may die alone."

"Merciful Heavens, Hal! Why did you not come to me at once, and say so? I will pack my bags immediately!"

"No, no, ma'am," he said soothingly. "She is with Tom Kingscott and his new wife at the moment, and will remain so until we join her. Tom's new wife is a sweet woman and an excellent companion to Aunt Margery. Hopefully she is enjoying the rest of not having to run a household, although of course, Jane does much of it now. So don't fret, she is quite happy at present, teaching my boys some manners. "

"Indeed, Hal, your lads have very good manners for their ages," said Aunt Kate relaxing a little at the thought that Margery was not alone. "Does the physician truly fear for her life? "

"I cannot deny that he does, ma'am," he replied realising how great her distress was, and seeking to calm her. "But he is also a fool of a man, who doesn't know Aunt Margery. I would that Phillipe Douy were still in the country. I know Aunt Margery holds him in dislike too, but at least we'd not be forced to listen to this charlatan. I think what is needed, is a lift to her spirits. If only we could get some of the old fight back into her she might make a better recovery. I was even toying with the idea of asking Sophie to make a visit. That usually rouses Aunt Margery into a passion."

"How goes that affair, Hal?," asked Kate, glancing to his impassive face. "Is anything settled between you?"

"Why, yes, ma'am, you know how it is settled," he replied at once, looking troubled. "Sophie declined to marry me last summer."

"Yes, I know that—and I know you are not a fool—

Hal, at least apart from your dealings with Sophie, you are not," she cried exasperated. "Yes, Sophie declined to marry you only days after her bridegroom had been murdered under her nose, with guests and members of the family dying like flies around you! Is it any wonder in such circumstances, she was a little disinclined for another wedding? What has happened? Surely you can come to some sort of an agreement, for it is as plain as the nose on your face, that you love each other."

"Is my nose so very plain?" he asked, trying to turn the conversation, which was painful, with a jest. He was still unsure in his mind whether Sophie had been indulging in one of her games as they had stood together just a few hours earlier, or whether she had been trying to tell him her feelings had changed.

"It is, as you well know, a particularly handsome nose," she replied tartly. "Don't think to turn my question aside, Hal."

"Dear Aunt Kate, pray do not chide me, I beg," he replied simply. "I am very weary, and the world has gone awry with me these days. I do not seem to be able to understand things as I once could, nor can I, it seems, expect happiness anywhere in my life. I am growing old and careworn."

"Careworn, perhaps," she agreed, "but not yet old,

just more sensible. Do you love her very much?"

"With all my heart, Aunt, against my better judgement, against any common sense, and certainly against my best interests," he replied, trying not to allow his voice to falter.

Aunt Kate sighed and nodded her head. "Yes, 'tis plain we have much to accomplish. A needless death to mourn and two love affairs to bring to a happy conclusion."

"A little more than that, ma'am, a murderer to bring to justice, too. Rosalind Pauncey suffered two blows to the head, making it most likely she was hit, and didn't just fall. If she wasn't dead then, she was left to die," said Hal gently. "And that brings me onto another, rather unpleasant subject, which I have been hesitating over ever since I first arrived."

"Oh, Hal, never say Rosalind was killed deliberately!" Aunt Kate cried, in horror.

"Perhaps not deliberately, ma'am," he said carefully, "but she was certainly allowed to die. If she had possibly been given better attention, she might have lived. You see, I think she either saw something, or overheard some words, and it was felt she had to be kept out of the way for a while. During that time she died."

"Oh, Hal, what a tragedy," cried Kate in distress. "Her poor mother—my heart grieves for her."

"Mine too, ma'am," he agreed, "but mostly it grieves for you."

"For me, Hal?" Kate turned to him in surprise.

"Aunt Kate, I would give anything not to have to say these words to you, but we have—it has been discovered—something has been discovered, about Sir Richard Harrison."

"About Richard?" she repeated blankly. "Why, Hal, what can you mean? Richard is a fine man, everybody says so.

"I'm sure reports make him so, dear Aunt Kate," he said, catching her fluttering hands in his, and squeezing them gently in comfort. "But I made a discovery, through my friend Philippe Douy—you do recollect him, don't you?"

"Well, of course I do, Hal, he cured the pain in my knee last winter. His recipe for a rub was most excellent. Indeed it might be the very thing for Margery's chest, you know; for it was powerful."

"I am hopeful you may help her health in many ways, ma'am," he agreed, "but Philippe as you know, travelled to Virginia back in the summer with his new wife."

"I recollect you telling me of his disappointment with his reception in his ancestral home in France, and how difficult he found it to settle," she agreed.

"Well, as I said, he took ship to Virginia, and went to visit another old acquaintance, who by chance is the schoolmaster of a settlement which might be familiar to you."

"Familiar to me—why what do you mean, Hal?" Kate looked puzzled. "Are they not happy there?"

"I don't think he has had time to find out, he merely relayed some of the local gossip which he had heard, because he recognised the name of Sir Richard Harrison from my correspondence."

"Oh, I see, Phillipe is in Virginia, in the settlement where Richard lives, is he? Isn't life a curious thing? And yet, when one considers, there are limited choices in Virginia. The population is so small, everyone knows each other, or has at least heard of them, it would seem," Kate said, looking relieved.

"Yes," again Hal hesitated.

As he was seeming unable to continue Kate was forced to ask unhappily, "What is it, Hal? I can see something is troubling you."

"Dear Aunt Kate, there is no other way to say this.

Sir Richard Harrison is not held in esteem in Virginia. It seems when he left, on hearing of his inheritance, he departed bearing money raised by his church for books for the school, and some furnishings for the church."

"Well, that doesn't sound like Richard," said she indignantly. "Depend upon it, Hal, there will be an explanation for such a rumour. Recollect what hotbeds of gossip our own villages and towns are. Why, I am surprised you give credence to such gossip, when you have suffered the same sort of thing yourself."

"Yes, Aunt you are quite correct," he agreed, with a sigh. "I even abandoned my wife and children, too."

She stared at him as if transfixed. "Wife and children?" she whispered.

"The tale from Philippe is that one Sir Richard Harrison left his home, his wife and family, and set off to claim his inheritance in England, some two years ago. It seems he returned home last summer, after an illness, to find the reports of his wife dying had been false, and that his family had increased in his absence. He stayed but a month, then disappeared in the dead of night, taking the funds supplied by the church for the purchase of school books."

"Oh, Hal, it cannot be so! There must be some mistake," Kate, who had turned pale, was moved to protest.

"I would that there were, ma'am," he replied quietly. "I have barely had a chance to talk to the fellow, he appears to be avoiding all my attempts to talk to him, but Aunt Margery has made extensive enquiries about his movements amongst her acquaintance. And I have to say, that I think this is at the root of her illness, for she is so grieved that it was through her agency that you met this man. From all the reports she has received, it would seem there can be no mistake. Did not Sir Richard Harrison take ship for Virginia in 1659, at the fall of Cromwell's son?"

"Yes, yes, I think so, but Hal, surely there must be some mistake? I cannot believe that Richard of all people..."Kate turned her face away in distress, biting at her soft lips.

Hal reached out to take her hand, his heart wrung. "I am so sorry, Aunt Kate, I would have given anything to save you this. You deserve better."

"Oh, Hal," she replied, resting her head on his chest, as tears slid down her cheeks, "now I know how poor Sophie felt. Oh, Hal, the relief of it all!"

"Relief?" He repeated blankly, "Sophie? I am sorry— but what are you saying, Aunt Kate?"

"Hal,I have been in such an agony of guilt all these months, because I allowed Margery to persuade me against my better judgement, to enter into a contract with Sir Richard. It was when Sophie was being so difficult last winter, and within weeks I found myself in a similar situation to her," she replied as tears slipped relentlessly down her cheeks. "

"You mean you don't wish to be married, ma'am?" Hal asked blankly, feeling the world turn upside down.

"I never wanted to be married. Oh, yes, I was flattered by Sir Richard and his attentions, and I lost my head for a while, but marriage, no! I so love Westwood. It has been my home for such a long time, it felt like ripping my heart out to think of leaving. I love you children so much that I feel you are like my own, and to think of leaving you all and crossing that vast ocean, to that wild, untamed land! I am not a brave woman, Hal. I have always been a coward, which is why I have been prevaricating so long, making every excuse to not be married, that I am ashamed of myself."

"But Aunt Kate, why are you ashamed? You are the bravest woman I know." Hal was bewildered by these revelations and uncertain, as she continued to weep into her handkerchief, just what to do. "How can this be? I know I speak for us all, when I say you are the mother we never had, but why then did you not say something? If you feel as you do, how could you ever think of leaving us?"

"You'll remember the big quarrel you had with Aunt Margery last winter, Hal? It was when you returned from France, you were ill and Philippe Douy was with us?" Kate replied, mopping up her tears and blowing her nose with a resolute air.

"Yes," he replied. "How could I ever forget such a dreadful time? It will be forever etched upon my memory! My wife Libby had just died and I hadn't returned in time to see her before she died. I'd found Stephen and Cordelia, and brought them back from France. I knew that would cause trouble, yet I couldn't abandon them. It was without doubt the darkest period of my life. Without the help and support of my family, I often felt I must lie down and die. You speak of being ashamed, you have no comprehension of the sense of shame I lived with then."

"You had nothing to feel ashamed about. It was an unfortunate set of circumstances," she said quickly, "but you do recollect how it was? How you came home to find everything all awry? How Sophie was being so impossible? How everyone seemed at odds with each other, and you dismissed the cook?"

"The cook?" he replied blankly, then casting his mind back, he added, "Oh, yes, I do remember the cook, why that woman berated me for the quality of my guests! Why, what had she to do with Aunt Margery?"

"Margery has run Westwood for more years than I can remember, Hal. Henry explained it to me when we were first married, how she had been the mistress of Westwood since the death of her mother, and how he didn't want me to bother my head over domestic drudgery so I must leave it all to her," she smiled up at him through her tears. "Dear Henry, he was so like you, Hal, he understood people so well. He knew to remove all power from Margery would crush her. Even when Henry was alive, neither of us would have dreamed of dismissing a servant without discussing it with Margery first," she replied gently.

Hal nodded. "Yes, ma'am, I recollect you saying so at the time, and realising I was in error, I did apologise to Aunt Margery once I wasn't feeling quite so ill."

"By that time Margery had fallen into a fit of the glooms," Kate replied with a sigh. "She said we were relicts of the past, of no use to anybody and plainly a cause of annoyance to you, and that she for one didn't intend to remain where she wasn't wanted—or be a nuisance to a new generation of impertinent young people who imagined they knew better. It was then she decided we must find ourselves a new home," said Aunt Kate with a small sigh.

"Aunt Kate, I am deeply grieved," cried Hal clasping her hand, as she wiped her eyes again. "I deserve to be whipped for my insensitivity. I never meant to cause you both such pain, I was just so beset by my own devils. Surely you knew, ma'am that my anger was mostly against myself? That my short temper was..."

"Yes, yes, I know, Hal. Good heavens, you are your uncle again!" she exclaimed at once. "I never thought to meet another man with such a conscience, and it is a great joy to know that his legacy continues, but Margery was adamant. She said we had no right to expect you to house us, and that plainly you wanted a new order of things and that we had no choice but to relieve you of the encumbrance we represented."

"Oh, Aunt Kate, how you shame me," he cried in dismay. "And you were to be the sacrificial lamb in finding a new home, I suppose?"

Kate gave a watery chuckle. "No, it wasn't entirely

like that. Richard was, and can be, quite charming. I was flattered by his manners. It had been such a long time since I had been the object of anyone's attention, and I so enjoyed being courted again," she sighed. "So, I was paid out for my vanity, it wasn't me, but the Westwood name and connections he desired."

"More fool he then," said Hal warmly. "Anyway, it was Aunt Margery's vanity, not yours which led you amiss. Left to yourself, you would never have thought of marrying again."

Kate sighed, and she wiped her eyes again. "Probably not, although, like Margery, I did feel Sophie resented us, and wondered if our presence at Westwood was the cause of all the quarrels you had."

"Sophie loves you like a mother—we all do—your Westwood orphans, " he replied quickly. "Our relationship with Aunt Margery is different. There is respect and dutiful affection of course, and there is none other I would sooner turn to in a tight corner—although I often would prefer not to hear her opinions of my character." He grinned suddenly. "No doubt I'll be informed of it again when I make her a sincere and heartfelt apology, but ma'am, there can be no further talk of either of you leaving me, in that I am absolutely adamant. Wherever my future lies, we shall all be together at Westwood."

"All?" she asked. "Does that include Sophie, too?"

"Certainly, I have hopes that she, Adam and Cordelia might be persuaded to return with us. More than that I cannot guarantee," he replied, "but I am relying on your good offices."

Chapter Eighteen

Hal finally left his aunt as she went to relieve Sophie, who was sitting with Bella. In a thoughtful mood, he waited for Sophie to appear outside the chamber. "You managed to deal with Pridow, then?" he asked, as Sophie appeared.

She smiled at him and said, "Yes, the fool! Aunt Kate had given Bella something to help her sleep, and he ranted on a bit until Brendon came to whisper into his ear." She gave a sudden shudder. "How I dislike that fellow!"

"Do you?" Hal asked warily. He was aware he had betrayed his feelings earlier, but in spite of his words to his aunt, he was still unsure of how to proceed and felt this was neither the time nor the place to enter into any discussion of their own affairs. "We need to discuss many things." he said, thinking rapidly. "Did you make any progress with talking to various people in my absence, or was everyone too distressed? Did you make any discoveries of importance?"

"Other than the obvious?" she murmured demurely, with a sidelong glance.

Hal chose to ignore this, hoping the gloom in the gallery would hide his countenance. "Obviously not then," he said. "I imagined it would be so."

"No, I did make some progress," she replied with a frown, wondering at his coolness, and whether she had misread his embrace. "I found the opportunity to speak to Louisa Pridow..." She hesitated and glanced about her. "Pray, step into my chamber here. As we know these walls are paper-thin, and we don't want to be overheard."

She opened the door, and led the way into a chamber not unlike the one inhabited by Bella Craven, where a fire had been kindled, and hangings shut out the grim weather. She indicated a chair for Hal, and sat on a chest at the foot of the bed. Hal, filled with misgiving, took the seat.

"Louisa Pridow," she continued, "I spoke with her at length. Not a pleasant woman; not a pleasant family;"

"No, but Mistress Pridow appears gentle," said Hal, frowning a little at the thought. "From my observations

Pridow's children run to her, rather than to their aunt."

"Yes, she is gentle, whereas Louisa is a sharp-tongued, bitter woman," Sophie said, nodding. "She is desperate to get a wealthy husband and will do almost anything to achieve her ends but not, I think, kill. She doesn't like Bella and considers her brother slighted by her putting off the wedding earlier in the year. Louisa is eager for the match, but only because she is expected to help with her brother's children, and she doesn't like them. In fact, I don't think she likes anyone. She is however, looking for a husband, and she is looking your way."

Hal grimaced. "I am not looking for a wife," he replied incautiously. "I am especially not looking for a sour-tongued shrew. So you think Louisa is not like to have killed Rosalind Pauncey from envy?"

Sophie eyed him uncertainly, wondering who his words were aimed at. "I don't think so," she said slowly. "I imagine she'd not worry if any harm came to Bella, but she deals in the most deadly of weapons, nothing as quick or clean as a blow. She is full of malice and envy."

"But if she were angry enough to say, push one who had a weak constitution?" he asked.

Sophie considered the question. "More of an unlucky accident? It could be a possibility, but not likely. Louisa has an innate dislike of taking any trouble for another. If she pushed Rosalind and she fell, knocking her head, Louisa would have run for help, then made sure the blame fell upon Rosalind herself, saying she was clumsy, or some such thing."

Hal nodded his understanding. "I did wonder if she and Rosalind might be in a conspiracy to fool her brother into marriage. Recollect Rosalind was wearing Mistress Bella's wedding gown."

"Yes, but Louisa wouldn't promote a wedding between her brother and Rosalind. The Pauncey's have too few connections—and too little money. Louisa is eager to improve her own social position. And by a marriage with her brother, Rosalind would have gained higher status than Louisa."

Hal nodded frowning over the words which would never have occurred to him. "I see, yes, that makes sense. She most certainly doesn't speak to any of the Paunceys as if they are her equals." He paused thinking deeply. "No, you are right, it doesn't hold together, does it?" he said at last, adding, "Did you get a chance to talk to the Pauncey sisters?"

"Yes, I did," said Sophie, frowning over the recollection. "Both are still much shocked and grieved, of course, and I would say that Helen bids fair to become as wilful as her elder sister."

"And the middle one—Beatrice is it? She struck me as a sweet young woman," remarked Hal, unguardedly. "She is most certainly the prettiest of them all."

Sophie subjected him to a searching look. "Yes she is pretty, and has a pleasant, open character, however she wouldn't be interested in a widower with children."

Hal frowned and looked nettled. "I merely said she seemed a pleasant sort of young woman," he said sharply. "I believe I said earlier I wasn't looking for a wife."

"I was speaking of Ezekiel Pridow. I have no interest in your matrimonial plans," snapped Sophie, in return, suddenly feeling very tired as she overcame the desire to weep.

"I believe you have made your feelings on the subject clear on several occasions," he agreed, rather dismayed by this, and rather glad he'd not made a fool of himself earlier. "Why do you consider Beatrice wouldn't accept an offer from Richard Pridow? Her mother might wish for her to do so, as I understand it they are not well-dowered young women, and might struggle to find a match."

"Beatrice already has a lover," replied Sophie, unaccountable tears stinging at her eyelids. "Hugh St John, her sister-in-law's brother is her choice—and she his. Unfortunately, the St John family doesn't agree, and at present Mistress Pauncey is wary of offending her step-son and his wife, so who knows what the future holds for the sisters."

"Who knows what the future holds for any of us," he replied, suddenly feeling rather depressed. "So, Mistress Beatrice's affections are engaged, just like Mistress Bel-la's were. Did you get to have speech with anyone else?"

"No, the older women were all too busy taken up with Mistress Pauncey and her grief. Catherine, Simon's wife, was busy with her children, and helping as much as possible with the Pridow brood, and I did my best to avoid Mistress Hollingshead. But I did have something of a conversation with Sir Richard."

"Sir Richard Harrison?" Hal sounded surprised. "Did you indeed, I wouldn't have thought he would speak to you. He seems to be avoiding me, and would surely view you with deepest suspicion?"

"As you say, he looks upon me as a scarlet woman," she agreed, her voice shaky. "I was taken by surprise at finding him alone in a parlour, and only paused to be polite. It was the man himself which held me. I have never been in the company of such utter misery before; it surrounded him like a mist. It was as if for those moments I, too, tasted his despair and felt my soul was lost." She seemed to make an effort, and literally shook herself, as if wishing to get herself free of the corrosive emotion. "I merely wished to express my condolences for the loss he had suffered, which I did, and he felt obliged to converse with me about Aunt Kate and his own family."

"You certainly fared better than I have." replied Hal with a sigh. "You plainly have the knack of getting people to talk to you, which it seems they won't to me."

"You come not only with the title of a Justice, which makes many wary, but the reputation for rooting out secrets, 'tis no wonder everyone avoids you like they would the plague," she replied candidly. "Whilst am perceived as a lost soul myself, they feel superior to me, and have no need to be on their guard."

He frowned over her words, looking dismayed. "Do you truly see yourself as a lost soul? I cannot believe you are considered such by these people. They are but country people like ourselves. How can they consider themselves superior to you? They must have uncommonly small minds to think you a lost soul," he said, in annoyed tones.

"A lost soul, a voice calling in the wilderness, I am all of these things and none of them," she replied, a little consoled by his defence of her, but turning from him to hide her feelings.

"They appear to be hidebound people for the most part," he said dismissively, "although the Hollingshead's improve on acquaintance, and I like the Cravens. However, I am sorry they view you with contempt and very little favour, when you are doing them such a service."

"Indeed," she agreed, hovering on the verge of tears, "but I am well used to it. Very few people view me with any favour, anyway. Are you finished with me now, for I promised Catherine Craven I'd help her with the Pridow boys?"

"I had thought it was you who had done with me," he replied, frowning. He was aware something was amiss, but did not want to provoke the tears which seemed imminent, or get caught in what so easily could become a quarrel at this juncture. He instead chose to take refuge in formality. "I must thank you for your assistance and beg that you will continue to observe what goes on about you, and inform me of anything you find amiss. Please be assured that I very much need your help and do appreciate it."

"I will, if it truly is your wish to continue to observe all that goes on about us," she replied as he rose to take his leave. "But I honestly doubt the wisdom of sharing my observations with one who seems to be so very determined to be blind!" she added, as she, too, got to her feet.

"I am not blind, Sophie," he snapped back, totally at a loss as to what he had done wrong. He opened the door and glanced out into the corridor. "I have just learnt that in dealing with you, it is often better to be blinkered."

"Certainly safer for a steady old cart horse!" she cried to his retreating back.

He hesitated, plainly stung enough to wish to answer, but on hearing the opening of another door, he shrugged his shoulders, and continued on his way whilst Sophie stood fighting back the tears, and wondering why it was they could not be in each other's company for more than a few minutes without descending into a squabble.

She finally knew her own heart. He was the only man she would ever love. She saw no future for herself unless he was by her side. She had tried her hardest these past six months to forget him, and she had managed to convince herself she had, and that marriage wasn't for her. Even with the daily felicity of observing her companions at Bickmarsh, she had come to the conclusion that such bliss would never be her lot. Yet he only had to appear once again in her orbit to make her foolish heart beat faster and all the old longings she had managed to suppress rise up anew.

When they had stood so close on the stair with his arms firm about her, she had felt so safe, as if she had finally come home, and he—he had not held her as if she were a stranger, more as if she were part of himself. In that moment she had known that he was still as much a part of her as he had ever been. It was as if they were separated only by her intransigence.

She sank back down to the chest and began to consider the matter. It was plain immediately it would take something momentous to make him ask her to marry him again. She had refused him, and made him look a fool before others. She could see now how that had hurt and angered him, although such had been her own confusion at the time that it had never occurred to her. He had no plans to marry, he had said. That was indeed a relief. All of the summer and autumn she'd been expecting word of his betrothal to a young woman selected as suitable by Aunt Margery, but he had said he had no plans to marry. How could she change that, given their propensity to dispute every matter within the compass of their existence? She sank her chin to her hand and turned her brain to the task.

Hal meanwhile retired to his chamber prey to many doubts. Like Sophie, as they had stood locked together in that embrace on the secret stairway, he had known with blinding clarity what a fool he had been. Their love was never going to be a passing fancy, soon forgotten. Indeed thanks to his folly it looked as if it could be a mortal wound to both of them. He had suffered torments of jealousy this past year, and for what? A mental picture he carried in his mind of the perfect man? A fear his reputation might be compromised? Who was he trying to fool but himself? He was terrified of committing his love totally to Sophie, because he knew once he did so there would be no going back. Yet why would he want to go back? He had done so these last six months and his life had been dire. A desert of care and longing, with no joy of her presence to alleviate his despair. He reviewed the last half hour filled with gloom, but with enough hope, as he thought on her answers and made ready for sleep, to give him impetus to make some decisions about the morrow and his own future.

Chapter Nineteen

Hal, who had been alerted by a pre-arranged message from a groom, went to meet Nick Revesby as he arrived in the hall the next morning.

"Sir Henry, I am glad to meet you again so soon," he said at once, clasping his hand warmly.

"And I, you, Nick," he replied pleasantly. "Now, before you ask, Sophie—Mistress Redcroft—sent word that Mistress Bella slept well all night, and has awoken feeling much happier, mostly I imagine, because of the discoveries of yesterday. Simon saw her briefly last evening and they are reconciled, which is excellent news. Now Pridow is, as we imagined, pushing for the wedding to go ahead, but I have encouraged Simon to hold out against this, citing that it wouldn't be seemly in view of Rosalind death. So he has refused to agree to Pridow's demands."

"Praise be!" Nick said in heartfelt relief. "I have been

imagining arriving to find Bella already the bride of that man!" He retained his hold on Hal's hand, adding, "Sir Henry, pray allow me just to express my most grateful thanks for all your patience and good advice yesterday. I have already committed it to paper, sir," he added, taking a folded sheet from the top of his boot. "I thought it possible I might not get a chance to see anyone, but be simply ushered away out of sight." He grinned suddenly. "You'll be glad to know I have used both Latin and Greek in its composition, and I mean to do so each day in future, in honour of my father, and so that I never grow rusty again."

"I am honoured that you would take such trouble," replied Hal smiling at his enthusiasm. "I only hope my brain is up to the translation."

Nick chuckled, "There is no fear of that, sir, my work is pitifully rudimentary! But stay, I heard Mr Craven's voice. I must not offend him with my high spirits." He instantly sobered, and turned to bow politely, as a grave Simon Craven entered the hall.

"Sir Henry, Mr Revesby, good morning," he said his voice cool, as both nodded in acknowledgement. "I am of the opinion our interview should be a private matter, and thus propose to hold it in my book room, if you will follow me."

Hal directed a warning glance at Nick as Simon turned away. Nick grimaced back, but checked his exuberance, as he bent to pick up his heavily-laden saddle bags. As they entered the rather spartan chamber, his demeanour was as cool as his host's. Simon Craven indicated seats, and offered refreshment, which both declined, then Nick plunged recklessly into the matter at hand.

"I have come this morning, Mr Craven, to offer you an apology for the considerable inconvenience I have put you to with regard to dear Bella. Sir Henry pointed out to me what a hare-brained scheme it was, and was kind enough to say that although he could clearly see it had its roots in desperation, there really was no excuse for such behaviour. He has made it very plain that I have wronged both you and your sister. I have come today to ask your pardon for my foolishness, which has brought this trouble upon us, and to beg that I might be allowed to make amends for any damage done to the reputation of my dearest love. I also wish, if you will be so good, to seek your advice on a legal matter.

Hal's lips twitched and he had to master an urge to smile. The speech was so patently rehearsed and not only well-learned, but said with such honesty as to put

Simon Craven into difficult position. Hal could read the reactions to it in his face: surprise, irritation, astonishment, and the desire to vent at least some of those reactions on one whom he saw as the author of his misfortunes.

"Before you speak, Mr Craven, may I add a few words?" Hal asked quickly. "As you know, I spent some hours yesterday in company with Mr Revesby, and as a consequence have come to admire much about him. However, youth is very much upon his brow, and caution a long way from his mind. Nick, allow me to speak first, please."

"Naturally, Sir Henry, if you will be so good, I'm obliged to you," replied Nick instantly. "I know I lack tact and blunder into situations without thinking them through."

"I am relieved to hear you accept that much responsibility," said Simon icily.

"Nick is prepared to accept responsibility for his actions, Mr Craven," agreed Hal. "He is ready to accept the blame quite cheerfully, but I do believe you, too, must accept a share of it."

Simon met his eyes blankly, and then recollected the circumstances. "Well, yes, Sir Henry, indeed, I believe

I have already expressed my apologies for making the error of challenging Mr Revesby to a duel."

"Indeed you have, but only to me in my capacity of Justice of the Peace, as far as I am aware you have made no apology to Nick," replied Hal

"You are expecting me to apologise to Nick?" Simon Craven repeated blankly.

"I believe it to be essential if this meeting is to progress. You are, after all, wishing to effect reconciliation with a neighbour, and Nick has already apologised to you," Hal replied gently.

An abrupt silence fell as Simon digested the unpalatable truth and Nick, seeing the various emotions flitting across his host's face was moved to protest.

"Sir Henry, I don't require an apology," he said, seeing refusal on Simon's face. "I have admitted I am to blame for persuading Bella to elope with me."

"Quite!" Simon snapped.

"I believe what is required here today is a new beginning," said Hal, refusing to be daunted by his host's annoyance. "Mr Craven, if you can find it within you to apologise to the Law, why not to a neighbour?"

Simon reddened as he realised the point of Hal's words and then said curtly, "Like Nick, I will allow myself to be guided by you, Sir Henry. Mr Revesby, I extend my apologies for aught that I may have said or done amiss."

"Excellent," said Hal, as Nick looked amazed but hastened to accept his words. "Now, shake hands upon it please, for you are to be family."

Nick was from his chair immediately, his hand held out at the ready. Simon was more reluctant, but he extended his hand with a thoughtful air.

"Even better," said Hal. "Now to business! No Nick, business first, pleasure second. Mr Craven, Mr Revesby asks for your assistance in a matter of business. He has large sums of money to repay to Mr Brendon, and asks if you will be so good as to bear witness to the transaction."

"Money?" Simon asked blankly, looking from Hal to Nick and back again. Then as Nick hauled one of his heavy saddlebags to the desk and opened it, the coins spilled out in a golden splatter across his papers, he added, "Gold?—Good God, Nick, never say you have found your treasure!"

"No, Sir Henry did!" he replied with a grin.

"No, you found it, Nick, I merely said where I thought it might be found," said Hal.

"But, this means you can pay off the mortgages on your property, doesn't it?" Simon asked. "Which means you'll not lose Weston Revesby? Good heavens! Oh, Nick, I am so pleased for you!"

"Pleased enough to consent to my marriage to Bella?" Nick countered swiftly.

Simon stared at him, immediately sobered, and then a small embarrassed laugh escaped him. "You can have the pick of all the young women locally, Nick, if you have found your famous treasure!"

"I don't want the local young women," replied Nick crisply. "I only want Bella. I always have, ever since we were children. Everyone will say I have ruined her with my folly, and I think I should make it right again in the eyes of the world, besides which, I love her with all my heart."

Simon sighed thoughtfully. "Yes, I know you do, Nick, nor can I deny you are the man she wants, but you see, she is still contracted to Pridow at the moment."

"She hates him and says the thought of his clammy embrace gives her the horrors. The thought of being married to him makes her want to sit and weep forever. I can't have Bella unhappy for the rest of her life. I can't have her unhappy for one moment more," said Nick.

Hal laughed at his unashamed avowal of love, but felt a twinge of envy at its simplicity, too. "Mr Craven is explaining that we have yet to find a way of extricating Bella from this projected marriage. It will take a little time, Nick, and recollect, because of Rosalind's death it wouldn't be seemly for you to be married at once either."

Nick nodded his understanding. "Yes, you kindly explained all this yesterday, Sir Henry, all I am asking is for a private betrothal, if Mr Craven will allow it."

"I'll be happy to do so, Nick, as soon as I may," agreed Simon. "Although you must understand it isn't a thing easily accomplished. Pridow was here again first thing this morning, pushing for the marriage to go ahead privately, and I must confess I was never more thankful than to be able to tell him I did not think it right to do so when one of our family was so lately dead. I cannot feel it seemly for Bella to enter into any contract until Rosalind is buried and mourned."

"I rather think we might have a key to that matter too," said Hal. "Nick, show Mr Craven those title deeds we found in the chest hidden with the money."

"Title deeds too? Where did you find all this, Nick? You have been looking for it for many a long year!"

"Mistress Sophie found a paper in my library. Sir Henry had said the library was the perfect place to conceal something, and we went to look and quite by chance Mistress Sophia, who was helping to dust the books, dislodged a single sheet of what I took to be one of my father's poems."

"Which it was, Nick," said Hal.

"Yes, so it was—and Sir Henry worked out the clues which led us to the holy well in the wood. The treasure was concealed in the well."

"Holy well—good heavens, Hollywell Wood! You mean the well, there in the wood? Why, I often stopped there as a child."

"Yes, it was in a niche cut into the wall," said Nick, producing the bundle of documents from the other saddle bag, and handing them to Simon. "These were wedged into the top of the chest, along with the money. Sir Henry is of the opinion that my father concealed them too, lest my grandfather gambled them away, never realising how he would be forced by the incessant fines to raise funds on them."

Simon frowned and glanced sidelong to Hal. "I'd have thought he'd have been hard pushed to raise funds without them," he said slowly.

Hal nodded and asked, "Did Mr Brendon follow an occupation in past times? As I understand the matter, his is not inherited wealth."

"His grandfather was a tenant farmer in reasonably comfortable circumstances," replied Simon. "Brendon's father was the second son. He became an attorney and later inherited the farm when his brother was killed in the war. Brendon had already followed his father into the law, and both were employed by Parliament, dealing with land taken in fines from the Royalists."

Hal nodded his understanding, and after a pause Simon looked up to ask directly, "Do you suspect foul play here?"

"I am a Justice of the Peace, Mr Craven," he replied dryly. "It is part of my occupation to be suspicious of almost everything."

"Well," Simon hesitated again, wrinkling his nose in dismay. "I have heard tales," he admitted reluctantly, "but in truth, no more than that. You know the sort of things, rumours on market day?" He was silent for a space, which lengthened as Hal made no reply. Nick glanced from one to the other, puzzled, and Hal shook his head, indicating for Nick to hold his tongue.

"I can also recollect my father speaking of the many

dubious goings on immediately after the war," said Simon finally. "I remember him saying how Jack Hollingshead's father was buying up parcels of land all over the area, and especially how he snapped up his cousins' place at Bickmarsh. Royalist land seemed to go very quickly. I remember my father calling it a damned free-for-all, but that could have been because we never had enough money ourselves to buy anything of substance. It had been something of a struggle to retain what we did have, because in the beginning my father tried to stay out of the conflict. He always insisted no good could come of it and that the King would always be the King, even if they did chop his head off. Of a consequence we were looked upon as unreliable and seldom included in anything which was going forward. In truth we only started to be part of local society again after my father's death, and later when I began to pay court to Cathy Hollingshead."

"I gathered from something my aunt said, that yours was a love match, Mr Craven. There must have been a lot of competition for a Hollingshead bride?"

Simon grinned and suddenly looked a lot younger. "Yes, there was, but I was fortunate in that I was the youngest suitor by far and that Cathy very much has a mind of her own. There are times when she makes Jack look pliable."

Hal smiled politely and paused before asking, "Am I in error, or to your knowledge was the priest hole in your house never brought into use during the war?"

Simon looked very uncomfortable. "I was taught to be very careful never to discuss the matter," he replied. "All I do know is after Naseby, such was the situation at the time that my father decided it should be sealed up and forgotten about. Recollect the uncertainty of those days? I was but a youngster—I am a little younger than you, Sir Henry—but I remember how frightening it all was. What with the King being imprisoned in various houses round the country, and groups of armed men forever on the march from one place to another. It seemed all over for the Royalist Cause, and those in power were looking to target any they considered not loyal to Parliament. My father knew we had to be seen to be with them, that it was no time to relax our guard. Nick's father had returned wounded from Naseby, and my mother had been a frequent visitor as he lay dying. Then when his grandfather came back from exile, my father said although he would never speak against a neighbour, he was no longer happy to be seen aligning ourselves with so prominent a Royalist." He glanced unhappily to the younger man. "I am sorry, Nick, but no doubt you'll know that in the first war my father had helped as many Royalists as he could, and that your grandfather was hidden in the priest hole for almost a week, having escaped a group of Cromwell's Ironsides. I can remember the terror of waiting as they rampaged through the house looking for him, but fortunately for us all, they found nothing. After that date we came under such increasing suspicion that my father decided to block off the tunnel and shut up the priest hole. We set about it methodically, removing everything from the chamber which pertained to religion, and creating a fall in the tunnel. I was confident in my mind it had remained so until this week. That is why I was so angry with Bella. Obviously she being the younger by some years, cannot recall the terror we all went through."

"Well, sir, Bella only really knew about it because I told her. My grandfather told me all about it when I was a boy, but warned me never to speak of it. I knew how much your parents had assisted us at various times. I remember your mother's visits as a child and her kindness to me, which is why I hold her in such great affection. Her visits, especially when she brought Bella with her, stand out in my childhood. As we grew older we met up whilst out and about, and during one of these occasions I showed her the tunnel. We often explored it, playing games as children, then one winter day, on a rare visit to your house with my grandfather, we explored the other end and found the priest hole full of old furniture. We went down the stairs to the underground passage, and followed it until we came to the fall in the roof. It didn't take much digging to open it up again, for we reasoned once the King was returned there was no fear of Roundheads anymore."

Simon grimaced, "No, but by that time I had thrown in my lot with the Hollingsheads, and didn't want anything to spoil my relationship with them, or to make them think they had made a mistake in allowing Cathy to marry me."

"Indeed, who would want to offend his wife's family?" agreed Hal kindly. "But you are familiar with the arrangement of the priest hole, staircase and tunnel, I assume?"

"Yes," Simon pulled a wry face, "I went over the whole thing with my father, prior to sealing it all up; just to make sure there would be nothing for prying eyes to see. My error has been in imagining it would remain so."

Hal nodded, "I ask because I need you to understand what happened next. You will have guessed it was our method of return last evening. Your sister led us back though the tunnel, and up those tortuous stairs. The whole thing is an amazing construction, but she impressed upon us the need for silence as we went. Thus, at one point we had to remain still and silent for some minutes, as we could quite clearly hear voices from a chamber we were passing. Mistress Bella had gone on ahead, but Mistress Redcroft and I were trapped, separated only, I imagine, by the thin panelling of the chamber, where two people were quarrelling." He paused, glancing sharply to his host. "We heard Brendon and Pridow in conversation. Their words were low, sometimes annoyingly inaudible, other times when they grew angry, we heard them with utter clarity. They spoke about 'the damned wench who had overheard them earlier', and discussed how they were to get themselves out of the trouble they found themselves in!"

"Were they speaking of Bella?" Nick cried in dismay.

"No, Mistress Pauncey, I rather think," said Hal in soothing tones.

"Rosalind?" asked Simon quickly.

"I rather fear so," Hal nodded. "If she heard voices

as she passed on the stair, would she have stopped to listen, as we did?"

"Oh God, yes!" Nick cried, before Simon could even consider. "Listening behind doors and spying on servants was one of her favourite occupations! That's how she came to know about Bella and I—and she was forever repeating every bit of tittle-tattle. That is what made her so unpopular, so Bella said."

Hal looked grave. "Well, I rather suspect she overheard a piece of tittle-tattle, which she took back to the conspirators in an effort to persuade Mr Pridow to marry her, instead of your sister, Mr Craven."

"But did she really believe he would agree to this sort of deception?" Simon asked blankly. "Or that none of us would notice the substitution? She is a good half a head taller than Bella!"

"And at least twice as wide!" added Nick indignantly.

"I believe her powers of self-delusion had led her way beyond such petty details," said Hal thoughtfully. "You see, Bella had got herself a lover with all the attributes of romance. Her younger sister, Beatrice, had attracted the attention of a kinsman, who was impatient for them to be married, yet none thought to offer for Mistress Pauncey. She had before her the evidence of what happened to sharp-tongued spinsters, in the form of Mistress Louisa Pridow. I think she felt time was escaping from her. When she discovered Mistress Bella's plan, it must have been too great an opportunity to resist. That was compounded by her over-hearing Ezekiel Pridow and Jacob Brendon talking. I think she must have overheard something which she thought gave her the power she needed."

"What?" asked Nick blankly. "What could she have possibly overheard to make her think they would consent to such a charade?"

"We can never hope to know, but I surmise it must be something to do with you, Nick, for what else would bring two such unlikely characters together? Pridow likes to think of himself as the soul of rectitude, whereas Brendon is plainly a scamp of the highest order. What do men such as these have in common, Nick, but that one is stealing your land, and the other wants to marry your beloved?"

"Why?" Simon and Nick asked in unison.

Hal smiled. "Doesn't crabbed age always envy gilded youth?" he asked in reply. "What chance would a fellow like Pridow have of Mistress Bella, if Nick had still his land, and his home unencumbered by debt?"

"None!" agreed Simon instantly.

"No, none, and thus was formed an unholy alliance to cheat poor Nick out of almost everything," agreed Hal.

"An alliance I was fully prepared to endorse!" Simon said blankly. "Dear God, what have I been doing?"

"You have been blinded by constant care and anxiety," said Hal kindly. "Those of us, who come over young to responsibility, often make quite foolish errors. The only crime is in refusing to recognise them."

Simon met his eyes, and relaxed into a smile. "Sir Henry, meeting you has been a revelation for me. I do not know what to say. If another man had come to me with such a tale, I would have dismissed it out of hand, and in doing so would have felt mean and unreasonable. Yet you explain everything so clearly, and more importantly make no harsh judgement on my more crass errors!"

"Mr Craven, you give me hope that I have become a good Justice, not only because such judgements as I make are tempered with mercy, where ever possible, but because the errors I witness, I have often made myself. When I was first made Justice, at a foolishly young age, I was in the care of a wonderfully wise man, who taught me all I know about the sense which we call common. He insisted it should renamed rare sense, because as he used to say, so few people use it. It is, he said, the most important of all our senses. Justice is mostly a matter of interpretation, and he concluded that without that helping of "rare" sense, it could so easily become a mockery which brought both men and the law into disrepute."

Both young men nodded their understanding, looking thoughtful, and after a space Simon Craven said, "Indeed, Sir Henry, how right you both are—and I for one shall take great care to cultivate this 'rare' sense in all my dealings."

"Then I feel my time here will not have been wasted," replied Hal, "although I am still at a loss as to how we prove foul play with regard to Mistress Pauncey's death."

"Could we not call both Brendon and Pridow to account?" asked Simon Craven after a moment's thought. "After all, a goodly piece of this skulduggery has occurred under my roof. We should also investigate how it is Brendon holds deeds to Nick's land, for if he does they can only be falsified documents, in which case, Nick probably doesn't owe him a penny."

"No," said Nick quickly. "If my grandfather borrowed

against deeds, false or no, I must repay what is owed."

"Indeed you must, Nick," agreed Hal, as Simon looked surprised, then as he considered the words, pleased. "But not if the monies charged were exorbitant, as I suspect, or indeed extracted from your grandfather under duress. When I first arrived and heard about all that had gone on, it rang a bell with something else my brother-in-law is looking into for me. There has not yet been time for a reply, but it could well be this is another of the abuses we have uncovered with regard to the Court of Sequestrations."

"That is a name to strike fear into the heart of many a man," said Simon Craven. "What do you suspect, Sir Henry?"

"Ambrose and I appear to have uncovered considerable discrepancies, not just in our own area, but in others, too. Ambrose has noted it was not uncommon that many of these local men of law were given tacit 'permission' to 'bleed' certain 'Malignants' of their livelihood in order to pay these unscrupulous men."

"My grandfather was accused of Malignancy," cried Nick at once. 'A persistent disregard for the newly formed government of the Realm and Commonwealth of England' is what they said!"

Hal laughed bitterly. "Indeed, Nick, my father was also accused. We were more fortunate in that my Uncle Henry remained in England after he was wounded, and paid fine after fine. It became a source of rancour between him and my father, but by dint of great economy, he managed to conserve most of his land, and provide a home for my brother and sisters. He also, by great shift, found the money to purchase the ruin which was my father's home, but was unable to restore it. That took my brother Ned and I several years, and a good proportion of my wife's dowry to restore it fully. The point is, Nick, was the land sequestered, or sold to pay the fines imposed by the Commonwealth? These documents suggest some shady goings on."

"I agree," said Simon, decisively. "There is more to this, I think. We should call a meeting of everyone to discuss what exactly did go on. If Nick and his grandfather were cheated..." Hal hesitated and suddenly asked, "Was your grandfather the scoundrel and rake they claim, Nick?"

"My grandfather?" Nick chuckled. "I cannot judge, nor deny he liked a pretty face, yet he talked with great affection of a lady in the Low Countries, who was a long-time companion of his. He said he'd been hoping to bring her back home with him and marry her, but that she died of a fever the summer before the King returned. I cannot say that I know it was not something we discussed. He was rather a handsome man, so it's possible, I suppose."

Hal smiled ruefully, "A well-looking man can suffer from rumours equally with a pretty woman, Nick, so you'd best beware."

Simon grunted as Nick laughed. "I begin to think I've been totally blinded by a clever smoke screen. Sir Henry, if invited, would you consider holding an inquiry into Mistress Pauncey's death?"

"I could only do so informally, Mr Craven. I must have great care not to step on the toes of the Crowner—and we should also pause, and take thought. Often one can find out things which will leave you less comfortable when seeking the truth."

Nick and Simon exchanged a look, then as Nick gave a nod, they said in unison. "Come what may, we'll have the truth."

"You are sure?" Hal asked doubtfully.

"Yes, but perhaps a little later if you please," said Nick. "It will give me time to seek the assistance of one who may be able to clarify certain matters." ⚜

Chapter Twenty

It was not half an hour later that Hal, having drunk a toast with his host and the jubilant Nick Revesby, went to his chamber to find his ever-increasing bundle of notes, they would be put into some order if he was to ask questions of people. He picked up the papers and ran into Sophie as he returned along the corridor. His eyes lit up at the sight of her, then a gloom descended as he recollected how he never seemed to get any further forward in understanding her. Irritation, born of fatigue followed, as he paused to say, "Sophie, will you do me a service?"

Sophie smiled. "But of course I will, Hal, I am yours, as ever to command!"

"Except into marriage?" The words came before he could prevent himself, and cursing inwardly he hurried on, "I find I am nearing the end of my time here. There is talk of holding an informal enquiry into Rosalind

Pauncey's death, since the coroner and his man seem stricken with the ague, or are using it as an excuse not to deal with the matter. Should this be the case, I might in my official capacity, be called upon to summon the sheriff, and detain members of this household. Should this occur, and it appears to be increasingly likely, I would like Aunt Kate to be taken from here as soon as possible."

Sophie, who had gone pale at his opening words, raised her brows in quick comprehension. "Yes, I understand. Have you thought out a reason for an abrupt departure?"

"No, I have only just seen it may be necessary in the course of justice, to distress further one who is very dear to me. There is no help for it, but it did occur to me that nothing would appear more normal to these people than that we should quarrel—as we invariably do—then you and she could flee to Cordelia's home." He spoke lightly, but his voice held more than a tinge of bitterness.

"Yes," she agreed quietly. "That would strike them all as a very likely tale. I would think almost all of them would be happy to believe such a thing. Will you send me word when it is to happen? Or will you suddenly pick a quarrel before everyone, as usual, to make it more believable?"

"Naturally I would prefer to send you word and save myself the shame of further exposing my feelings before all," he replied, and the bitterness was very strong in his voice now, as he half-turned away.

"Then shall we leave it so? Unless, of course, I inadvertently irk you, and the plan happens as it usually does, with you holding me at fault for all that has occurred?" Her enquiry was cold enough, in her distress, to make him turn back.

"Did I hold you to blame for all the deaths at Harcourt Hall?" he cried, rare anger in his voice. "Did I ever level one word of accusation at you? No, I was too terrified to do so, lest they settled upon you as the murderer! Did I desert you? No, I remained in that God forsaken house to ensure your safety, and you rewarded me by making me look a fool before everyone, including my own kin, and then, finally after all that, you declined my offer of marriage!"

"Is this the quarrel, or just yet another lecture?" snapped Sophie as resentment flooded her face with colour. "God, how I long to be free of your eternal censure! Is it any wonder I refuse your offers of marriage, when they are couched with such loving respect?"

They stood glaring at each other in fury, oblivious as

the doors opened all along the gallery in response to the raised voices. Then as Hal realised they were being observed, he bowed curtly and turned away, walking off.

"Oh, Sophie!" Aunt Kate came quickly to her, as she too turned away, tears spilling from her eyes. Her arm came about the younger woman's waist and she compelled her to walk into the sanctuary of her chamber. "Sophie, Sophie, what have you quarrelled with Hal about now?"

For a few moments Sophie sobbed on the shoulder of the older woman, as if her heart was breaking, then, finally regaining the use of her voice, she took the handkerchief Aunt Kate pressed upon her, and wiped her swollen eyes. "I never realised he was so bitter and angry," she said. "Oh, it hurts me so to see him thus!"

"That's because you love him so deeply, silly." Kate could not but smile, although her face was anxious. "Do you not see, if you quarrel with Jack Hollingshead, or Margery or Adam, you may be a little sorry, but you don't truly care, but to hurt the one you love is to inflict pain upon yourself."

"I don't seem to be able to find a way of not doing it," said Sophie tearfully. "Every meeting between us turns bad. I so wanted to help him, to make up in some way for all the trouble I caused him. Why I had just…" Sophie stopped realising she was not sure how much the older woman knew of what was going on. "Oh, what is the use?" she asked in a petulant manner, turning aside. "We may indeed have deep feelings for each other, but we plainly do not suit, and the truth is I am better off away from Hal! Aunt Kate, I am minded to return to Cordelia within a day or two, won't you come with me? Hal will be here another week at this rate, and as you are going on to Tom Kingscott's home, won't you stop for a few days with Cordelia and Adam to reassure their fears with regard to their baby?"

"Well, yes indeed, Sophie. Hal said we could break the journey for a few days at Cordelia's home," said Aunt Kate, a little surprised at her sudden change of subject. "You know I am anxious to see she is well and happy. I worry so much about her, so far away from all those she knows, but my dear, that is all settled. The matter of you and Hal is not. To say you are not suited is nonsense. It is plain to all you are very well suited indeed, and that he loves you with all his heart." She sighed and shook her head a little, "His poor wife Libby, for all that she worshipped him, he never gave her a second glance, you know. Oh, he was kind to her; it is not in his nature to be anything other. He was patient and affectionate, much as he is with all his family, but I have honestly seen him more distressed over the fate of his dog. To him, Libby was like one of his sisters. Someone to be nurtured and made safe, but his emotions were never greatly stirred. I remember saying about it once to Margery, for he had a way of smoothing things over. In her wisdom Margery said she feared if Hal ever did feel great love, he would be consumed by it."

"Is that why Margery is still so angry with me?" asked Sophie dully, still much upset by the bitterness of the quarrel.

"I suppose it is," replied Aunt Kate thoughtfully. "He has become like a son to us both, you know. I suppose we women must have something to love. One day you'll come to understand how much the happiness of those you love is important to you."

"I do now, ma'am," she replied with a sniff. "I wish with all my heart Hal could be happy."

"Then why did you refuse his offer of marriage?" Kate asked sharply. "Having pursued him so single-mindedly for such a long time, why did you refuse him when he asked you to be his wife?"

Sophie wept again for a few seconds. "Don't you see,

ma'am, that was all part of it? Pursued him so single-mindedly that I became known as a byword for un-maidenly conduct! He felt I made us an object of yet more gossip, and forced him into offering his hand to me. He said—he said—"

"Hush, hush now," Kate came to hold her again and pat her back, as she sobbed out her pain and confusion. "What did he say? He does have a sharp tongue when he is angered, I'll admit."

"He said he was relieved to be rid of me into marriage to Gervase Harcourt," she whispered. "That at last he might be free of my tantrums and fusses!"

Aunt Kate allowed herself a half smile as she sighed. "Yes, that does sound like a man driven to the end of his tether," she agreed.

❧

Hal, once he had managed to calm his annoyance, was cheated of his chance to organise his papers, for no sooner had he begun to sort them into piles, than Jack Hollingshead appeared to tell him that the Coroner had reluctantly dragged himself from his sick bed to attend to his duty, and required the assistance of any with information.

"This is some progress then," said Hal carefully, putting the relevant stacks of paper away inside his book. "Perhaps if this fellow is competent we can turn the whole affair over to him," he added.

Jack's face mirrored his thoughts. "Simon's lack of enthusiasm says it all, I would say!" he replied diffidently.

Hal glanced up quickly, thinking how much his companion had improved lately. Now that Cordelia was married, the antagonism between them had disappeared almost completely, and he had plainly made strenuous efforts not to fall out with Sophie. "He doesn't fill one with confidence?," he asked, with a sigh.

Jack grinned. "I have never met the man before," he admitted, "and I understand he has the ague, but I'd sooner set my dog onto the problem, than this fellow."

Hal's heart sank, and any hopes that he could make a swift departure with it. Even as he acknowledged it, he knew he had to remain and sort out this affair not only with regard to Rosalind Pauncey, but also the matter of himself and Sophie. It could go on no longer. The six months separation which he had confidently assumed would give Sophie's volatile emotions time to either settle or find another outlet hadn't worked. Not for either of them. He'd known it the moment he'd set

eyes on her at Bickmarsh Hall, and he'd guessed with
the sixth sense of lovers that she felt the same. From
the joy of once again being in the company of one with
whom he felt at total accord, to the bliss of holding her
in his arms as he had in the stairway, he could no longer
deny either of them the happiness of a future together.

Yet he had backed away more than once from the
prospect and in doing so robbed Sophie of that instinctive trust which is the hallmark of true love. He felt
small and demeaned, yet knew his own behaviour was
to blame. The fear of being rejected by her again, of
enduring a repeat of the humiliation he suffered at her
hands not six months ago, was still in him. He must
plan this with care, but first things first, business before
pleasure as he'd told Nick.

He followed Jack from the chamber back to Simon's
book-room to be presented to one of the worst speci-
mens of a band of officials he had come to admire. Whilst
he could agree with Jack that the man was in the grip
of a particularly unpleasant form of ague, he could not
but feel that the coughing, sniffing and groaning which
accompanied the interview, were all more designed to
make them aware how inconvenient the whole affair
was to him, and how unreasonable the general public at

large, and the people at Haceby Hall in particular, were to expect so much of him.

The result was inevitable. The inquest was delayed until the health of the Coroner was improved and the body was released for burial, to ease the suffering of the family of the deceased. With that ruling they had to be satisfied.

"Well, I have to say," said Simon after the man had been escorted away and they sat back to consider, "that I am positively ashamed of these proceedings."

"Indeed," said Jack Hollingshead, looking disgusted. "The fellow is a fool; I can't believe he is talking of bringing in death by misadventure!"

Hal sighed accepting the goblet of wine Simon offered. "He reasoned it soundly enough," he said.

"He reasoned it around the house and back again," said Jack bluntly.

"I must admit it smacked of sophistry to me," agreed Hal.

"Presumably pressure has been brought to bear upon him," said Simon dispassionately. "Both Pridow and Brendon have friends in high places."

"Do they?" Hal asked in some surprise.

"Not a great deal has changed in this part of the

world," said Simon, having taken a sip of his drink. "True, the King sits upon the throne again, but locally those who were for Parliament are still very much in control. This has ever been a radical thinking area, and resentment at what many saw as a freer England in the form of the Commonwealth being destroyed, has meant that any changes have been slow and reluctant. Sir Harold Ainsworthy is a dyed-in-the-wool Parliamentarian even now, and he blocks any change."

"Yes, I have heard of him," said Hal thoughtfully. "I have heard it said he opposes any moves to install any he thinks might be King's men, but his tenure cannot be indefinite."

"He certainly is of a good age," agreed Jack, "but he has picked men of his own inclination these last ten years. All the local Justices are of his ilk."

"Time is ripe for a change then, and I can think of two men who would make excellent Justices."

"Do you mean Jack and I?" Simon asked in surprise. "Are we not rather young? I thought it was a position for a man of mature years."

"The main requirement is wisdom," replied Hal. "Age nor condition admits that as a right. Nor is it achieved easily. I was younger even than you, Jack, having barely attained my majority, when I took over from my uncle on the Bench, who as you know had been murdered. My guardian was also the Justice, and he thought it right for me to assume all the responsibilities of my uncle's position. The King favours younger, perhaps more loyal men, too."

"Well, I am happy to do any duty, if called," said Simon. "Especially if it gives us influence over the positions of lesser officials, so that we can see fairness for all."

Hal nodded, "And on the credit side of this affair, Mr Craven, if the inquest is delayed, fewer people will know of your sister's escapade, and that must be for the best."

"Indeed," said Simon with feeling. "Yes, there is nothing quicker forgotten than a nine day wonder. So all in all, it is settling down a little. My Aunt Pauncey speaks of leaving soon, to take poor Rosalind home for burial. I shall of course accompany her and her daughters."

"Is her home a great distance away?" Hal asked thoughtfully.

"Fifteen miles or so. My mother is most anxious for me to accompany them, indeed I would not wish to show my aunt any discourtesy, and I suppose now that

Bella is safely back at home, I am at liberty to do so."

"If it would aid you in any way I'd be happy to undertake such a duty, Craven," said Jack diffidently. "I am not sure that I could provide the support you would, but I can engage to escort them safely back home."

Simon smiled a little. "That is a very kind suggestion, Jack," he replied, "but I really couldn't ask you to escort half a dozen weeping females and a corpse across the county. They are my kin, and as the only male in the family, it is my duty. If only we didn't have this trouble here, there would be no difficulty."

"Perhaps we should revert to our original plan?" Hal suggested, as a silence fell. "I do not think our friend the Coroner would object more than for form's sake, if we were to present him with a tidy solution to his problem."

"You mean do it for him?" Jack asked, a shade indignantly.

"Well, it could be argued that if he is too ill to attend his duty, we are within our rights to call an informal meeting, to establish certain facts and put paid to unpleasant rumours," suggested Hal. "Your aunt could hardly be expected to leave her bed today, when she is in such deep distress. Can you not persuade your mother to keep her sister and nieces here another day? After all, it can hardly make any difference to poor Mistress Rosalind anymore."

Simon's eyes brightened. "I am in favour of that plan," he said at once. "I have the feeling that if we allow these fellows to disperse, that will be an end to it all. The truth will be hidden, and they will escape justice in one form or another."

"Few ever escape justice entirely, I notice, but it the interests of not only having justice done, but being seen to be done, I think we should proceed with an informal enquiry into what has occurred here, and ask all to account for their movements and behaviour. After all, if there is nothing to fear, there is nothing to conceal."

"Indeed," said Jack, with enthusiasm.

It was agreed between them, as they finished their glass of wine, to do exactly that, and they dispersed to make arrangements for the proceedings.

"Sir Richard! Sir, a word, if you please," called Hal as he caught a glimpse of the man in the long corridor as the gloom of the afternoon progressed. Indeed Hal had the impression Sir Richard had dodged back from view, on catching sight of him. He made a note to warn Sophie and his aunt.

"Sir Henry?" he bowed warily but didn't advance, so that Hal was forced to walk to him.

"I have been anxious to have some discussion with you since I arrived," said Hal as he smiled pleasantly, trying to keep his instinctive feeling that the man was avoiding him under control. "We both have the best interests of my aunt close to our hearts, I am sure."

The man sighed heavily. "Katherine is a good woman," he agreed, reluctantly.

"Aunt Kate is an excellent woman, greatly beloved by all who know her," said Hal, rather irked by his lacklustre response. "To know her is to admire her. I do not know what I—and my brother and sisters—would have done without her love and attention."

"Katherine spares herself so little," he replied. "I have remarked upon it often, indeed occasionally to the detriment of her devotions, I am grieved to note."

"I am sure the Lord sees her good works and counts them as devotions," said Hal, his hackles rising further.

"I would not presume to comment," he replied coldly. "I only know that there is little more powerful than constant prayer."

Hal repressed a sigh. He felt the man was eluding him still, hiding his faults under an air of sanctity. "Sir

Richard, it is essential we have some discussion over certain rumours which have come to my ears. That and the situation we find ourselves in here, mean…"

He broke off as open fear showed in the other man's face. "It is not possible," Sir Richard stammered quickly. "I know nothing of the situation here, or of rumours. I have been ill, I tell you. I have been in a fever. I understand little of what has occurred."

"You do not strike me as a fool…" began Hal, as another door opened and voices were heard on the stairs.

"I am ill!" Sir Richard cried, glancing about him as if looking for an escape. "I cannot be tormented in this manner! You will excuse me, Sir Henry, I am waited for!"

Without giving the astonished Hal a moment to protest, he pushed past him and clattered down the stairs almost thrusting aside Louisa Pridow, who was coming up in company with the Pauncey sisters.

⚜

Chapter Twenty One

The progress they appeared to be making much improved Hal's mood, so when a tap sounded on the door of his chamber he went to answer half-hoping it might be Sophie. He opened it to see Simon Craven standing there.

"Sir Henry, I spent some time with Bella last night and we now have a better understanding than we have had since she was a little girl. So I have come to thank you for all you have done for us."

"I did no more than listen to her and young Nick Revesby," he replied. "I must confess I have taken both of them to my heart, and would see them happy if it were possible, but at least we got Bella back home, and gained her some time to come to a decision about her future."

"Yes, that is not a matter for this evening," he said, "but I do think we need to make some progress with regard to the matter of my Cousin Rosalind's death."

"You think the coroner will prove ineffectual?" Hal asked bluntly.

"We know the man is a fool, in the pay of those who seem to control the law in this part of the world." Simon replied with equal bluntness. "I think, as was suggested earlier, we should make the excuse of the man's ill health, to hold our own enquiry so we can present him with a neat solution he can't dispute.

"I like the idea, but cannot vouch for it being a success," said Hal doubtfully. "Recollect we have no jurisdiction, no power to get anyone to answer questions they don't want to."

"But we do have the power of public opinion," said Simon eagerly. "If any should refuse to answer any question, it will soon be common currency, and the talk of Market Day."

Hal nodded, "True, there is that power, but do remember it works both ways, you'll not want to see your sister the subject of common gossip, too. And if we can't prove these men guilty, they may well take that revenge."

"They may well do it anyway," replied Simon grimly. "If it is going to happen, let it be as a result of our calling them to account, not as vindictiveness."

This agreed between them, Hal returned to making his preparations. Word soon got round that something was afoot and Sophie hurried to support Aunt Kate.

"Have you heard Aunt Kate? Simon, Mr Craven, is to call a meeting after all," Sophie called as she entered Aunt Kate's chamber, only to find her in tears. "Oh, ma'am, what is amiss? I am so sorry to intrude upon you."

"Thank you, dear, yes, Hal came to warn me that most likely everything would come out—and you could never intrude upon me," she replied, hastily wiping away a few tears and summoning a watery smile.

"Is something amiss, ma'am?" Sophie asked, clasping her hand in sympathy.

"Only my foolishness," she replied, with a small sigh. "Hal was concerned that in the course of establishing what has happened to poor Rosalind Pauncey, my feelings might be hurt."

Sophie frowned. "How is this? I thought Hal had determined to get you away from here before all this came out."

"Had he?" she asked in surprise.

"Well, he asked me to go with you to Cordelia's home to await him, but that was before we quarrelled, so he probably thought I wasn't to be trusted—oh, no matter!" Sophie shook her head, looking far from happy. "Did he mention why you might be hurt, Aunt Kate?"

"Yes, he did. He is reluctant to talk of it, but he seems to fear Sir Richard is not the honourable man I believed him to be," replied Kate. "Oh, Sophie, I still can't believe he could be so very dreadful as to cheat all his people. All those poor souls, the settlers, cheated out of money, especially money intended for church furnishings and schoolbooks!"

"It does sound quite dreadful," agreed Sophie, "but we don't know the circumstances, Aunt Kate. I am so sorry, you must be feeling so confused. You admired him so."

"Yes, I am most terribly disappointed—but in a way, rather relieved, too." She sighed heavily, and more tears welled up, "Oh, Sophie, I am so wicked, for it is my vanity which irked. I am going to look such a fool before everyone!"

"You could never look that ma'am," said Sophie, patting her shoulder in comfort. "You always look so calm and dignified when confronted by trouble. Rather like an outraged kitten, as Hal once phrased it, when I'd made both you and Aunt Margery cross on one occasion." A smile flitted across Sophie's face at the recollection. "Aunt Margery, he said, was roaring like a lion at my iniquity, but you sat with your paws tucked in, and a surprised frown on your face, just like an outraged kitten!"

"Oh dear!" Kate laughed and cried at the same time. "Yes, how acute an observer Hal is. That is exactly so. Margery is a lion, and I am an old tabby-cat."

"A very pretty tabby kitten, Hal was firm about that," said Sophie. "Come, ma'am, tidy your hair, and we'll go down together. Recollect, you are the one who has been slighted. You need not say a word. Merely look saddened and pensive."

"Yes, perhaps we can get a place by the fire and I can look into the flames with that wise expression my poor Tabitha used to have, and none will think the worse of me."

"You shall have another cat when we return to Westwood," Sophie soothed, settling the lace collar about her neck.

"Margery doesn't care for cats," sighed Kate. "Even she hasn't had a dog since poor Worsley was killed by Ned's hounds."

"Just because Aunt Margery doesn't have a dog, and doesn't care for cats, doesn't mean you cannot have one," said Sophie gently. "Hal would want you to have any animal you chose, I am sure."

"Yes, he is a good boy—man," she agreed, with another sigh, "but as I was to be married too—and Richard said there is no place for a beast that doesn't earn its keep in the settlement—I decided it would be better not to have one." A sudden smile lit her face, driving away her haggard frown. "When 'we' return to Westwood?" she repeated.

Sophie looked stricken. "I meant when you and Hal, return to Westwood, of course," she said quickly.

"Sophie, what has gone amiss between you and Hal? I see him talk of you with such a lost, desolate look in his eyes. I hear you talk of the future, and Westwood and Hal are there in your mind. You simply belong together. You both will be miserable apart."

Sophie's mouth went suddenly awry, and tears glistened in her eyes. "I cannot deny what you say is true, ma'am, but we would be equally miserable together. Hal will never see me anything but a nuisance. The woman who chased after him until he felt he was an object of derision. You know how proud he is. He would hate all the comments which would be made if we were to be married. How I finally caught him with my wiles and my money, how he was obliged to marry me because my reputation became so tarnished no other man would."

"Such foolishness and nonsense!" Aunt Kate declared sharply. "If Hal has learned anything, it is that there will always be gossip. People invent it if it isn't there. You are both being very silly. He won't ask you to marry again for fear you'll reject him again, and you won't encourage him because you think he doesn't value you! Tell me, Sophie, what did Hal do when he found young Bella and stopped Simon Craven from challenging Nicholas Revesby to a duel?"

Sophie shook her head. "I don't know. I wasn't there," she replied.

"Neither was I, but Simon Craven came back in a pretty temper, saying Hal wanted you at Weston Revesby, didn't he?"

"No, that was Jack Hollingshead." she replied, as she understood. "But Simon Craven was in a rage, wasn't he? I heard him as I arrived, but he wasn't angry with anyone, not Hal, or even Bella and Nick."

"He was angry with himself," agreed Aunt Kate, "but you are missing my point. Hal found himself in a dilemma, so what did he do? He sent for the one person he knew would come immediately, not raise a silly fuss whatever situation you found, and who would work with him, without question, to resolve the problem."

Sophie nodded her head. "Yes, yes, he knew that I would do that."

"So, don't you see, child, you are both so very close, that you understand without question each other's motives. You didn't bother him by asking what had gone on, as Jack Hollingshead would have done. You weren't shocked as I would have been. You took your cue from Hal and helped him unravel the tangle those silly children had got themselves into. Yet you don't seem to be able to unravel your own tangle!"

"The knots are pulled too tight, Aunt Kate," Sophie replied, her voice almost a whisper. "They cannot be unravelled so easily without a great deal of pain, and yet more suffering. It were better they were cut, and we both went free."

"Well, if that is truly how you feel, I don't wonder Hal despairs," said Kate sharply. "Who are you to turn aside because the road looks rocky ahead? Pain and suffering? I have never heard such nonsense, Sophie! There is no pain like having lost a loved one to the grave. You know nothing of suffering until you look ahead to endless, empty years. There is no romance in a lost love,

Sophie, just the dull misery you endure today and will for the rest of your life. You have the power to change that. What if the knots of your love are pulled tight? You are young and strong. You'll have to work on loosening them, so that they don't chafe—but don't, don't cast them off, or you'll never know a day's contentment!"

Sophie, who had listened to this impassioned speech in amazement, bit her lip to hide a smile, for Hal was right, Aunt Kate was like an outraged kitten. Love filled her heart for this kindly woman, who had done her best to help her these past few years. She bent and kissed her faded cheek.

"I beg pardon, ma'am," she said, her voice choked with tears. "I am sorry to have put you to so much trouble, and I thank you with all my heart for your kindness and sense. I will try to do as you say, I promise you."

"Good!" Kate nodded her head in a satisfied manner. "This has all been rather a shock to me, Sophie, but it has shown me that I must speak up more often. I am too reluctant to speak out, and always think others have a better grasp of the situation than I. So often I defer to Margery or Hal, but in future I shall say my piece. Now, if you truly mean what you say, you will assist me in persuading Cordelia and Adam to return with us to

Westwood, too," she replied. "In fact, we can all travel back together, after Hal and I have visited Cousin Tom and his new wife."

"Cordelia and Adam come back to Westwood?" Sophie repeated blankly, "Cordelia is to have a child, ma'am, and Adam has the land to attend to."

"He must have a man he can trust, or he can get Jack Hollingshead to attend to things for him," replied Kate firmly. "Cordelia cannot have her child miles from anybody she knows. The pair of them are so very miserable here anyway, it will be better for all, if they sell the place back to Jack, and return to Old Manor Farm."

"Oh, Aunt Kate, wouldn't it be wonderful?" Sophie cried. "I do so hate to think of Cordelia alone up here. They've not been well received, you know."

"Two lone children of Royalists in Puritan East England, I am not surprised, neither of them have any roots here. I'll talk to Madeleine Hollingshead about it all, and see what can be contrived, but not until after this meeting is over." said Aunt Kate, with a sigh.

"Yes, we'd best present ourselves, ma'am," Sophie agreed. "There will be enough showing reluctance to attend, muttering that Hal has no jurisdiction. He doesn't need us to be laggards, too."

"Indeed, no, that would never do," agreed Kate gathering up her sewing hastily.

In the event, they were amongst the first to take their places in the vast hall, earning a nod of approval from Hal, who was deep in conversation with Simon Craven. Kate was able to establish herself close enough to the fire to be able to set some further stitches on the baby clothes she was sewing for Cordelia's expected child before dusk fell, and the attention required kept her anxiety under control.

Sophie sat at her side, pondering on what she had said, and earning another nod of approbation from Hal when she resisted all Sir Richard's efforts to gain access to his betrothed on his belated arrival.

"Well," said Simon Craven uneasily, as Jacob Brendon and Ezekiel Pridow hesitated in the doorway behind Louisa. "Thank you all for assembling like this. Jack, can you make space for Mr Pridow and Mr Brendon? Ah, excellent, thank you. Helen, are you sure you'll be comfortable on that stool? Now, gentlemen, Mistress Hollingshead will be more than happy to accommodate you on the settle with her, and Jack, take this joint stool so you can sit alongside. Yes, that is just right. Now, Sir Henry Westwood is known to us all by now, and he has kindly agreed—as the Coroner, poor fellow, is still suffering with his ague—to hold an enquiry into the circumstances of young Rosalind's death. Just so that we can all be easy in our minds as to exactly what did happen. However, Sir Henry wishes to make in very clear there is no compulsion for any of us to speak, if we don't wish to." Simon smiled brightly on them all and indicated Hal.

"Good afternoon, friends," said Hal promptly, before any could raise an objection. "I'd like to add my own words to Mr Craven's. This is a purely informal gathering, not a court of law, but much more like the meetings our ancestors would have been used to, when long ago, they would gather to discuss an event which had occurred. In effect it is the very root of our trial by jury system, where available evidence is presented by all concerned, and the facts, rather than being whispered about and distorted, are brought forth into the clear light of day."

Hal paused, scanning the various faces, noting that already some were ill at ease. "In my experience, very often people will not tell the truth for a variety of reasons," he continued. "The biggest barrier to clarity is often embarrassment. How often our petty foibles catch

us out. Those small uncharitable actions we are all privy
to at times. A disinclination to take trouble for another,
when we are weary at the end of a long day. A feeling
of resentment over a slight, often unconsciously given.
We all have some meannesses within us, and are usually
deeply ashamed of them and would hide them, if we
can, from our neighbours. On this occasion, I would
beg you will not. I cannot say your neighbours will not
judge you, none of us are perfect, and that must be our
guiding light. None of us are without sin, and all of us
can only judge with that guiding knowledge."

"Oh, well said, Sir Henry," cried Mistress Hollingshead as she turned to her audience. "Most of you will
know Sir Henry and I were out of charity with each other." she explained. "We had been negotiating a match
between Jack here and Sir Henry's ward, which came to
nothing, and I will admit freely I held him to blame for
it, and so was piqued with him."

"And with me too, ma'am," said Sophie quickly, "for
I, not Sir Henry, was the one who assisted Cordelia in
her elopement with the man she loved."

Madeleine Hollingshead's steely eyes fixed for a few
seconds on Sophie's lovely face, and then she nodded.
"Yes, Mistress Redcroft, you are right. I blamed Sir

Henry for your behaviour, when in truth Jack and I were more concerned by our desire to retain the land we'd spent many years restoring, than any true desire for our kinswoman's happiness."

"Not an unreasonable desire, surely?" Ezekiel Pridow remarked. "Everyone knows how much money Jack, and his father before him, had spent on that land. Why should he be dispossessed, by an unknown daughter of a man many held to be a traitor?"

"Because the law, Mr Pridow, in the form of the Act of Settlement, says the heirs of Basil Sandys own the estate, and Mistress Sandys had the proof required to support her claim. Neither Mistress Hollingshead nor Jack wished to dispute the law, however unfair they might have felt it."

"In his favour, I have to say that Adam Blackwell, my cousin Cordelia's husband has offered to repay much of what we paid out on the property," Jack Hollingshead added woodenly.

"So you see, by establishing the truth of what has occurred, however uncomfortable it may be to our particular feelings, we all at large come to understand how misunderstandings occur, and how they can, with good will on all sides, be resolved," said Hal smoothly.

"By discussion and openness, we can reach a resolution which possibly is not perfect, but perhaps all can agree is fair."

"How fair is it for Jack Hollingshead?" Jacob Brendon asked nastily. "He has lost not only the land he worked for many years, but his bride, because of your inability to control an interfering wench."

"The other rule it is essential we adhere to, of course, is to mind our manners," remarked Hal mildly, as Sophie threw the man a look of contempt.

"Exactly!" said Jack sharply. "As the one deemed to have been slighted, I object to Mistress Redcroft being addressed in such a manner. I would think it beneath me to do so, and I have greater cause. As Sir Henry pointed out to me at the time, land is just that, but domestic harmony is priceless."

"Well, to move on to our present problem," said Hal hastily. "We come to the needless death of Mistress Rosalind Pauncey. This seems to have occurred because of the proposed match between Mr Pridow and Bella Craven. We are not here to discuss the wisdom of such a match in the light of our discussion, and Jack's excellent reminder of how important hearth and home are to us all. As I understand the matter, Bella, being both young and inexperienced was guided by her mother and brother, away from her natural inclinations, toward a marriage which on the face of it promised a steadier, more solid future. Bella, uncertain, and only partially convinced by her elders, soon confided her misgivings to Rosalind, her former companion. And as the time for the marriage loomed ever closer, they hatched a foolish plot to rescue Bella from the match she had given her consent to."

Bella, red-faced at this open discussion of her affairs, hung her head in shame. "I am so very sorry," she said quietly. "I would that I had the courage to have acted honestly." She turned to Ezekiel Pridow, tears in her eyes, her hand half extended. "Believe me, I am very sorry, sir, that my behaviour has been so ill. I must tell you to your face, before these witnesses, that I cannot marry you."

Never had she appeared to more advantage, the picture of shy supplication, but Ezekiel Pridow was however, offended. "I am greatly shocked," he cried, in harsh tones. "I would not have thought it in your power to dismiss me so, like a servant, without your brother's consent!"

"Which she has, sir," said Simon sharply, turning to smile encouragingly at his sister. "Well done, Bella that took courage."

"How is this?" Pridow cried, getting very angry. "It was my understanding that we had an agreement, Craven. I have spent a good deal of time and money on preparations for this wedding! I have already told you I am generously prepared to overlook your sister's disgraceful behaviour, and even wait until you are out of mourning for your cousin. I see no need for my suit to be dismissed on the whim of a girl not properly left the schoolroom!"

As Sophie's eyes flashed and her mouth dropped open in astonishment, Hal fixed her with a look, which allowed Simon Craven the opportunity to reply

"I am very sorry, Mr Pridow, that you feel as you do," he replied, in measured tones, "but you seem to have forgotten in all this, that the consent of my sister is a legal requirement. My position as her guardian is but to protect and guide her, and in that capacity, might I advise you to moderate both your tongue and tone with regard to her. Bella has told you honestly, and to your face, before witnesses, she will not marry you. As her guardian, I stand willing to reimburse you for any unnecessary expenses you feel you may have laid out in your preparations. And with that assurance, I feel certain the matter may now be considered closed."

Hal hid a grin as Ezekiel Pridow, red-faced with fury, stuttered and gobbled over a reply, finally crying furiously, "I am not obliged to endure such insults at your hands! I tell you, Craven, you'll live to regret this day!"

"No, sit down, Mr Brendon, and you, too, Mr Pridow," said Hal, keeping his voice even, as both men got to their feet angrily. "Recollect we are gathered here to discuss the death of Rosalind Pauncey. I do believe you both may have information which will be of interest to us all."

Both men stopped dead in their tracks, and at this opportune moment, Nick Revesby suddenly appeared in one doorway, and an older man, entered from another, effectively blocking their exits.

"Ah, Nick, welcome to both you and your companion," said Hal smoothly. "You arrive in good time."

"Good-day, Sir Henry, Mr Craven, ladies and gentlemen," said Nick politely. "Allow me to introduce my companion, Mr Jem Attwood."

❧

Chapter Twenty Two

Amid the surprised looks and murmur of greetings, Hal noticed the pale face of Jacob Brendon, and a puzzled look passed between Ezekiel Pridow and Sir Richard Harrison.

"Mr Revesby has come to transact some business with Mr Brendon, which he requires us to witness, but he will, I know, not mind delaying it a little, as we continue our enquiry into Mistress Rosalind Pauncey's death." Simon explained, as everyone looked a little mystified.

"He may indeed be an important witness," suggested Ezekiel Pridow, his face suddenly pale. "Wasn't his company the destination of Mistress Arabella and her companion?"

"It was most certainly mine," said Bella sharply, "but Rosalind did not travel through the underground passage with me. She went back up the secret stair."

Again there was a buzz of murmurs, quickly hushed. "Yes," said Hal, "it is this stair we would like to discuss. Mistress Redcroft and I followed Mistress Bella back through it last night. It was an amazing progress, and Mistress Bella, being well used to it went ahead. Mistress Redcroft and I, being novices, hesitated and looked about us."

"For rats mostly!" Sophie confided, with an eloquent shudder, which helped to ease the tension a little.

Hal continued, "It was Mistress Redcroft's predilection to squeak at the sight of a mouse, which brought us to a halt, because I had caught the sound of raised voices." He paused glancing about him. "We are all connected here. What is said need go no further. I imagine some of you are familiar with the priest hole and secret passage leading from the wood into this house? I have seen others in the past, and this one, like them, winds its way around one of the chimneys which goes up through the house, until it comes out to a concealed chamber in the roof. Of a consequence, in the course of our journey we passed many and various chambers. Some had thick stone walls, which concealed the sound of our footsteps, so we need have no fear of being heard. Others appeared to have but the thinest piece of panelling between us and the occupants. It was the sound of raised voices from one such chamber, which gave us pause, for we reasoned if we could hear them, then they surely would hear us. So, as we stood, frozen in panic, we inadvertently heard a conversation not intended for our ears. It was however, of such import, that on arrival at our destination, I asked Mistress Redcroft to write down her recollection of what she heard, and I separately wrote my own. I have these depositions here." Dramatically Hal took two sealed documents from the cuff of his sleeve.

The chamber was now so quiet, that if a mouse had dared to squeak, all would have heard it clearly as Hal continued, "I later got Mr Craven to witness the sealing of these testimonies, so there could be no dispute as to their authenticity. He has sealed them for me and I have brought them hence. Anyone who wishes to see them may freely do so, when we have finished here. In the meantime, Sophie—Mistress Redcroft—will you recount what you recollect you heard, and then I'll add what I can remember."

Sophie looked up, her face rather pale and serious. "At first, because of the mouse, I didn't understand why Sir Henry was hushing me. Then I heard the sound of men quarrelling angrily, and I recognised the voices of Mr Pridow and Mr Brendon." She paused as if she expected them to object. Neither spoke, but rather sat as if turned to stone, and so at a nod from Hal, she continued: "I don't recollect the exact words," she admitted, "but it seemed to me Mr Pridow was angry with 'the long-nosed, tiresome jade,' and 'vowed it was none of his doing that she had fallen and hit her head'."

A gasp, and a quickly-muffled sob from Mistress Pauncey, followed by a murmur, ran through the hall again. Sophie paused and as silence fell, continued, "Mr Brendon grew even angrier at that, and cried that it was surely none of his. He said Mistress Rosalind was nothing to him, and had Mr Pridow but agreed to her proposal to substitute herself for Mistress Bella Craven as his bride, the accident need never have happened."

Mr Pridow made as if to protest, but Jacob Brendon caught his arm in a painful grip, to keep him silent.

"After that there were many hot words, both often speaking at once, and in truth, all I could make out were but odd phrases, 'that Sir Henry Westwood was known to have a long reach', and 'that it was typical of Jack Hollingshead to ride off to fetch him, without a word to anyone'—oh, and finally, 'that if they could but weather the storm, there was no proof of anything against them'."

"Exactly!" Jacob Brendon cried in triumph, as she finished. "All noise and hearsay, from a foolish wench of dubious reputation! We deny this meeting ever took place! Whose word do we have here? A woman whose bridegroom died in suspicious circumstances only last year!"

"Be very careful, Mr Brendon!" Hal said quietly. "This may be an informal meeting to enquire as to how Mistress Rosalind Pauncey met her end, but there are many witnesses, too, should Mistress Redwood wish to bring a suit for slander."

"Hold your tongue, you fool!" snapped Mr Pridow, as Brendon suddenly glanced about him to the assembled faces.

"Yes, Mr Brendon, there is no judge or jury, just your neighbours and those who call you friend. They will be the best to judge if you had summoned help when Mistress Pauncey fell, then she might still be alive today," continued Hal calmly. "Or was she indeed dead as soon as she fell."

"She wasn't dead!" Ezekiel Pridow lost his head, seeing the reply to this rhetorical question in the shocked faces of his neighbours. "We picked her up and she recovered her senses, but then she started wailing and screaming, and threatening us both, saying she'd tell everything she had heard! It was Brendon who grabbed her and shook her, just to frighten her into silence, you know!"

"He most certainly achieved his object," agreed Hal coldly. "Your secret is very safe. Mistress Rosalind is as silent as the grave."

"We didn't know she was so sickly!" cried Jacob Brendon indignantly. "I tell you I did no more than take her by the arms, and give her a shake, and she went limp in my hands! What was I to do?"

"Return her to her mother?" Hal suggested, at his most severe, casting a hand toward Mistress Pauncey, who was silently weeping. "Call a physician to assist her? Anything other than what you did do, which was to abandon her in the priest hole in the dark, and tell no one."

"I wanted to call Craven," said Pridow, in a whining voice. "I thought we could explain, but Brendon said we had to have time to think. It all happened so quickly. If only she hadn't been such an interfering sort of…" He broke off, as Mistress Pauncey with a cry, hastened from the chamber, followed by her tearful daughters and sister. He read only further condemnation in the faces around him.

"I don't understand, what was it Rosalind Pauncey

overheard?" demanded Jack Hollingshead testily. "What made her think Pridow would accept her as a bride?"

"Ah, yes, now we came to the main part of the story, not just the tragic circumstances of a young woman's death. Mr Pridow wanted a new bride, and Bella Craven caught his eye. Mr Craven, her brother, knowing Mr Revesby was very young and penniless, decided a match with an older, steadier man, was probably the best for all concerned. He could not have known, of course that Nick and his grandfather had most probably been cheated out of a vast deal of money by Mr Brendon over the years, when he was concerned with the Committee for Sequestrations."

"Cheated, Sir Henry? How dare you accuse me of such a thing? I merely did my duty! I am within my rights to demand satisfaction for such an insult!"

"As a Justice of the Peace, I would be obliged to arrest anyone foolish enough to fight a duel," replied Hal, his deliberately moderate tones at a variance to Brendon's. "You naturally meant legal satisfaction, I assume? Yes, whilst you think about that, Nick will produce those papers.

Brendon began to rant at him. "No, sir," Hal added, "Stay both your hand, and your tongue. You claim to hold the deeds to Mr Revesby's property and are about to call in your mortgages, yet Mr Revesby found these deeds yesterday, concealed with the treasure his father had hidden. Now I am not a lawyer," he added, "but I do know, that the deeds predate any you must hold, and therefore, I wonder how you came by them, for if these were concealed by Nick's father along with the treasure, whilst his grandfather was still in exile, then ones you hold, cannot be the original deeds. Furthermore if—as is suggested by this—much of the land held by Mr Christopher Revesby was sequestered by the Committee of Sequestrations, in lieu of fines, then by the Act of Settlement, the land must return to the heirs of original owners."

Jacob Bredon fell back onto the settle, his face a picture of astonished consternation. Pridow sat with his head in his hands.

"But Sir Henry, I have here the money owed, to pay in full," said Nick Revesby, indicating his saddlebags. "I have come to pay the debt, like an honourable man, and to ask for Bella's hand in marriage."

"I am aware you have the best, most honourable of intentions, Nick," replied Hal warmly. "Should we find on investigation, all is in order that is exactly what you shall do. However, if we find the irregularities I suspect…"

Brendon began to protest heatedly as Hal continued, "May I add, Mr Brendon, that one of my brothers-in-law is already investigating a like case for me in the records of the Court of Sequestrations, and his preliminary letter, suggests that some of the fines awarded to the Weston Revesby estate, are *not* in accordance to those awarded against Mr Christopher Revesby."

Jem Attwood, who had accompanied Nick Revesby and stood all this time in the doorway, looking puzzled interrupted, "If that be so, Sir Henry, I for one shall be mightily interested. I am the son of Master Revesby's agent, aye, and his father afore him, too. I have with me the books of the Weston Revesby estate, with all the transactions regular and irregular, that have taken place these past five and twenty years.

Ezekiel Pridow got swiftly to his feet. "I just want to say I know nothing of these matters. My only interest was in making an alliance with the Craven family, to find a good mother for my children and a helpmeet for me."

"For someone with such modest requirements, you took a great interest in Bella's dowry," said Simon Craven contemptuously.

"Naturally, in the course of matters such as this, one

must enquire as to—to—"

"Damn you, Pridow!" cried Jacob Brendon furiously. "You were the one urging me to foreclose on Revesby, so that the Craven family had no choice but you! You insisted that we need not do anything about the silly wench when she keeled over!"

"I begged you to help me carry her back to her chamber!" Ezekiel Pridow looked appalled at this accusation.

Brendon jumped to his feet. "I see it is your intention to lay the blame on my shoulders, but that won't hold water, Pridow! I don't have to remain here and listen to this!"

"I rather regret that you do," said Hal. "Pray resume your seat, Mr Brendon, or I shall be obliged to arrest and confine you, until such time as we can establish exactly who is to blame for what."

Brendon looked about him wildly, and then losing his head, he grabbed the arm of Kate, who was looking rather amazed, and jerked her to her feet suddenly, holding a knife at her throat.

"Stand back," he cried, his voice cracking in fury. "Stand back I say, or I'll slit her throat!

"Aunt Kate!" Sophie cried in terror. "Let her go, you coward, let her go!"

"Hush!" Hal commanded his own voice taut with rage. "Sir, I insist you release my aunt immediately, before some harm is done!"

"Get out of my way, all of you or there'll be more than harm done! Pridow, Sir Richard, get some horses arranged! I shall go out through this damned priest hole! Meet me at the end of it with horses, or I'll cut her throat and leave her in the passage!"

"Give it up, man," said Pridow, appalled. "Have you taken leave of your senses? Let Mistress Westwood go at once!"

"Sir Richard?" Brendon swung Kate about, as Nick Revesby made a sudden move. "Be still, all of you, I warn you, I am not to be trifled with!"

"Hold, Nick, Simon!" Hal's voice cut across a babble of words. "Please, everybody, be calm! Sir Richard, it would seem some action is required of you by your companion."

"He is no companion of mine!" said Sir Richard, his colour ghastly. "I barely know the man!"

"Never the less, it would seem he requires your assistance in this matter," continued Hal, his voice rigid with fury. "Pray do as he bids. You cannot wish to place the life of a loved one in danger!"

"I'm ill," he bleated, looking about him in a panic. "I cannot do this thing, you must excuse me!"

"Richard!" The name was wrenched from Kate's lips in despair.

"Excuse you!" Hal exclaimed with disgust as tears ran from Richard's eyes and down his ashen cheeks unheeded, while he sat with arms crossed over his body, rocking back and forth in despair.

"Brendon, I'll saddle your horses, but I warn you, if one hair on the head of my most beloved aunt is harmed, I'll hunt you down as the worthless cur that you are!" said Hal.

"No, not you!" screamed Brendon, getting more and more agitated. "You stay here! I won't have you following me! I'll kill her, if any of you attempt to follow me!"

"I'll get the horses and meet you at the tunnel entrance," said Nick Revesby quickly. "Jem, come, help me saddle the horses. No, Simon, I am the one who could find the tunnel easiest anyway! Calmly now, Brendon, none of us wants trouble and it will serve no purpose to harm the good lady.

"Get going then," said Brendon, seeing no other help for it, "but I warn you, all of you, that if any attempt to follow me, I will kill her!"

Sophie stood up, barring his way. "Take me instead, I am younger, and will be able to keep up better. I beg you, let Aunt Kate go—she has done you no harm."

"Get out of my way, wench, I'd sooner take the devil himself than you! No more, any of you! Craven, you'll have to lead me to this priest hole, and I warn you, all of you, stay back, or I will kill her!"

With Kate clamped to his chest, a knife held to her throat, he walked backwards toward the stone stairway, all those in the hall moving aside for their progress, helpless with impotent fury, but terrified that the man was clearly beyond the reach of reason.

Nick and his companion headed out of the house, back into the rain, making for the stables, whilst Simon Craven followed the unreasonable Brendon after a nod from Hal. Then as Brendon and his hostage were half way up the stair, Hal called out, as if he could not stop himself, "Please do all he asks, Aunt Kate!"

"Do not worry for me, Hal," she replied calmly. "Mr Brendon's not an unreasonable man, I am sure. He knows I represent no threat to him. Once he has achieved his object I am certain he will be pleased to release me." A final little quiver in her voice gave a lie to her brave words.

Those left in the chamber were not so sanguine. Madeleine Hollingshead informed Sir Richard of her opinion of his character as he sat weeping helplessly, whilst Jack and Hal held a short conference.

Bella came to tug at Hal's sleeve and said in an undertone, "Sir Henry, do you remember as we made our way back through the passage, I told you I had often heard the steward singing as we passed by that old wine rack? And how Nick and I have always thought that there might be a way to the tunnel from the cellars in the house? Now, Brendon must go past this place, but before he gets to it he must negotiate the secret chamber, and come down the staircase in the dark, with Mistress Westwood, all of which will take some time. If we could find this place, could you not be waiting for them there, in the passage, and get Mistress Westwood free?"

Hal turned to her in hope. "How big is this doorway? Can I get through?"

"I do not know, sir," she replied, "but do you not think we should at least try?"

"Indeed I do," he replied. "Lead me to the kitchens at once!"

⚜

Chapter Twenty- Three

Kate, meanwhile was beginning to suffer from shock. As they came to the head of the stairs and went up a few more steps into the gallery, tears welled up and slipped down her cheek, but she took herself to task, knowing if she gave way, she would be in trouble.

"Mr Brendon," she said, in as calm a manner as she could, "I have to say I find this method of progress rather uncomfortable. Could you oblige me, by letting go of my neck, and allowing me to walk forward, with your knife held to my back?"

"Or better still, let Mistress Westwood go, Brendon, and take me hostage instead," said Simon, who was following at a distance, and had just reached the head of the stairs.

"No, stay there, Craven!" The man cried, panic rising in his voice again. "Do not think to out manoeuvre me!"

"I have no desire to do anything of the sort," said Simon. "My intention is to expedite your removal from my home without harm to any of my friends. You insisted I came with you. All I ask is that I take Mistress Westwood's place that she might return below to safety in the hall."

"No, hold your tongues both of you! I'll not be distracted by all this nonsense!" Roughly he pushed Kate forward, and caught her arms pulling them behind her. "Craven, come bind her hands, then you can lead the way."

"May I have them bound in front of me?" Kate asked mildly. "For I fear if I am bound with them behind my back, I may irritate you further, by tripping on my gown hem."

"Do as you please, only do it quickly!" Brendon snapped, his knife held poised at her throat again as Simon came to take her hands in his, and bind them with the sash she offered.

"My dear Mistress Westwood, I can't say how sorry I am that this—"

"Hold your tongue man!" Brendon cried, beside himself with rage and fear. "Get on with it, or I'll do you both an injury!"

Simon averted his eyes to hide his fury and reached

out to gently wipe away Kate's tears. "All will be well," he soothed.

"And all will be well and all manner of things shall be well," returned Kate, with a tremulous smile. "Lead the way, sir."

Simon walked the length of the gallery, as Kate followed him, the knife Brendon carried pressed hard by the small of her back. Their rate of progress increased and Kate kept a firm hold on her gown and her emotions, as they passed through a small door in the panelling she had often noticed, and along a narrow corridor leading to a suite of chambers. Simon opened the door to one of these and passed across the floor into a closet, and from thence out into another long corridor he had paced with Hal previously.

"We must climb these stairs, so have a care, Mistress Westwood, you don't slip," he said over his shoulder. "The way becomes increasingly dim, there should be a lantern ahead in the priest hole, and I'll pause to light a candle if there is still one to be had."

"Hurry, you fool, never mind your silly chatter!" Brendon cried, his voice showing clearly how jangled his emotions were.

"Foolish or no, I shall pause to light a candle. I give

you fair warning. It would be the height of folly to attempt the stairs out of the priest hole without a light,"
said Simon, recollecting in time, for Aunt Kate's sake,
that it was probably better not to tell the tale of the
ghost of a recusant priest who had met a nasty end in
the dark.

Brendon waved him ahead irritably, and Simon
climbed the narrow staircase swiftly, looking back to
make sure all was well. He extended his hand to help
Kate as she followed as best she could with Brendon
close behind her. Once in the narrow confines of the
priest hole he lit a candle and fixed it securely in an ancient lantern, before the others joined him.

"I sorry this is so cramped," he said, stepping aside to
make way for Kate. "It wasn't designed for so many at
once."

"Open it out onto the stairway," commanded Brendon sharply. "The sooner we are out of here, the safer I
shall feel!"

"Brendon, for God's sake let Mistress Westwood go,"
said Simon reasonably. "Here is the means of your escape." He turned a carved angel on the wall at an angle
and a dark, narrow opening appeared in the panelling.
"I give you my word none will follow you down these

stairs, and by now Nick will have brought the horses to meet you at the end of the tunnel. Make your way to freedom, it matters not one whit compared to the safety of this lady."

"That is not how Westwood will see it!" the man snapped. "He will have gathered a force by now and be waiting for me in the woodland there. A hostage will be my only safe conduct, and she is perfect, for from what Sir Richard says, she is like a mother to him. He'll take no chances with her life!" He jabbed at Kate with his knife, piercing her gown and slightly pricking her flesh, so that she walked forward, bending to get through the aperture. He followed her, and turned back to Simon to take the lantern. "Show me how this thing secures from this side," he commanded. "It must do or they could have merely chased the priests down it and slaughtered them in the tunnel, with none the wiser!"

Reluctantly Simon showed him the companion angel just outside the door on the stair way and three well-oiled metal bolts creaked out of the woodwork, showing how the small door was kept concealed in the usual run of things. "Once you are the other side of that door, none can follow you. You'll be quite safe."

Brendon nodded, and indicated Kate. "Release her

hands, she'll need them free to get down the stairs, and you stand there, whilst she ties yours with the cloth. I'll leave you here in the dark. I don't want you following us down those stairs, and I am sick of the sound of your voice."

Simon took a deep breath to control his fury, and having released Kate's hands, submitted his own for her to tie. She did so competently, looking up into his darkened face. "*All will be well, and all will be well,*" she said.

"*—and all manner of things shall be well,*" he replied nodding.

"Pull it tighter than that, woman!" cried Brendon impatiently "You don't want him to follow us. The second I hear a step on the stair, you'll breathe your last breath."

"There really is no need for all these violent threats, Mr Brendon," remarked Kate calmly. "I have offered you neither abuse, violence or resistance. I am not a fool. I am well aware my best interests lie in accommodating you. May we please proceed and get this adventure completed as soon as is possible?"

Simon hid a grin, and his last view was of Kate's encouraging smile as Brendon closed the door and he was left in the dark.

❧

Bella, leaving her shocked sister-in-law, with the remaining guests who were still all of a flutter in the hall, led the way to the kitchens beyond the screens passage just off the hall were they found the servants gathered about a fire. Tulley, the butler got to his feet as they entered. "Mistress Bella?" The man's tone was wary, as if he did not relish this incursion into his territory.

"Good evening," Hal took control of the situation, nodding to the assembled servants. "I think you will be aware I am Sir Henry Westwood. This is Mistress Redcroft and you'll all know Mr Hollingshead. Pray excuse us, we wish to inspect your cellars."

"My cellars?" the man repeated blankly. "I don't know that Mr Craven would care for that." He glanced beyond Sophie, as if expecting Simon to be following.

"Mr Craven is occupied at present, but will be back shortly, in the meantime, Mistress Bella will show us the way, if you don't care to," said Hal evenly.

The man glanced to the cook who sat over the fire, her face sullen. She shrugged her ample shoulders. "We should best wait for the master," she muttered unhelpfully.

"No, we'll see them now," replied Bella sharply. "Tulley, light a lantern and lead the way."

"You've caused enough trouble these past few days, young mistress," said the man, in an insufferably patronising manner. "Happen Cook is right. We'll wait upon the master."

Hal placed a soothing hand on Bella's arm, as she bridled with indignation. "No matter, if you are not prepared to oblige us, Tulley, we can find our own way. Lead on Mistress Bella, you'll have some idea of the direction."

A young boy, who had been crouched in a corner, at some distance from the fire, got warily to his feet. He was dressed in a dull grey jerkin, which had seen better days, and his bones were barely covered in as little flesh as is possible, so that his nose appeared overlarge, and his ears huge. His eyes however, were alert and intelligent.

"I'll lead the way, Sir Henry," he said simply. "Mr Craven said you were to be shown every courtesy."

"This is Rupert, Hal, the lad who escorted me to Weston Revesby. He is bright and helpful," said Sophie, with a quick smile for the lad.

"Sit down, boy," snapped the cook. "You are already

in trouble, this day. Sit down and know your place."

"I think he already knows his place," said Hal, grasping the lad's thin shoulder kindly, "Lead on, young man. Your master will be pleased that you have listened to his instructions."

Hal waved the reluctant steward aside, who, having had time to reflect realised his error. Hal followed the boy out of the kitchen and into a narrow passage. Here the lad hastily caught up a candle and used it to light two lanterns. He then indicated a door which led to a flight of steps. They gave a lantern to Jack Hollingshead, who was following with Sophie, whilst Bella lingered to vent her annoyance in an undertone to those remaining in the kitchens.

Down the steps they went, still in single file, and into another chamber and from this, Rupert led them into the cellar.

As the boy hesitated, Bella caught them up. "Keep going, Sir Henry, right to the back of the cellar," she called. "As I remember from playing Hunt the Thimble with Nick as a child, there is another, smaller cavern beyond, and by my calculations, the door we seek should be at the back of that."

"We are certainly moving in the right direction, and

most certainly underground now," agreed Hal softly. "However, please remember how sound will echo about these underground caverns, so hushed voices only from now on."

They nodded in agreement, and set off again making for the back of the smaller cellar. It was the boy, who tapped Hal's arm and indicated another undercroft leading off. There they were forced to duck their heads to avoid the low roof. At the far end of this larger cavern, well-hidden behind large barrels and sacking held in position by planks, was what amounted to a room formed by the bare rocks.

"Yes," whispered Hal, "this looks very much like an entry into another cavern, and these planks are not held very fast either." He stood close to the wood, listening intently, and then nodded. "I can't hear a sound, so we'll have to take a chance this is the place. Here, lad— and you too, Jack—give me a hand. Sophie, Bella, hold these lanterns, and be ready to cover them if I give the word!" Then as Sophie opened her mouth to speak, he hissed, "Everyone, as quiet as possible!"

The sound of the wood being twisted and wrenched from the nails seemed to rent the air, but once released, Hal indicated the space beyond which stretched away into a black void. "There is no help for it. Pass the lantern, Sophie."

She handed it to him silently and he allowed the dim light to reveal the tunnel, just exactly where Bella had said she thought it would be.

"Oh, well done, Bella!" Sophie whispered.

"The question is whether Brendon and Aunt Kate have al…"

The sound of footsteps, and a man cursing at a distance, came to their ears. Hastily Hal gave the covered lantern back to Sophie and indicated for them to remain where they were, whilst Jack noiselessly joined him, concealed behind a rock in the tunnel. The boy glanced to Bella, and at her nod, stepped out with the men, possessing himself of a stout length of wood.

"Pray, Mr Brendon, do not tug at me so," Aunt Kate's voice drifted ahead of her, and they could tell how anxious she was, by its quaver.

"Go more quickly then!" the man snapped ungraciously. "Do not seek to delay me!"

"My dear sir, the very last thing I want is to delay you," she replied, in the nearest thing to tartness Sophie had ever heard her use. "I can't wait to be rid of you and your companions!"

"Aye, Sir Richard did not show to advantage," the man agreed unpleasantly. "They say his wife has sucked all his lifeblood away."

"You tell me no news, sir, that my nephew didn't bring earlier," retorted Kate. "What a pack of scoundrels you all are!"

"Don't take that tone with me Mistress! You just hold up the lantern, so we can see our way, and keep a civil tongue in your head."

"It is you who needs to keep a civil tongue!" Hal nodded to Sophie, who uncovered the lantern, as he stepped out in front of the man, whilst Jack came around the back of them, his sword ready drawn. "Release my Aunt at once, and I'll not run you through as you deserve, but take you back with me, so you can have your neck stretched by the hangman!"

The man glared at them, and grabbed at Kate's arm to pull her closer, but Jack's sword was before him slashing across his wrist, whilst the boy Rupert, who had scrambled up the rock earlier, leapt on his back, taking him by surprise, and bringing him crashing to the ground.

"Oh, well done, Rupert!" Sophie cried, coming to clasp Aunt Kate in her arms.

"Well done indeed, boy!" Hal said, then as the sound of horses hooves came to their ears, he drew them all aside and stood guard. Jack jerked Brendon to his feet, and with the help of the boy began to bind his hands tightly, only relaxing as Nick Revesby and Jem Attwood, almost laying along the length of their horses' backs, came into view.

"We heard voices," explained Nick with a grin for Bella, "and so rode hell for leather, in case something was amiss!"

"You are quite mad, Master Nick," said his companion, looking white-faced. "I don't know what you thought you were doing, to ride like that in the dark, in a low tunnel!"

"I know this tunnel very well," said Nick, "I told you to keep your head down, or you'd regret it." He got off his horse, still grinning. "Anyway, you kept up, I notice!" He turned to Bella who had joined them all in the tunnel and was commending the boy for his quick wits. "You remembered, Bella, about the noises we heard, and Tulley getting drunk on your brother's wine, and how we thought that it might be an opening there into the cellars? I wondered if you would. So, you didn't need me after all!"

"I'll always need you, Nick," she replied, with a smile of adoration. "Although, this young man has been invaluable in helping us, this evening, which is more than can be said for Tulley and that miserable female who presides over the kitchen. Make your bow, boy, your master will be pleased with you when he hears of this evening's work."

Grinning, the lad did as he was told. "Well it would seem you've gained the admiration of your mistress, Rupert, if not the other servants," remarked Jack Hollingshead.

"My admiration, too," said Hal, as the boy grew very pink about the ears. "His quick thinking led us swiftly to this place, and he assisted in the release of my aunt and capture of this rogue. But where is Mr Craven? I half expected him to be with you, Aunt Kate.

"I am afraid he is tied up and locked in this now-famous priest hole, poor man. Someone should go and release him at once," said Kate. "He is beside himself with anxiety."

"I'll go," said Nick, "it won't take me a moment to run up those stairs! Jem take my horse back to the stables, and come back to the house, for a cup of wine. Oh, perhaps I shouldn't have said that, it's not my house, I don't want to offend Simon further."

"I should think Simon will be so grateful to you, as to lavish entire bottles of wine on you," said Jack.

"I am extremely grateful to you all," said Kate, quietly, "but could I be more grateful in another place, which isn't home to rats and spiders?"

"Not to mention bats," said Sophie, giving her a hug. "Come, ma'am, we'll lead the way back into the house, and young Rupert will light our path."

Chapter Twenty Four

Left alone in the hall listening to the retreating steps and the murmur of voices coming from the kitchen, those still sitting remained so, half afraid of what might occur if they tried to move, still inclined to talk in whispers.

"Brendon has run mad, Ezekiel," said Mistress Pridow, with an anxious glance at her companions. "What can he be thinking of?"

"Escape?" Louisa suggested contempt in her voice. "He is leaving you with all the trouble and explanations! You are such a fool, Ezekiel."

"I don't see that," replied her brother, frowning. "Why should I be left with trouble? What explanations?"

"Why you left young Mistress Pauncey in the priest hole of course," said Sir Richard, coming out from behind his handkerchief. "Oh, my poor Kate! What shall I do? If only I were a stronger man!"

"If only you had some backbone you wouldn't be in this fix," said Madeleine Hollingshead at her most forthright. "There is nothing you can do. You must leave the fate of poor Mistress Westwood in the by-far more competent hands of her nephew. He is not the sort to sit and weep over spilt milk!"

"How can I be held to blame for Brendon's actions?" Pridow cried indignantly. "I never said I'd be prepared to wed the wench. It was all his idea! He got me to that damned priest hole by trickery, and then expected me to go through a form of marriage with her! It was Sir Richard, who insisted it wouldn't be legal, then she started screaming and wailing and we knew if we weren't careful we'd be caught. All I wanted was to get some rest, and there we were with a screaming wench! Brendon did no more than give her a shake and a slap, and before we knew it she collapsed on the floor!"

"It was horrible, terrible!" Sir Richard looked haunted. "I had to get away, I couldn't stay!"

"What use are you to your Community?" Madeleine turned upon him. "As I understand it, a minister in Virginia is called upon to aid his flock in many ways, are you as weak-willed there? You did not stay to consider that if she was as we now know—dying—your place was with her as she breathed her last?"

"I am ill; I can no longer deal with these problems."

"Don't bleat at me, man, I have no time for sheep," declared Madeleine roundly. "You, Pridow, what excuse do you have for not calling someone to aid this young woman? You have a sister. She is older 'tis true, but would you have left her in a dark priest hole, when she had clearly fainted?"

"I wouldn't get myself into such a situation!" Louisa cried indignantly. "I am not so desperate to be married I'd try to trick a man into it."

Cathy Craven exchanged a look with Mistress Hollingshead, and as she held back the obvious retort, merely snorted and changed it onto an unconvincing cough. The sound of voices coming back from the kitchens, made them all turn their heads.

Brendon, looking much battered and with his hands tied together, was pushed into the hall by a young boy, followed by Hal supporting his aunt, and Sophie and Bella, with Jack bringing up the rear.

"My dear Mistress Westwood, you are safe!," cried Cathy. "I thank heavens, and are you all well? None of you are hurt?"

"Aunt Kate has a scratch, and Mr Brendon is rather

battered, but most of us are well," said Sophie, cheerfully. "You'll never believe how easy it all was! Brendon just walked into Hal's and Jack's arms, and this lad Rupert hit him over the head for good measure."

"Katherine, come to me, I beg!" Sir Richard made some effort to rise, "Oh, my dear, I have been so anxious! You don't know how my heart has been racing—come, sit with me, that I can be sure you are unharmed!"

Kate glanced across the hall to him, her face grave, as Hal stood with his arm still gently about her. There was no constraint, she could have walked across the floor to him, but she stood her ground.

"I am sorry you are unwell, Richard," she said coldly. "I feel a little unsteady myself. Sophie, may I sit with you?"

Hal helped her to the settle beside Sophie, and Cathy brought her a cup of wine, whilst the chatter went on around them. In a short while there was a noisy furore in the hall as Nick and Simon—released from his imprisonment in the priest hole—came clattering down the stairs. Barbara Craven came to see what had occurred and more wine was procured as everyone sat down again and peace was restored, before proper explanations began with Simon outlining all that had happened to himself and Nick.

"What a pretty pair of villains!" Madeleine Hollings-head said as Bredon began a faltering excuse, and Pri-dow was moved to protest. "It seems to me you are all as bad as each other. How can you be so ready to lay all the blame on your companions? See here Pridow, Sir Richard, you allowed this man to take control of your miserable lives and think for you. I will not scruple to tell you to your face I am disgusted by you, Sir Richard. How could you let this man take your future bride as hostage like that? I repeat my question—what kind of man are you?"

"And I reply, a sick one, madam," he muttered taking a kerchief from his sleeve to mop his heated brow. He cast a doubtful glance at Kate who sat with Sophie, tak-ing distasteful sips from a glass of strong wine.

"Brendon, you are beyond words. You systematically cheated an ageing soldier, who had only just returned from exile. You must have previously put pressure on his dying son, in your capacity as Parliament's toady! Who knows how much you may have shortened poor Philip's life with worry, and you compound all this, by trying to cheat the next generation! And you, Pridow, aided him in all this in the hope of getting a good alliance to further your pretensions—the pair of you sicken me!"

"I assure you, madam," cried Ezekiel Pridow, "that Sir Richard and I had no hand in this, we were not aware…"

"Save your breath, Pridow," interrupted Simon curtly. "You also, Sir Richard, who came to my house masquerading as an honourable man, for I cannot abide liars and cheats. I do not know how guilty or otherwise you are, but I vow I will not have either of you under my roof a minute longer."

"Oh, well said, Simon!" cried his mother, as Sir Richard, who had been sitting with his eyes downcast all the while, now looked up in amazement, a horrified expression on his face.

"I beg pardon, C--Craven," he began. "I—I—"

"The masks are coming off, Sir Richard," said Hal, who had received an assenting nod from Aunt Kate. "No more lies! All shall be known, far and wide. I suggest you saddle your horse and make for the nearest port. You need have no fear; I dispatched the altar-sticks, the Bible and the school books back to your colony last month. They should be in the hands of my good friend, the physician Philippe Douy in time for Easter. You however, must follow, for I understand your wife is expecting to be brought to bed with her next child, before that date."

Absolute silence filled the chamber at these words and Kate dropped her eyes to hide her shock. Sophie slipped a comforting arm about her shoulders and gave her a hug, whilst Madeleine Hollingshead drew in her breath with a hiss, and the deserted bridegroom stood stuttering and stammering in his rage.

"Come, Simon," Jack Hollingshead got decisively to his feet. "We don't need men such as these! Help me kick these hypocrites from our society."

As Simon got to his feet with alacrity, and Nick came to stand shoulder to shoulder with them, the two impostors, with cries of mingled rage and fear, wasted no time in getting from the hall.

"Well, that's improved matters enormously," said Madeleine, with satisfaction. "Louisa, I suggest you and your mother might be more comfortable following your brother. The Pridow name is not one to be proud of at the moment."

"I am sure poor Ezekiel has been sadly led astray by those men," said Mary Pridow, looking shocked. "I swear to you, Barbara, I had no idea of any of this!"

"Perhaps not," said Madeleine, as Barbara Craven

hesitated, "but it would be best to draw a veil over these proceedings if you wish to remain in the district. We give our word to say nothing further, if you'll remove yourselves immediately. And Louisa, if I ever hear one uncharitable word from you about Bella Craven, I will have no hesitation in recounting the whole of this wicked tale to all of your acquaintance. I trust you understand me?"

Louisa huffed and got to her feet, assisting her distressed mother. "I am only too happy to forget all that has gone on," she snapped. "I have never been in such a place as this, where one is insulted as one sits, by people one doesn't know from Adam! Come, Mother, let us be gone, before Ezekiel rides off without us."

"I am sorry, Barbara, and I apologise to you, too, Catherine," said Madeleine, suddenly stricken as she turned to her hostesses after they left. "I shouldn't have interfered. This is your home, but these people have made me so cross!"

"It is of no great matter, mother," said Catherine calmly, "we, like you, are glad to be rid of the pestilence of their company."

"I feel I should explain some things, Madeleine," said Barbara uneasily. "I am sure you'll remember what great friends my husband Charles and Christopher Revesby were. It was only natural for him to conceal so close a friend from Oliver Cromwell's men."

"My dear Barbara, I couldn't abide Noll Cromwell myself," said Madeleine heartily. "A sanctimonious sort of fellow. I know John was for Parliament, but in truth he found some of those he had to deal with strange bedfellows. He knew all about Christopher being concealed in your priest hole, and did his best to get the Ironsides called off."

"You knew that Charles was assisting the King?" cried Barbara in dismay.

"My dear, in the beginning we also sent money to the King," she replied candidly, "but he was such an unreliable fellow, you know—and John just couldn't abide the thought of Irish Catholics being brought over to fight free-born Englishmen—and then, situated here as we were, well, we were all forced to trim our sails to the prevailing wind, so to speak." She turned in appeal to Hal.

"Indeed, ma'am," said Hal, "I think I can safely safe we endured many strange bedfellows in exile, too, and trimmed our sails out of existence for the most part. That is all in the past now. The King is returned to us, and we are at peace again. Peace for our land is a great victory."

"Well said, Sir Henry, and thank you for your assistance in putting us to rights," said Madeleine with a twinkle. "Once again neighbour shall know and trust neighbour, and all shall go well with us. We shall see to that."

A tap sounded on her door as Kate began her packing. It had been agreed between them they would leave first thing next morning, and as it was too painful for her feelings to be part of the general mulling over of the events enacted below, she had sought refuge in her chamber.

She paused, frowning, for Sophie has just left, after insisting on applying a salve to her wound. Kate had changed her gown, contemplating the blood-stained one, and recollected with a wry twist of her lips how excited she had felt when she had worn it, for it was the height of fashion, and she had thought it made her look younger. She knew Hal was drinking a celebratory glass or two of wine with Simon, Jack and young Nick Revesby, and suspected Madeleine Hollingsworth had come to take her back into company.

"Come in," she said, and regretted it instantly, as Sir Richard Harrison, dressed for a journey, hesitated in the doorway.

"Please don't send me away, Kate," he said immediately, seeing intent in her face. "I can't leave you without an apology and an explanation."

"I want neither," said Kate, surprised to hear the hauteur in her voice. "Save them for your wife!"

"I have to tell you how sorry I am," he said quickly. "I have been in such torment, since my return from Virginia. I didn't know how to even begin to explain."

"I have told you, I require no explanation, merely your removal from my company," Kate said, her eyes flashing, although she kept her voice calm.

"Then I will go," he said, his voice full of abject misery. "I assure you I have no desire to further insult you. I merely wished to tell you it wasn't a lie. I love you with all my heart."

"You have no right to tell me so. You are a married man, and will soon be a father—again," snapped Kate, suddenly very angry. "Explain your conduct to your wife, Sir Richard."

He nodded miserably. "Yes, I knew it would be so.

You are too fine a woman to listen to me. When we first met, when I fell in love with your gentleness, I'd had word from Virginia that my wife had died six months before, in childbirth and the baby with her."

Kate frowned. "Yes, I recollect you were still grieving," she said more kindly.

He smiled bitterly. "No, Kate, you imagined I was grieving. I was grateful that I had been released from marriage to a shrew, who had made my life a hell on earth for years. I was lost in wonderment at the kindness and goodness of you."

Kate stiffened; she'd not be beguiled by sympathy. "All this is no concern of mine, sir," she said sharply. "I am not required to listen to you. You are nothing to me."

"Don't say that, Kate, I beg of you," he cried "You don't know the despair I suffered on my return to Virginia in the summer, to find my wife alive and well, and that it had all been a mistake. It seems it was generally believed she would die. The child was already lost, and it seemed likely that she would follow, her fever was so great."

"Then the Lord has been kind to you," she replied coldly, "and the only mistake is the one made by you, in thinking I could ever have any association with a man who despaired at the sight of his wife alive, when he thought her dead."

He nodded his agreement. "I was appalled at myself," he admitted candidly. "And all my neighbours expected great rejoicing, but I could only grieve for what I had lost—you."

"Yet this grief did not, I notice, stop you siring another child on your wife who had so recently lost one," she snapped, unable to stop herself.

He frowned. "How could I deny her that solace, when I was already denying her my true affection? My wife holds her children in deep affection. It is in this one sees so clearly how…"

"I have no desire to hear another word from you, sir," cried Kate, angrily. "I have listened to you when I had no need to, so now get you gone from my sight!"

He stood so rebuked for a few seconds, with his eyes closed, to hide his despair. "Madam, I will obey your instructions immediately, but by your charity of heart, would you please give a message to your nephew, Sir Henry for me? I know if you are the bearer of such a message, he will heed it."

"Tell me your message and then be gone, you are not

wanted here," replied Kate, suspecting this was another trick to play upon her sympathy.

"Pray, tell Sir Henry, if you please, my dearest Kate, that I am not guilty of the lesser charge. I am only guilty of the folly of being afraid of exposure. Brendon got to know of my wife's survival. He has been extracting money from me for his silence. I had charged him, when I first returned, as my man of law, to send the Bible, the books and the candlesticks, back to the settlement on the first available ship. He assured me he had done so. I do not offer this as an excuse. It was a matter I should have attended to myself, but as you know, ill-health overtook me."

Again Kate nodded, hardening her heart. "Then let that stand as an excuse for the lesser crime," she replied curtly. "I'll relay your message to Hal."

"I would greatly prefer to reimburse him for his expense," he added tentatively, "but I suspect he'll accept nothing from one so base as I."

"Then you wrong Hal," she replied. "He is a fine man and a good Justice because he is only too aware of how folly can befall us all."

"Then will he accept this do you think?" He took a heavy purse from his coat and held it out to her hopefully.

"No," she said simply. "As I know Hal, he'd prefer you to take more books back for your school, and in doing so perhaps make some reparation for the damage you have allowed to be done here."

"No, you'll have nothing of me, will you—and who can blame you? Goodbye Kate, I'll see you in my dreams."

"I'll remember you in my prayers," she replied, stony-faced, as he bowed and stepped out of the chamber and her life. Then she sank to the bed, her knees suddenly weak as tears filled her eyes and she wept hopelessly for some minutes. Then she got up, washed her face and stoically continued with her packing.

✤

Chapter Twenty Five

Once this was accomplished to her satisfaction, Kate glanced to her mirror, and having tidied her hair, stepped along the corridor to the chamber of Mistress Hollingshead, knocking firmly on the door.

Madeleine herself opened it, and smiled a welcome. "Come in, do, Mistress Westwood. I was just changing my gown, it seems there is to be a celebratory dinner, but you will not feel like celebrating, I imagine. My dear, I am so sorry that fellow abused your kindness."

"Oh, do not fret for me, truth to tell, I am half relieved," said Kate. "At least I shall not be obliged to sail that vast ocean now!"

Madeleine smiled, "Come sit by me, Mistress Westwood. I cannot tell you how much I admire your courage. Now, you must call me Madeleine, and I shall call you Kate, not Aunt Kate as it seems almost everyone else does, but Kate, for I very much hope we shall become friends, even though we shall never be related."

"Indeed, that is my hope, too," replied Kate.

"I am sorry for as I understand it, none of your children lived, but by heaven, you have a brood in those Westwoods."

"My brother-in-law's children were a godsend to Henry and I," she admitted. "We took in the girls and young Ned and Hal more as a duty, and because Margery, my husband's sister, had been a good friend of their mother, but by heaven, we were rewarded by their unfettered affection."

"I suspect they were glad of a stable home life, poor things," sighed Madeleine. "The war parted so many families. I never saw my brother again after Edgehill. "

"Indeed, my own brother died at Newbury, where Henry was wounded. It was some time later the children came to us, and we were amply recompensed for taking them in, for in time they became like our own children. Certainly young Ned, who was with us from his birth and his sister Hetta, too," said Kate.

"Now they are all married and left you, it is no wonder you considered Sir Richard's offer," sighed Madeleine.

"It was more that Margery and Sophie don't agree. I

could see how Hal was constantly divided by his duty to us, and his adoration of one of the most lovely, but spirited young women I have ever met."

"She certainly is a handful," agreed Madeleine, "but on better acquaintance, a good-hearted girl, I think?"

"Indeed, I am very fond of her, but I thought if I re-married a man of substance, then Margery could make her home with us, leaving Hal free to follow his heart."

"Will he do so? Jack says they quarrel all the time, and that Sophie never listens to a word Hal says."

Kate laughed. "I imagine Sophie to be the worst kind of female to your son, Madeleine?"

"A few weeks ago I would have agreed with you, but it seems she is gaining ground with Jack," she replied with a wry smile. "He still thinks she is a nosy, inter-fering girl, but he now adds she is very brave and has marvellous spirit."

"Good heavens!" Kate cried in dismay. "Sophie is de-voted to Hal, you know!"

"And he to her—yes I do see something in front of my nose," laughed Madeleine, "but his words gave me to think. Jack is proving very difficult to find a wife for, and I have heard that your sister-in-law Margery is very good at making matches. Do you think she might come to my assistance? If I were to write to her, do you think she might know of someone who would suit Jack, for it is plain none of the females hereabouts will do."

"She does invariably know of a host of young females just ready to make a suitable mate for almost every un-matched gentleman of her acquaintance," replied Kate, with a half laugh. "Come Madeleine, I see we must be-come co-conspirators, for I have a favour to ask of you."

"Ask and be welcome," replied Madeleine looking in-trigued.

"My dear, ma'am, you must have observed how poor Cordelia and her splendid husband Adam are strug-gling at Bickmarsh Hall?"

"Indeed I have, and Jack at my behest, has taken the tenants to task for their surly behaviour." she sighed, making a wry face. "The truth is, my dear Kate, Basil, Cordelia's father—and my husband's cousin—was not a good landlord. Even before the war there is no dis-guising that he was an indolent fellow, ever given to easy promises, and his poor people were let down again and again. When the war came, he lost no time and he was off to join the King, taking the best of everything with him, leaving the land only further impoverished. From what Jack has told me, Adam Blackwell is making good progress, but the east country mind is not adaptable. It will take many years for them to accept Cordelia or her husband."

Kate nodded her comprehension. "The greatest trouble, as I see it, is that neither have any true roots or friends in the area, and so feel dreadfully isolated."

Madeleine looked uncomfortable, "Kate, you rightly reproach me. I fear I haven't been as welcoming as I could have been," she agreed. "I have been nursing a sense of chagrin, as I mentioned earlier, and so told myself I need make no special efforts on their behalf for people who were but the merest connection. I feel heartily ashamed of myself, especially when I consider how you, Sir Henry, and Mistress Redcroft have made such efforts to assist us. I do beg your pardon, and I'll put the matter to rights as soon as we return to Fordham Manor."

"You are most kind to suggest it, Madeleine, but do you know, I am of the opinion, both you and Jack will always be galled when you visit Bickmarsh," said Kate candidly. "I have been thinking about it, and to my mind the solution would be for Jack and Adam to come to some sort of agreement. "

"An agreement? Why do you think they might be

prepared to sell?" Madeleine asked.

"I cannot speak for another," replied Kate, "but Adam does still have his own farm near us in Gloucestershire. He purchased it only recently, and it requires a lot of work. His own land was forfeited by his father, who unfortunately sold it off, rather than it being sequestered. Cordelia's was—which was of course, bought by my niece Mary's husband. The Old Manor is nothing like as grand as Elmley Park, but it has the advantage of being close to the places where Adam grew up. Cordelia, poor dear, has few ties in any country, but to my mind it makes more sense for them to live where at least one of them feels at home, and closer to those who have a fondness for them."

Her companion nodded her head, "I understand what you are saying, and I know Bickmarsh is legally Cordelia's property, but we spent a lot of money on it and it is so galling to have it taken back in this fashion."

"There is no dispute that so many people have lost so much these past years. Kings can, and do, make decisions about our futures. They can precipitate us into terrible wars, which set brother against brother, father against son, and left women and children bereft. There can be no going back to the past. What is done is done.

All we can do is accept the here and now, and try, with goodness of heart to go on."

Madeleine nodded, "Yes, much of what you say is true. My husband got Bickmarsh for very little, because it was ruined. He spent much money, but even more time on its restoration. Basil had only further plundered its resources, and the various armies had been marching back and forth several times. I don't think there was a beast left on the place, and the barns, never well maintained, were falling down."

"Yes, Hal told us how you had turned it into a prosperous estate. You are indeed to be congratulated on that, but I don't think Adam will be unmindful of these facts. Life has been very difficult for him too, you know."

"Really? From what I understood of the matter, he was previously an innkeeper," said Madeleine bluntly.

"No, indeed, you have been listening to ill-natured gossip, at least—yes, in a way he was. His father was another such as your cousin, Basil Sandys. A feckless sort, by all accounts, he was injured in the war, and lost almost everything but the best inn in Chawchester, the market town closest to us at Westwood. He moved himself and his young son into the inn at the end of the war, and married the young widow of the former landlord. Poor Adam, who was but a lad, grew up there, and when his father died, only further burdened with debts, he had no choice but to work with his step-mother to free her from them."

"Good heavens, I had no idea. That must have been very hard for him," said Madeleine, rather more interested.

"Yes," agreed Kate. "According to Hal, when he first met up with him, he was a surly young brute, who was courting Sophie, and not unnaturally they took an instant dislike to each other. Which was fuelled I imagine, by Sophie falling head over heels on love with Hal."

"Who was, so gossip says, a married man at the time," remarked Madeleine blandly.

"If you are to have any dealing with Sophie, you'll have to accept that she is unlike anybody you will have met before," replied Kate. "That was why Hal attempted to leave Chawcester as soon as the Sessions were finished, but the death of Sophie's guardian, Edmund Benton prevented that. Then things began to get really out of hand, several of the inhabitants of the town were cruelly murdered. Sophie was abducted by the murderer—a most unpleasant young man—before she could be rescued."

"But wasn't there much talk of her being Hal's mistress?" Madeleine asked slyly.

"You are acquainted with Hal, so you can only be aware that he is an honourable man," replied Kate firmly. "At Edward Benton's death, Hal and his brother-in-law Justin—whom you'll remember from the tragic wedding we both recently attended—found to their great dismay, they had both been named as guardians of Benton's heiress, Sophie."

Madeleine nodded, smiling a little, "Yes, now you recount it, I recollect all that was being said at the time. Guardianship of Sophie Redwood must be something of an unenviable position, I imagine. Is that why Sir Henry decamped to France?"

"Hal went abroad in search of the truth concerning his father's death, and to see whether or not his step-mother had survived. He found that she had perished leaving a baby, his half-brother, whom he brought home, along with Cordelia."

Madeleine nodded. "Yes, the remainder of the tale I know, for this is where Jack and I join it." She glanced curiously to her companion. "Excuse me for saying this, Kate, but your nephew does seem to seek out trouble."

Kate chuckled, "He does have what my sister-in-law, Margery calls an unfortunate tendency to attract trouble brought about by his desire to assist those less fortunate than himself."

Madeleine nodded, "Sir Henry and I had a short discussion about the dilemmas we all face still since the war. Naturally we never thought that would be the end of it, once the King returned, but…" She paused sighing and then nodded, "Yes, I'll talk to Jack about Bickmarsh Hall. What you say makes sense, but how he will view having to repurchase a property he had come to consider his own, I cannot say."

"There is no great hurry," said Kate. "It is my intention to persuade Cordelia and Adam to remain at Westwood with us until after the birth of their child. Adam can travel back and forth should the need arise, but I was hoping you might suggest to Jack that he keep a neighbourly eye on things in their absence."

Madeleine sighed. "Yes, that might answer, if he were to get involved in the place again, he might be more inclined to think of retaining it. I have heard Jack and his steward both complain bitterly about what they term Blackwell's soft West Country ways."

"Unfortunately, Adam's knowledge of farming is limited. By the time he was an age to learn these things they had lost all their holdings, and once his father died he had nothing he could do but assist his poor step-mother at the inn."

"Poor young fellow, put like that 'tis no wonder he struggles," said Madeleine mildly.

"But back in Gloucestershire, of course, there are all manner of folk to assist. Sir Henry, his young brother Ned, Guy Armstrong, husband to Mary, Sir Henry's sister. They will all be glad to help Adam bring his farm about, and of course, as it is close to Westwood, Margery and I can help Cordelia with her baby."

"I can see it is all settled on your mind, Kate," said Madeleine with a laugh. "I am happy to do my best to assist you where I can. Now, I think we should go down to supper before aught else befalls us."

❖

Chapter Twenty Six

"So, Hal," said Sophie, entering the small parlour shortly before supper to find him alone, composing a letter. "We leave in the morning Aunt Kate tells me."

"Yes, have you spoken to her? How is she taking Sir Richard's disgrace?" Hal asked quickly.

"She appears to be quite philosophical at the moment, but you know how she hides her pain," replied Sophie, with a grimace.

"To my shame, I did not know she hid any pain," he replied, frowning. "She invariably says she is happy and well, and I accept her words at face value."

Sophie smiled faintly. "Naturally you do. You are a man."

He glanced to her still frowning, as he sealed his letter. "I am aware of that fact, but not that it was a matter for commiseration."

Sophie laughed, her spirits rising, as she realised they

would be leaving soon, and that she would be in his company for the next few days. "Aunt Kate says she'll persuade Adam and Cordelia to return to Westwood for a visit."

"Yes, that is her intention. She says she will ask Mistress Hollingshead if Jack will watch over Bickmarsh for them, so they may be easy." He hesitated, and then added. "I can see no reason to remain now. Simon and Nick are firm friends and he has given Nick his word he and Bella can be married as soon as it is right to do so. Simon is to escort his aunt and cousins home tomorrow and stay with them to arrange the funeral. The word is that the Pridow family has departed, and Sir Richard, with them."

"That is excellent news," she replied. "God is in Heaven surrounded by his angels and man is safe on earth. It is plain Sir Henry Westwood has passed by."

He glanced sharply to her. "Better, surely that leaving a trail of havoc in my wake?"

"As I do, you mean?" she replied sharply.

He blinked in surprise, "No, that wasn't my meaning at all," he replied, carefully keeping his voice neutral. "I was thinking more of Brendon and the trouble he has caused. All too often, as I have said before, a murder leads to further tragedy. Here at least the death toll has been but the unfortunate girl, Rosalind Pauncey. It was reputations which were destroyed here, not lives."

"And only the reputations of the undeserving," she agreed. "For Nick's family reputation is restored along with his fortune."

"The two frequently go hand in hand," nodded Hal. "Few very wealthy people suffer from a bad reputation; they merely become eccentric."

Sophie laughed, "True enough, although women suffer if considered eccentric."

"Yes, I am sorry it is such an uncharitable world," he agreed, "but beautiful women who have a fortune are ever in the forefront of peoples' minds."

"Even yours?" she asked with a hint of irony.

"Especially mine, when I am her guardian," he agreed, wariness in his tone.

Sophie cast him a speculative glance and then sighed. "What do we do now, Sir Henry?" she asked.

"We return to my cousin Tom's home, rest there for a few days, then as soon as my aunts are ready, we go back to Westwood, of course," he replied. "Adam and Cordelia are to make a visit. It would seem your presence isn't required at Harcourt at present, and in future matters can be settled either by Justin or I."

"Return to Westwood to do what?" she asked. "To Aunt Margery finding me another unsuitable bridegroom?"

Hal glanced away from the appeal in her face, seeming to withdraw into himself. "Strictly speaking, it was agreed you'd not marry for the year of your mourning for Gervase Harcourt. So you need have no fear of Aunt Margery's machinations until the summer."

"I do not fear Aunt Margery's machinations at all," she replied candidly. "Neither do I begrudge them, for it is her only form of entertainment, besides which, the rumour is Mistress Hollingshead has retained her services on behalf of Jack. "

"Has she, by Heaven, poor Jack!" he exclaimed ruefully. He glanced at her, as a thought entered his head. "You don't think…"

"Aunt Margery is no fool. Even she would know at once Jack and I would never suit, however much she may want to be rid of me quickly to protect you."

"I do not need protection," he said hastily. "I can take care of myself. "

"Can you?" she asked with a direct look.

He hesitated, then said slowly: "Yes, I can. You see,

I am armed against all comers now, for my heart is already given, so none of Aunt Margery's plans are of any use against me."

"What, your heart, too?" she asked with an air of innocence. "My eyes are bedazzled by a perfect, gentle knight, and I will love no other."

He laughed abruptly, taking her meaning. "Poor you, perfect gentle knights seldom wear well. Now, I am besotted by a tempestuous beauty with the temper of a vixen, who will never allow me one moment's peace."

"There is peace aplenty in the grave," said Sophie, with a laugh in her voice, "Whither we are all bound. In the meantime, this tempestuous vixen, is she free to give you your heart's desire?"

"No more than your perfect gentle knight, I expect," he replied with a sigh.

"No, my perfect gentle knight is free, but is grown afraid," said Sophie.

"Knights are never afraid," he replied, with a short laugh. "You have been betrayed, bedazzled by an old man!"

"Perhaps, but he is my old knight," she retorted, laughing.

"Vixen!" he cried, delighting in her sharp wit.

"Old Knight!" she retorted.

He crossed the parlour, to catch her by the arms, shaking her gently. "I swear you are a witch!" he cried. "I'll not ask you to marry me, so you can refuse me again. I swear I won't !"

"And I swear never to refuse you anything again," she replied swiftly.

He pulled her to him roughly. "Truly?" he asked his voice husky. "Do you swear you'll never refuse me again?"

"No," she replied. "I swear I'll marry you, and love you for all time!"

"And never give me any peace," he said, his lips hovering over hers.

"Not even in the grave," she agreed, surrendering.

"So," he said, when they felt their pact was sealed well enough. "*Will you come with me and be my love, that we might such pleasures prove?*"

She glanced to him, slightly puzzled, then her brow cleared. "Christopher Marlowe? Does he mention marriage? I thought it was more about birds singing bright madrigals?"

"Melodious madrigals, yes it's Marlowe, a Christmas gift from cousin Tom," he replied, not mentioning its companion gift had been *The Taming of the Shrew*:

'*And I will make thee a bed of roses, and bring thee a thousand fragrant posies, a cap of flowers and kirtle, embroidered with leaves of myrtle.*"

"Still no ropes of pearls and rubies and emeralds, " she sighed in mock dismay. "How like a poet to promise all and nothing in the same breath."

"*And buckles of the purest gold, with coral clasps and amber studs,'if you will but come with me and be my love?*" he continued smiling.

"I never intended anything else," she replied candidly. "Although I must admit I haven't be quite sure lately how it was to be achieved."

"*The shepherds' swains shall dance and sing, for your delight each May morning: if these delights thy mind may move, then live with me and be my love.*"

"I will live with thee and be thy love, I give you my hand and promise on it," she replied.

"Come then, we shall go and announce it to all. This time neither shall change their mind, none shall stop it. We shall be married very soon."

⚜

Simon looked up as Hal and Sophie entered the hall hand in hand, where the other guests had gathered to discuss all that had gone before. Simon grinned at Nick, who was sitting alongside Bella.

"I owe you a guinea, Nick, but I plead mitigating circumstances. Sir Henry most definitely told me earlier, that Mistress Sophie had declined his offer of marriage."

"I have finally got her to consent to be my wife," said Hal smiling at him. "So I hurried her here to call upon you all to witness it. Sophie, you have promised to marry, haven't you?"

"I have, Hal, and to love and honour you," she agreed gravely.

"I am so very pleased!" Aunt Kate said quickly. "And so will Margery be when we get to Cousin Tom's home."

"Pleased? Aunt Margery?" asked Sophie blankly.

"Yes, it has been her desire to see Hal happily married this winter past, and she has come to see that this will only happen if he marries you, Sophie."

"Well, this calls for a toast, Simon," said Barbara, as everyone looked very pleased. "We'll all gladly drink the health of Sir Henry and his lovely betrothed, who have come to our aid, not forgetting to add our deepest thanks."

"And we'll ask each of you to join us at Westwood for the celebration of our marriage in due course," said Hal.

"That will be lovely," said Bella. "I would so like to see you married, Sophie."

"Indeed, won't we all?" said Madeleine Hollingshead, as Simon called the boy to bring wine. "Do we not all enjoy a happy ending? And today has bought us two such events, to perhaps counter the tragedies we also endured. Does your poor mother still keep to her chamber, Beatrice?"

"Yes, Mistress Hollingshead," she replied dutifully. "She is laid upon the bed with the headache. She says she cannot believe Mr Brendon could be so very wicked."

"I do not think it was his intention to hurt your sister, Mistress Beatrice," said Simon kindly. "I think it is more that he panicked when she went limp on him. I know it is not any excuse that his cowardice—the cowardice of all of them—caused her death, but perhaps it does explain a little."

"It goes to show how one can never be sure. If he and Pridow hadn't been so intent on cheating Nick of his inheritance, they would never have got themselves into such a situation." said Jack.

As the others nodded or sighed according to their inclinations, Sophie, who was filled with such happiness she wanted everyone equally at peace, smiled at Beatrice. "At least you can be married now, once your mourning for Rosalind is over, so something good may come in due course, from this painful time."

Beatrice smiled doubtfully. "Perhaps," she agreed hesitantly.

"We can always hope for a happy outcome, my dear," said Madeleine Hollingshead. "I believe your mother told me your sister-in-law is one of the St John family, I think we share a connection somewhere in our family. I must try to discover it, and get to know them again. I am sure something can be contrived. You are both such good, biddable girls, you and your poor mother deserve a little assistance from your neighbours and family."

"Well," said Simon, as the boy brought the wine and began to hand it round to everyone gathered there, "Friends, please raise your glasses, and join me in drinking the health of Sir Henry Westwood and his lovely bride-to-be—Hal and Sophie!"

⚜

Chapter One

Summer 1667

Hal glanced across to Sophie, as Ned and Cecily set off on horseback down the avenue in the moonlight. She was smiling as she returned Cecily's wave, and a moonbeam struck her hair making it glow with an unearthly beauty.

"Come," he said extending his hand. "Walk with me. It is a beautiful evening."

"The night air is dangerous," said Aunt Margery, as Sophie turned to him with a smile of delight.

"Not on such a night as this," said Aunt Kate, touching her sister-in-law's arm and shaking her head. "The air is as gentle as a lamb. It is a night for lovers." She took Margery's arm through hers and turned with her back toward the house. "Don't stay out too long or you'll get dew-damped!" she called over her shoulder to Hal.

Hal chuckled and hand in hand he and Sophie strolled under the trees in the wake of the riders. "I have been thinking," said Hal, after a few moments of companionable silence, "We should probably make plans for our wedding before some disaster comes to spoil the enchantment of these past few months, or there is another crop of babies."

Sophie gurgled with laughter, "Oh, I think we have a good six months before Cecily will be bought to bed. "

"Cecily?" Hal said quickly. "Is she…?" Then adding in a slightly hurt manner—"Ned said nothing to me."

"I would imagine she forbade him to do so. Indeed, none spoke a word to me either, but she has a look about her, and Ned was filled with such joy, wasn't he?" Sophie replied, detecting the disappointment in his voice and wanting to ease it. "I imagine after all the disappointments they've had, they'll want to be sure."

"Yes," Hal nodded, "yes, of course, that will be it." Then as he recollected how tenderly his young brother had helped his wife into the saddle, he nodded again. "Yes, he was very happy wasn't he? Well, that is splendid news and it gives us a time scale."

"Not one as large as you might imagine," said Sophie. "I'm obliged to remind you of Jane, who is due in October, and I believe Mary said something about having a full autumn, too."

"Oh, Mary has a baby every year," said Hal. "They don't seem to incommode her or Guy one bit, but Jane, that is something different, she is a little old to be having her first child."

"Not so very old and she will be very well looked after by Aunt Kate and Aunt Margery," said Sophie. "Who could have any fear with Aunt Kate at her side? She has helped so many Westwood babes now."

"I could," he replied, tightening his grip on her slender fingers.

She smiled up at him. "I am very healthy, Hal," she replied gently.

"I couldn't lose you," he said, all the happiness draining away, leaving his face stark. "I can't contemplate life without you."

She smiled again. "Then perhaps we'd best not marry?" she suggested mischievously. "For I gather that babies tend to follow on as a consequence."

He hugged her to him. "There can be no question but that we shall be married," he said.

She returned his embrace but asked after a moment's hesitation, "Where do you imagine we will be married, Hal?"

"Where?" he looked at her in astonishment. "Why,

here at Westwood, of course!"

"Yes, of course," she agreed quietly.

He had begun to walk on but stopped at this. "Where else?" he asked bluntly.

She shrugged her shoulders, and smiled a tight smile. "In the church, you think, alongside Libby's monument?"

"Oh—I see!" He turned to look back at his home, bathed in the glory of the moonlight. "I am sorry, it never occurred to me. It just seemed the most natural thing to do."

"Oh, I'd want the feast to be at Westwood—where else, as you say—but, Hal, could we not be married in the Abbey?"

"In the Abbey?" he cried. "In that god-forsaken town of Chawcester? Never! Did I not vow I would never set foot in that place again?"

"Yes, you did, "she agreed, "but Chawcester was my home. My mother and father are buried there; and Uncle Edmund, and Aunt Hannah."

"Aye, along with Robin Tripp, Master Benton's apprentice, the cooper, Will Greenaway, Wat Rose, the baker, and Sam Hedges, the tailor, indeed most of your acquaintance."

"Indeed, but for dear Mistress Blackwell and Sally

Rose, who is making my wedding gown," she agreed mildly. "But Chawcester is closer for Mary and Guy. Mistress Blackwell, oh, I can never get used to her new name, Mistress Capel, I should say, has suggested I might wish to be married from my own home."

"Will you be happy to be married from the home of tradespeople?" he asked, in a disparaging manner

"Indeed, for I am the heir to one, and in truth, I am happy to be married anywhere, if you are to be my bridegroom," she said placidly. "I merely mentioned that I would quite like to be married at the Abbey in Chawcester. I used to dream of it as a little girl running in and out among the gravestones."

"I had forgotten your parents are buried there," said Hal, who had not truly given them a thought since the demise of Edmund Benton, feeling suddenly ashamed of his introspection.

"Yes, they are both buried in the plot Uncle Edmund bought when my mother died—alongside Aunt Hannah," she replied. "Uncle Edmund is buried within the Abbey itself, but he managed to get consent for my father to be put in the same grave as my mother, after he died of the fever in prison. "

"Yes, I remember you telling me now. I am sorry it

had escaped my memory. Well, I suppose it was more that I put it all from my mind after I left," he added truthfully.

"Yes, I know, but don't you see, Hal, if we were to be married there in the Abbey, it would bring it all full circle," she said quietly. "The people of Chawcester would take us to their hearts, and make us their own. All the bad gossip would be forgotten. They are to a man so very proud of their Abbey, having raised the money themselves to buy it from the King."

"Yes, I recollect being told the tale when Edmund Benton died," said Hal. "It was the fact that his grandfather had contributed to the sale which meant he could be buried within the Abbey itself." He shrugged his shoulders adding, "I am of the opinion it will just rake up all the old gossip."

"Our marriage will do that anyway. Sally Rose says the whole town was full of it as soon as we returned from Lincolnshire with Adam and Cordelia."

"Mistress Blackwell, no doubt?" Hal remarked grimly.

"Mistress Capel, since her marriage," Sophie reminded him. "You have to remember, your coming to Chawcester, and the events which followed were the most exciting thing to happen in the town since Oliver

Cromwell marched through during the war. You were a figure of romance and drama long before you arrived. Once you came and everyone saw your modish coat and good looks, the town was abuzz."

"Yes and we left it in a high frenzy, " he replied sharply. "I was too ill to care, but as I understand it, you were got away to Mary and Guy because the scandal was so great."

"I was sent away to Elmley Park because Justin couldn't bear the sight of me and wanted to protect his sister," said Sophie candidly. "He made Libby send me away—'in everyone's best interest,' he said."

Hal nodded, recollecting those dark days. "I am sorry I was too ill to protect you properly," he apologised formally, adding with a heavy sigh, "well, if it is truly what you want, to be married in the…"

"No, no!" she said, appalled to see how much he disliked the idea. "No, I don't want you to dislike it and do it just for me, so that it robs all the joy from our wedding. If you hate the idea of it so much, then we shall be married at Westwood as you say! Don't you understand, I love you, and want more than anything to be married to you, as you see fit. The where and when are but mere trifles."

He caught her to him and said with all the warmth

back in his voice, "It is no mere trifle to be married to me, Miss! It is the most important occasion of our lives, and if it is your wish to be married in Chawcester Abbey, attended by all the good gossips of the town, that is where we shall be married!"

"And so Aunt Margery shall be told?" Sophie suggested, a challenge in her eyes, as she withheld her lips.

He smiled wryly, as he saw the trap too late, "And so Aunt Margery shall be told!" he agreed.

"By you?" she added.

"By me," he sighed in resigned tone, as she finally surrendered her lips.

⚜